IRIS

IRIS

by Janine Veto

Boston: Alyson Publications, Inc.

Published as a paperback original by Alyson Publications, Inc.

Typeset and printed in the United States of America.

First edition, first printing, November 1983.

ISBN 0 932870 32 5

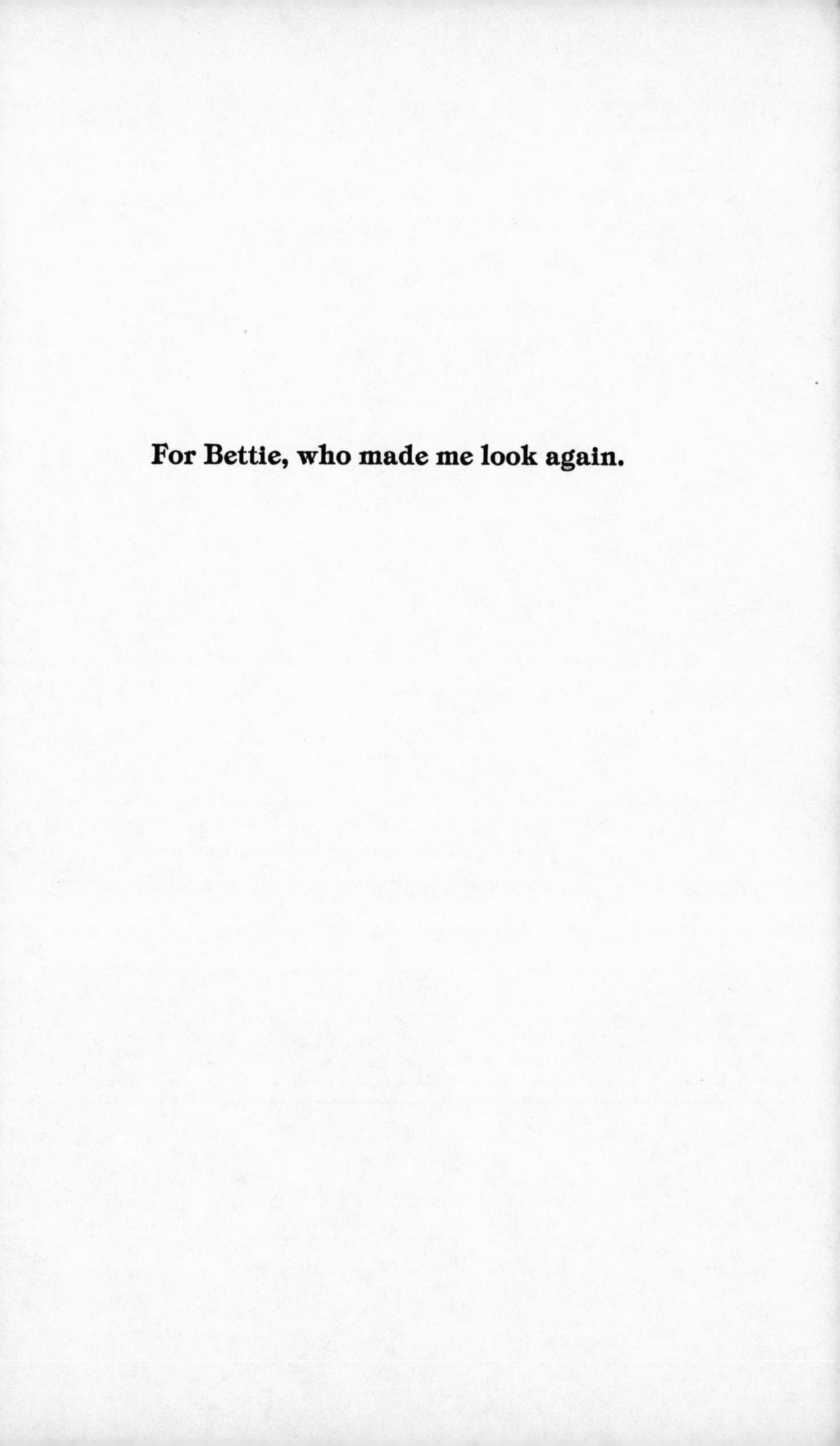

For Bettie, who made me look again.

I.
Rainbow Cradle

One

Hawaii is America's most exploited resource; a media event extravaganza. It is a thick, spine-cracked novel worth millions; a movie with embarrassing roles for Julie Andrews, Richard Harris, the once noble Max von Sydow.

Hawaii is a Southern California surfer's dream gazing west, a poster in a teenager's bedroom, a T-shirt to wear while washing your car. It is a violent television regular, a Continental Airlines special package tour, the pensioner's release from cornfield boredoms.

Hawaii is a rapacious fantasy of bare breasts, an excuse to enter a world war, the proper paradise in which to launch the proper marriage.

Iris had no such remotely fashionable reasons in mind when she purchased her one way ticket to Honolulu on one of New York's most unyieldingly grey afternoons. She was operating on command, from duty, in response to an emphatic vision.

For days she had tossed about feverishly in her one room walk-up above an importer of fake African artifacts on Second Avenue. Propped up in the musty cushions of a once-plush sofa, Iris slowly felt the wind gathering in her head that signaled the advent of voices, the onset of visions. In a holier time Iris might have been hailed as a saint, or stoned as a heretic, but as a young woman in the 1970s she attributed her "spells" to the chemical distortions wrought by her teenage adventures with LSD.

She felt herself being lowered from a great height, from a region of pure light into a tunnel with a speck of blue and green at the far opening. She was weightless, without support as she moved through the quiet tunnel. As Iris brought her vision into focus she could perceive that what lay before her was clearly an island, rhythmically washed by the sea. She took it as a directive, a direction of flight from a city that held her in a confusion of memories.

"Quick, someone's going to die. Pray." It was her mother's voice. She was seven, her sister Phyllis, twelve. They were kneeling in front of the statue of the Blessed Virgin Mary lighting candles when a sudden draft extinguished the flame in the red votive cup in front of their mother. The two girls bent their heads in feverish prayer. They knew a dying flame signaled a soul to heaven.

"Christ have mercy on their soul," chanted Phyllis.

"And on the souls of all the faithfully departed," responded Iris, her eyes drifting up to the benevolent face of the Virgin, the mother of God, who seemed to have considerable influence on the salvation of the souls. She was infused with faith and confidence. "I think we saved it."

"Don't be silly," whispered Phyllis with authority. "You can't know that. It's a mystery."

"Not to me," boasted Iris.

"Shh, girls, that's enough," said their mother. "Time to go home." She rose stiffly to her feet and turned down the aisle of the nearly deserted church as the late winter light fell through the stained glass in muted patches of color. Two weeks later she was dead. And the two fidgeting girls who trailed in her wake were orphans.

Iris shook her head to clear it of the memory and forced herself into quick action. Within three hours she was seated on the afternoon Aloha flight, accepting a Piña Colada from a lei-bedecked steward and the attentions of a businessman seated next to her en route to Los Angeles.

"Say, anyone ever tell you how much you look like Lindsey Wagner? You know, that Bionic Woman on TV?"

Iris had the problem of all pretty women on planes: whether silent or attentive, any gesture short of a slap was taken as encouragement.

"Dead ringer. I mean that as a compliment. She can act, too. You an actress?"

It was only when Iris stared at him, her green eyes boring

through his skull as if it were air that he stuttered into silence and finally moved to the piano lounge in search of more sociable, if less attractive companions.

Iris often had this disquieting effect on people. Her attention would last long enough to determine if she could pick up a signal from them. Once satisfied, her eyes would cloud over in mid-sentence, mid-job, mid-affair. She became unreachable; and all around her men and women would be left, listening to their own voices in a new, uncomfortable way.

"Hey, doll, looking good," said the handsome man, the dark man with flashing teeth. His hands grazed her shoulders and slipped down the curve of her spine.

"You want me to call Phyllis? She's upstairs combing out her hair."

"Naw, naw, no hurry, honey. Why don't you tell me all about school. You like high school? Got any boyfriends?" His arm was around her waist now drawing her body up against his hard torso.

"School's fine. I like my English class."

"No boyfriends? A knockout like you?"

"She's only fourteen, Dion," said Phyllis evenly. She stood in the doorway, awkward in her high heels and fresh bubble hairdo.

"Don't mean nothing," responded Dion smoothly as he loosened his grip on Iris. "In some parts of the world that I've seen, they're married by her age and having kids."

Iris looked pleadingly to Phyllis for help. What she saw was mistrust, a flicker of doubt in her sister's eyes. And between them stood Dion, smiling.

"Fasten your seat belts for landing. We are beginning our descent over Diamond Head, which is visible from the right side of our aircraft. We hope you have enjoyed your flight. Aloha."

Iris was startled from her reverie and peered eagerly out the window. Yes. It matched her vision, this blue vista speeding up to the dense green in the fading afternoon light. Iris nudged her flight bag under her seat with her heel, then shut her eyes, as she closed her hands lightly over the armrests in anticipation of the jolt of landing.

Two

Captain Gustav Monenschein was the last member of his crew to roll into El Toro's on sea legs that night. He had stayed behind to have a beer with Mr. Pringle, the wizened harbor master, in his cramped corner office in Aloha Tower. The winter sun was just slipping behind the buildings that blocked the view of Diamond Head when he crossed Keamouku Boulevard to the slightly derelict adobe façade.

Nothing seemed changed since their last docking five weeks before. A few crewmen infiltrated the handful of diners seated at tables in the restaurant. But most of the men were crowded into the bar and around the piano, flirting with the coolly beautiful bartender, Nancy Chin.

Owner Hans Voorman, "Dutchman" to the regulars, was already slightly drunk and telling a bored first mate about his meeting with Edith Piaf twenty years before in Paris.

"I was too shy, a young man. I didn't take command like she wanted. I lost my chance. She wasn't a beauty, understand — never took a bath, her teeth were rotting." He stared at the ice cube diluting his Scotch, tears welling up in his yellowed eyes. "But she was all woman; she hurt, she suffered, she understood, you see." He shook his head, unaware of the first mate's indifference.

"Why Captain, I was beginning to think you jumped ship on us, you naughty boy."

Gustav turned as the claw-like hand of Dutchman's wife closed around his muscular forearm. She was not a woman that appealed to him. Thin and cunning, the protruding tendons in her neck betrayed the anxiety underneath her fading Southern belle exterior.

"Ach, Hattie, this I'd never do. At sea I dream of your steaks and barrels of good beer."

"So it isn't me that brings you back?" She feigned a hurt expression, batting her eyes circled with heavy black liner.

"This is not becoming, Hattie," Gustav waved a schoolmaster's finger across her hawked nose. "You're a married woman with a grown daughter and I must have respect for you."

They both burst out laughing, Gustav's good humor rolling across the room in waves. Women were compelled to flirt with him. It was his knowledge of water, of mood, that made him seem wise. His blue eyes looked deep and far from the wide face framed by the neatly trimmed black beard sprinkled with grey. Virility in open collar and short khaki pants.

"Hattie, I'm a hungry man. Have Rosa bring me two steaks," two sausage-like fingers were waved in front of her face, "and one large stein of beer right away, yes?"

"No. . . and yes, Captain." Hattie inclined her head toward a small table for two. "You'll have your steaks and beer, you brute. But no Rosa. Her baby's sick. But I think you'll like Iris just fine. Now sit down and behave yourself ya hear?"

Hattie gave him a wink as she gestured to a girl swinging through the kitchen door at the back. Gustav watched with mounting approval as Iris approached his table. Yes, this girl was to his liking. She was at that stage between adolescence and full womanhood that appealed to him. A good figure, with breasts and hips a man could hold onto, yet slender and firm at the same time. Very American looking with long blond hair tied back in a paisley scarf.

"And just keep the beer coming for him, darlin'. Don't bother asking."

Iris took one look at the confident sea man and turned on her heel when Hattie caught her arm.

"Now, honey, don't you run off so fast. I want you to meet our Captain."

"Pleased to meet you, Captain Monenschein. But if you want those steaks, I better place your order." Iris nodded briefly and was gone.

"Well, I declare," exclaimed Hattie, placing her hands on her hips, an exasperated Madame. "I'm all for efficiency, but she goes too far."

"No, no, Hattie," said Gustav. "She's right. She doesn't waste time."

"But I thought she'd be perfect for you," protested Hattie. "That is, since you don't want *me*."

"But I like her, Hattie. I like it that she doesn't go right away for me. Means she's not every man's woman. That's good. Now you go. She's coming with the beer. Go get Dutchman away from my first mate if you must make matches. Let Claus have a chance with Nancy without Dutchman around his neck, eh?"

Gustav ate his steaks quickly with great relish, washing the meat down with streams of beer supplied by the professionally attentive Iris. He watched her serve the other diners with the same efficiency and detachment, keeping to herself amid the clatter, seemingly unaware of how her disturbing beauty drew the eyes of the men.

Gradually the other patrons cleared out, leaving El Toro entirely to the crew. The tipsy Dutchman drifted to the piano for an off-key rendition of "Je Ne Regrette Rien." Goaded by the Germans, he finally gave way to the more measured rhythms of German drinking songs.

One by one, Iris finished resetting the tables around Gustav for the next day. He watched as she untied her apron and pulled the scarf from her hair, releasing the long waves down her back. Crossing to the bar, she edged in next to Claus, leaning close to Nancy to be heard above the singing. Nancy nodded, setting aside her cigarette to pour a clear stream of tequila into the blender for Iris' nightly drink. The self-absorbed Claus was shaken from his lethargy by the sudden gift of a woman's body next to his. He quickly produced a match for the cigarette Iris was drawing from Nancy's pack on the bar.

Gustav grew restless as Claus and Iris engaged in conversation, their bodies leaning at angles toward each other to be heard. He drained his stein and strode over to the bar, the men parting like water to let him pass.

"No, I don't know Schiller and hardly enough Goethe," Iris confessed to Claus. "I suppose I'd have to look into them before I can appreciate Nietzsche or even Mann, for that matter."

Stoop-shouldered and grave, Claus bobbed his head as if in agreement, while in reality more at sea in the conversation than when thrown from his berth above Gustav in a storm.

"Ja, ja," agreed the amused Gustav, slapping Claus on the back. "This reminds me. We must get more books before we sail again, no? And tapes. Opera is good away from land."

"I never realized culture was so elevated on the high seas," said Iris in a mocking tone. "And what opera do you like, Captain?"

"Rossini, Puccini are excellent," said Gustav as he reached between Iris and Claus to claim a fresh stein of beer. "But I *am* German, so Wagner says many things to me. Do you know German opera?"

"Only 'Der Rosenkavalier' and some other Strauss. That I like. But Wagner frightens me."

Claus turned his attention back to Nancy Chin, relieved that Gustav stepped in to handle this woman who wanted to show off so much in front of men. Gustav spread his pillar-like legs, a hand on his hip, a Colossus rooted in his harbor home.

"So it's through Hitler you know Wagner, no? Like most Americans. You were not even alive those years, right?"

"No, you're right. But I did see some of Leni Riefenstahl's films, with Wagner's music backing up the Führer's ravings. How can you forget? How can you separate the two?"

Iris looked at him with frank eyes, like an equal, like a man. Gustav's curiosity was piqued. This very desirable woman could get much from a man. Yet she challenged instead of charmed.

"There was Wagner before Hitler, when I was a little boy. But understand. I don't disown Hitler. He did many good things for Germany. My father was in the Luftwaffe; shot down three times and up he would go again." His thumb pointed up to the skies.

"At least you learned your lesson and stuck to the water," goaded Iris.

"Ach, just another part of the family. My grandfather was captain of U-boats in the First War. And you need another drink."

Gustav was surprised that she did not fight his ordering the drink. In such a short time the only constant thing he felt from her was resistance, as if each time she answered him she was indifferent as to whether he would continue or not.

"So, Iris, tell me about your family."

Gustav offered her a cigarette from his pack and cupped his hand around the flame as she bent toward him for a light. She threw back her head, tossing her hair over one shoulder to clear her line of vision.

"Nothing to tell. They're all dead or indifferent. Same thing, isn't it?"

"There must be more to this story," said Gustav shaking his head.

"Not much." Iris was uncomfortable with the question. She felt the shadow of memory start to descend over her mind. "My father was in the Navy, killed in Korea. My mother's dead. And then there's my sister. I don't know about her anymore."

"Yes?" prompted Gustav. "You don't get along with your sister?"

"Not exactly," said Iris. "We used to get along very well; we were inseparable. But then mother died and things fell apart. I haven't seen Phyllis for years. She married a sailor when I was a teenager and went south. I think that covers it." But once triggered, the memory couldn't be covered.

It was hard to think back to her childhood, because to go straight backward in time she had to cross the memory of her mother's ghastly death and how she had sat for hours at her piano teacher's house, waiting to be picked up by her mother who was already dead, twisted up inside the carcass of their old grey Oldsmobile in the Jewel parking lot all because some suburban wino was in a hurry to get home with his bottle. They never did get around to figuring out where she was. Her piano teacher finally called her house and a policeman answered. Iris could hear Phyllis screaming in the background while the color drained from her teacher's face.

With no living relatives, they were sent to live with her mother's friends whose charity wore thin as their own personal tragedies overshadowed concern for the orphaned girls. Always close even when their mother was alive, Iris and Phyllis clung to each other more fiercely than ever. Phyllis stepped into her mother's role and protected her younger sister from the jolt of their frequent moves. Iris was included in the older girl's games, dreams and longings — until Dion Panagakis took Phyllis away to an island off Florida. Then Phyllis was no longer hers.

"Your drink," announced Gustav, nudging the glass toward her on the bar. "So you are alone?"

"I can take care of myself," said Iris curtly. Gustav studied her fine-cut features, the pain in the drawn-down corners of her mouth.

"Yes, yes, of course. And it seems you did well. You sound like you have an education, no?"

"Yeah, I've put in my college time." Iris took a quick drink and half turned away from the insistent Gustav. After Phyllis' abdication Iris had grown quiet and studious. She put herself through school on a scholarship for the bright children of dead American heroes. After school she held good jobs, but always quit after a matter of months, feeling comfortable only on islands. The mainland was too expansive and familial to seem real. Islands at least reminded her of her own isolation, gave her boundaries and the notion of vast depths of nothingness that surrounded her.

"Excuse me if this is private," persisted Gustav, "but if you went to college, why do you work here?"

"Simple. I need the money."

"But you were trained differently, no?"

"Look, I think that's my business. I'm sure sailing around the world is a barrel of laughs. We're not all that lucky, you know."

"Sailing is not just for fun, you know. It is my duty. But I also love it. I am a fortunate man."

"Ah, fortunate indeed to be so at one with yourself... or so successfully repressed..." said Iris with an ironic smile.

"This psychology is German, too, Fraulein," Gustav waved his finger across the bridge of Iris' nose. "If you know this then you know also what Freud says is good for women."

"Only too well." Her tone was a whispered wound. Gustav felt her sudden retreat as her face froze into mask-like perfection. He felt a panic to draw her to him before she ran through his fingers.

"Iris, take me home with you," he poured softly, urgently into her hair. For an instant his sea-trained eyes spotted a weariness washing across her young face. Iris rubbed her hand roughly across her temples and squinted at him in an effort to focus his features.

"All right."

A quick jerk of her wrist knocked the ash off her half-smoked cigarette. Gustav slipped his hand under her elbow, guiding her through the wake of crewmen to the door. He wished there was another way to leave, away from their mocking, knowing gazes and lewd gestures. No, he wanted to tell them. She is not like others. She is different.

The men's bodies closed behind them as Gustav and Iris stepped into the fresh air of the tropical night.

"Take off your shoes, Captain."

"My shoes?" Gustav glanced down at his laces.

"Yes, your shoes. We have a Japanese landlord who is in love with his carpet. Just leave them by the side of the door."

Iris slipped out of her sandals and lolled against the white balcony that led to her door, waiting for Gustav. On the mainland this would be an enclosed corridor, affording the habitants of the large apartment building protection from the elements. But in Hawaii everything was left open to the trade winds; buildings were innocent skeletons, elevators opened to the air.

In the distance across the Ala Wai Canal a glow hung above the commercial night life of Waikiki. Iris turned her gaze *mauka*, towards the mountains, past the roofs of the University buildings, following the diminishing trail of light to a vanishing point deep in the Manoa Valley.

"I'm ready," said Gustav.

Iris turned her key in the lock and swung open the door. Two closed bedroom doors faced the hallway leading to the living room. And beyond that, sliding glass doors to the *lanai*. The decoration was sparse, the bare minimum, an obviously "furnished" apartment of an indifferent blue tint. Iris rolled open the glass doors to admit the breeze, the flimsy curtains billowing out in slow ripples.

"Drink, Captain? All I have is wine."

"Ja, that's fine." Gustav settled into the cushions of the one couch. He studied Iris as she unscrewed the cap of the half-gallon bottle and poured the deep red wine into thick glasses. Did she do this often, pick up strange men and take them home with her? She didn't seem the type. And yet she went with him so easily. He would like to think that she found him exceptional, but he had an uneasy feeling that she chose him quite for her own reasons and purposes.

"You live here alone?"

"Hardly. I've got two roommates. Students. But they're home for the holidays."

Iris handed him his glass and folded her legs beneath her, leaning against the smooth edge of the coffee table. They sat in slience a few moments before Iris drained her glass in one quick motion and jumped to her feet. She crossed to the *sohji* doors that enclosed an area off the living room, sliding one of the framed rice paper panels to the side.

"My room," she intoned softly.

Gustav looked up. What was it in her voice? A command, an inevitability? She lingered for a moment, her hand reaching between her breasts to undo the pearly buttons of her blouse. In the shadows behind her he spied a narrow bed against the wall; Iris followed his gaze with an enigmatic smile and turned her back, letting the blouse fall from her shoulders like a shawl in suddenly warm weather. She stepped out of the skirt that pooled at her feet.

Gustav passed his tongue across his upper lip, tasting the sting of salt and sour wine that clung to his beard. A thirst welled up from deep in his loins, burning through his chest and drying the inner membranes of his mouth. Her naked body was a veiled whiteness, a trick of moonlight, deep in the room.

Gustav moved toward her, his desire mounting. Iris stood motionless, hardly breathing as he loomed through the shadows. For a moment she felt a wild doubt, a foreboding of powers released beyond her control. In a flash – was it memory or prophecy? – the image of Dion filled her inner vision. She raised her arm as if to shield her eyes from a blinding sun.

Then Gustav was upon her, closing out the light from the other room, closing over her, relentlessly pounding against her till all she heard was the roar of water in her ears.

Hattie took full credit for the affair, fussing over Iris in the way her own daughter wouldn't allow.

"Now darlin', here you come in again all sunburned. You *know* how that dries up your skin. The Captain'll be back in two weeks, and you with that lovely fair hair turnin' to straw from the elements."

Iris laughed in spite of herself as she tied the red apron across her hips.

"The next thing you'll have me doing is drinking buttermilk to bleach out the freckles. And wearing a wide-brimmed hat whenever I venture forth into the sun."

"All right, have your laugh," Hattie sniffed, counting out Iris' meal checks for the night. "You're as bad as Virginia. Ever since she's been working for that women's lib psychologist at the University she just won't listen to sense. You both think you'll be young and beautiful forever."

"God help us if we've got to make it on beauty alone. I think Virginia's Dr. Hartman has got the longer view in mind. Besides, I can hardly believe a sunburn will keep a man away."

"Suit yourself. But a man like the Captain don't keep interested for nothing. And it ain't your brains he's looking at."

"Well, he's going to have to take me like I am, freckles and all. I wouldn't trade my afternoons for the world, let alone Captain Monenschein."

"Where do you go off to? Waikiki?"

"Not a chance. No, another place I've found. More private." Iris finished tying back her hair and slipped the meal checks into an apron pocket. "I'm going back to see if Nancy needs some help setting up the bar."

Iris needed to get away from Hattie's probings, and didn't want anyone intruding on her retreat. For now she found sustenance each day in her small niche by the sea where she could look out across the water, feel the sun and fine spray pepper her upturned face and just barely discern shadowy forms on the horizon through the dance of a thousand rainbows.

During the next few months Gustav found excuses to dock the *Lorelei* more often than was necessary in Honolulu Harbor. The winter rains gradually brought forth a profusion of poinsettias and African tulips in the thousands of backyard gardens throughout the city. It was not the most fragrant season in the Islands. But February carried the deepest colors – reds and midnight purples – which appealed to Gustav Monenschein's European eye.

He guided his vessel to the familiar slip, clipped and professional with his orders, keeping his men in line as they strained eagerly toward shore. His eyes swept across the dock and he smiled with satisfaction. She was there, waiting, her hair and light skirt lifting slightly in the breeze. He made a mental note to send Mr. Pringle a keg of beer for relaying his radio message to her. Gustav felt generous.

First mate Claus Klein scowled his disapproval, the bones of his face tight against his clean-shaven cheeks. He had served with Gustav Monenschein for years and never had he seen him lose his head over a woman. It was not fitting for such a man. Claus had been horrified when Gustav had peeled off the dull black and white photos of his wife from their cabin wall and replaced them with new color studies of this Iris. The pictures of the three daughters were not touched, to his relief. But to have a port woman replace a wife, no matter how estranged, was not proper. It was a weakening of the moral order, as far as Claus was concerned. His attempted liaison with Nancy Chin could never affect the status of his wife and son in Bremen.

Claus hung back as the men filed off the ship. He did not want to encounter Gustav or Iris. Look how the men raked Iris with their eyes as they passed! How could a captain command respect from his men when a woman like that met him on the dock? Finally Gustav descended the plank, encircled Iris with one arm and guided her quickly into a cab. Claus breathed a sigh of relief, smoothing his hair with one hand before seeking his ease along Hotel Street with the other men.

"Any place but Waikiki," said Iris emphatically as she and Gustav drove out of the harbor.

Within the first few weeks of her arrival on Oahu, Iris had learned to avoid Waikiki with its inflated prices, its obsequious "native" Hawaiians and the reddened, fat American tourists, husband and wife in matching Aloha shirt and *muu-muu*, the unwashed cotton material still stiff from the racks.

The Japanese tourists were hardly a more heartening phenomenon. While the Americans came as the result of years of sacrificial saving, the Japanese-Hawaiian tour was often a prize awarded to the most industrious division of a company. The most diligent, devoted and fanatic won the trip, bringing their obsessiveness and mechanical response to order with them to paradise.

A red flag would shoot up on Waikiki Beach. Two dozen Japanese would scurry from the crowd and line up in perfect pairs behind the leader with the flag waving from his rigid arm, and they would march as a military body down the beach.

"Kahala Hilton?" Gustav took his eyes from the road long enough to cock an inquiring eye toward Iris.

"Fine." Iris smiled contentedly as Gustav piloted the bright red rented car around the curves of Diamond Head past her secret niche below, toward the elegant calm of Kahala. A flash of color caught her eye.

"Look, Gustav." Iris pointed inland with excitement. "Rainbow over the Pali. Think we'll find the pot of gold on the other side of the island?"

"Pot of gold, is it?" Gustav glanced at the arch of color streaming over the mountain and smiled. "That must be the American story. In Germany we would say at the end of the rainbow is Hawaii. This is every sailor's fantasy."

"And here we are," pronounced Iris. "And where do you go, Herr Captain, after you reach your fantasy?"

"You stop sailing," he answered softly, closing his hand over Iris' hand on the seat between them.

Gustav had become totally enraptured with Iris. It was her otherworldliness, her elusiveness that impassioned the methodical Captain. Variances in mood he understood in women. He was accustomed to calm seas turning treacherous with a shift of the wind and undertows that could claim the strongest swimmer. But Iris was different. Sometimes in their lovemaking as they moved together in exquisite fluidity, their bodies sleek with briny sweat, Iris would open her eyes and look at Gustav, or rather *through* Gustav, in a manner that shot a cold chill to his heart. Her body never missed a beat; every pore seemed open and receptive to him. And yet that detached, faintly mocking stare removed her from their act as if she were watching from an Olympian vantage point and found him too fleshy and rather ridiculous. This perception spurred Gustav in his efforts to tumble Iris from her superior pose and bend her totally to passion.

They never spoke of this mighty struggle between them or of Iris' stubborn withholding of the part in herself Gustav sought to the point of obsession. As the weeks passed they found they spoke to each other less, their primary communication molded in the swirling contours of sweaty sheets.

After a few days at the Kahala Gustav was baffled. If he couldn't reach Iris with the insistence of passion, perhaps he could find another way to own her. They lay in long afternoon shadows on chairs near the dolphin lagoon. Early diners drifted into the lobby, winding up the circular staircase to the Maile Restaurant, orchids dotting the lava walls along their path.

"I'm not a poor man, Iris. Why won't you let me do it?" His face was reddened as much from frustration as the sun.

"No, Gustav," sighed Iris. "You can spend as much as you like when we're together. But I won't take a penny from you. And I don't want you to rent an apartment for me, either. That's final. I need to feel free."

Iris' gaze drifted to the lushness of the Kahala grounds. It was a sophisticate's notion of paradise, with bamboo groves shielding the intimate, fragrant gardens of rare planting tinged a delicate purple. Near the hotel the gentle murmur of waterfalls served as natural dining music for the outdoor restaurant lit by island torches. And on the other side of the lagoon the wide beach was raked smooth to the lip of the surf.

Gustav's fist rapped the arm of his chair. His eyes traveled the length of Iris' lightly tanned body. He must have her without seeming to beg.

"I want you for my wife."

Iris turned with a jerk, nearly upsetting her beach chair and lifted the sun glasses from her eyes. This was one tactic she hadn't expected. She examined his face.

"My god, Gustav. I do believe you mean that."

"Of course I mean it!" Gustav slapped his thigh and jumped to his feet.

"Aren't you forgetting one tiny detail? Remember your wife, the mother of your daughters?"

Iris drew her legs up quickly, narrowly missing a crushing as Gustav dropped his bulk on the end of her beach chair. His finger was wagging now, a storm warning against the setting sun.

"I've taken care of that. I wasn't going to tell you before all arrangements were made, before it was done. But you force me to tell you now. In a few days I won't go back with the *Lorelei* when she sails. I go back to Germany for meetings with the company. I'll make a settlement with my wife; some money and papers and it'll all be through. She wants this, too. I just haven't been in Germany to make it final."

"I'm not interested in marriage." Iris hugged her knees against her chest as the evening trade winds gently stirred the air.

"No, no, think about it, Iris. I'll be gone for some time and then you can tell me. I'll be free when I come back. We could marry right away. I won't change my mind."

"Gustav, what difference does it make?" Iris sighed and released her grip on her knees. "You're gone most of the time, anyway. And when you're in port, I stay with you. Why get married?"

"It is not proper." Gustav's face clouded over. "You're not that sort of woman."

"And what sort is that, Gustav?" Iris squared her shoulders in defiance. "I don't see where it's so great to be married to a sailor. And I don't much like your attitude."

Gustav's eye was drawn to a bead of sweat that broke and ran a rivulet between Iris' breasts. He passed his tongue quickly over his upper lip.

"I won't always be on the sea, Iris. This is why I go back to Germany. There'll be changes."

"What sort of changes?" Iris' eyes narrowed. "I know the *Lorelei's* a research ship, but what exactly are you researching? You've never told me."

Gustav drew in his breath, a flicker of indecision crossed his eyes. He let out his breath in a gust, nodding toward Iris.

"All right, all right. I'll tell you. But you must keep this secret, ja?" Iris nodded. "The *Lorelei* is owned by the company with the German government. We look for metals on the ocean floor."

"So what's so secretive about that?"

"Not just ordinary metals. Metals Germany needs for space travel." His thumb jerked up to the heavens. Iris let out a low whistle.

"Ah, and your 'changing role,' Gustav?"

"We're almost done with this part of the Pacific. The *Lorelei* must move on. But instead of Captain I will ask to work from Germany, checking her several times a year out of

Durban, Rio, Hong Kong and maybe here. You could come with me... as my wife."

Iris saw the romance of the world's harbors open before her, purchased for one gold ring and the glory of a rising Germany. It was the same seductive sailor's song that wooed her mother, that Dion Panagakis used to entice her sister. Iris stared at Gustav, trying to penetrate the meaning of his words, to look for a confirming signal and finding none, shuddered.

"I'm cold, Gustav," she said abruptly as she stood up. "I'm going in to change."

Three

It was because his countryman was teaching the course and because he was struck with an uncharacteristic nostalgia for his first island home that Harold Upton signed up for the Modern British Poetry class at the university that spring – as an auditor, of course. At thirty-five, Harold had no illusions about degrees... or about committing his thought and attention to any one person or task long enough to see it bear fruit. So auditing the small class was ideal; it afforded him the opportunity to exercise his mind, expound his worldly ideas and show off his upper-class accent to an appreciative audience at the same time.

Harold arrived early the first day of class, positioning himself on the far side of the sun-filled room to allow a clear view of the students as they entered. It was a stark, squared-off modern room, indistinguishable from its beige-grey cousins throughout the modern world. But the architectural blandness of Hawaii was overshadowed by the complex arrangement of genes that produced the unique beauty of its inhabitants. A delightful island mixture, Harold decided, as he ticked off each entrance with a habitual toss of his head. Wholesome, lithe boys, delicate girls with a fresh hibiscus behind one ear, a few sun-streaked *haole* mainlanders.

Harold snorted. What would these innocents know of Yeats' visions, the measured scream of "The Waste Land," the magnificent roarings of a Welsh lush? Europe didn't bear down upon them with the force of twisted ancestors. The anger that lay so near his surface rose quickly to flood his cheeks with red, to pop his perpetually bloodshot eyes, to stand his wispy hair on end like haphazard tongues of flame. Take a class? Indeed. He should be teaching it!

The professor, Anthony Douglas, made his entrance followed by a young woman Harold took to be a teaching assistant. Brisk and efficient, she took a seat near the front and opened a notebook, pen poised above the paper in anticipation. He's probably fucking her, Harold decided, and turned his attention toward a slender Japanese girl across the room.

Just in time, thought Iris. She hated arriving on the heels of the instructor the first day of class. Not that this class mattered in the academic sense of the word. She had signed up to distract her mind from the tropical stupor and from the anxiety she felt over Gustav and his offer.

Should she leave the island, and commit herself to Gustav and his travels? She sensed that she had not yet fulfilled her purpose on the island. I can't believe I'm meant to retire from life and practice the wifely arts for one man, Iris told herself. I must stay, she decided. Though she wasn't through with Gustav she knew she couldn't be his wife, nor leave the island.

Slowly, Iris' attention drifted back to the sounds in the room. Nightingales and kingfishers turned through the occult gyres of imagination. The lecture transformed into a dialog, a bantering of embroidered English tongues. Iris turned to fix upon the face of the professor's alter ego on the far side of the room. Feverish, fitful, he tossed his head in enunciation, closing his eyes in intensity, his hands foreshadowing the ends of thoughts, scooping the air in great circles toward his body.

Deceptive, she decided. The flourishing moustache designed to divert attention away from a weak chin. But bright, articulate; a counterpoint to the commanding masculine self-assurance she knew in Gustav. There were few silences in a man like that, his words a flow of hot lava from some internally erupting source.

Iris smiled, sensing that this wild man might prove an antidote to the Captain. Whenever she let herself drift in one direction for any length of time, something inside urged her to turn around, to draw back and to proceed in a direction at right angles to where she was headed. She would look further into this impeccably toned Englishman.

"Actually, I think you are due for another drink." Harold flicked a finger at the lumbering Samoan bartender and turned on his stool toward Iris. Her eyes were becoming glassy, slightly out of focus from the rum.

"Oh, I don't know," she mumbled. Alcohol took away the illusion of uniqueness in Iris. It could be any time, in any place now, instead of a beautiful mid-May afternoon in the heart of downtown Honolulu.

"Nonsense," declared Harold as the new drink in a spotted glass was sloshed down in front of her. "I'll see you home."

"Oh, that's a comfort," hooted Iris.

"My dear," Harold feigned a hurt expression. "Upon my honor as a gentleman, I would not leave an engaged tipsy woman alone in a Hotel Street dive, ripe for the pickings of any wandering sailor, or worse."

"Didn't you say you were a sailor once? Or was it worse?"

"Both." Harold tossed his head. "I was given the sack from every job I ever held. Insubordination or booze. But don't worry, my dear. You are not my type. I go for those slender Oriental women with no hips." He held his glass of rum with his finger extended straight out, as if they were sitting at high tea in the garden.

"Why don't you just settle for boys? Sounds like that's what you're really after."

"My, my, aren't we clever?" Harold's mouth twisted in a sneer. "And how did we come to that conclusion?"

Iris shrugged and sipped at her drink, idly watching a Filipino youth at the pool table unintentionally sink the eight ball.

"Simple deduction, my dear Watson. That upper-class background of yours gone wrong and the habits in English boys' boarding schools, not to mention the life of horny sailors at sea."

"What one does in a pinch and what is done with the choice of options are two different things." Harold pursed his lips and gave his rangy moustache a twist. "Oh, and you left out jails. One doesn't have choice in matters of sexual encounter in cells. Particularly if one is slight of build." Harold tossed back his drink with a flourish and nodded toward the game. "I'm on intimate terms with a cue stick, as well."

"Sorry," said Iris, shaking her head. "Seems I get nasty in direct proportion to the volume of rum I consume."

"Not at all, not at all." Harold waved an indifferent hand.

"Drinking makes *so* many things much more bearable. Like having to be kept, don't you agree?"

Drinks appeared before them, the bartender well acquainted with Harold's capacities. Iris drained her glass.

"Wrong track, Harold. I'm not kept. I pay my own way."

Harold wheezed a thin laugh. "You're really too good to be true. But you'll not be free if you marry, correct? Seems he controls the situation *off* the island, wouldn't you say? Not that I'm criticizing, you understand."

"I told you. I'm *not* going to marry him, Harold. Jesus. My mother and sister married sailors and look what it got them."

"Really? What did it get them?" Harold twisted the ends of his moustache in preparation for his next drink.

"Nothing. The men gallivant all over the world and they stay home to raise kids. Big deal. I'd rather be alone."

"Bravo," applauded Harold. "Spoken like a true liberated woman. It's so easy to feel liberated when young, don't you think?"

"You know what I like about you, Harold?" Iris took a quick sip of her drink and caught a trickle from the corner of her mouth with her finger. "You don't make a big fuss over how I look. Most men do. Idiots. The important part is inside my head, you know?" She tapped her temple with her free hand.

Harold nodded in solemn agreement. She was half slumped on the bar, sipping her drink from habit rather than thirst, becoming drowsy and drunk as the rum spread through her system to the beat of the single blade fan above their heads. Harold had caught on early to Iris' habit of gulping great quantities of liquids whether it was coffee, wine or water. He kept the rum before her, distracting her with chatter and watched with satisfaction as her speech slurred and her head finally came to rest on the edge of the bar. He gestured to the bartender, peeled off crisp bills onto the bar and pocketed the rusted key tossed in front of him.

"'Let us go then, you and I,'" he quoted, slipping his arm around Iris' waist and half lifting her off the stool. "Time for your next poetry lesson."

Iris' head flopped onto Harold's shoulder as she stumbled, half carried and half pushed, through the darkened hall and up the rotting staircase behind the ever-active billiard table.

"'There will be time, there will be time,'" chanted Harold, his newest student passed out, pressed against his side.

A thousand snakes thrashed through her system, tossing her feverish body from side to side. Iris tried to hold her body still, sensing it would ease the pain. But when she succeeded, horrific images thrashed through her mind, satanic laughter ranted in her ears. Demons with enormous red-hot penises were violating every hole in her body, whipping her with razor sharp palm leaves, riding her like a crazed bronco. It was Harold. It was Gustav. It was Dion. It was all of them at once, then in turn.

Gradually, she felt rather than saw that she was in her own bed in the room sided with opaque rice paper. At times she was aware of other presences in the room, of an arm that would support her shoulders as she spewed green bile into a pail or the placement of a cool cloth across her eyes. But they were creatures from another life or another planet, impossible to contact, to speak to through the impenetrable atmospheres that divided them. She gave herself up to these disembodied, ministering hands and prayed for the blessed bouts of unconsciousness.

Cora slid the door to the sick room closed and joined Audrey in the kitchen.

"She any better?"

Cora nodded impatiently, hooking a length of her lank hair behind one ear with a pudgy finger.

"Yeah, she's out cold for a while, I think."

"What could have happened to her? Did you see. . .?" Audrey poured a steaming cup of coffee and handed it gingerly to Cora as she sat down heavily at the formica counter.

"Well, it's more than a hangover, that's for sure." She looked up to Audrey's frightened face. "I know. I know. Those welts across her ass, the dried blood down her legs. Some bastard sure went wild with her. Probably when she was high. It's a miracle she made it back here alive."

A shudder passed through the wide-eyed Audrey.

"What should we do?"

"Change the locks on this place," snapped Cora. She swung her book bag across the sweat-soaked spot between her shoulder blades and heaved herself off the stool. "I got a class."

Audrey stood helplessly in the kitchen as the front door slammed loudly after Cora. Behind the rice-paper doors of the living room there was a rustling of sheets and low moans as the fever gripped Iris once again.

Iris was more withdrawn than ever when she returned to work three days after the incident with Harold. She hardly spoke and shied away from any boisterous although innocent gesture from a customer. Hattie was worried.

"Are you sure you should be working, honey?"

"What's the matter, am I hurting business?" Iris was mistrustful even of concern. She watched Hattie's owl-like eyes for the truth.

"No, no, you know that's not it. I just don't want you doin' yourself any more harm."

"No, it's worse at home," Iris shook her head as she reset the table for the next day. "It's better when I'm busy. I don't even want my days off this week. I mean, I'll even work in the kitchen, do salad or something."

"I understand," Hattie hesitated a moment before continuing. "Listen. Why don't your run up to the University and talk to that Dr. Hartman? Maybe she can help you work it all out."

"I don't think talking is going to help anything, Hattie."

"Virginia says she's very sensitive, you know? What have you got to lose?"

"Not much, that's for sure," responded Iris with a short laugh. "I don't know. Let me think about it."

"You do that, sugar. I'll give you the number. Oh, and one other thought."

"What's that?"

"I wouldn't tell the Captain about this when he comes back if I were you, Iris. Men don't understand."

"Why not? It wasn't my fault, now was it?"

Hattie caught her lower lip in her jagged teeth.

"Doesn't matter. You were out drinking with this man, weren't you? The Captain's old fashioned. It looks like you were, well, not exactly asking for it, but you certainly put yourself in a place where it could happen."

Iris stiffened, her green eyes sharp with anger.

"My God, Hattie, you can't think. . ."

"Not me, no, not me, darlin'. I'm talking about how a man sees things. Just keep your mouth shut, honey, and get your protection where you can. It can be mighty wearin' on a woman any other way."

Iris studied the thin, grim line of Hattie's mouth and nodded mutely, laying out a fork, a knife, and a spoon; then another fork, knife, spoon with an acceptance of the inevitability of formal, set patterns.

Four

"Got a minute, Dr. Hartman?"

"Exactly how many, Virginia?" asked Dee Hartman, peering over the rim of her reading glasses at her secretary. "I was hoping to get away early today."

"Well, a couple, I guess. Remember that girl I told you about? You know, the one who works for Mom down at the restaurant?"

"Oh, yes. The one who was raped?"

"Yeah, well, she's in the reception area. I guess she just decided to stop by and see if you were in."

"Of course," said Dee, closing the file she was studying and setting it neatly on the corner of her desk. "She probably needs to talk. Tell her to come right in."

It had been a long day and Dee was eager to get home and prepare dinner for her son Toby. She wanted to spend as much time with him as possible before he left for his summer in California with his father. But an extra half hour wouldn't hurt and the need of this girl certainly was genuine.

"Dr. Hartman?"

Dee looked up. A young woman stood hesitantly in the doorway.

"Yes. And you must be Iris. Please come in. Have a seat."

"Thanks." Iris took a chair near the window and smiled weakly at Dee Hartman. "I don't know where to start."

"That's all right. I know the general story from Virginia. But I want to hear it in your own words. And how you're feeling."

"Confused. Anxious."

"Understandable," said Dee. There was something familiar about Iris that she couldn't quite put her finger on. She was sure they hadn't met before, but Dee had a sense of knowing her. "You've had quite a shock."

"Oh, it's not all from the – incident – though I'm still shook from that. It's what to do next in my life."

"It would seem one would have quite a bit to do with the other, wouldn't you say?"

"I suppose," said Iris slowly.

"Why don't you start with what happened and we'll go from there," suggested Dee. She listened attentively as Iris told of her relationship to Gustav, the proposal, her doubts and the attack from the man in her poetry class. Watching her gestures and movement, it gradually dawned on Dee who Iris reminded her of. Iris was her younger self. Of course. Why hadn't she seen it? The physical resemblance was striking.

"...and so finally I figured it might help to talk it over with you. Virginia thinks you're the Goddess reincarnate."

Dee smiled. "How flattering. I don't pay her enough to get that kind of buildup. Tell me, what are you feeling right now?"

"Relief," sighed Iris. "I haven't said the whole thing out before. Must be my Catholic girlhood."

"How's that?"

"You know. Confession. Getting things off one's chest. Cleansing yourself of sin and starting fresh."

"You feel you were in sin?"

"Not sin, exactly. But I sure was in hell. Now it's more like purgatory. But if there is a devil, then Harold Lloyd Upton is certainly one of his agents."

"Who did you say?" Dee stiffened in her chair.

"Harold Upton. The Englishman. The bastard."

"Yes, well," Dee was having trouble regaining her composure. "I'll tell you what, Iris. I really must leave here soon. But I want to see you again. Tomorrow."

"Oh, I'm sorry, I know I just barged right in," said Iris, standing up quickly from her chair.

"No, no, that's all right. That's fine. I want to see you. How about tomorrow morning?"

"Sure. I don't have to be at work until late afternoon. What time?"

"How about ten?"

"Ten it is." Iris smiled at the older woman. "And thanks."

"Of course." Dee rose to her feet and walked Iris to the door. "Tomorrow morning."

Dee watched Iris disappear down the hall and turned sharply towards Virginia.

"Hand me Harold Upton's file, would you please?"

"Sure, Dee," responded Virginia reaching into the files next to her desk. "Mind if I take off?"

"No, go right ahead, I'll be a little while yet. Have a good evening."

Dee returned to her office and sunk into the soft leather of her desk chair. Harold Upton! The man had completely fooled her. He must have been playing games with her all along. Dee shook her head as she scanned the file. Her mentor, Dr. Wulff from Los Angeles, referred Harold to her six months ago and Dee had thought she was making headway with him. But he was obviously still drinking, which triggered his rage against women. And her miscalculation had cost Iris dearly.

Dee passed her hand across her eyes. No wonder Harold had cancelled his appointment that week. She felt an obligation towards Iris. In the brief session she sensed her deep hurt as well as her intelligence and sensitive nature. She wanted to help. And she also wanted to draw closer to this younger variation of herself.

During the next few days Iris opened up more as she gradually came to trust Dee.

"You see, I can't marry Gustav. And I can't leave the island. I know it's not all rational, but there are other powers that give me direction in life. I'm not that connected to people; I seem to have a stronger affiliation with dreams." Iris looked into Dee's clear blue eyes to see if she was with her.

"I believe in very primal things – good, evil and fate. Oh, I know that polite psychology doesn't admit to all these forces. Just symbols to you, aren't they? But there are dark powers that antiseptic science tries to ignore. And that pristine attitude allows the Harolds of the world to walk unimpeded and do their evil."

"Go on," prompted Dee. Mention of Harold made her uneasy. Her attempts to locate him had failed. He had cancelled his last appointment with her and had checked out of the transient hotel where he had been living. It was obvious that he had no intention of continuing sessions with Dee.

I'm sure you've got me figured out by now in your terms," continued Iris. "That I'm going to reject Gustav because he's a sailor like my father who deserted me by death and Dion who took away my sister. And I can talk to you because you're a stand-in for my mother – or sister – who also both deserted me. But it isn't all that simple."

Iris' steady gaze challenged the self-possessed Dr. Hartman. Dee smiled at her with amusement.

"That would be the classic interpretation. But what makes you think that I ascribe to it?"

"Assuming too much, am I?" Iris sat back in her chair. "Sorry."

"Nothing to be sorry for," assured Dee. "You're not used to talking things out, are you?"

"No, you're right there," agreed Iris. "I usually find my own way. I don't expect people to understand – or care. Not since I lost Phyllis. People are attracted to me, sure, that's easy. But not the caring. And I don't mind if I can be left alone to work things out. I used to have a place where I could do that here. But since yesterday, well, I've even lost that."

"What do you mean?"

"I know I shouldn't be that upset, but I am." Iris lit a cigarette and watched the smoke spiral to the ceiling before she started her story. "I had a special place down a small path along the rocky face of Diamond Head. I had found a niche in the rocks a third of the way up from the narrow beach. It was perfect. My hips fit exactly into it with a smooth rock at my back. I could read or look out across the water or watch the tiny marine life in the tide pools formed by the rocks and sand.

"I rarely saw anyone. I'd hear footsteps further up the side of Diamond Head once in a while where it was steeper and covered with foliage. But I never really paid much attention to the men I saw – or, more precisely, sensed – above me.

"Until yesterday. I was there reading, and suddenly a shower of pebbles bounced off the rocks around me. I turned, and on a ledge above me stood three naked men masturbating.

"I turned away, but not before I sensed their intent to ban me from those rocks. The dark hairy man on the left was hunched over, leering at me while he jerked his penis like he was sharpening a weapon. The man in the middle didn't seem to know I was there at all. His eyes were on the enormous penis of the man on his left. This third man was the youngest of the three; he had a trim, athletic surfer's body with long blond hair that brushed his brown shoulders. His eyes were fixed in a drugged stare at the horizon as he slowly and lovingly stroked his swollen penis.

"As you can imagine, I got out of there fast. I'm sorry to lose that place, but I won't risk calling down the inherent violence of trysting males. It's the same on islands as in mainland cities."

After her last words, there was an imperceptible click behind Iris' green eyes, then a slow smile spread across her features as she reached to stub out her cigarette in the ashtray on the desk. Dee was enthralled. She wasn't sure if Iris was telling her a true story or trying to impart a curious brand of wisdom to her by fable. It didn't matter, really.

"Am I projecting?" Dee asked herself. She felt drawn into a

very unscientific occult frame of mind around Iris, as if she were a messenger from an ancient order that gently mocked the proud upstarts of modern science. Try as she might, Dee could not dismiss a feeling that Iris possessed a strange aura of power, of knowing, that was alien to her. It was not linked to any pathology she was trained to unearth, and although she had not known Iris long, Dee felt a growing respect for her.

"Don't you have anything to say?" queried Iris.

"Should I?"

"No, I guess not," admitted Iris. "In fact, I don't know if I want – or need – to be a 'patient' anymore. I enjoy talking to you. But I'm no longer upset. I know what I'm going to do."

"And what's that?"

"Gustav's due back from Germany tomorrow. I'm going to meet him at the airport. And then I'll tell him I can't see him anymore. I've got my balance back now. I'm just going to bide my time here on the island. But one thing." Iris hesitated.

"Yes?"

"Is there a chance we could be friends? Like I said, I don't want to be a patient. But I like you."

"Thank you. And I like you. I agree that you seem to be back on balance now, though I wouldn't take things too fast right away. And I see no reason why we couldn't keep in touch, have lunch, something like that."

"Good," Iris let her breath out slowly. "I'd like that too."

"Then give me a call. Let me know how things work out with Gustav. Nonprofessionally, that is." Dee smiled a full smile towards Iris for the first time.

"You can count on it," said Iris firmly, as she rose to leave the office. "I have a feeling that we're going to be very close."

Dee just smiled her response. But as she watched Iris' receding figure she allowed herself the pleasure of anticipating their next meeting away from the office and without the roles that kept Dee from drawing as close to Iris as she desired.

Five

Iris arrived at the gate as the cluster of mainland vacationers poured forth from the jumbo jet. Her eyes cast nervously into the stream of bodies that trickled past her, looking for the broad, healthy span of Gustav's body. Suddenly, her eyes met those of a stranger behind steel-rimmed glasses. Iris gave an involuntary step backwards. It was Gustav, standing before her in an ill-fitting grey tweed sport coat and out-of-date skinny tie that made him look chunky and overfed.

He did not move to greet Iris, but stared through her as if trying to remember, to match a nagging memory. Fresh from Europe, he looked with displeasure at the Polynesian print shorts she wore and the string of shells around her neck. It was not dignified. She would need a new wardrobe before leaving for Germany. Then she was kissing him, turning her face against his chest as if it were a great shell, as if she were listening for the roar of the sea. Gustav drew her arms away from his body and held her at arms length.

"What's wrong, Gustav? You look so strange."

"Nothing. I'm free. I got what I asked for. Everthing is closed with my wife. I won't sail with the *Lorelei* again. We'll marry now." Gustav was sweating, the few extra degrees of Hawaiian summer making him curse under his breath and to dream of skiing in the Alps in the dead of winter, invigorated and alone.

"Not so fast, Gustav. We have to talk."

"You don't want to marry? After all this?"

"It's more complicated than that. And I never did say I'd marry you in the first place. And we can hardly talk here."

Gustav looked around, as if aware of the airport for the first time.

"Your apartment then?"

"No, Cora and Audrey are both there. Let's go someplace else."

"Come. We will go to Makapuu." Gustav clapped an iron grip on her elbow. "I need the water."

"Wait," pleaded Iris. "I don't even have a suit with me. Gustav, what's wrong?" She tried to keep the panic from her voice. The grip tightened on her arm painfully.

"We will buy a suit at the shop here and rent a car. Now come."

The car swerved dangerously around the curves of Route 72 on the way to Makapuu. Iris was frightened; Gustav was not acting at all like himself. And in the mood he was in she was afraid that her refusal of marriage would push him over some edge. The emerald and turquoise waters of Hanauma Bay appeared over the lip of the highway. Iris tried to tempt Gustav into the calm pleasures of the bay in an effort to calm him down.

"Remember the day we snorkled here, Gustav? How the blue reef fish and yellow tang ate from our hands? How happy we were?"

Gustav glanced at the bottom of the extinct volcanic crater that formed the sheltering hollow of the bay and shook his head.

"No, Iris. It is too crowded with tourists. We will go to Makapuu Point."

"Gustav, please, you must tell me what is troubling you."

"I will not be Captain again," said Gustav through clenched teeth, his eyes riveted on the road in front of him.

"Isn't that what you wanted?"

"Yes, for a time. But this is not my choice, this never to be Captain again. I wanted a year for the honeymoon. Now the company does not *want* me for Captain anymore. This is a difference. They do not think me fit." Gustav turned to Iris, a flash of hate across his eyes. Iris recoiled as from a slap.

"Surely you can't blame—"

A thought, a kindness dropped over the naked barbarism of Gustav's gaze. He shook his head as if clearing it from a drug and returned his eyes to the twisting road.

"No, Iris. This is not your fault. This is me. I did it."

The car hugged the coastline around the sheer volcanic cliffs that fell to the boiling sea and past the Blow Hole geyser. Finally Gustav pulled the car off the road above Makapuu, jerking the hand brake to stop the rocking motion of the car on the steep incline. His eyes searched the air far out to sea then snapped back to the roll of giant waves breaking on the beach.

"Not as high as winter," he muttered, "but still this is good." He nodded his head in satisfaction and turned to Iris.

"Makapuu is very important to navigation, yes? The easternmost point of Oahu." His hand waved above the water. "It is here the trade winds divide. And where the waves are always high." His hands swirled away from each other and crested over the horizon.

"Yes, it's magnificent." She gazed out to the lighthouse,

isolated on a protrusion of porous rock, her mind a blank in her confusion. Gustav was climbing out of the car, peeling the clothes from his body.

"Come. We swim. Then we talk." He was halfway down the steep path before Iris could follow, her new suit uncomfortable and unfamiliar, too tightly tied behind her neck. But she didn't stop. Gustav was throwing himself into the waves, slapping the water and shaking his head like a sea lion, the beaded sprays catching the light like a halo around his head.

Iris hesitated at the shore, drinking in the cavorting figure as it receded further and further out to sea. She was struck by the transformation in Gustav, his reunion with water. Gustav behind a desk would not be Gustav. He would be the boys she grew up with; precise and responsible and devoid of vision.

It was then that Iris realized why she didn't want Gustav at all. The fear she carried with her for weeks drained from her body. It was the water, the certainty of motion, a movement without traces, that she desired. She entered the water and took her first strokes against the powerful onrush of the ocean. A few hearty body surfers shot past her, their bodies planed out horizontally on the crest of a wave speeding toward shore. Her breath came in gasps as she lifted to meet each wave before it could close over her head.

Suddenly Iris felt a snap and a sharp sting across her right ear. The band that held back her hair had given way. Her long hair broke free, falling over her face, cutting off her vision just as a twelve foot wave rose in front of her. Confused, Iris stopped her stroke, not knowing for an instant which way led to shore, which way to sea. And in that hesitation, the wave consumed her, making her the center of its tumultuous rolling toward completion.

Iris' gasp of surprise filled her mouth with the briny sea. She was choking, gasping, rolling over in a whirlpool of water, unable to find the surface. Would forceful motion bring her to the top or drive her deeper toward the bottom? She could see no light. She gulped for air and half filled her lungs with water.

And death was elemental, a dark whirlpool without air, a spinning. Iris stopped struggling and sank into the slow loss of consciousness, the end without answer, neither cheated nor exhausted, her body relaxed into a curve.

A sudden punch in her stomach reopened her eyes. She was being propelled in a straight line motion against the turn of the wave, pulled limply backward against an inevitability of darkness. The water became lighter. Her head broke through the surface and the air filled her nostrils mixing with the water in her lungs. She still could not see clearly, her hair clinging like seaweed over her face and neck. But she perceived her motion as shore-directed, moving with the waves on top instead of within their motion.

This must be Gustav, this pressure pushing her breasts against her body, this dragging along like a cartoon caveman. This must be Gustav arranging her limbs on the sand, crushing her back with his weight, forcing this racking cough to spill salty pools from her mouth into the sand.

Finally Iris felt her body being turned over, hands brushing the hair from her face. She opened her eyes not to Gustav, but to a slender island boy, his black wet hair plastered against his head. A sudden certainty drove panic to her heart.

"Gustav? Where's Gustav?"

The boy turned to the cluster of people surrounding Iris and shrugged.

"Was there someone with you?"

Iris sat up, her eyes raking the horizon, following each set of waves, searching for a dark head bobbing in the trough of a wave or riding on top like a rightful heir. Nothing.

Iris sank back on the sand with a moan, flinging her arm across her eyes, oblivious to the young men rushing to make rescue dives, the woman weaving about her with awkward gestures of consolation. Iris knew it was futile. Gustav was gone.

Harold sat in the Kuhio Grill near campus, sipping a beer, nibbling fantail shrimp and gloating over his latest cat and mouse game with Dee Hartman. Giving her the slip was child's play. And when he finally showed up she would pretend that nothing was wrong. He'd walk into her office or stop by that little house in the valley and take up as if he had never missed a session. It would drive her buggy, take the wind out of her pompous sails, show her her place. What she didn't know was that he knew just about as much psychology as she did and was on to her method of operation. What fools women were! The educated were even more stupid than the common variety. There was nothing to challenge the cunning of the male.

Harold absently flipped pages of the *Honolulu Star Bulletin* while indulging his favorite fantasy when an article caught his eye: the drowning of a sea captain off Makapuu. The irony appealed to him. He enjoyed it when people failed in their own element. He excluded himself, of course, pouring the rest of the Primo into the beer glass and signaling the bartender for another. What he did best was drink, and no one could claim he failed at that endeavor.

Raising the glass to his lips he read down the column with pleasure when it struck him. "Good Lord." The exclamation spewed golden droplets across his moustache. Of course. Captain Gustav Monenschein. Iris' almost-fiancé.

Harold rushed out of the bar and turned the corner onto University Avenue, quickening his stride. Iris' apartment was only a block away. He hadn't seen her since her "lesson" the month before; probably she had gone whimpering to the safe marriage with the Captain with just a disturbing memory of the alternatives. It's all he could hope to do with the short time he had to work with her. But now, now, she might be ready for more. Life had dealt her the next blow for him, the deeper despair, and had cut off her possible avenue of escape. Each death drew her closer into the demonic territory he knew so well.

Harold rapped on the white door and worked his face into a mask of concern. He was about to repeat the gesture when a sharp voice demanded,

"Who's there?"

"Harold Lloyd Upton. A friend of Iris'. I must see her."

"No, I don't think so." There was a hesitation. "She doesn't want to see anyone but Dee Hartman."

"Ah, but you are wrong," responded Harold. The mention of Dee's name startled him. What was the bitch doing with Iris? Harold collected himself and renewed his plea. "Believe me, I can help."

"Oh, all right." The door swung open to reveal a chunky girl with limp, nondescript brown hair wearing an exasperated expression. "Maybe you can do her some good. God knows I can't."

"Thank you... what is your name? Ah, yes, Cora. We will bring her through it." Harold grasped her dimpled hand and squeezed it with sincerity. Cora blushed, uncomfortable with her hand clasped against Harold's thin chest.

"Ah, sure. Listen. She's a roommate, not a friend. I feel sorry for her, but Jesus. I think she's jinxed or something."

"Yes, yes, an unfortunate period for her and it must be a strain on you." Harold slowly released his grip. He leaned close to her ear, forcing her to retreat a step from his insistence. "She's an heiress, you know. Family doesn't have a clue to her whereabouts. A grand show of spunk on her side, wouldn't you say? Trying to make it on her own merit, finding her own way?"

"Well, I never knew," Cora's eyes widened, her fleshy mouth hung open moistly. Harold put a finger to his lips.

"Now, not a word that I let on to you, understand? She would be furious."

Cora nodded energetically. "Why, of course, I see, well, I never..."

Harold smiled, tossing his head and stepped into the apartment, closing the door discreetly behind him.

"And where is she?"

"Oh, in her room, of course... behind the rice-paper doors." Cora gave a slight involuntary bow. "And I'll just stay in my room here. Homework. Plenty of it." She stepped backwards through the door and closed it with a click.

Harold smiled to himself, twisting the frayed ends of his moustache into obedient smooth tips like a matinée villain as he slid back the wooden cross-hatched doors with a gentle restraint. Iris sat huddled in the corner of the small room on the rumpled, wine-stained sheets of her single bed. Her eyes, when they lifted to meet him, contained no trace of surprise. This is good, noted Harold to himself. Already she has the pose and attitude of receiving inevitable blows. For an instant he wondered if she had ever served time.

"May I join you, Iris?" Harold bowed as he stepped into the room.

Iris tipped the half-filled wine glass in her right hand toward him. Dipping gracefully, Harold hoisted the jug of wine next to the bed and refilled the glass, closing his hand over Iris' on the stem. She had been drinking, but she was far from drunk, the wine serving merely to deaden and not to obliterate her mind. Bending over her, Harold drank deeply, still holding her hand with the glass and looking for any spark of resistance in her eyes. Finding none he pronounced his command over her.

"To the dregs, my dear, drink it."

Harold guided the glass to her swollen lips and held it steady as Iris gulped the last of the red wine, her head tilted back, exposing the smooth whiteness of her throat. Satisfied, Harold let the glass fall to the floor and drew Iris off the bed.

"Come. We have someplace to go."

Endless rows of identical markers lined the crater. White dots ran like perforations across the renewed lushness of an extinct volcano. Punchbowl; the interracial graveyard of the military dead. Harold's grip was painful on Iris' upper arm, but she did not move or speak to ease the pressure. It was all part of her lesson, she was certain, part of what she must endure before meaning of any sort would grace her once again.

"Do you see all these deaths, my dear?" Harold hissed into her ear, stirring the air in the perfect calm and quiet of the colossal open pit tomb. "What makes you think your little death is so important, has any meaning, deserves attention?"

There was no response, no resistance from Iris as he drew her toward a cluster of blossoming shower trees.

"I'm going to fuck you, do you understand, Iris?" Harold's hot sour breath was heavy upon her as he jerked her forward. "You must rise above the self-importance of your own little ego, my dear." His reddened eyes widened as he pushed Iris to the ground, slowly unbuckling the worn leather belt of his rumpled trousers. "I'm going to fuck you back to the life you deserve, do you hear?"

Iris lay inert, her body at a right angle to rows of other lifeless bodies, her deadened eyes open to the even blue of the sky, motionless as a still-born sea. Her passivity excited Harold, her surrender more complete than he had dreamed.

"Turn over," he commanded. And she obeyed.

Iris' eyes lost the light, her face turned toward the ground. Then his awful weight was upon her, each cruel thrust into the dry tissue of her body causing her to bite the earth in pain, her mouth filling with dirt, chewing out her own narrow grave.

Six

Kiyo Slowkowski's almond eyes squinted against the sun from behind his black horn-rimmed glasses, trying to place the figure that scrambled from behind the shower trees toward the dilapidated red Volkswagen near the curb. Something about his movements aroused Kiyo's suspicion, a quality encouraged by the military training he was trying to forget. The car swerved close to him before careening against the opposite curb, righting itself and speeding toward the exit. In that confused moment Kiyo recognized the driver as someone he had seen around the campus. This character had stood out in his memory, with his strange head-tossing tick; obviously not a professor, yet older than most of the other students.

Kiyo hesitated a moment, his arms dangling at his side, his father's broad shoulders much too wide for the narrow Japanese body he inherited from his mother. Was it the breeze, or was there movement from behind the shower tree? Kiyo crossed the road swiftly with his silent tread, a sense of dread mounting as he peered around the trees.

His outward expression didn't change. At such times his Oriental demeanor was in command. But inside, from the pit of his stomach, he screamed at the sight of the young woman's twisted, half-naked body with the face turned to the ground. Newsreels of Vietnam flashed through his mind. All the reasons he chose dishonor over duty surfaced in the instant of awareness that one never escapes horror, not even amid the safe islands of home.

He turned her body gently, brushing clots of dirt from her face, not knowing which he feared more; her death or the obligation to take further responsibility for her welfare. Her eyes fluttered slowly, trying to focus on the smooth face obscured by the black beard, the smooth long black hair that feathered in the breeze.

"Don't be afraid," he soothed. "I won't hurt you."

Iris gazed up at the benevolent figure crouching against the slow-moving sky and fainted. Kiyo slid his arms under her knees, around her shoulders, and with surprising ease scooped Iris into his arms in one seamless motion. He walked with her against his chest down the hill to the old white Falcon parked in front of his father's grave on whose clean surface fresh-cut Birds of Paradise nodded slowly on their stalks in the wind.

The physical damage dealt Iris by Harold was not severe, but the healing came slowly. Fortunately, there was no sense of urgency in the house where she woke. With just a few utilitarian pieces of furniture, the sunny, well-swept rooms exuded a sense of quiet order, disturbed only by the hollow bamboo clatter of wind chimes.

Iris slipped fitfully from awareness into unconsciousness during the first days, noting movement and presences in short spurts. Besides the quiet glidings of Kiyo, she became aware of a young Japanese woman slipping through the house, a different fresh flower behing her ear each time Iris awoke. And there was another man, taller, with a lumbering gait, who struck poses more like those of a Chinese warlord than a Japanese master.

Her dreams were a United Nations horror show, with English lords in pink coats, blind Samurai and the entire force of the Luftwaffe pursuing her across the Pali, down Oahu's windward coast, around and around the island, her lungs about to burst as she ran into the sea for relief, only to trip over the bloated corpse of Gustav floating, eyes bulging toward the sky.

And then a scream woke her into the bare room, a woman's cool hand on her head.

"Just Rita," she reassures, then is gone, a book of Japanese poems by the bed next to a delicate hibiscus blossom in a hand-painted vase.

The presence of Rita triggered old memories in Iris; memories of her own childhood and the years she shared with her mother and her sister Phyllis. They were hard years, to be sure, those years after her father's death when her mother was away so much to earn their living. But Phyllis was always there; fixing her sandwiches, holding her hand on the way to school, telling her stories of Greek heroes far into the night. Even before her mother's death Iris was aware that they lived in a fragile universe, but that there was a fine web of women holding them safe, preventing them from falling into that darkness surrounding the pinpoint of stars.

Iris woke from her stupor refreshed, as if she had sweated out the past in her long delirium. After weeks in bed she opened her eyes to find herself installed in a gentle household of poets who asked nothing in return for great kindness and who also respected her long silences.

As soon as she got her bearings, Iris called Dee and Hattie to let them know she was safe but couldn't bring herself to leave the peace of the little mountain house. Hattie took it in stride, but Dee was disturbed.

"Are you sure you're all right?" she asked. "I don't know if it's so good for you to stay up there so isolated... and with strangers."

"It's all right, Dee. I appreciate the concern. But I just don't want to leave here now."

"I can understand. But how about a visit? Want me to drive up?"

"I want to see you, too, Dee. But not just yet. Maybe in about a week."

"I'm going to hold you to that, Iris. And please call any time, night or day. I'm frightfully concerned about you."

"I promise, Dee. Next week, then. Lunch or a drink, all right?"

"Okay. And I promise not to be doctor. Just let me be your friend."

"I know you are, Dee," said Iris softly. "I'm counting on it."

Iris hung up the phone and felt a new sense of security knowing that Dee was there for her. During the next week Iris learned to relax. Never before had she noticed, let alone enjoyed, the simple necessities of daily life. Iris would watch Rita with admiration as she arranged a simple egg dish, balancing color and texture with a fresh green sprig on each plate, as if each meal were going to be immortalized by a gourmet cookbook photograph.

"The palate is further pleased by the eye, but the real point is that it doesn't last," she told Iris when complimented. "Each moment can be beautiful when you don't need to hold on to it."

Iris tried to absorb this lesson, to learn the gentleness and acceptance that seemed to be the key to the harmony of the household. Never did she hear one of them reproach another, never did they sit in judgment, even when Michael became drunker than usual, reciting poetry fragments at the top of his voice and taking Rita away from her own work to make love in the back bedroom they shared. At such times Iris became uncomfortable, left alone with Kiyo, the night suddenly too quiet around them with not even a breeze to stir the air.

One day when she was handing flowers to Rita for an arrangement, Iris asked about Kiyo.

"Where's he from, Rita? He never talks about himself."

Rita smiled, looking up from her work, balancing the long stalk of a bird of paradise against her small breasts.

"He's from Kaneohe, on the windward side near the Byodo-in Temple. His whole family is from the military. His mother's family were samurai, his father from West Point. But Kiyo refused an appointment and he is not close to them. Inside he is much like you."

"What do you mean, Rita?"

"You both have your lonely distances from people. But you are changing him whether you realize it or not, as you are changing."

Although nothing more was said, Iris understood that Rita approved of her for Kiyo; that when she healed Rita hoped he would join Iris in the near bedroom he had gladly given up to her for her convalescence.

But most of the time that week was quiet and unpressured in the house near the mountains. The four of them spent most of their time at home, reading or composing poems separately or as a group in the soft light of evening. They laughed at Iris' first poems about flowers and island fauna. Her natural tendency was to make objects symbolic, to represent a thought or emotion.

"Relax, Iris," they coached her. "Just see what's in front of you. Don't make more of it than it is."

So she would laugh self-consciously and revise. But always there was an edge to her poems, a certain hardness and dramatic quality.

"You're a city poet, grown from concrete. Of course you're different from those of us who hardly ever leave the island. Just so." Then Kiyo would smile and refill her delicate white cup with warm sake.

Dee was uncommonly nervous waiting for Iris to make her first visit to her home, tidying up the house with uncharacteristic vigor. When she finally did walk up the drive just before eleven Dee had been ready – and not ready – for her since ten. Iris stepped into the house slowly, her eyes moving over the room like the hand of a blind woman over braille.

"May I look around?" she asked.

"Of course." Dee followed her as she examined each room. In Toby's disheveled bedroom she stopped and smiled.

"Your son's room?"

"Yes," Dee answered. "He's at school. Punahoo. A freshman."

Iris nodded her approval of him, of Dee, of the school, Dee didn't know which. Through the rest of the tour she moved like an amnesiac, as if every space and object had the sensation of memory, of long association rooted in a forgotten past.

"I like it here," said Iris simply. "It's very much like I imagined it."

After the tour they settled in the kitchen and drank coffee, cup after cup, trying to know each other, exchanging anecdotes about the islands and their lives. When the second pot of coffee was drained, Dee opened the wine and went about putting the final touches on their lunch of Chicken Risotto. She was vain about her cooking, considering its mastery one of the few worthwhile accomplishments from her years of service as the expensive, decorative wife of a rising young corporate attorney.

As they were about to sit down for the meal the front door slammed and a cry went out.

"Mom, I'm home!"

The two women turned simultaneously to face Toby as he burst into the kitchen on his straight line course to the refrigerator. He stopped dead in his tracks at the almost twin smiles that greeted him. Dee laughed and waved him to the empty chair at the table.

"Great timing, kid. Have a seat. Toby, this is my friend Iris. Iris, Toby."

Iris smiled her greeting as Toby slid into the chair.

"Geez, you had me confused for a minute. You look a lot like Mom."

"Yes, I know." Iris stopped herself from reaching over and straightening his carelessly rumpled hair. She was too new here to make such gestures.

Dee looked fondly at her son as he dove into the lunch. What a joy he was – and to think she didn't want him at first. Things had gone wrong so early between Tom and her that the thought of raising a son who might duplicate his insensitivity repelled her. Dee always wondered whether Toby ever sensed this early rejection. Did all mothers think of their children as bruised angels – and feel responsible?

As she leaned over to touch the nape of Toby's neck where his hair pushed up over his collar, she met Iris' eyes. They held a look of such tenderness, of longing, that Dee blushed and dropped her eyes for an instant. Once again Dee felt a flutter in her breast, the sudden shortness of breath she had experienced that day in her office. Raising her head, she returned Iris' gaze over Toby's head and nodded her head slightly, acknowledging the current that ran between them.

At the sound of wheels on gravel, Iris flipped the switch of the rice cooker, crossed the kitchen and opened the door to greet Kiyo. She had been daydreaming, turning over in her mind and heart the sensations of her day with Dee.

Iris stepped out onto the wooden stoop but could not find Kiyo. The white Falcon stood deserted in the drive. Then she spied Kiyo's squatting figure along the other side of the house, and she smiled. At the garden again. Kiyo would spend countless hours weeding, pruning, rearranging the flowers and plants covering the small plot of land. Although the house was in a populous area, the foliage was arranged in such a manner that walking out the back of the house gave the sense of cloistered seclusion under a faultlessly blue sky. Small birds bobbed around Kiyo, going about their business undisturbed by his quiet labors.

"Yo, Kiyo. Careful they don't nest in your beard. You've become as crazy as old Han-shan, treading trails of Cold Mountain."

Kiyo looked up smiling, his bright black eyes dancing in merriment.

"Burn the texts, burn the texts. And let the weeds run wild!" He rose, brushing the dirt lightly from the knees of his jeans, inwardly pleased that she had read the *Cold Mountain* poems he had left her the day before.

What a lovely man, she reflected. And yet, and yet... Perhaps she couldn't feel passion for any man yet. Gratitude, warmth; yes, that was possible. But passion? She shook her head slightly. What passed between them was more spiritual than physical. And then there were these growing feelings for Dee. Maybe sex wasn't important to Kiyo? He never pressured her. And that was the greatest pressure of all.

"I have a special treat, Iris-flower."

Iris reached out her hands to receive the two ripe mangos from his hands, their smooth skins of green and sunset pink cool to the touch. She hefted the heavy ripeness of the fruit.

"Are they ready?"

"Yes, Iris," assured Kiyo, stroking his beard. "It's summer harvest. Time for much ripeness in the mountains. Guavas line the trails. You should see them. How about taking a hike tomorrow, bring the tent and stay in the mountains for the night?"

Iris set the mangos down quickly on the stoop and sat down, her knees drawn close to her body.

"I thought Michael and Rita had to work tomorrow."

"They do. I thought you and I might go."

Iris hesitated. "There's something I wanted to discuss, Kiyo. I'm going back to work, part time. I'm strong enough now. And the restaurant wants me back. I called Hattie today."

"Good, if you're ready."

Iris rushed to complete her thought, the evening breeze

clacking the bamboo chimes over her head.

"Yes, I'm fine. And I want to contribute. You've all been so kind, but now that my money is gone, I want to keep pitching in, you know?"

Kiyo's small firm hand closed over Iris' fidgeting fists in her lap.

"Easy, Iris. You're our guest. For as long as you want to stay. Don't worry about money."

"Thanks," said Iris, drawing a deep breath. "But I need to work, Kiyo. To be at peace I have to feel I have earned it."

"All right." Kiyo's fingers pinched the air, flapping an imaginary cloth. "So back to El Toro with you."

"Thanks for understanding, Kiyo. I'll start next week."

"Then you can still go hiking tomorrow?"

Was he being innocent or knowingly insistent, wondered Iris. She sensed another question behind the stated purpose of the hike. She did care for him, she argued with herself, and she would like to see the mountains with someone who knew their way. Standing up, Iris gathered the mangos in her apron.

"Would you like them for dessert tonight, Kiyo? Or do you want to take them with us on the hike tomorrow?"

A wide grin spread across Kiyo's rounded features.

"Let's share these with Rita and Michael tonight. There's so much fruit on the mountain now. We'll have our pick."

They entered the kitchen together and silently went about preparing the dinner, Kiyo unwrapping and dressing the fish, Iris setting aside the mangos and filling the sake bottles to warm on the stove.

A half hour later Rita and Michael entered together as Kiyo and Iris were arranging the dinner on plates.

"Ah, this is even better than the service of twenty trained geisha," pronounced Michael, reaching for a delicate warm bottle of sake and downing two small cups in rapid succession. There was something in the way Kiyo and Iris smiled in unison that caught Rita's eye.

"I'll be right back."

Taking the small shears by the door she searched for flowers in the garden, choosing white ginger and wood rose blossoms for the arrangement. Smiling to herself, Rita gathered them, laying the stems gently in the crook of her left arm. The summer dusk settled, pink and orange and deepening blue around her. Harmony in contrast, she reflected, comparing the blossoms in her arm and looking up through the kitchen window to two heads of long hair; one black, one golden, bent over the freshly split mangos before them.

In a climate of unending perfection for the human body, one day could hardly be deemed more beautiful than the next. But Kiyo found the next morning exquisite as he jumped from his narrow bed on the living room floor and folded it quickly in thirds to store in the nearby closet. He stretched his small strong body with its oversized shoulders and slipped on his black horn-rimmed glasses to bring the room into focus. Running his fingers through the tangle of his beard and hair, Kiyo crossed to the kitchen to put on the kettle for morning tea. He became aware of the simple fact that he was smiling, a throbbing happiness seeping below his cultivated serenity, a sense of joy spreading through his system unlike the peace he found in the solitary moments on the mountain. Images of flowers and fruit filled his poet's inner vision. He heard Iris stirring in the nearby room. By the time he poured their morning tea he had composed a poem owing more to Western romantics than to Chinese sages.

They hardly spoke the entire morning of the climb, Kiyo setting the pace, light on his feet despite the tent and gear strapped to his back. Iris admired the way his thong-clad feet threaded their way among vines and protruding air roots from old banyan trees with never a falter. Her own progress was less sure, and she suffered a stubbed toe more than once through the flimsy canvas of her old smudged sneakers.

"Thimbleberries," Kiyo would say simply, pointing to a cluster a short distance from the moist, hard-packed mud of the trail. Or, "Guavas," indicating the hard greenish-yellow spheres dangling around them like so many Christmas ornaments. Further up the trail, where the more direct sunlight ripened them sooner, hundreds of squashed guavas lined the path, the deep pink softness of the fruit darkening like a wound. Birds with long thick tails and fruit flies buzzed through the heavy, sweet air, celebrating the banquet of decay. Kiyo noted Iris' irritation.

"Not much further," he reassured her, raising his finger to the sky with the mystic, mysterious smile of DaVinci's St. John. "We are nearing the top of the ridge."

Sweating slightly, Iris adjusted her small pack and hurried to follow Kiyo as he disappeared around a curve in the trail. Making the turn, she gave an involuntary gasp. In front of her was a forest, a curtain of bamboo ten feet tall. She saw the slight swaying of the stalks, and heard the hollow sound of bamboo struck against itself, the sound of a natural ceremonial. It was the sound she slept and woke to, the sound of the gentle wind chimes at the back of the house far down the side of the mountain. But here it was different, more measured and less random. Of course, Kiyo. Somewhere hidden among the towering bamboo he was playing the stalks like a giant xylophone.

"Kiyo, where are you?"

Only the hollow rattle of the bamboo answered. Iris grew uneasy. Was he trying to teach her a lesson or was he merely so absorbed in his artful play that he was oblivious to her?

Iris turned on her heels and followed the path out of the bamboo forest to the sunlit ridge alone. She had to start finding the way for herself.

One morning a few weeks after her lonely lesson on the mountain, Iris woke in her sun-filled room in a panic. She had an urge to be alone, to drive up the North Shore to a rocky promontory near Laie and just sit and think, looking east. It was September, a quiet time between the summer rush of tourists and the November rains.

She found Kiyo in the living room, folding up his mat to put in the closet.

"Take the car," he urged, sensing her growing irritability. "Just drop me at the airport and be on your way." He pulled a clean T-shirt over his head and tucked it smoothly into his jeans.

"Are you sure..." she trailed off, vaguely annoyed that Kiyo always seemed so eager to back up any mood or whim. She was spending more and more time at Dee's house. But he never asked about her whereabouts nor made a definite move towards her.

"Sure. In fact, just take the car to work with you and I'll have one of the guys drop me by El Toro's after my shift. You'll have the whole afternoon that way." He squinted at Iris, trying to focus her face as he replaced his glasses.

"The whole afternoon." Iris snagged the car keys on the way out the door. "I'll drive."

They were silent as Iris swung the car down the twisting mountain road. Iris was working against a sense of foreboding, a restlessness she tried to attribute to a form of "island fever," a mainlander's inevitable reaction to months spent on an island in the middle of the ocean. But it was not that, she knew. If anything, the island was a comfort to her. Maybe Dee could help. The point was that she was dreaming again, curious idyllic dreams interspersed with violent intrusions and culminating in a rush of wings.

Seven

Dee hummed to herself softly as she daubed the mayonnaise into the mixture she was preparing for deviled eggs. She had cancelled her appointments for the next day so that she, Toby and Iris could have the entire day at the nudist colony beach. Dee smiled to herself. She hadn't been sure at first that Iris would go along with the idea, but with a little coaxing she came around. Dee had a hidden motive in mind, beyond the unencumbered pleasure of the sun and sea: she wanted to check Iris' reactions to her "liberated" life style... she didn't want any barriers between herself and Iris.

The sound of the phone interrupted Dee's musings.

"Hello, Hartman residence."

"Dr. Dee, I presume?"

Dee detected the unmistakable wheeze of Harold Upton and a very unprofessional hatred shot through her system.

"Harold, where are you?"

"Oh, around, love. Rest assured. I'm around."

"Do you want to make an apointment?"

"Dear god, no. I think I've had enough of that game, don't you?"

"So you're drinking again, is that it?" Dee tried to keep her temper and to flush Harold out into the open. While she couldn't press criminal charges, perhaps she could be instrumental in getting Harold institutionalized for intensive treatment. And keep him away from Iris.

"Of course, dear Dee. It's what I do best, as you know. Lord, what a fool you are. You were almost too easy a quarry."

"Is that what you wanted to say, Harold? I would think you'd like to deliver that message in person."

"I'm no fool, Dee. You're not going to throw the net over me. I think you should save your 'treatments' for other quivering little souls. Like Iris."

"What about Iris?" Dee drummed the countertop with her fingers. How did he know the connection?

"I know everything, Dee. Everything."

"So what is it that you want?"

"Nothing. I just wanted you to know that I'm around. That's all."

"Harold, listen to me. . ." There was a click on the other end of the line and a long buzz. Damn him! Dee replaced the receiver and tried to slow her breathing to a normal pattern. *That bastard.* Dee tried to expel the image of Harold from her mind, replacing her fear with hopes for what the next day would bring. She had no intention of spoiling their time with the specter of Harold. She wouldn't tell Iris of the call. Dee squared her shoulders. That was settled. On with it, she instructed herself. Now if only I can find that old picnic hamper in the closet. And by such an act of domestic will, Dee banished Harold from her conscious life.

Dee, Iris and Toby escaped early the next day before the rush hour traffic could clog the overloaded streets of Honolulu. There was a perfect ease among them in the morning light; Toby telling the details of his favorite class, football practice, his progress as a surfer. It was only when they approached the sun-bleached wooden gate of the nudist colony that Iris stiffened and fell silent.

Dee eased the car down the sandy road past a few naked cultists who waved amiably at their approach and brought the car to a halt beside a simple, one-room cabin. Toby leapt out of the car, ripped off his clothes and left them in a crumpled heap as he dashed for the water. Dee climbed out of the car with a sense of purpose, grasping the heavy double handles of the picnic basket and swung it easily into the doorless mouth of the cabin. Iris unfolded herself hesitantly from her seat, not sure whether she should follow Toby or Dee.

Before she could decide, Dee reemerged and stood framed in the doorway, slowly removing her clothes while she looked absently towards the beach. Iris didn't know whether to watch or turn away. Unknown to Iris, Dee was fully conscious of the effect she was having on her. She was proud of her body. In spite of the Caesarean scar that bisected her abdomen and the hips and thighs that were heavier than current fashion would condone, Dee's tanned body was pleasing for a woman of forty. And she wanted Iris to see it.

After a slight hesitation, Iris slipped out of her print shorts and scoop neck top, neatly folding each piece with great concentration and care. Dee suppressed a smile. How shy she was! And then Iris was naked, too. Dee allowed herself the pleasure of drinking in Iris' form. How glorious she was. Dee wanted to weep for the perfection of her body, the softly rounded breasts, still pink and undarkened by childbirth. Her stomach lay flat, between her hips, her thighs long slender tapering stalks supporting the full flower of her young womanhood. Dee tried to conceal her pleasure with sophistication.

"Iris," she said, stepping forward and taking Iris' hands in her own. "Now, let's look at each other frankly and get used to it. The greatest gift of this island is naturalness in all its forms. Don't you enjoy being naked?"

"Yes," responded Iris. "But I've only been naked in houses, or at night to take a dip in the ocean. Never like this."

She was about to say something else but Toby came up behind her, shaking the water from his blond hair. Iris laughed.

"And never have I seen a mother naked with a grown son."

In the late afternoon pastels they drove home slowly; sunwarmed, salt-encrusted, a bit weary from food and wine, feeling oddly readjusted to their civilizing clothes. Iris and Dee were silent as Toby nodded drowsily in the back seat. As they approached the city, Dee reached for the stick to downshift the car and accidentally brushed Iris' thigh. In an instant Iris placed her hand over Dee's on the shift and held it as if waiting for a signal. Dee glanced over in surprise and met Iris' eyes boring through hers with the intensity of lasers. Without thinking, Dee nodded back to her, her heart turning over in her chest like a hibernating animal waking to spring. That night, after Toby went to bed, they became lovers.

Months later Dee would look back in wonder, trying to unravel the rich tapestry of that time. There seemed to be no linearity to their love but a series of interwoven experiences that built upon and enriched their time together. They became lovers. Just so. The shock came not from the fact that they were both women, but from the memory of the intensity of the lovemaking itself. Call it mythic, something removed from time, an interruption in the rational order of things. Dee perceived them to be not so much lovers as celebrants, priestesses in some forgotten order, using hands and tongues to articulate patterns that etched them around the very curve of space.

Does Paradise only exist as memory, she asked herself, an

impossible state to recognize as it is lived? It was only later that she could say it simply. They were happy together. They were in love. During the entire month of September they lived in an idyll: Iris and Dee and Toby, too. But Dee resisted a total giving of herself; she hid behind her professional demeanor to give herself time to adjust to the powers she had so naively unleashed.

So she quizzed Iris on her attitudes toward men; more precisely about Gustav, Harold and Kiyo. Dee told herself that it was in order to find out if Iris' attachment to her was neurotic or compensatory. In reality she wanted to know how truly Iris loved her.

One afternoon as they walked in Paradise Park admiring the yellows and pinks of the Rainbow Shower trees, Iris gave Dee the final word on the subject of the recent men in her life.

"I represented a different quality to each of them," explained Iris, breaking off a sprig and placing it in Dee's hair. "I was despair, salvation, the perfect victim. But they had a lot in common. For all of them, whether kind or cruel, I was unreal in myself; a projection of flesh or spirit. But not real."

"How about that brother-in-law of yours? How do you feel about him?"

"Dion?" Iris' face darkened. "I hate him. I realize now that he was trying to molest me as a child. Then he ends up marrying my sister and taking her away. But what does that have to do with us? I love you, Dee. Can't you just accept that?"

Dee hung her head. She could no longer dismiss their relationship as a novelty, nor was it her first encounter with a female lover. During the first wave of the women's movement she had had an affair with a lesbian painter from her consciousness-raising group in Los Angeles. But there was no passion amid the paint tubes; just intellectual justification and revenge on Tom for his latest mistress. Dee wasn't proud of herself for the pain her indifference must have caused when her ignoble ends were met and she stopped seeing the woman.

After confessing the story to Iris that afternoon, Dee asked if she had ever slept with a woman. They were laying in bed after their excursion deep in the valley; Mahler's First Symphony on the stereo, the curl of smoke from Iris' cigarette winding in counterpoint to the riot of hair on the flowered pillowcase. She turned to Dee with one of those faraway looks that dissolved her very presence.

"Once before, in college, I loved a woman. Matter of fact, she seduced me. But the morning after we made love I woke up and she was gone. It must have unnerved her. I only saw her in crowds after that and she'd run away from me. Of course *I* took the blame. I felt grotesque, like a monster." She reached her hand to Dee's breast and smiled, coming back to the present. "But you've made all that go away, Dee."

Iris' hand slipped from Dee's breast down her torso and disappeared between her legs. Dee gave an involuntary gasp.

"You're wet," Iris said softly.

"What do you expect?"

"Want me?"

"You know I do."

Iris rolled over on top of Dee, fitting the curves of her body into the hollows of Dee's body.

"And I want you. God how I want you, Dee." Iris pressed her mouth to Dee's, her tongue probing her mouth as her body undulated with the rhythm of their mounting passion.

"I want you inside me," gasped Dee between the thrusts of Iris' tongue.

Iris slid her hand into Dee's moist welcoming vagina and let out a groan as she felt the muscles contract around her fingers. She turned and brushed Dee's torso with light kisses as she worked her way down her body and took Dee's swelling clitoris in her mouth, flicking it with her tongue as Dee twisted with intensifying pleasure until she could take it no longer and burst into orgasm that shattered the light into a thousand rainbows.

The next day Iris moved in with Dee and Toby, appearing near noon with her single suitcase. Dee's heart lept with joy. She had not dared to hope that Iris would take up her offer to live with them.

"What about your friends?" she asked, trying to be fair.

"Oh, it's time to move. I'll always be grateful to them and of course I'll keep in touch. But I don't feel comfortable there anymore. And Kiyo was starting to get on my nerves. If he wanted me, why didn't he say so? He was *too* passive, *too* accepting. I was beginning to feel sorry for him; but angry, too. I wasn't going to get further involved out of gratitude or pity."

"So you're clear, then," said Dee. "About us?"

"Absolutely," said Iris quietly. She stopped unpacking for a moment and unwrapped an antique gold locket set with diamond chips and held it out to Dee. "Here. I want you to have this."

"No, Iris, I can't take that."

"Please," urged Iris. "It's all I have from my mother, who got it from her mother. And I want you to have it."

"But shouldn't it stay with you? It's a family heirloom."

"You are my family, Dee. More so than my sister Phyllis. I haven't seen her in years. Besides, I have every intention of staying with you, so it'll be with me anyway."

"All right, love, if that's what you want," said Dee as Iris opened the delicate gold chain and fastened it around her neck. "Because I have every intention of staying with you, too."

Iris turned Dee toward her to take her fully into her arms, the cool gold locket pressed between their breasts as they embraced.

And so one routine was exchanged for another. Iris still worked three days a week at El Toro's but avoided Hattie's probings into her private life. Her love for Dee was something she would share with no one.

"I never see that Japanese boy around here anymore, honey. You two have a fight?"

"No," said Iris. "I just moved out."

Hattie's eyes narrowed. "Find yourself a sugar daddy, eh?"

Iris laughed. The image of Dee puffing a cigar, dangling expensive baubles in front of a coy, negligee-clad Iris was hilarious.

"No, nothing like that at all. I'm staying with Dee Hartman. It's better that way."

"Hm. So I hear from Virginia." Hattie brushed Iris' cheek with a red lacquered forefinger. "That color in your cheeks don't come from the sun, baby. Since when do you have to hide from me?"

"I'm happy, Hattie." Iris stepped back, coloring even more deeply. "Just let me be, all right?"

"I hope you know what you're doing, sugar," sighed Hattie. "Something in my Indian bones tells me you're not through with your troubles."

Iris smiled and counted out her tips, setting aside a dollar to buy anthuriums for Dee on her way home. She loved the bold, waxy red beauty of the blossoms, so blatant and sexual and unashamed. Iris had been on the island for a year now and for the first time felt herself free from the tyranny of fate. A year, and here she was, happier than she had ever been, buying flowers for a woman who had broken the curse, taken over after the abdication of her mother and sister. She had come home.

In an effort to maintain her professional decorum, to make up for all the cancelled appointments during the first weeks of the affair, Dee stayed in her office on campus until three to see patients, arrange meetings and to generally reinforce her sagging image as a serious doctor of the mind. But once off campus she let herself return to her newly rediscovered status as a student of the heart. She stopped by the fish market to inspect the day's catch and selected fresh crab flown in that morning from Alaska. She wanted to make a special dinner for Iris. Toby would go straight from football practice to the Aloha Week celebration, foraging for his dinner among the food stalls set up for the festival. They had the entire evening to themselves.

It was about five when Dee heard the screen door slam. She was busily prying open the crabs in the sink with an ice pick to get at the tender meat.

"In here, Iris darling," she called out, mentally checking down the menu – crab, asparagus, white wine already on ice, a green salad and a special mousse for dessert.

Dee looked up eagerly, only to see Harold's form filling the doorway, his weight on one hip, a sneer on his face, his eyes slightly out of focus with alcohol. A *lei* hung wilted and stained around his neck. Her heart stopped for a moment in fear while her mind raced through the tools of her profession, hoping to find a protective shield or weapon to use on him.

"Well, well, Iris *darling*, is it?"

"Why Harold, what a surprise. Did you decide to come back to treatment after all?" Dee felt absurd, chattering like a hen, but she needed desperately to buy time.

"Oh, come off it, Dee. I told you I'm through with that little game of yours." He tossed his head and bared his yellow teeth in a menacing manner. "I repeat. What's this about Iris?"

"Iris? We're friends."

"Don't insult my intelligence, Dee. I may be mad. But I'm not stupid. I told you I know everything. Sit down."

Dee moved toward the kitchen chair slowly. Harold reached for the open bottle of cooking wine and took a large gulp before speaking. Drops of wine clung to his moustache. His eyes stared red and vacant.

"You really should draw your bedroom curtains at night, darling. I happened by last night. Did you know that by standing on a cinder block one can peer directly through the slats and be treated to Sapphic scenes of delight? The two of you really are lovely, all naked and intertwined in your innocent sleep."

Dee tried to interrupt, to steer the conversation back to him, but he held up a finger and commanded, "Quiet, bitch! I'm a sophisticated man. Do you think I'm upset by anything as trivial as women sucking each other off?" He gave a hollow laugh as he took another gulp of wine. "This sort of thing happens in the absence of the male. But I'm back, you see. And you both need a little lesson."

Dee opened her mouth, but before she could speak his hand shot out like lightning, delivering a stinging blow across her face. "I said quiet!" he screamed.

Without words she could not touch him. And he knew it. Then he was upon her, his hands around her throat, choking her, dragging her off the chair and onto her knees.

"You bitch, you cunt-sucking bitch."

He slapped her, tore at her clothes. His strength was enormous. Dee thrashed wildly to free herself but her struggle just prompted more blows from Harold.

He pinned her to the floor by her throat with one hand, his other hand unbuckling his belt, his body poised above her for one long terrible moment. Dee closed her eyes; the sight of him just added to the nightmare. Iris was right. Harold was evil. And he couldn't be stopped by reason or compassion, nor kept at bay by love. She was struggling for her breath, knowing that this time Harold meant to kill.

Then suddenly his body gave an odd jerk. A scream rose above her as the grip loosened on her throat. Then a spasm of jerks and Harold's entire weight slumped onto her own body and lay still. Dee opened her eyes in surprise. The ice pick jutted from the back of Harold's neck, blood trickling from either side. And standing above them was Iris, her face contorted in hate and triumph.

She rolled Harold's body off Dee and half lifted her to a chair.

"Are you all right, Dee? How hurt are you?"

"Not too bad," mumbled Dee.

Iris stepped over Harold's body to get water from the sink, brushing aside the anthuriums whose crimson blossoms mocked the wounds of Harold's body. She moistened a towel and applied it to Dee's bruised face.

"Just relax, darling. Everything'll be fine."

"We better call the police," said Dee in a groggy voice.

"Fine," agreed Iris. "I don't care what they do to me."

"No, no, wait a minute. It won't work." Dee shook her

head as it started to clear. "You never reported the rapes, the beatings."

"No, you know I didn't, Dee."

"Then they won't buy it." From some deep reserve Dee found the courage, the knowledge of how to save them both. She took the towel from her face and bent over Harold. Carefully, she wiped the handle of the ice pick still lodged in his neck, then gripped it firmly in her own hand, leaving clean new prints.

"There," she said, sitting back in the chair to relieve her dizziness. "Now get packing. You can't be here when the police arrive."

"I'm not going to leave you here," protested Iris. I'm not going to let you take the blame."

"It's the only way, darling. I've got my professional credibility. And there's a ton of documentation on Harold's violence. Besides, I'm the one with the fresh bruises. They'll believe me. You'd be harder to explain."

"I can't leave you like this," wailed Iris, reaching out for Dee.

"You have to, my love. Just for a little while. Now get everything into that suitcase. Fast."

Iris tore herself away from Dee, the old foreboding of abandonment rising in her. She was packed in five minutes and waiting by the door.

"Here," instructed Dee, handing her a billfold. "It's all the cash I have. And a credit card. Take the first flight out of here. Walk over to the intersection and call a cab from the Kuhio Grill. Have coffee, take your time. And don't try to call me."

"I'll write to Rita, tell her to let you know where I am. She'll do it and not ask any questions."

"Good," approved Dee.

It was the parting moment, both of them too full of raging emotions to speak. Dee reached out and held Iris' trembling body to her own.

"I love you, Iris," she said finally, simply, without qualifying statements or hesitations.

Stepping back, Iris held Dee's head in her hands, looking deeply into her eyes, her own fine eyes filled with tears. Iris gave a slight nod, kissed her, then was gone. Dee waited until she rounded the corner, then walked purposefully to the phone and called the police.

Kiyo Slowkowski walked slowly toward the employee parking lot after his shift. His long arms swung loosely at his side, his mind clear of thought. It was better this way, this uninterrupted peace of mind, this solitude apart from the passions of others.

His beard lifted gently in the early evening breeze as he opened the door of his old white Falcon. Overhead one of the last flights of the day, a 747, nosed higher into the cloud-dotted sky. He looked up at the plane's belly that he had just stuffed with cargo and felt a pang. His heart fluttered with regret, with acknowledgement to his ancestors that he was afraid to fly.

The plane edged higher to gain the altitude it needed to clear the high ridges of the Koolua Mountains bathed in late afternoon light. Shadows were already creeping up the base of the mountains where King Kamehameha's enemies leapt to their deaths in the wake of his drive to unify the islands. The plane leveled off as it passed over the Pali. Off the right wing, weary body surfers caught one more set of foam-crested waves, their bodies skimming past the lighthouse of Makapuu Point to shore. In the opposite direction, off the plane's left wing, a small band of naked people crouched around a fire on the beach, their tanned bodies taking on the russet tones of ripe fruit, of innocence, on the dusky shore.

Then the plane took a sharp inclination upward, lifting higher into the region of light above the clouds. The island receded until it appeared only as a mote in the eye of the ocean.

II.
The Obscure Oracle

One

After the middle of October even the ferry from Crete ceases its sixty-mile voyage across the crisp southern Aegean to Santorini. The cruise ships do not risk calling, afraid of unexpected high seas that could maroon their high-paying clients on the foreboding island for weeks, cut off from the mainland and illusions of power over the heavy sea. Few non-natives would choose to spend a grim, isolated winter on the white marble surface of this extinct volcano, prey to the forces of ancient ghosts and dark mysteries.

Santorini lies nearly equidistant from the Peloponnesus, Turkey and the island of Crete – a lonely sentinel of the Aegean, belonging to none, the renegade of the Cyclades. The very shape of the island serves as a disquieting reminder that all is just half done, still to be completed, unresolved. The inner lip of the crater forms the eighteen miles of curved coastline in the shape of a sickle with its mouth open toward mainland Greece – shouting a curse across the water to the thriving, the secure, the satisfied.

It is said by many – peasants, folklorists and geologists alike – that Santorini is the most likely site of Plato's fabled Atlantis, that the eruption that started here caused the tidal wave and subsequent flood that swallowed the ancient world in one colossal deluge. The flood. All traditions speak of it. Versions of this disaster are depicted in Egyptian hieroglyphics, in Plato, in the sacred writings of the Jews, the Muslims and the Christians. A flood of such magnitude that it lingers as our most primordial fear. Each time we feel the pull of undertow or stay one second too long under water, we re-experience the horror of knowing all our labors to be soluble in a roaring wall of water that sucks everything before it into the final entombing silence. Triggered by sudden volcanic eruption or nuclear blast or by the slower but no less effective melting of polar ice caps, all cities are doomed to become Atlantis. And all destinies are ultimately subterranean.

In the dawn light the cliffs of Santorini display a muted striation of green, scarlet, mauve, cobalt, grey and yellow impressed upon the twisted convulsions of rock by terrible heat, some eon before humans began to record time. These cliffs are nature's Parthenon, testifying to a force greater than the ordered powers of civilization.

The smell of sulphur still lingers in the air as the boat crosses the very center of the extinct volcano to land on the rim of the shore. Bits of pumice float in the bay like an omen, a warning of impending explosions. Wisps of steam still appear around the two small islands floating in the warm water of the bay. At night the silence is profound, the islands black in their steaming caldron.

By mid-November the Pleiades begin to rise in the early evening. Rain squalls are frequent. Fishermen draw in their nets and seek winter quarters. Women gather at the communal bakery, sharing their secret knowledge in low voices as the bread rises. The men congregate in the cafe to drink arak or ouzo, to discuss news of Europe from month-old papers or to stare mutely into space when a distant howl cannot be attributed with absolute certainty to the wind.

All is not dead in winter on Santorini. The purple saffron crocus is in bloom; its stigmas prized as an aphrodisiac. Tangerines and oranges take on their first blush of color. But no one ventures into the fields in winter. Since the recent disturbance of the archeological excavations, there are too many distraught ghosts wandering the countryside, accompanying the more familiar witches, vampires and random apparitions.

The town itself hangs nine hundred feet above the harbor and can only be reached on muleback by way of a perilous, twisted path. It is here that the Hotel Atlantis is situated, facing the volcanic bay and the open sea. It is here that Iris found her winter home in the dying year far from the mainland and the delusions of civilization.

Like so many before her, what drew Iris to the island was

her own despair. The euphoria of escape, of fully vented revenge, gave way to a terrible loneliness. She feared that her meager portion of love and happiness had been used up in one perfectly-orchestrated interlude that now was done, its echoes a maddening, melancholy harmony that played only to her inner ear.

The despair did not grip Iris all at once; her hopes had still been high when she landed in Athens after her flight from Hawaii. She was convinced that a letter sent to Rita for Dee and a short wait for response would serve to reunite them in a matter of weeks. Iris had checked into an indifferent hotel in Athens, leaving her room only for meals in fear that she would miss a message, a phone call or a telegram announcing Dee's arrival. She slept fitfully, kept awake by her muddled dreams that left no trace or direction upon waking, and by the incessant bouzouki music that played far into the night, the last strains floating out to meet the first dawn rays over the tiled roofs of the city.

On the tenth day the yellow envelope appeared in her pigeonhole behind the front desk. The middle-aged desk clerk smiled archly as he handed her the envelope.

"For you. I think you were waiting for this, no?"

Confused and anxious, Iris threw a folded bill from her pocket onto the counter, snatched the envelope from his hand and ran out the door to the nearby cafe where she took her meals. She did not want to open it until she was safely off her feet with a fiery ouzo on her lips to give her courage. It was just a telegram, she told herself. How much could be given in a telegram? A flight, a time; no more.

Iris ripped open the envelope, oblivious to the eyes that watched her from the corners, the men who passed and stopped to preen in front of her, dreaming of America and the fortunes to be won by making love to rich women. Iris neither heard nor saw any of them as she carefully unfolded the message with shaking hands.

CAN'T COME NOW. AM FREE BUT BEING
WATCHED. INQUEST FORTHCOMING. ALL
WILL BE FINE. MONEY TO FOLLOW. I WEAR
LOCKET ALWAYS. LOVE DEE

Iris jerked her wrist to order another drink, fighting for clarity of thought and feeling. Dee wasn't coming. There was trouble. Why had she left the island so thoughtlessly? Would it have been so very bad to try and clear herself? But then it was sure to come out about their affair and that would only serve to cast doubt on motives once again. Dee would have even more problems, not the least of which was the threat of losing Toby in an ugly custody case. No, they did the only thing they could do under the circumstances. Dee couldn't join her in Greece and she couldn't go back to Honolulu without further jeopardizing Dee.

With no reason to wait in her room Iris was seized with a desire to walk, to roam the noisy city and to mix with the crowd of parading Athenians and meandering tourists. She rose from the table abruptly and tripped down the rough cobble of the street. But her progress was impeded by the men buzzing around her like flies, proud men, their hair thick with the sheen of olive oil, who ran after her or leaned from automobiles, offering her exotic ecstasies in languages she could not understand.

"Make me a hag," she begged the presiding deities. "Let me go unnoticed among crowds of people."

Finally she freed herself from the sticky cluster of men and rounded a corner. A group of stocky Aryans, the men dressed in shorts and loaded with cameras were orderly filing into a small bus. They reminded her of Gustav's crew and their familiarity was welcome to Iris. She approached one of the more pleasant-looking women.

"Excuse me, do you speak English?"

"Ja, some English."

"Good. Where are you going? This bus, where is it going?"

"We see the Acropolis."

"Please, could I go with you? I'll pay."

The woman hesitated, her Germanic sense of procedure resisting the suggestion. But the warm sun, the woman's sense of holiday and compassion won out.

"You are alone?"

"Yes, I am alone," Iris assured her.

"Ah, so. You wait here." She turned to a companion, spoke a few words of German, then approached the tour leader with explanations. Iris watched his face darken as the woman spoke. When she pointed out Iris the man's features softened and finally his head gave way to a nod. The woman executed a half bow to the man and returned to Iris.

"This is fine. But you know the instructions are in German. You will not hear the history."

"Oh, no, that's fine," beamed Iris. "I know a lot from school. I just want to walk around. That's all."

"Good. Follow me."

The woman rejoined the line at the bus with Iris at her heels. The bus carried them through the streets at speeds Iris felt were unsafe for passengers and pedestrians alike, but no one else seemed to feel in peril. They drove up the approach to the Acropolis, feeding into the stream of bodies, cars and buses and two-wheeled conveyances of all descriptions headed for the crumbled pile of stones that Western man clings to as his prime symbol of harmony, order and beauty in the universe.

"One hour," the German woman instructed her, tapping the watch strapped to her ample wrist. "Come back here in one hour, we leave."

"Thank you, yes, I'll be back."

Iris walked slowly up the path to the Parthenon, remembering all the things she had read and imagined about the meaning of the building. When Iris was a little girl her sister Phyllis had been enamored with everything Greek. She would tell Iris stories from mythology by the hour, about the battling Zeus. and Hera, the beauty of Aphrodite, the wisdom of Athena, the power of Ares and the disruptive charms of Dionysos. While other children repeated Mother Goose, Iris learned of the battle of Troy, the wanderings of Odysseus, the quest for the Golden Fleece and the unthinkable revenge of Medea.

Perhaps it was Phyllis who was responsible for Iris' notion that gods and spirits could enter directly into her life, give her instructions in dreams and determine her fate. The thin veneer of Christianity that was laid over this early indoctrination never sunk into the grain of Iris' character. A host of half-human deities with faults intact was always more appealing than the stern monotheism that demanded allegiance to one perfected and untouchable god.

As Iris approached the ruins her heart beat faster. She anticipated an avenue back to the pagan perfection of childhood. She could hear Phyllis' voice, remember her plain, kind face framed in unflattering bangs and inappropriate ribbons. Phyllis was not a pretty child like Iris, although her features had promised a handsomeness in womanhood. But she was not here, not among the ruins of a civic center thronged with tourists and besieged by the acidic, polluted Athenian air that promised to hasten the ravages already inflicted by war, bombings, English lords and time.

Despite the Parthenon's dedication to Athena, the Acropolis was a monument to men. The plateau above the city was designed to impress its power upon the citizens, free men and slaves who labored below. This was not the site of oracles and dreams. There was no humility about the place, no recognition of intervening powers. It was quite simply built in homage to the glory of men.

Iris' disappointment was palpable. She gazed out past the crisp blue and white Greek flag snapping in the breeze, across the jumble of flat rooftops pierced by the occasional long finger of a cypress tree, out further to the mountains barely visible through the haze that settled over the city. She had to get out of the city, back to an island. It was a mistake to wait on the mainland; she never received instructions in the confused, contorted corruption of landlocked cities.

Iris circled the Parthenon, more to take up time than to drink in the sight. She knew there were occasional ferries to the larger islands and decided to let chance take part once again. Whatever ferry left from Piraeus the next day she would board and wire her location to Dee.

That resolved, Iris could relax, feel the warm sun on her head and arms. She lit a cigarette and looked at the tourists snapping each other's pictures against the backdrop of the still heroic Doric columns. Why did men insist on throwing up stones against nature in some petulant, fruitless gesture of defiance? Iris made her way slowly back to the bus. Calm down, she instructed herself. Tomorrow, the islands.

When she arrived at Piraeus a ferry bound for Crete was about to leave. Of course it had been scheduled to leave a full hour before Iris' arrival but delays were common enough not to be solely attributable to Iris' singular fate. Without further hesitation Iris boarded the large ferry bound for "the big island" and hung over the rail as the last cars were driven into the boat's belly. She was struck by the number of Scandinavians that lined the deck, their blond heads burnished platinum in the Greek sun.

Iris sighed with satisfaction as the ferry pulled away from the harbor. It would be a long journey across a roughening sea and they would not see Crete until the morning. Like many Americans Iris' idea of Crete was a jumble: Anthony Quinn as the irrepressible Zorba crossed with the image of the terrible Minotaur at the heart of the maze.

She kept to herself for most of the voyage, not caring to

strike up any acquaintance with the other tourists or Greeks on holiday. She wanted to absorb the rhythm of the water as she once again was at sea, rocked by the element from which she took her strength.

Iris woke early the next morning so that she could be on deck when Crete came in view. She didn't have to wait long. In the early morning the broad rocky back of the island filled the horizon. How large it seemed. Iris felt disappointed at the size; what she longed for was a solitude free of the distraction or the temptation to explore such a wide terrain. As the ferry drew nearer she could make out the walled city of Heracleion that still retained the architectural flavor of its former Venetian masters.

Too busy, she murmured as the tourists poured down the plank on foot and by car. Too much like a Mediterranean Honolulu, prepackaged for the unimaginative. She noticed that most of the tourists veered to the left on disembarking from the ferry, heading for the ruins at Knossos five miles away or to hotels in the more fashionable area of the town. Without reservations or guidebook, Iris chose to follow a quiet middle-aged Greek couple down the ship's ramp and trailed them at a slight distance.

The man wore a crisp white shirt that caught the early light and reflected it back onto his wife's traditional shapeless black dress. The way they turned to the right without a glance in any other direction gave Iris the impression that they had been here before and were on private business rather than holiday. She followed them for a quarter of an hour, turning in the crooked streets until she was totally lost. They finally stopped in front of a modest whitewashed house indistinguishable from the others, and knocked on the weathered wooded door. It was flung open by a man who bore a strong resemblance to the woman. There was much excitement; kissing and embraces and the presentation of gifts tied in brown paper extracted from the worn bag the woman carried on her arm. Then the couple disappeared, the voices muted as the wooden door slammed shut and Iris was left alone in the strange street.

She looked around the area in which she found herself and continued her wanderings unperturbed. The first hotel I find will be mine for tonight, she decided and soon she passed a modest hotel next to a taverna whose rough latticed roof was choked with grape vines, providing a dappled shade as the sun rose higher above the city.

It was on that afternoon, lulled by the many glasses of ouzo and the kind attentions of the owner, that Iris felt relaxed for the first time since leaving Hawaii. Free of the smog screen of Athens, the sun's rays soaked directly into her body and bathed the entire courtyard in the fabled haunting light of antiquity.

Seating herself in the semi-shade, Iris had uttered "Ouzo" to the old man who approached her, wishing she knew even the simplest word for please or thank you in Greek. He shook his head sadly.

"And nothing to eat? Ouzo on an empty stomach will make you sick."

"You speak English!" exclaimed Iris.

"I should," laughed the old man. "I lived in New York for thirty-two years."

Now it was Iris' turn to laugh.

"I should have known. Come halfway around the world and across a rough open sea and who do you meet but another New York Greek running a restaurant."

"Come. It's easier for you, no? At least I can understand what you need. If it would make you more comfortable, I could speak in Greek and you could get frustrated and hungry." His craggy face and nut-brown arms belied his Manhattan connection.

"And why are you here now?"

The old man made a sweeping gesture with his arm, taking in the sea, the sky, the mountains in back of them.

"You see all this and you ask me why I'm here? Since the time of Odysseus every Greek wishes to end his days in his home. I saved all the years I lived in New York to come back here and live where I was born. Five years now I'm back. I'll never leave."

"Understandable."

"Call me George. Now, if you still want that ouzo I'll bring you something nice to go with it, OK?"

"Fine. I'm in your hands." Iris leaned back and pushed her single valise under the table. It seemed so long since someone had wanted to nurture her that she entirely gave in to George's command. He reappeared in a moment, a bottle of ouzo and a small glass on a tray and a plate adorned with a generous wedge of feta cheese and honey-covered dates.

"Eat, drink, be Greek, my beauty." He slid the contents of the tray onto the small table in front of her with perfect ease. "You stay with us long, eh?"

"I don't know. Crete's so large, hardly like an island at all."

"Oh, it is an island, all right. It'll take you at least two weeks to see it all. You can stay two weeks, can't you?"

"I don't know." Iris swallowed her mouthful of cheese, honey and fig. "I really want to go some place else. A smaller island, more isolated."

George seemed offended. "If it's the real Greece you're looking for, then this is it. Crete's the most Greek of all the islands. Don't make up your mind until you go to Knossos. You have to see Mount Juktas through the Horns of Consecration above the ruins."

Iris downed the first ouzo with a quick twist of her wrist. "No, I didn't come to see ruins, George. I need to be alone. I need to hear the spirits of Greece, not see its stones."

"Ah, you have had a tragedy, then," said George softly. "Even the young and beautiful have tragedy, no? The gods are jealous. I understand."

"Do you know a place where I might go?"

George hesitated and flicked his damp towel at a fly that dared to trespass on a honey-soaked fig.

"Santorini is such a place. You wouldn't be bothered there. But it's not safe."

"Not safe? What do you mean?"

"There are many ghosts and not all of them kind. And vampires."

"Vampires?"

"Yes. And not the sort you see in the movies on Forty-Second Street. But there are wise women there, too, who know the spells to keep them away. They are witches."

"This Santorini sounds better and better. Is it far?"

"This is no joke, young lady. You don't know about the powers that are loose on these islands. This is not New York, where you can call the police or hop in a cab to take you to a safe East-Side apartment. This is Greece. And you must have respect."

Iris bent her head, studying the thick liquid ouzo in her glass.

"I'm not playing, George. I'm familiar with the powers you talk about. I'm beginning to think I'm part witch myself." George reached out his hand and patted her golden head bowed over the plate of figs and cheese.

"Excuse my anger, little one. Not many your age have such knowledge. Yes, Santorini is very close to here. If you like, I can make arrangements. A cousin of mine runs the Atlantis

Hotel. There is a boat that makes the trip once or twice a week in good weather, less during the rainy season. If you must go, I'll send a letter with you. You'll be looked after."

"It's where I must go, George."

"Then so be it." He crossed himself backwards in the manner of Greek peasants and retreated into the shadows to leave Iris to drink undisturbed and to reconcile herself with her decision — a winter of exile on the island of Santorini while waiting to be reunited with Dee.

Two

From the port of Piraeus it is a short bus ride to the Devil's Tower jutting out into the Gulf of Athens. Only a narrow channel of water separates the mainland from the island of Salamis. It was at this particular spot that the over-confident Xerxes set up his golden throne to witness the inevitable Persian victory over the Greeks. He commanded over two thousand ships while the entire Greek force consisted of only four hundred vessels. But the sheer size of the Persian ships were their downfall. The small, skillfully maneuvered Greek vessels were able to sink the lumbering Persian ships which could not respond in the shallow narrows near Salamis. Over fifteen hundred Persian ships were disposed of that September day, four hundred and eighty years before the birth of Christ. Xerxes was forced to flee and Persian culture was kept from spreading throughout the Mediterranean.

Naval history cites the Battle of Salamis as the archetypical example of victory for the skilled underdog. It was for this very reason that Dion Panagakis wanted to visit the Devil's Tower on his first trip to Greece. His parents were from Rafina, near Marathon where the young messenger died of a burst heart after delivering his message of victory.

Dion always seemed situated near the site of a battle. He was born prematurely on board an overloaded cargo ship headed for Florida. That same day, the officially neutral Greece was invaded by the Italian army and plunged once more into war. After a brief sojourn in a colony of relocated Greek sponge divers in Tarpon Springs, Andreas and Sophia Panagakis moved down the coast with their new son, seeking a quiet corner to set down roots in their new land. And when they ran out of coast they boarded another boat and came to rest, finally, on Key West.

Young Dion grew up to tell time by the movement of tides and the arrival of boats from the mainland. His father returned to fishing, the one trade he knew, and signed on to help draw fish from the warm Gulf waters onto the decks of other men's boats. Weeks would pass when Dion had only his mother for company. She didn't learn English at first, stubbornly preferring her deep Greek silences. She spent her days weaving, preparing their food and praying to the ikon she brought with her from Rafina for the blessing of more babies. But no more babies ever came to her.

By the time Dion was ten his father purchased his own boat and took his son on as apprentice to teach him about prevailing winds and the living, silver treasures that could be coaxed from the depths of the sea. Dion came to love the sea as much as his father. He grew impatient during the long months in school, dreaming of the summers when he and his father would haul nets of squirming fish over the side of their boat, the sleek silver bodies flicking rainbows of color in the sun.

But as he grew older he grew ashamed among his schoolmates.

"Hey, Stinky," they would call, "what's the special today?"

Not for him did the golden-haired girls wait after school. Instead they attended the captains of basketball and football, whose fathers ran polite, sweet-smelling hotels where rich guests from the mainland would sip drinks on the veranda, contemplating the sunsets.

In time young Dion grew ashamed of his father, too, and found a summer job in one of the hotels to avoid shipping out with him. His father was deeply disappointed, but he did not want his son to be an outsider in his own land. He himself had been an outcast, and would not be in Florida now if he had found a way to remain in his homeland without bearing arms.

Andreas Panagakis was the rare Greek who chose pacifism over conflict, an unheard of and undervalued choice in the shadow of German and Italian fascism. Like many simple men, Andreas held deep convictions. He embraced the Sermon on the Mount as his guide to daily life and read everything he could about Gandhi and the power of civil disobedience. But his arguments had fallen on deaf ears. The citizens of Rafina called him a coward, a faggot, a woman. They believed his presence in their town would bring them dishonor and defeat. Sadly, Andreas sold his boat and took his pregnant wife to America so that their child would not be born in shame. And now that child stood in front of him, trying to avoid his eyes.

"Go then, Dion. Be like the American boys. Learn about hotels and football. But always be the best you know how to be. Be proud." The boy squirmed like a young octopus in front of his father. "Go. Be home for dinner. Don't worry your mother." Dion's wild eyes met his father's in disbelief, gratitude, exaltation.

"Thank you, Papa. Yes. Yes. I'll be home for dinner," he called over his shoulder as he ran down the pier, the vibrations of his footfalls traveling up his father's body as he sat on the pier opposite his boat. Andreas watched his son's young brown body pumping down the length of the pier. He was losing him.

Dion thought of his father's words as he stood at the site of the battle of Salamis. He had learned to belong, but it was always a battle. Shorter than the rest of the boys, Dion had been a fierce fighter. His tightly wound muscles, developed during the long summers on his father's boat, stood him well in many fights. He made the football team and was feared as a defensive tackle who broke more than one bone in his desire to prove himself. He was not a good team player, but if directed properly his energy was invaluable. There was even talk of an athletic scholarship to college. His parents were as proud as the parents of any ancient warrior. The summer before his senior year everything seemed possible for their son.

And then the inexplicable tragedy. How could it have happened? Andreas Panagakis knew the winds and the sea better than any conch, any native of the Keys. What fate singled him out for a watery death in the swirl of a Florida hurricane? Did he miscalculate, wishing to haul in his catch before heading for a safe harbor? Dion would never know. In the days when hurricanes were still all named for women, his father was lost: he disappeared with his boat, the *Rafina*, vanished without a body left to mourn or a relic by which to remember him.

His mother let out a moan that rivaled the force of the hurricane. For days her keening echoed through their small white stucco house near the harbor. She would not go out into the sun. She kept all the curtains drawn and the ends of her black shawl drawn over her face so that only the pain-pierced redness of her eyes was visible in the mound of black folds.

Dion never returned to school. He stayed on at the hotel, asking for a raise to help support himself and his widowed mother. What had once seemed the job of his dreams turned into an ill-fitting yoke around his neck. He was another man's servant, owning nothing, obliged to wait upon the foolishness of vain men and decorative women. Finally, he could take it no longer; the humiliation on his job, the mute grief at home. He lied about his age and joined the Navy to fight in Korea.

For twenty years he sailed from port to port as a navy diver, going where orders sent him, always sending money back to his mother in Key West but avoiding visits as much as possible. He would go down for Christmas when stationed on the East Coast to spend the holiday eating his mother's honey-soaked pastries and drinking in her perpetual sorrow. He could not wait to return to the cool, overseas duty, never tiring of long voyages and new sensations. But after twenty years he could retire from the Navy with a small pension and the freedom to direct his own destiny.

Handsome, virile and not yet forty, Dion decided it was time to marry and have a son of his own. He received his discharge papers in Norfolk, Virginia, and headed straight into town to find a wife. It didn't take him long. He sauntered into a Big Boy hamburger restaurant and spied a young woman all in white sitting alone at one of the booths in imminent danger of dripping catsup on her snowy skirt.

"Look out," he called to her. "You're going to drip."

Startled, she looked up, jerking the hand that held the hamburger just enough to shake the liquid loose and drip it with a soft plop onto her lap.

"Oh!" she exclaimed, dropping the hamburger back onto the plate and attacking the offensive spot with a flimsy napkin. Dion slid into the booth opposite the distressed young woman.

"Sorry, didn't mean to scare you. Just trying to sound the warning." She looked up at him with pale blue eyes, confused.

"Oh, that's all right. It's not your fault. I'm just clumsy sometimes." Dion appraised her slim figure, her light brown hair drawn back in a bun, her carefully manicured nails.

"You a nurse?"

"A nurse? No, not a nurse. Receptionist, at a doctor's office." The stain was a ruddy island on her skirt.

"You don't mind if I sit here, do you?" He flashed her a wide smile, knowing well the effect his rugged features had on women.

"Well, I suppose. . ." The young woman was confused and flattered.

"What's your name?"

"Phyllis," she smiled shyly.

"Glad to meet you, Phyllis." He thrust his hand across the table to shake hers above the pile of French fries on her plate. "My name's Dion. Dion Panagakis."

"Oh you're Greek," she said with interest.

"Yes, yes I am. Both sides. Pure Greek."

"Oh, I've always wanted to go to Greece. Tell me about it."

"I've never been there." Phyllis was disappointed.

"Oh, it's just that I've always been drawn to Greece."

"Then I'll tell you the stories my father told me about Greece," said Dion, slapping his hand on the table. "Will that do?"

"Sure." Phyllis smiled her shy smile once again. "That'd be great. But I've got to be back at the office in twenty minutes."

"A short story then. About how Pan climbs into the lemon trees and seduces village girls with his sweet music from the branches."

Phyllis blushed. Dion launched into his story. After the twenty minutes expired he walked her the two blocks to her office. A few dates, a quick courtship with no parents to stand in the way, and they were married.

Dion brought his bride home to Key West to meet his mother. The old woman's eyes filled with tears at the sight of her son and the shy, awkward girl at his side. She might live to see grandchildren after all. A rare smile played across her features as she crossed herself and touched her gnarled, dry fingers to her lips.

The newlyweds stayed in Sophia's house until Dion could figure out what he wanted to do. Most of the friends of his boyhood were gone from the island that was more of a tourist trap than ever thanks to the long highway that connected Key West directly to mainland Florida. A few old friends remained to run the hotels passed on to them by their fathers.

Dion wandered among the ships of the harbor, noting the number of pleasure boats that dotted the bay. He hit upon the plan to buy his own boat and guide the rich tourists on fishing expeditions, taking them to places he knew of from his voyages with his father. Dion paid calls on his old football cronies, the self-satisfied men of forty with thickening waists, established families and the smugness of provincial power. Dion charmed them, offering kickbacks on high fees if they recommended him as guide to their guests. Bargains were struck, the boat purchased and christened the *Rafina* in honor of his father and his dream. At last Dion was his own master on the sea.

He was no less fortunate in his home. Sophia offered up incessant prayers before the weathered, peeling ikon.

"A grandson, give me a grandson and I will never ask anything for myself again."

The gods who decades before had ignored her prayers for more children of her own, looked kindly on the old woman's prayers this time. Five years after Dion's discharge from the Navy, a son was born into the house of Panagakis.

It was time that Dion returned to Athens. Kostakis should be back in his office after the long afternoon rest that Athenians prize so dearly. They lived two days in one, resting for a few hours midday so that they could dance or scheme far into the night.

Kostakis was a kinsman, a cousin on his mother's side and a wealthy man. Dion hated to be in the position of a poor relation, but he had nowhere else to turn. All his monied friends on Key West shied away from such a long shot investment; they could make more ready money by backing the lucrative drug trade that criss-crossed the Keys and fed into Miami. Why bother with fantastic tales of treasure aboard Spanish galleons that sank off the reefs hundreds of years ago?

Dion hurried back to his hotel to shower and put on a fresh shirt before meeting with his wealthy cousin. Kostakis. Make him a dreamer, prayed Dion. Let him have affection in his heart for the son of his mother's sister. He buttoned the cream-colored silk shirt across his wide chest and adjusted the tasteful Dior tie. The brown pin-striped suit was of a good cut and tailored to reveal his athletic body.

Dion took the bottle of Johnnie Walker Black Label from his suitcase and placed it on the night table as he finished dressing. Kostakis must not suspect that his savings account was on his back and in the single bag he carried with him. He must appear as an equal, not a beggar, or all could be lost. It was time his luck returned to him.

The first few years with his wife and son had been happy ones and his mother was joyous for the first time in over two decades. The two women doted on the boy whose strong sturdy body and dark curls made him a miniature image of his father. Dion had wanted to give him a simple American name so that he would not suffer the teasing he had received as a boy on the first day of school when his full name was read aloud: Dionysos Aristotle Panagakis.

But his wife protested. No common Tom, Bob or Joe for her. If he couldn't be named for a god, he must at least carry the name of a hero. Ulysses, Heracles, Achilles, she offered. Dion shook his fine head. No. After days of quarreling a compromise was struck. Jason would be his name. Jason Andreas Panagakis; the name of a hero and a fisherman.

While they never grew rich, they were comfortable in the small house by the water. The money Dion made at the height of the tourist season was sufficient to take them through the lean times with the help of the Navy pension. But after twenty years of wandering Dion found it difficult to stay in one port a full turn of seasons. He was restless.

And there was the issue of the boy Jason. As long as he was an infant, there were no problems. But as he grew older, he started having friends, playmates, and Dion was struck once again by his old sensitivity about status. He did not want Jason to grow up ashamed of him as he had been ashamed of his father. Yes, he had the *Rafina,* and his trunkload of stories from around the world. But he was still a guide, a man for hire to other men's pleasure. A man over forty should have more than that to pass along to his son.

Dion got in the habit of dropping by a local bar for a few drinks in the afternoon. It was frequented by the islanders and an occasional sailor. Few tourists found their way to its dimly lit interior. The facade was uninviting with its peeling, dirty whitewashed face and windows with cracked casements and smudged glass. Men gathered in the afternoon to get out of the sun and away from their wives, or to discuss the last televised Sunday football game with their friends.

It was in this bar that Dion first heard about the treasure of the Spanish galleon *Annuncion* from two divers on holiday. Rough, embittered men, they had been on the first expedition under the direction of the half-mad Frank Taylor. They had discovered a dozen wrecks on the coral reefs near the Matecumbe Keys but none were the *Annuncion*. Taylor had to return broke and defeated after years of research and obsessive searching. But he didn't give up. Raising more funds through investment bankers, Taylor returned once again and found another team of divers to uncover the wreck that haunted his gold-struck dreams.

Dion was seduced immediately with the divers' tale. He pumped them for information, buying their drinks and plotting late into the night. Yes, this was the way he would make his fortune. There were more ships at rest in the sea waiting to give up their treasures to clever men who knew the waters. These divers were sent to him from the gods. It was his destiny. He would be a king among men and his son a prince.

Drunk on whiskey and dreams Dion stumbled from the bar down to the harbor. He stood on the pier remembering the patient teachings of his father as he watched the *Rafina* rock gently in the moonlight.

"Papa, hear me. It's Dionysos, your son. You taught me how to bring up fish from the sea. You died hauling fish, old man. For fish! Now I'll bring up more treasure than you ever dreamed of. I'll be rich. And my son after me. And his son after him, damn it. Panagakis will be a rich man's name. We'll buy and sell little islands like these." Dion waved a drunken arm toward shore.

"No more fat tourists and fags." He spat on the rough concrete near the water. "From now on the name Panagakis will command respect from all men."

Dion raised his arm in farewell to his father's ghost and wheeled around to make his way home. In the bay the *Rafina* rocked as before, indifferent to the shouts of her master as she lay bathed in the silver white light of the moon.

Dion was kept waiting for over half an hour in Kostakis' outer office. He tried to appear nonchalant, leafing through magazines and gazing up at the photos of sleek merchant vessels rimmed by expensive walnut frames. Kostakis' fleet. A rich man's harem more enviable than any sheik's collection of women.

He took a deep breath as he was finally led through the heavy carved doors into the inner office. Kostakis was in a leather chair behind an exquisite antique Mediterranean desk. A small man, overweight, balding, Kostakis sprang to his feet with the energy of a boy as Dion entered the room.

"Cousin!" he exclaimed as he rounded the desk to embrace him. "Come sit. Tell me about your mother."

Dion eased into a chair and studied this jovial cousin with

the deep-set eyes like two translucent olives. Those eyes! They seemed to absorb the light in the room and reflected back nothing.

"She's good, cousin. She's good now that she's got a grandson to spoil."

"Ah, yes, this is good. A man is an animal without a family." He turned a photo on his desk toward Dion. "My family," he announced. While Dion concentrated on the photo of a heavy-set woman and four childrem with varying combinations of their parent's features, Kostakis flicked an intercom. "Coffee. And ouzo, please."

"Nice-looking family, Kostakis."

"Thank you. But, please, call me Alexis. Come. You must have photos of your wife and son."

Surprised, Dion reached into the pocket of his coat, thankful that he had the required proof of his humanity for his cousin. He drew the photo out of its plastic cover and handed it to Alexis.

"Ah, how handsome the child is, Dionysos. What's his name?"

"Jason. He's a real tiger."

Kostakis nodded his approval. "Yes, he has the figure of a hero. Very like you. And your wife. She's Greek?"

"No, American."

"A good family?"

"They were, I guess. She's an orphan."

"Then all her attention is on you, my friend. Not so bad." He waved his hand. "The trouble my dear wife's family gives me." He handed back the photo. "You are fortunate. She has kind eyes."

"Thanks. Yeah, she's an okay wife." He suddenly remembered the scotch. "Oh, and a little gift, Alexis." He drew the bottle out of his bag and placed it on the edge of the desk.

"How generous, Dion. Would you care for a drink?"

Dion shook his head. Of course he wanted a drink. But he did not want Alexis to see his nervousness.

"I'll wait for the coffee. . . and maybe a little ouzo."

"Fine." As they spoke the tray was delivered to them and the heavy door shut discreetly to leave them in privacy. Kostakis poured the coffee and ouzo and edged them over the desk to be within Dion's grasp.

"Tell me what I can do for you, Dionysos. You didn't come to Greece just to visit your cousin."

Dion reached into his pocket and placed a sea-worn coin on the desk. Kostakis took the coin in his hand, stroking the smooth edges and the embossed shield at the center.

"This is Spanish."

"Yes, once upon a time. But for over three hundred years it's been in the Caribbean. Now it's yours."

Kostakis raised his eyebrows. "A generous gift. And what can I give you?"

A slow smile spread across Dion's handsome face.

"Help with getting more of the same. And not just coins, but gold chains and bars, ornaments, quicksilver and jewelry. A lot of stuff worth millions to collectors and museum people."

Kostakis' black eyes gave no hint of his feelings; their satin patina sealed thoughts from intruders. "And you wish to take all this from the ocean like so many fish waiting for your net? What about the governments?"

"Sure, they take their cut. But there's still plenty left over."

"If there's so much for the taking why haven't others done it?"

"Oh, they try. But most of them don't know what they're doing. I know these waters. I was a Navy diver myself. And I've signed up divers who worked with the guy who brought up that eight reales piece there. I've got a cesium magnetometer that'll pick up traces of the wrecks on the coral reefs."

"What remains to be done?" Kostakis folded his small manicured hands over his ample stomach.

"The *Rafina* – my boat – needs some equipment. An air lift to suck the debris, for one thing. The divers gotta be outfitted and paid. And there's some other instruments. It could take six months, maybe longer."

"How much?"

Dion licked his lips and took a quick sip of ouzo.

"A million dollars. American."

"A million dollars, eh?" Kostakis' eyebrows arched once again. "A million dollars for you to scout the ocean for ships for six months?"

"No, no, not scout. I know the ship I want – the *Toledo*. She was carrying rich colonists headed for Spain. These guys wore a fortune in jewelry to dodge taxes. They were smugglers, too; they put gold and silver in false bottom trunks. All this loot, *plus* the legit cargo of gold bars and coins minted for the King. A million dollars could bring back fifty, easy," claimed Dion.

"And where is this *Toledo*, eh?"

"She sank in a storm off the Florida Keys. Look, I've researched this. I was in Spain on my way here, looking through the archives in Seville." Dion reached once more into his bag and spread documents and old maps in front of Kostakis who fingered them slowly as Dion talked. "Most of the old treasure galleons have been worked over. But not this baby. She's in deep water; too deep to reach until all this new equipment was invented. None of these guys could've reached her where she lays without busting a lung. I can find her with the cesium magnetometer this guy Taylor developed. It's a sure thing. And we gotta do it now. Now, before Taylor turns around and moves in on the *Toledo*." Beads of sweat dotted Dion's forehead. He stopped abruptly to pour himself another ouzo.

"What you say is very interesting, cousin. But you must give me time to study the proposal and to talk with my associates. If I do this thing it would be as an investment with others. As a relative I could personally help you with the outfitting of your *Rafina*. This is, after all, my business," he smiled a cordial, but humorless smile. "But the raising of capital I do with others."

"Whatever you want, Alexis."

"You dream like a Greek, Dionysos. But we must do business like Americans, no?"

Dion tried to force a laugh. Kostakis gathered the papers in a neat pile in front of him.

"May I keep these a short time?"

"Sure. Take your time."

"Good. Enough business. I think we understand each other. You must come to my house for dinner tonight with my family. They are anxious to meet their American cousin."

"Great. I'll be there."

"Good." Kostakis hesitated before continuing. "This business may take a few weeks. Can you stay that long in Greece?"

"If I have to, sure."

"This is your first trip, no?"

"Yeah, first time."

"Ah, then you must see the islands. They're beautiful now, before Easter, before the heat of summer and the planeloads of tourists."

Dion forced an amiable smile. "Sounds good."

Kostakis got to his feet, extending his small hand across the vast expanse of the desk.

"Till this evening then, Dionysos. About eight."

Dion grasped the other man's hand in his firm grip and rose to his full height. Look him right in the eye, he told himself. Inspire confidence. But the flat black pools of Kostakis' gave back nothing in return.

Three

As spring spreads across the islands a new flowering takes place; orchids, narcissi, irises, orange and lemon blossoms and the white flowers of the arborescent heath burst into profusion. It is spring and the sun grows hot once again, capable of inflicting a sunburn on those foolish enough not to wear a red and white thread around their wrist to ward it off.

For the Christians there is the anticipation of Lent and the forty days of fasting before Easter. But in Greece there is an awareness of the more ancient mysteries behind the Christian festivities; the Eleusinian mysteries, which in essence belong to women, an echo of the time when they had power in the heavens and on earth.

The forty days of fasting correspond to the time of Demeter's refusal of food as she searched for her daughter Persephone who was raped and abducted by the King of the Underworld. As the fruitful goddess mourned, the earth grew barren and knew its first winter. It was only when Demeter and Persephone were joyfully reunited that the earth could bring forth life once again.

The Christians perverted this wisdom, attributing the arrival of spring to the rising of a man from the underworld of death. Fertility celebrations and joy in natural forces have no place in the hearts of Christians whose only idealized woman is a virgin; a mother subject to the rule of her own son.

In Greece it is still possible to believe in the power of women. The temples of stern Artemis pepper the islands and people still speak in respectful tones of her followers, the fearful Amazons, female warriors that stormed Attica, challenged Heracles and came to the defense of Troy.

The most famous and celebrated mortal woman produced by the Greek islands is undoubtedly the poet Sappho. Even today stuffy professors in obscure college towns around the world are forced to admit this. But is was not her poetry alone, powerful and beautiful in its directness, that attracted Iris. It was the mystery surrounding her life and her love for other women. To Iris the idea of a community of women devoted to the cultivation of the arts, sufficient unto themselves, guided by the care and genius of a woman such as Sappho, was irresistible.

One of the few books she had with her the long winter on Santorini was a copy of Sappho's poems. The poems sunk into her consciousness deeper than any of the works given her by the company of poets she lived with in Hawaii. Phrases played back to her during the silences when she was learning to listen in new ways to the forces and spirits all around her.

Her only contact with the world off the island was the letters she received from Dee. They would arrive out of sequence, in clusters, sometimes at intervals of weeks during the uncertain weather of the winter Aegean. Iris liked this syncopation of messages; stories and news free from time and logic but consistent in the thread of love that tied them all together.

And now Dee was finally coming, due in Athens in a matter of days. Iris' excitement mixed with apprehension. Would they still share what they had in Hawaii? Would time and the very fact of Harold's death separate them despite the longing expressed between them in their letters?

Iris packed slowly, laying the volume of Sappho on top of her few blouses folded neatly into the valise. And her silences. She had almost lost her habit of speech the past few months on Santorini. George's cousin spoke broken English and she learned just enough Greek to let her basic needs be known. They were kind, leaving her alone for the most part, respecting her solitude as if she were a recent widow. Some days she would not even emerge from her austere room for food, forgetting hunger in her search for the center of her visions.

Other days she would appear early in the kitchen and ask for food – cheese, bread, fruit, almonds and the local red wine that carried the slight fizz from its volcanic source. She would pack the food and wine into a knapsack and not return until the late afternoon light lit up the cliffs above the crater. On these days she would climb up past the church with its three towers and pale blue dome, up above the town and into the countryside to listen to the winds and the creatures that roamed the deserted fields. Often she would encounter nothing more mysterious than a fox trotting through a vineyard. On more than one occasion, however, arriving just before sunrise, she perceived a ghostly white haze, sensed apparitions retreating from the rising sun, and listened as low moanings echoed through the mountains.

Iris grew to understand the voices of these fleeting ghosts who could pass knowledge across the barriers of language and time before the sun consumed them. She had learned to read the future in dreams, to read the texture of a life found in the aura around a body. And now it was time to gather up her new-found wisdom and step back into her interrupted life, back into the unraveling of her own peculiar destiny.

"I have become strange," reflected Iris as she looked into a mirror with objectivity for the first time in five months. Her hair was full, wild, and streaked with the sun. But it was her face that carried the marks of change. She looked older, a woman's face now looked back at her in place of a girl's. Fine lines gathered around her green eyes that stared out almost luminescent from her tanned face. If anything she was more beautiful than ever, but no longer in a cosmetic, fashionable American way. Iris had always felt different, and separated from others; more tuned to an inner voice. Hearing that voice more clearly now, her face, her eyes, her gaze, were more unsettling than ever before.

As much as Iris longed for Dee, she could not bring herself to return to Athens, to the bustle of a modern city, to the mainland. Instead they arranged to meet in Mytilini, on Lesbos. Iris smiled softly to herself. Of course she picked Lesbos because of Sappho and the ancient practice of love between women that borrowed its name from the island. Iris turned from the mirror and closed the old leather suitcase with its silver clasps. She must hurry to catch the ferry at the foot of the steep, rocky path. She had a long journey in front of her that would require stops at nearly a dozen islands as the ferry made its way slowly north through the Aegean to Lesbos, nestled close by the shores of Turkey.

Iris was struck by the lushness of the islands as the ferry approached the port. After the stark beauties of Santorini she was not prepared for the more sensuous offerings of Lesbos. The houses were painted an array of blue, pink and white, a bouquet of pastels.

Iris spent her day scouting the choicest offerings of the town; the best restaurants, the most romantic hotel. She took dinner in her room that night, the late sun filtering onto the tray set on the rich wood of the table by the window. She sipped the good white Lesbian wine and allowed herself to lapse into fantasies of Dee and their lovemaking that she had pushed from her mind the entire winter. The warm wind rustled the ivy on the courtyard wall and blew the fragrance of narcissus into the room. Iris set down her glass and watched dreamily as the last light caught the glass and threw a rainbow across the white cover of the wide bed.

Dion Panagakis reluctantly boarded the cruise ship at his cousin Kostakis' energetic urgings. Usually he would have been excited to be exploring new territory, but his preoccupation with Kostakis and the gold that lay at the bottom of the Florida straits took all the joy from his current journey. He had an uneasy feeling that Kostakis wanted him out of the way, out of Athens, as he negotiated the deal that could bring in a million dollars within a few weeks.

As the ship pulled out of the harbor and Dion felt the rush of sea air once again, he found himself grateful for his cousin's insistence. The ship headed south, bypassing the islands near Athens that served as weekend getaway resorts for weary urbanites.

As the ship approached the islands of Cythera and Anticythera off the Peloponnesus, Dion's thoughts turned to activity below the surface of the waves. He was passing over an area where many ships had gone down through the ages, buffeted by storms, and also where twentieth-century salvage had its first big successes. It was here, in 1900, that sponge divers waiting out a storm on their way back from Tunisia happened upon a wealth of statues, bronzes and artifacts that had lain undisturbed since before the time of Christ. Stretching the limits of human endurance, the divers plunged into 150 feet of water to retrieve enough artifacts to fill an entire gallery at the National Museum of Athens. One diver died in the effort. At least two were disfigured by the bends. But the treasure was retrieved and modern marine archeology was born.

Dion was oblivious to the tourists milling about him, taking the sun and reading on deck chairs. His eyes strained against the brilliant blue of the water, trying to see deep into the bay as if looking for the ghostly shadow of a wreck, a statue, a column.

Stories of treasure played endlessly across Dion's mind. His original motivation had melted away months before. No longer was the treasure hunting merely a way to support his family. It was the search itself that preoccupied him. He thought little of his wife and son and mother waiting patiently on Key West for his return. He had already mortgaged his mother's home to purchase the essential $30,000 magnetometer. There was no money left in their savings account and little immediate prospect for cash unless Kostakis came through. The very thought of a return to fishing tours filled him with revulsion.

Dion lit a cigarette, promising himself not to have another until dinner. He did not want to damage his breathing for the long months he would spend underwater uncovering the Spanish galleon and gold that waited for him below centuries of salt and debris, hard up against an ever-growing coral reef.

Dion disembarked at Rhodes and decided to stay a few days and wire his location to Kostakis in case there were any developments. He was restless and spent his time visiting the supposed site of the Colossus of Rhodes and wandering the streets of the town. He tried to calm himself at the tavernas, sipping the sharp resinated wine of the island, sitting in the midday sun that turned his naturally olive skin a deep, rich brown. So absorbed in his own thoughts was he that he did not take notice of the women who stole glances at him from downcast eyes, swishing their skirts flirtatiously with the island breezes.

Only once was his interest piqued. Two old men sat at an adjoining table the third day of his visit talking of dreams.

"I saw gold, I tell you, first one circle of it, then more until there was a whole pile of it on the deck of a ship." The old man's battered hand shaded his eyes from the sun as he spoke with great excitement to his friend.

"Gold, ha! On ships? There's no gold in the sea here." He filled their glasses from the half-empty bottle. "Even your dreams are drunken, my friend."

Dion smiled to himself. It seemed that the two men had been friendly adversaries for years.

"Do not be so quick," snorted the dreamer. "Remember how I dreamed of the rock formation on Castelorizo where they found the buried pirate treasure? Don't be so quick to laugh."

"Ha! Yes, you dreamed that. But another man found the gold. What good does it do to dream of other men's fortunes?!"

"It's true." The old man sighed and grasped his glass. "All my life I have been like Cassandra, predicting things no one believes, seeing treasure that other men collect. It's a terrible curse."

"Then tell me and I'll find this treasure and give you half. How about that?"

"Don't mock me, Demetrius. Even if I told you it would not do you any good. In the dream the waters had a different look than those around here. It could be halfway around the world for all I know. There was a woman with golden hair that stood between the boat and the coins. The coins, yes, the coins. They had shields on them, not like the Roman ones we see here."

Dion's patronizing smile faded as he listened to the old man. He was describing Spanish reales pieces. He tried to lean casually into their conversation.

"Excuse me, but I couldn't help hearing your story. My mother's Greek, from Rafina. She used to say that dreams give clues to treasure. But until I heard you I always thought she was just telling stories."

"She is right. You should listen to your mother, my friend. The young people no longer pay attention. They want cars and radios and movie stars."

"Yeah, well, I know what you're saying. Now, what else did your dream say?"

"An anchor. Before the first gold coin there was a very large anchor; dark, old. And I saw the sea at night, with lights on the water."

"And this woman? What's she doing?"

"I don't know,"the old man shook his head. "But the man who holds the anchor is not the one who piles the coins on the deck."

"Anything else?"

"No, no, that's all. But there's trouble with this woman. And a child. Sorrow. That's all."

Demetrius twisted in his chair. "From drinking. That's where his dreams come from. They're hallucinations from ouzo, nothing more."

"But a good story, no? Here, I'll buy you another bottle of ouzo so that you can always dream of treasures." Dion called over the waiter to order the extra bottle for the two old friends and brushed aside their thanks. "No, take it. A gift of respect. In honor of my mother."

He left them at the table in the shade of a lemon tree and hurried back to his hotel. Something in the story excited him and he could not help believing that it was meant for him. So he would find the treasure, eh? It seemed destined. But when he asked the desk clerk for his mail there was only another telegram from Kostakis that gave no news and asked him to relax and enjoy the islands.

Dion was seized with restlessness once again. He checked out of the hotel and headed for the harbor to take the next ship bound north. His encounter with the two old Greeks set Dion to thinking of his father, the gentle Andreas. There was a dimension in these men, a sense of spirit that was lacking in Dion. He was a man of action, of the physical world. But since he entered Greece he was nagged by the notion that a more subtle purpose lay behind the drive to action.

From the rail on the second deck of the ship he gazed at the monastery of St. John on the barren hill of Patmos. It was not uncommon for the most bloodthirsty and passionate of Greek adventurers to retire and live their last days as monks in such monasteries, shut away from women, newspapers, the opinions and values of the world. Here St. John had visions and dictated the splendid *Apocalypse* in one rush of the spirit. Poetry, vision and mysticism came together in the ancient light of the islands.

Dion could imagine his father retreating to just such a monastery in his old age had he lived. Dion lit a cigarette, unconcerned for the moment about the capacity of his lungs. If his father had lived, perhaps he could have explained this unease that gripped him. It was too easy to attribute it to mid-life crisis, male menopause or other facile explanations of pop psychology.

His brooding was disturbed by a woman near him at the rail who was having difficulty lighting her cigarette in the wind.

"Need help?" he asked, producing his lighter.

"Yes," she sighed. "I can't seem to get a light in the wind and of course the more I struggle the more I need the damn cigarette."

Dion cupped his hand around the tip of her cigarette and held the flame steady as she bent to catch the light. An attractive woman, thought Dion, about his age. A faint scent of jasmine hung around her.

"Thanks," she said, exhaling a plume of smoke. "Keep trying to give them up but I guess the pleasure outweighs the warnings."

"I know what you mean. I've been trying to give them up, too. Not much luck."

They smiled cordially at each other and having no one else to talk to at the moment decided to carry on the pleasantries a little longer.

"So you're an American, then. I thought you looked like a Greek."

"Yeah, I'm American. But both my parents are from Greece. So you weren't so far off at that. And you?"

"From Hawaii, by way of California."

"Great place. I'm from Key West myself."

"Island people. We're both island people, then. It's a type, you know."

"Really? What do you mean?"

She drew another long drag on her cigarette.

"Oh, island people tend to think of themselves as 'different' – loners, misunderstood. They're not comfortable on the mainland, in the mainstream. They have an absolute horror of being thought to be like everybody else."

"That's me, all right," laughed Dion. "How'd you figure that out?"

"It's my business to figure out such things."

"You a tour director?"

"Of a sort." A smile played at the corner of her mouth. "I'm a psychologist."

"One of those." Dion extended his hand. "The name's Dion Panagakis. An island person."

"Dee. Dee Hartman. Another one. God. Dion and Dee. Sounds like a fifties rock group."

"Your first time in Greece?"

"Yes, first time. And you?"

"Me, too."

"Holiday?"

"Not really. I've got business in Athens. And you?"

"Pure pleasure." There was a twinkle in Dee's eyes, but Dion did not perceive it as a flirtation directed at him.

"Are you alone?"

"At the moment. But I'm meeting a friend in Mytilini."

"Ah, I'm going on to Samothrace." He threw the glowing stub of his cigarette into the sea. He liked her; she took his mind off his preoccupation with gold and the dreams of old men. "It's a long stretch to Lesbos. Want to have lunch with me?"

Dee hesitated a moment, but saw no harm in the man. His company would make the time pass more quickly and would help steady her nerves for her meeting with Iris.

"Sure. Why not? And I promise not to psychoanalyze you over the soup."

"Too bad. Thought I'd get a free shrinking if I bought you lunch."

"In that case I'll just read your palm and have the next seven years of your life spread out for you before dessert."

Dion offered her his arm and they strolled down the deck for all the world like two characters from a British upper-class comedy of another era. A casual observer would have perceived them as a handsome couple, vigorous, on the kind side of middle-age, affluent. Perhaps they had children at school and were taking the time for a second honeymoon. Or so they might have appeared to the other passengers who cared to notice. Until their coffee. It was then that the wallets were produced on both sides and the pictures of children exchanged to be admired.

"My son and wife," said Dion, handing her the same photo he had produced for Kostakis a few days before.

"He's the image of you," commented Dee. "And your wife has such soulful eyes. You must miss them very much."

"Yeah, sure do," lied Dion, a bit ashamed that he felt so little for them at the moment. "And your kid. You got a picture of him?"

"You had to ask?" smiled Dee, detaching the plastic windows from the center clip in her billfold. Dion studied the hearty, smiling face on the Kodacolor print.

"He's got your looks. Nice."

"Thanks."

Dion was about to return Toby's picture when a photo on the opposite side of the plastic sleeve caught his eye.

"A daughter, too. . ." he started to say and caught himself. "No, you're too young for a daughter that old."

Dee blushed as Dion studied the photo carefully. There was something very familiar about the girl's face, around her unusual eyes. Was it the family resemblance to Dee, perhaps? "A niece?" he asked handing back the photo.

"No, a friend," stammered Dee, suddenly uncomfortable. "The one I'm meeting."

"Oh, I see. She looks like you though."

"Yes. Others have said the same. Coincidence. Or maybe

just a more extreme example of friends choosing others like themselves. Shall we go? I have to gather a few things together before we dock." She was on her feet and moving away from him quickly, giving him no time to protest. He threw down some money for a tip and hurried after her, catching up at the door to the deck.

"Nice meeting you, Dee. Maybe we'll see each other again."

"Maybe. And thank you for lunch, really. I didn't mean to be rude. I, I just remembered that I still had so much to do."

Dion nodded politely, baffled by the sudden change in her. One minute a sophisticated, self-assured woman and the next moment she was totally off balance.

"Have a good time. With your friend."

"Thank you."

She was gone. Dion could feel the engines of the ship shift, a slowing of the mechanism as they approached Lesbos. It was late afternoon, the shadows lengthening into the valleys of the island, the stacks of the ship throwing large dark shadows across the deck. Dion walked to the rail and resumed his solitary vigil, smoking cigarettes absently, telling himself that he would cut back the next day.

A throng of people, a confusion of color swarmed around the dock as the ship approached: anxious taxi drivers waiting to snag the tourists for a guided tour of the island, relatives waiting patiently to collect their kin and take them to the feasts prepared by women awake since dawn, idlers who gather wherever there are crowds of people to observe. The plank was lowered and people started filing off in pairs, alone, their eyes scouting the crowd for something or someone familiar.

A bright spot of pink caught Dion's eye as he leaned from the rail. A blouse. A Greek blouse with fluted bodice and a satin ribbon that ran through it. And the girl. The girl was the one he saw in the picture. But transformed. Beautiful. Hypnotically beautiful. Her face was turned upward toward the ship, scanning the cluster of passengers gathering on the second deck to descend the plank to shore. The nagging familiarity of her face haunted him. He knew this girl, this woman, but from where?

Then Dee was descending the plank, her arms opening toward the other woman, calling.

"Iris, here I am. Iris!"

Iris! Of course! Iris, his own sister-in-law. In a flash he remembered the pretty, shy teenager who had attracted him so strongly years before. And here she was again, changed into the most beautiful woman he had ever seen. Dion was transfixed on the spot, unable to move as the women embraced and moved off through the crowd,their arms twined around each other's waist. Thoughts of Kostakis and Spanish gold fled from his mind. Iris. This was where he went wrong. He had married the wrong sister. The idea lodged in his mind like a ship worm in the hull of a galleon.

Once the women were out of sight Dion was jolted into action. He rushed back to his cabin and threw his belongings into his suitcase and rushed to the plank like a man possessed. He must find Iris, make her understand.

"Nothing is changed," whispered Iris as they lay naked on the wide bed, the early evening breeze caressing their smooth bodies. Dee turned into Iris, her lips brushing Iris' parted lips as if to silence her, not wanting words to break the unspoken understanding of their bodies. She ran her hand down Iris' spine, sending a shiver through her entire body. Dee's eyes filled with tears that squeezed out of the corners and ran a salty stream across Iris' cheek.

"Something wrong?" Iris raised her body slightly away from Dee to enable her to see her face. Dee shook her head on the pillow.

"No, silly. I'm just so very happy." Iris returned the smile.

"Me, too. Thirsty? Want a little more wine?"

"Wine? Are you sure that's all it is? Or have you been learning the art of charms and aphrodisiacs these months on strange islands?"

"Ah, then your passion needed prodding, is that it?" teased Iris as she reached for the two half-filled glasses by the bed.

"Hardly," retorted Dee as she raised herself on one elbow to watch Iris arch her exquisite body over the side of the bed. "You are perfection."

Iris handed her the glass and took a sip from her own.

"Stop it. You're going to turn my head. Anyway, it won't do you any good. You've already had your way with me. What else do you want?"

"More. Again."

"My dear Dr. Hartman. A lady of your position. What would your patients say?"

"They wouldn't be patients if they had a lover like you. You could put psychiatry out of business within a year."

"Very unscientific."

"Very."

They smiled across the rims of the glasses.

"I'm hungry," announced Iris, throwing her legs over the side of the bed.

"How unromantic. I thought we weren't going to get out of this bed for days."

"On the contrary," insisted Iris. "I'm very romantic. I have just the place picked out for dinner. By the water. Soft light. Excellent sea food. More wine. One sense to feed the others, so to speak. How about it?"

"Oh, all right," sighed Dee. "I guess you have a point. It's just that I can't touch you in public. I hate having to hold myself back with you."

"I know. It's not fair. No one even looks twice at a man and a woman holding hands. But we draw stares. Oh, well. It just builds the tension until we can get back here and work out all our frustrations, eh?" The twinkle was back in her eye, her mood too expansive to be swayed by Dee's reservations.

"Of course. But it's odd. I got so flustered on the ship on the way here this afternoon. I was having lunch with a man, having a rather pleasant chat and then got all confused about you, my 'friend,' the only one I really wanted to talk about but couldn't. It's so strange." Iris brushed Dee's lips with her own.

"Stop worrying. We're together. Nothing can harm us. Don't be preoccupied with men and things that don't count." She turned her back on Dee and bent over gracefully to pick up the pink blouse on the floor that was tangled up with Dee's silk scarf and the white bedspread that had slipped to the floor, unnoticed, just an hour before.

A bittersweet sadness tinged Dee's joy while she watched Iris dress, humming softly to herself. Maybe it was because she was older that she felt the impermanence of it all; the too-forceful intensity that could not be sustained. Or maybe it was the beauty of the islands themselves, a beauty so perfect, like the beauty of Iris herself, that was too ideal not to turn into tragedy. Or maybe I'm just an old Puritan, Dee scolded herself as she brushed back her hair with one hand, thinking there is always a heavy price to pay for pleasure. She unconsciously ran her hand over the Caesarean scar on her abdomen, the portal through which Toby had entered the world, and rolled to the side of the bed to reach out and touch, ever so lightly, the firm rounded hip of her lover.

Four

Finding Dee and Iris was a relatively easy task for Dion. By the time he had grabbed his belongings and raced down the plank he could not spot the glowing pink of Iris' blouse in the crowd nor down any of the streets that wound away from the harbor. But he knew both women's names and what little he knew of Dee Hartman led him to believe they would be registered at one of the better hotels in town. He collared a taxi driver and asked the names of hotels, then hastily jotted down three likely candidates as the evening shadows darkened the narrow streets. At the second hotel, he found Iris registered but was informed that the ladies were out for the evening. Dion tipped the clerk generously to ensure his silence and checked into another nearby hotel.

The next morning Dion positioned himself opposite the entrance to the hotel where Iris and Dee were staying, sitting at a table drinking strong Greek coffee through the early morning hours waiting for them to appear. He tried to put on a casual show, a well-thumbed Greek newspaper on the chair next to him, looking for all the world like a man of leisure. Finally his patience was rewarded. The two women emerged through the white stucco archway and were about to turn left when Dion waved his paper and shouted.

"Hullo! Dee, over here."

Dee hesitated, not recognizing Dion at first.

"It's me. Dion."

Dee smiled and leaned over to Iris to whisper in her ear as she nodded toward Dion. Iris shrugged and the two women crossed the street. Dion's heart jumped in his chest.

"I thought you were going on to Samothrace," said Dee, not unkindly. Dion inclined his handsome head and waved the two women to the empty chairs.

"I was, but I changed my mind. I decided to stay in Lesbos a couple of days, let my messages catch up with me. You ladies want some coffee?"

"Guess this is as good a place as any," said Dee as she took one of the offered chairs. Iris was about to follow her lead when she recognized Dion.

"Oh my god,"said Iris under her breath. Dion was smiling at her with the same confident attitude he had over a decade before.

"Something wrong?" asked Dee.

"Can I get you something?" offered Dion smoothly.

"Dion. You're Dionysos Panagakis, aren't you?"

"Why, yes. Yes, I am. Do I know you?"

"I'll say. I'm Iris. Phyllis' sister."

"No, you're kidding," exclaimed Dion. "Jesus, I'd never have recognized you."

"I'd never mistake you, Dion."

"You were a kid last time I saw you. What a coincidence."

"Is it?" asked Iris softly.

"Do you mean that this is your brother-in-law?" asked Dee in surprise.

"Yes," said Iris. "It's him." She stood frozen behind the chair, not one muscle moving as her mind raced back to her memories of Dion's visits, his stories, his hands on her body, his seduction of her sister.

"This calls for a celebration," declared Dion. "Jesus, wait till Phyllis hears about this. She never knew where you went off to."

"She didn't care," retorted Iris. Her knees were weak and she allowed herself to sink into the chair.

"Are you all right, Iris?" asked Dee, leaning toward her.

"I will be. Got a cigarette?"

"Here," offered Dion, lighting one quickly and handing it to Iris. "How about you, Dee?"

"Sure. Sure. I could use one, too."

"Now you're wrong about Phyllis," continued Dion. "She feels bad about losing touch with you. And you never took much trouble letting her know what's going on with you, either."

"There was no point." Iris' green eyes were feverish with churned-up emotion.

"Don't be so hard on her," urged Dion. "Or me."

"The picture," suggested Dee. "Show her the picture of Phyllis and the boy."

Dion reached into his pocket and produced the photo. Iris grabbed it from him and held it up in the air trying to get the best light on her sister's face.

"She's older," she murmured. "Older and better. And the boy. What's his name?"

"Jason."

"Of course," snorted Iris. "She would name him for a hero – or a god. That's always how she saw men." Her mouth twisted ironically for a moment as she looked back at Dion. "And which are you?"

"Neither. Just a regular guy."

"I see." Iris laid the photo on the table so that she could steal glances at is as she sipped the coffee that had been placed in front of her. "And where do you live?"

"On Key West, where I grew up. You gotta come and see us. Phyllis would be knocked out."

"Iris doesn't know yet where she's going next," explained Dee.

"Oh, yeah?" Dion was surprised. "Where do you live?"

"In these islands. Here."

"For long?"

"Since the fall."

"And before that?" Dion leaned closer to her to fall more directly into the beam of her eyes.

"Hawaii," she said simply taking a drag on her cigarette.

"Oh, I get it," Dion leaned back in his chair and looked at Dee. "Hawaii. Like you."

"Yes," said Dee. "We were friends in Hawaii and I'm trying to convince her to move back."

"Are you?" asked Dion, turning attention once again back to Iris.

"I don't know. I have a feeling that these islands aren't through with me yet."

"That's a funny thing to say. Don't you go where you want to go?"

"Not entirely."

"Sounds mysterious," said Dion.

Iris said nothing as she ground out the cigarette in the tin ashtray and took a long sip of her coffee. Dee jumped in to fill the silence.

"I think we better be going. We have to pick up a rented car."

Dion felt the women slipping away from him. "Have dinner with me tonight?"

"We won't be in town tonight," said Iris. "We're staying at Eressos. Maybe another night when we get back, if you're still here."

"Yeah, sure. I'll be here for a week. Until after Easter. Then I'll go back to Athens," he said, surprising himself with his newly-laid plans.

"All right. Wednesday night then. Okay, Dee?"

"If you'd like," said Dee.

"Terrific. I'll swing by your hotel around eight." He jumped to his feet as the two women rose from their chairs. "I'll write Phyllis right away. Boy, will she be knocked for a loop."

"Come on, Iris, we better get going." Dee touched Iris' shoulder lightly. "And goodbye Dion. Who would have thought we'd meet again like this?"

They moved away from him, both women in white slacks and colorful blouses, swinging straw bags. Dion licked his parched lips as Iris and Dee disappeared around the corner of a building. What was there between them? What secret communion? At least he had carried off the first encounter. Wednesday he would have a chance to take the next step. And then the next. And then?

Dion threw some money on the table and headed for the telegraph office to cable Kostakis his location. He had no intention of writing Phyllis anything about his meeting with her long-lost sister.

Iris reached out to brace herself as Dee swerved the car sharply to avoid a goat that jumped out into the road from behind a stone wall.

"Damn!" she exclaimed, barely missing the startled goat and running off the edge of the rutted road. "Guess I was going too fast."

Iris looked over at Dee's flushed features.

"You all right? Want me to drive?"

"No, it's all right." Dee shook her head and guided the car back onto the road. "I'm in the mood to drive."

"Something wrong?"

"No, not really. Just thinking about us."

"What? That we're silly going to Eressos just because Sappho lived there once?"

"No, that's fine. I think it's kind of fun to track her down, to see the places she lived and taught music and poetry. Let the fellows chase down the trail of Odysseus. Sappho's much more our cup of tea, isn't it, love?"

"Right. Then what's the trouble, honey? You've been so quiet since we left the city."

"Oh, just wondering when you'll make up your mind, what it will take for you to come back to Hawaii."

Iris turned her head and looked at the graceful olive grove they were passing.

"Not yet, Dee. Don't push me, please. Things aren't right yet."

"I'm sorry. It's a bad habit of mine. I just can't take the days as they come. I can't get away from the idea that this is a spectacular holiday and then, well, then there's daily life. I want you in my life, Iris."

"I suppose you couldn't stay longer in Greece?"

"No, I can't stay away any longer than three weeks from my patients. Or from Toby."

"I see."

"And I hardly think I could set up practice here."

"I agree with that. The Greeks don't seem to put much store by psychology. Here there's only problems of the spirit, of the soul; not of the mind."

"No wonder. It does feel different here." She waved her hand, indicating the generous landscape. "And unfortunately I can only make a living where neurotics flourish. A sad comment, isn't it?"

"Want some wine?" Iris reached into the back seat and uncorked a bottle of retsina, pouring a heavy portion into an earthenware cup.

"While I'm driving?"

"Oh, Dee, relax," laughed Iris. "There's no highway patrol. Any local police would probably be drunker than us in any case. Try to have a holiday, okay?"

"Oh, all right. Give me some." Dee guided the car with one hand as she sipped from the cup. "Love the sting of that wine."

"That's the spirit," approved Iris. She gazed out the window once more and spotted a small dark bird following their course for a moment and then swooping away to a nearby tree to join its mate. A sad, mournful call pierced the air.

"Look, Dee. A nightingale." Dee looked in the direction Iris was pointing but missed the small dark shape in the trees.

"Can't see it, but I think I heard it."

"'The nightingale's the soft-spoke announcer of spring's presence'" quoted Iris.

"What's that?"

"Sappho, of course. It's a good sign, don't you think? They used to call Sappho 'the nightingale,' you know."

"No, I didn't know. But it's such a sad sound."

"Well, she didn't exactly meet a happy end. And I think there's some myth about the nightingale, too; some sad story about a dead son and a rape, or something."

"Wonderful. That's a cheerful, romantic story. Why is there so much violence in all those myths?"

"They're just more honest, I suppose." Iris shrugged and swigged a mouthful of wine. "And maybe it's the light. All the passions seem unleashed around here. Everything more intense, as if centuries have accumulated an overwhelming storehouse of passion that can cut loose at any time. Hawaii was child-like compared to this. Maybe that's why I can't seem to go back. It seems like I've outgrown it somehow."

"And me?" Dee's eyes wore a hurt expression.

"No, not you, Dee. I love you. I want to be with you. I really don't know what's keeping me from going back to Hawaii with you just yet."

Dee returned her eyes to the road. "You're right. We should just enjoy this time together. How about another slug of that wine?"

"Sure." Iris handed Dee the mug and watched, concerned as she drained it in one gulp. She's afraid, thought Iris. She wants me and yet is afraid of what she would have to give up to have me. And me. I'm afraid, too. Every time I seem to set a course to happiness something horrible seems to intervene. And now there is Phyllis and Dion who pops up like a ghost from the past, sipping coffee across from their hotel. What does he want? She passed her tanned hand across her eyes to shield them from the glare of the sun. It was near noon. Everything was still, even the cicadas had ceased their chirping for the time being. The only sound was the hum of the small car as it carried Dee and Iris along the dirt road to Eressos.

Dion Panagakis had done his homework thoroughly before arriving at the hotel at eight in the evening on Wednesday. He had learned the location and times of the prime festivities for the Easter season and was prepared to offer himself as guide to the two women.

The past two days had been torture for him; he had barely slept as the image of Iris drifted through his dreams wrapped in a mist that made her seem more apparition than human being. She seemed to beckon him and yet always kept just out of his reach. Sometimes Phyllis would appear by her side, more beautiful than she had ever been in her life, a darker version of the radiant Iris. Yet she would mock him, too, putting her arm through her sister's as they turned away from him and disappeared behind a watery veil.

Dion would wake in a sweat, the linen on his bed soaked through from his strenuous nightmares. He would leap from the bed and throw open the wooden shutters on the windows and lean out to gulp the cool evening breeze that blew from the harbor. On Tuesday night he dressed and searched the area near the water for a taverna that stayed open until dawn and he drank ouzo alone, in a corner, stupifying himself with the liquor and the hypnotic bouzouki music until he was put out in the early morning to stumble back to his hotel and collapse, finally, into a drunken, dreamless sleep.

But tonight, Wednesday, he was the picture of a gentleman, his clothes freshly pressed, his expensive shoes polished with infinite care by the old man the hotel retained for such service. He paced the lobby nervously, passing his hand over his tie as if smoothing a bib over his soul. A few minutes past the hour Dee and Iris swept into the lobby, wearing light dresses, their hair full as if dried by the wind.

"Iris, Dee, how you doing?" He stepped forward to greet them, his lips brushing their cheeks in turn, hoping that the rapid beating of his heart could not be discerned at such close range. "How was your trip?"

"Good," offered Iris, swaying slightly. "Lesbos is so restful. A lady. Very different from Santorini where I spent the winter."

"Sounds like it suits you here. Both of you," he added quickly.

"Where are we going?" asked Dee. "At the risk of being crude, I'm starving."

"Oh, didn't you have lunch?"

"We had lunch all right." Iris suppressed a giggle. "But Dee worked it all off. We've had a very busy afternoon."

"And much too much wine," Dee blushed and touched Iris' arm imploringly. "We're not quite sober."

"But aren't all the shops closed in the afternoon?" asked Dion, confused by their banter.

"Yes, but we decided to get a little exercise to pass the time." Iris was enjoying her private little joke at the expense of her brother-in-law.

"Well, I thought we'd go down by the harbor. I know a nice little place near the water. It's really lively. Think you'll like it."

"I'm sure," agreed Dee, eager to get moving and to avoid any further allusions to their afternoon spent in bed.

They walked casually down the narrow streets, Dion

smoking cigarettes while providing a running commentary on the architecture and history of the village. Iris was surprised at the extent of his knowledge. He didn't seem like the kind of man who did a lot of reading of history, or even of guide books, for that matter. The more she thought of it she realized that she didn't know what he was doing in Greece. Dee had mentioned something about a business deal in Athens, but she knew little else, either. Iris had been so wrapped up in Dee that she hadn't had time to consider the appearance of Dion Panagakis. After their third glass of the good Lesbian wine Iris decided to interrupt Dion's discourse on the navigational aspects of the harbor.

"Excuse me, Dion, but I'm a little confused. Aren't you a sailor?"

"I was. But now I'm in business."

"What kind of business? I never caught that, I guess." She sipped her wine and was surprised to see him ill at ease.

"Salvage. Ships. Things like that. Off Key West."

"Then why are you in Greece?" asked Dee.

"To see a cousin. He's investing in one of my deals."

"Oh, then you are just starting this business," said Iris.

"In a way. I've got a boat, some equipment. But I need a little extra money to get it off the ground."

"I didn't mean to pry."

"You're not. Guess I'm sensitive. Some people think I'm crazy to go for treasure. To hunt for gold."

"Gold, is it?" Iris raised her eyebrow.

"And you," Dion shifted in his chair. "What do you do? I know Dee over here plays tour guide with people's heads. But how about you?"

"I travel," said Iris succinctly.

"For a living?"

"As a way of life. Don't I, Dee?"

"Yes, to an exasperating degree," agreed Dee.

"Maybe I'm dense, but how do you finance all this traveling?"

"Oh, I've had my little jobs here and there. But at the moment I'm a kept woman."

Dion's glass stopped midway on its course to his lips. Dee half rose from her chair, wanting to run from the statement she felt rising from Iris.

"Oh. A rich boyfriend, huh?"

"No, a comfortably well-off woman," Iris nodded cordially across the table to Dee who shook her head in disbelief, mumbling "Why?"

Dion followed Iris' gaze and set down the glass hard on the table.

"You don't mean. . . I mean, Dee?"

"Yes, me, Dion," said Dee, letting out a long sigh.

"Lesbians. On Lesbos," hissed Iris in a loud stage whisper. "Get it?"

"He gets it all right," said Dee. "But I don't. Why do you have to come out with that here?"

"Because he's my brother-in-law, Dee. We can't have family secrets now, can we?"

The wine had taken an ugly turn in Iris. The usual euphoria it gave her now turned to belligerence. She wanted to shock Dion, to pay him back for the hurt he had caused her. For the moment he had come to represent all the men who had betrayed her, who had used or abused her. He was so unquestioningly male with his strong body, his confidence, his good looks. . . . He was the man who took away her sister, the one person on earth who meant anything to her until she met Dee. And now he wanted to intrude in her life, as if he had a right to be there. Iris poured herself more of the wine and waited for Dion's response. Dee tried to save the evening.

"I think Iris has had a little too much to drink, Dion. I don't think she meant to spring it on you like this."

Dion's mind was aflame. Lesbians! He could not understand it. Why would two beautiful women shut out men? Is this better or worse than if Iris were married to a man? Dion had no point of reference. But his masculine perspective won out. No, it is better. A husband was a greater barrier than another woman. It could not mean the same thing, this affair with a woman. There was still room for a man. There was still hope for him.

"Well, I'm surprised, all right," admitted Dion, knowing that complete indifference would seem unreal.

"I bet," quipped Iris. "Now, aren't you going to ask if I hate men?"

"Iris, really. . ." Dee tried to divert her from her rampage.

"Do you?"

"Only when they try to interfere with my life. Or with the people I love. Catch my meaning?"

"I think so," responded Dion. "Cigarette?" He was going to play it like a man of the world, as if he ran across such arrangements every day of his life and was unconcerned.

Iris drew a cigarette from his pack and allowed him to light it for her. Now that she had made her point she could afford to lighten up a bit.

Dee watched Iris closely across the table. Was it just the wine talking or was there a core of anger, pain and vengeance in Iris that still was not resolved? She was complicated, all right. Spiritual, mystic and violent; the full range of passions. Yes, the Greek landscape suit her. Dee was growing to understand why the gentle Aloha land of Hawaii held little meaning for Iris. Though not of Greek descent, Iris seemed to spring from misted mysteries of the ancient world. And she wanted her. She had already unlocked Dee's dormant heart. Now she was going for her very soul. And Dee couldn't stop her even if she wanted to at this point.

"This is the best week of all in Greece," said Dion, trying to act as the tour guide once again. "Tomorrow, on Holy Thursday, they dye the eggs red. Then everything goes crazy for days, you know? Good Friday, they fix up this bier of flowers and perfume and carry it back and forth to the cemetery. Everybody sort of follows along behind it. Then on Saturday at midnight Mass they celebrate the Resurrection. The priest holds up this consecrated candle and everybody takes a light off it. If you can get it home without it going out they say you'll be lucky the whole year. Then Easter Sunday everybody eats themselves sick with all the lamb. Then they get up and dance. Yeah, it's a great time to be here."

Dion sat back in his chair to watch the two women, the lovers, as they listened to his story. To his surprise he did not find the idea of their sleeping together repulsive. On the contrary, it was appealing, very erotic. And he could imagine himself with both of them, at the same time, alternating between them. All the time while he spoke of Easter and peasant holidays he was turning this image over in his imagination.

Iris reached over and fingered a lock of Dee's hair and let her hand run lightly down her neck, along her arm and then stop to entwine her hand with Dee's.

"Want to stay, Dee? See all the celebration before we move on?"

Dee was confused. First Iris took great pains to put Dion in his place and now she seemed to go along with his suggestions. Was he to be included, allowed to share their precious little time together?

"Whatever you like, Iris. We don't have any set schedule."

"Good. Then we'll stay in Lesbos through Easter. And

you," she turned to Dion. "You can call for us on Friday to take us to the procession and then on Saturday to take us to this Mass. The other times we want to be alone, understand?"

Dion and Dee both jumped a little at her orders, for orders they were without a doubt. But the forces were so arrayed that they both had no choice but to comply with her wishes. From that evening on it became clear that Iris controlled all their lives. She had become the singular passion of both Dion and Dee.

They finished their dinner in relative peace, sticking to safe topics and observations. Filaments of lightning cracked over the harbor, zigzagging across the night sky, obliterating the pattern of stars for brief, brilliant moments. Iris was calm as the forces of nature gathered momentum. She had sobered up totally, as if the wine had never affected her at all. She glanced briefly at Dee and Dion and lifted her eyes to the sharp lines of light that split the heavens. Here, finally, she had connected with the source of her powers.

Easter Sunday dawned clear and warm. The natural congeniality of the Greeks was augmented even more by the festivities of their greatest holiday. It was a time to wake from slumber, a time of rebirth and new hope. Nothing was spared, nothing held back. Pantries and pockets were emptied in celebration. The best dress, the one suit, were taken out and cleaned with devotion. Devotion and exultation are closely entwined in the Greek spirit. Ecstasy is to be expressed, not suppressed. And Easter was the most exultant time of all, the Christian holiday capping the celebration of spring that reached back centuries before the thought of Christ.

As evening drew near the people gathered themselves for the culminating event. Symbolically, Christ still lay dead as any mortal in his tomb. The people made their way to the churchyard as the sun set, removing all hint of pagan color from the sky. Peasants, shopkeepers, village officials and tourists alike, they gathered in the churchyard to hear the Gospel read by priests newly delivered from their somber black vestments into splendid scarlet and gold robes.

Among them were the three Americans, the blond women and the swarthy man. A black lace mantilla draped the head of the older woman, a mark of respect to the local beliefs. But the younger woman was bare-headed, her wild hair standing out among the domesticated women around her.

As midnight approached, excitement passed through the

crowd. The old priest with his long beard was preparing his magic in the gold chalice. Iris shifted uneasily. She felt the other powers mounting as well, powers contrary to her own. She searched the sky for lightning, for any evidence of nature or ancient forces asserting themselves. Nothing. She looked at Dee whose gaze was intent upon the ritual of the priests. And Dion. She caught him staring at her with piercing intensity. Then came the sound of bells and the priest turned toward them, his arms raised.

"Christo anesti!"

"Christ is risen," translated Dion.

There was a burst of noise, of confusion. Small boys set off cap guns. Fireworks whizzed into the air, their light illuminating the dark, silent heavens.

"Alithos anesti," came the response.

"He is risen indeed," pronounced Dion with satisfaction. Dee turned to him with benign indifference, more taken with the festivity about her than Dion's pride in the proceedings. But Iris was troubled. It was as if Dion took personal credit for the rise of Christ.

In this light she saw him as the true adversary that he was. It was not even a question in his world vision that the male would rise above the female. He was not afraid of her powers at all. He was entranced with her, yes. But what she did was of little importance to him. Since he found her to his liking all he had to do was subdue her, as he had subdued her sister, as he wished to subdue the very ocean for his own glory. The gold on the priestly vestments was first cousin to the gold of the Spanish galleons, to the gold thread that ran through her hair. Men with gold fever wanted it all, everything golden melted down into their own self-image, the ultimate idolatry, murderous narcissism.

Now the priest was elevating the consecrated candle, imploring the congregation to "Come and receive the light," as the gongs and firecrackers added to the din. Couples were embracing as the candles were lit from the priestly source and passed back through the crowd, the light spreading in a wave across the churchyard.

Iris slipped her arm through Dee's and drew her closer. She closed her eyes and drew Dee next to her body, kissing her fully on the mouth, her back to Dion, closing him out from their embrace.

"I'm coming with you," she whispered through the delicate

black lace that fell over Dee's hair. "Back to Hawaii, or wherever you want to go. I won't let go of you again. Never again."

"Do you mean it, Iris?" Dee was incredulous. "What about Greece, about what you have to do, about. . ."

Iris stopped her questions with another kiss.

"I'm coming with you, Dee."

The candles were spread across the yard now. Dion held three in his hands, waiting for the women to part. Fnally, Iris broke the embrace and half turned toward Dion, a look of truimph in her eyes.

"Your candles," he said, offering a burning taper to each of them. As the candles passed from his hands to Dee and Iris a slight breeze wafted through the churchyard from the harbor, catching the unprotected flames, causing them to falter and fail, leaving the three Americans in a sudden pool of darkness.

Five

Wings of water sprouted from the nose of the *Sappho* as it cut the waves en route to Piraeus. From the lower decks the sound of goats headed for market drifted upward to the passenger decks, the low bleating interspersed with the lapping of the waves against the ferry. Near the island of Andros gulls circled the ferry, their cries intermingling with the wail of the goats in an eerie imitation of human keening; or perhaps it is humans in the throes of grief that imitate the more ancient articulation of animals.

But on the second deck of the *Sappho* thoughts of grief were far from the minds of three passengers — Iris, Dee and Dion. Two were in love and one in the grip of obsession; neither state permitting the presence of grief, though both may be avenues to the deepest tragedies.

She's coming home, thought Dee to herself with gentle disbelief. Iris is coming back to Hawaii. We will be a family again: Iris, Toby and me. We will match the happiness of last fall and there is nothing more that can harm us. Dee reached out and covered Iris' hand resting casually on the ship's rail next to her.

Her touch, thought Iris, sends shivers through my body. I am alive. And the happiness does not stop. The forces are kind. I have found Phyllis again through the agent of fate, through my brother-in-law Dionysos who broods so intensely in the shadows.

I must have her, thought Dion, biting his thumb in absent-minded frustration as he watched the two women at the rail from his deck chair in the dark. But how? What a rude shock to find her with this woman, in this way. She eludes me.

This was his last day with them, the day after Easter. Celebration was still running high in the islands. Men drank too much wine, too much arak, too much ouzo and reached out for their dreams. Women dispensed with the daily grind of denial and squandered whatever hoard they had accumulated through the long, isolating winter. Next week was soon enough to start hiding away that extra coin, refusing the extra cake to a village child, turning down the rakish man who had pursued them all year. This was Easter, the rising of the Lord, the advent of spring, the return of Persephone to the bountiful home of her mother.

It was the turning of fortune for Dionysos Panagakis as well. In his breast pocket was the telegram from Kostakis, bidding him to return to Athens to complete the investment deal. For months it was all he had hoped for, a chance to chase his wildest dream. Until his meeting with Iris. Instead of a clear joy, he was now riddled with conflict. Only a few more hours until Piraeus and then they would part – he to Athens and they to Patras to catch a boat bound for Lefkas, the last stop on the trail of Sappho. He didn't know which was worse; not seeing her or seeing her always in the company of Dee Hartman. She kept Dee next to her like a shield against him. She knew. She must know how he felt about her. And so she mocked him, asking only about Phyllis, about Jason, about a possible visit to Key West on her way back to Hawaii. As if she could feel his thoughts Iris turned toward him for a moment, an enigmatic smile on her lips.

I am fine now, she thought. How foolish of me to panic last night during the Mass. A hangover from childhood, she decided, when the church made me feel so small and the priests loomed so large. He can't hurt me, Iris decided, turning away from Dion in his deck chair. He is just a memory, a reminder of another time, or a past that I now can think about but that no longer owns me. Since Dee, she was able to ripple through her past and acknowledge all the wounds that never healed and soothe them one by one.

Dee turned her gaze from the water to the finely chiseled profile of Iris against the sky. How happy I am, she thought again for the tenth time that day. She is coming back to Hawaii. The light is so strange in Greece, she reflected. I was actually believing that she was right not to leave, as if geography has a greater significance than human love, as if love can only flourish in the right physical setting.

A gull dipped near the railing to scoop up a fish and then took to the heights once again, the late afternoon sun tinging its wing pink. Below the deck the goats joined in the chorus of the gulls once again, the mournful call echoing across the water and resounding in the bay of Andros as the ferry sailed on toward Piraeus.

Once again Dion was seated in the waiting room of his cousin Kostakis, gazing up at the photographs of his fleet of ships. But this time his wait was not long and Kostakis himself came to greet him rather than having Dion ushered in like a supplicant.

"Welcome, Dionysos," he boomed spreading his arms to embrace his cousin. "You look well."

Dion was encouraged by the greeting.

"Yeah, feel great, thanks. You had the right idea sending me off to those islands. They're really something else."

Kostakis nodded enthusiastically as he led Dion into his office. "Yes, talking about them does them no justice at all. But now that you have seen it for yourself, you believe, am I right? You will end up here one day yourself, you'll see. Every Greek wishes to end his days here. And I think you are more Greek than American."

"Maybe," Dion settled in a leather chair and tried to read the source of Kostakis' expansive enthusiasm, but his black eyes gave no more clues to his thoughts than they had two weeks before. "If we're partners there's more reason for me to come back."

"Ah, so you wish to get right to the heart of the matter, eh? Now this is not very Greek at all. First we'll have a drink of your excellent Scotch and then we can talk business."

Kostakis reached into the drawer of his desk to produce two glasses and the unopened bottle that Dion had given him on his first visit. He twisted off the cap and poured a generous portion of light amber liquid in each glass and handed one to Dion.

"A toast, my friend. To a profitable business and Spanish gold."

Dion touched his glass to Kostakis' and let the liquid burn down his dry throat.

"Ah, excellent," approved Kostakis. "Now, the terms. I have studied your ideas, looked over your figures. Everything looks reasonable and well planned. This is good. I have spoken with my associates and they are willing to join me in putting up some money for your expedition. You seem to have as much chance as any man of finding this *Toledo*. Maybe more. So we will put up the million dollars. You will have one year to bring in a return. If you do uncover the *Toledo*, or any other vessel with treasure, your share is ten percent of the profits after the government takes their twenty-five percent off the top. Now, is this agreeable?"

"Ten percent!" Dion jumped to his feet. "I risk my life and all I get is a lousy ten percent?"

"It's more than you have now, my friend." Kostakis shrugged and poured another portion of Scotch in his glass. "We are the ones who risk all the capital with very little chance of recovering any of it."

"But you want my boat."

"Worth less than $50,000 by this time next year. And the equipment, maybe another $25,000. It hardly compensates for a million dollars, wouldn't you agree?"

"I just expected more of the profits," Dion gritted his teeth.

"Let me be frank. You have no other choice. No American bank would give you a million dollars to search for gold. You have no collateral. I checked. Other than your boat and the magnetometer the only thing of value you had was this bottle of Scotch. It's only because you are my cousin that you have a chance at all of living out this adventure."

"Shit. Maybe I should chuck the whole idea."

"You won't," grinned Kostakis. "Or I should say, you can't."

"Why not?" demanded Dion.

"I've seen men like you. You can't stop now. You have gold fever. If I offered you five percent and demanded the life of your wife and son as collateral, you would take it."

"Son of a bitch. How can you say that?"

"Because it is quite simply true."

Dion paced the room.

"Then why are you helping me? If it's such a bad investment why waste your time and money?"

"I've told you. Because you are my cousin. But there is more, too, I admit. Yes, I could write off most of my losses if you fail. But if there is gold down there you are the man who will find it because you are willing to die in the effort. It's a splendid passion, worthy of a Greek man. You help live out the dreams I do not allow myself, you see?"

Dion stopped his pacing and came to a standstill in front of Kostakis.

"Let's cut the crap. Where do I sign?"

"Sure you wouldn't like to take this to an attorney before signing?"

"What's the difference? You've got me by the balls. I'd end up signing on your terms anyway. Gimme the papers."

Kostakis handed Dion a gold-tipped fountain pen. "You are not angry, are you?"

"Sure I'm pissed. I thought this deal would bring me some freedom."

"No man is free who is a slave to his passions, Dionysos."

Dion scrawled his name across the face of the document and threw the pen on Kostakis' desk.

"Thought you admire the 'splendid passions,' cousin."

"Ah, but what I admire in others and what I choose for myself are two different things. I chose power. Yours is the path of passion. We are different men. Like the old gods, each had his glory, and each his downfall. But Olympus was large enough to house them all. We live in a much more petty time, my friend."

"Well, so long, Kostakis." Dion moved toward the door.

"Not so fast. You must come again to my house. My wife has prepared gifts to send with you for your wife and son. After all, you do not have to hate me just because I know you."

"All right. I'll stop over. But I want to get the hell out of Greece. Fast."

"As you wish."

"I'll come by later. I gotta go pick up my tickets."

"This evening then, Dionysos."

Dion rushed from the office and back to his hotel to pack. He had just enough time to buy his tickets and rent a car before joining Kostakis. But the tickets he purchased were for Saturday. After dining with Kostakis he would head across land to the narrow strait that separated the mainland from Lefkas. . . and Iris.

Lefkas is by no means the beauty of the Ionian Islands. Ithaca rings with Homeric lengend and Corfu is graced with the architecture of Venetian elegance. Other islands of the group offer more natural beauty. But Lefkas has the White Cliffs. And surrounding the White Cliffs is the legend of Sappho and the controversy over the means and motivation behind her death.

Some sources claim that Sappho, a middle-aged woman of great accomplishment, fell into a passion for a young ferryman, Phaon, and followed him to Lefkas. When he refused her offer of love, she threw herself into the sea from the White Cliffs, the reputed gateway to the underworld.

But other sources refute this romantic tale. Sappho was a politically as well as artistically active woman who was jailed more than once on Lesbos for her outspoken ways. A temple of Apollo rests on the White Cliffs near a lighthouse and it was a common ceremonial practice for the priests to jump into the sea at this point to be retrieved by boats that waited below. The leap alone was not fatal. There is a suggestion of foul play connected with Sappho's death, a crime that was covered with a convenient romantic tragedy.

Iris had the notion that if she could stand on the spot, she would know the true story of Sappho's demise. And Dee was more than happy to indulge her on this last fantasy about Sappho before they returned to Athens to fly back to Hawaii. Reaching Lefkas was no great problem. Now that it was spring the boats were stopping once again on the island. They found a ferry at Patras that let them off on the southern tip of the island. But the real effort involved the trek up to St. Nicholas and the cliffs themselves.

They were forced to stay the night in the village where the ferry let them off before they could start the journey to the top. They spent the night sitting in the local taverna where the peasants gathered to continue the Easter celebrations. Women swathed in black kept time on the rude wooden tables as the men jumped up as if possessed and danced furiously. In solo display, or in a circle with other men, they draped their arms over each others shoulders as they dipped and swayed to the incessant music.

Dee and Iris had a difficult time persuading anyone to guide them to the top on the following day. They had no camping gear and had hoped to spend at least one night on the mountain after the great effort it took to reach the top. But the men would hardly listen to their request; thoughts of the next day and gainful employment were far from their minds or half drunken desires.

"Next week," they would say and try to draw the pretty Americans into their circle to dance. Unable to resist the genial good spirits, Iris and Dee joined the circle amid loud cheers and the offer of many glasses of ouzo. One youth in particular was taken by the women. Dark-eyed and handsome, he puffed out his chest as he danced, always checking over his shoulder to make sure Iris and Dee were watching his nimble performance.

"He's our guide," said Iris to Dee as they sat out a dance to catch their breath.

'What? Did you already ask him?"

"Don't have to," said Iris. "He's chosen us."

"Oh, really? What makes you so sure?"

"Watch."

Iris caught the young man's eye and raised a glass of ouzo in the air, beckoning to him. Hardly about to contain his joy, he rushed over to their table and bowed.

"Speak English?" asked Iris.

"Yes, some," he smiled with pride, his white teeth flashing in his face. "Do you want to make this dance with me?"

"No, not right now. Will you have a drink with us?"

He nodded vigorously and downed the ouzo in one gulp. "Good. Now we dance," he announced reaching out his arms.

"No, not so fast," laughed Iris. "Sit down for a minute. We want to ask you something."

He removed his cap with the narrow brim and straddled a chair at the table. "Níkos," he pronounced.

"Iris. And this is Dee. Glad to meet you, Níkos. Now, do you know the White Cliffs near St. Nicholas?"

"Yes, I know them. It is a hard climb."

"Well, we'd like to go there, but we can't seem to find a guide. Could you take us there?"

"Yes, I will take you Friday," Níkos nodded.

"No, tomorrow," insisted Iris. "By Friday we have to be back in Athens. We leave Lefkas on Thursday. So we have to see the cliffs tomorrow. And we need sleeping bags, a way to camp for a few days up there. We've looked at all the men here and it's you we want to take us up the mountain."

Iris nudged Dee's foot under the table to keep her quiet as she played to his ego. Níkos looked at the pretty American and hesitated. He was heady with the wine and dancing and had planned to keep on dancing and drinking for the next few days.

But the idea of being with these women on the mountain was more than he could resist.

"Wednesday. I take you Wednesday. We sleep on the mountain and I take you back for the ferry Thursday. Yes?" His bright eyes twinkled.

"No. Tomorrow. Tuesday. Two nights on the mountain."

Níkos threw up his hands. "But I must get the bags for sleeping. My tent, I don't know if it is ready. . ."

"Tomorrow," said Iris firmly as Dee looked on amused.

"Tomorrow," Níkos heaved a great sigh and struck his chest. "Okay, tomorrow. We leave at first light. Now we dance?"

"Yes, Níkos, now we dance." She threw Dee a knowing look and rose to dance with the enthusiastic Níkos.

"You, too," demanded Níkos, offering his other hand to Dee.

"Oh, I don't know, Níkos," protested Dee.

"You dance, or not tomorrow, yes? We all dance. It will be good luck for the climb."

"You win," sighed Dee, taking his hand and slipping her shoes back on her feet as she got up from the table. "I hope I have some energy left for tomorrow."

Níkos led the two women to the center of the dancers. One on each arm, the envy of the village men. His chest expanded suddenly; then he released their hands, spun on one foot, dropped to a squat and then sprung into the air.

"*Opa!*" shouted the crowd, as the dancing resumed with the blond heads bobbing along with the raven tresses of the Greeks in the circle.

At midnight Dionysos was able to break away from the home of his cousin and retrieve the car he had parked a few streets away. If he drove all night he hoped to reach land's end near Lefkas early the next day. He wound through the streets of Athens that were alive with the all-night festivities of the holiday.

Once outside the city he took the road to Thebes, which led along the Gulf of Corinth through Delphi, past Mt. Parnassus, and on up the coast toward Preveza. It was a moonless night and more than once he found himself off the road and sinking into the soft shoulders before he yanked the car back onto the pavement. He hadn't yet figured out how he would explain his appearance on Lefkas once he encountered Iris and Dee. He was out of credible excuses. And as soon as Iris had a chance to contact Phyllis she would realize that he had been lying to her about notifying her himself. All he knew was that he had to reach Iris, to confront her and have her before she had a chance to elude him once again.

He had studied the maps and calculated that he could easily cross the narrow channel between the mainland and the northern end of Lefkas by noon. Then there would be the trek up the mountains and across to the White Cliffs. He knew he would find her there.

In the morning a white mist rose from the sea and shrouded the rocky promontories of the cliffs. From her experiences on Santorini, Iris knew that if ghosts walked the land they were most likely to be found just before dawn, before the morning light could burn off the mist and send the spirits back into the shadows for the day. They had arrived exhausted the day before and had just enough time to pitch the tent before the sun set. Iris and Dee fell into the tent for the night, too tired even to make a fire and cook dinner. Níkos camped further down the slope under the protection of a rock that jutted out providing a natural canopy and protection from the cool wind that blew ceaselessly along the slope of the mountains.

Iris turned gently and disentangled herself from Dee's arms as she slept deeply by her side. She watched Dee sleeping as she drew on her jeans and nearby sweater and bent to kiss her lightly before turning back the flap of the tent and stepping into the cool, misty air. She picked her way carefully over the rocky surface as she made her way to the edge of the cliffs. Thorny asphodel caught at her ankles and she had to stop to disengage the plant from her socks, breaking off the white blossoms in her efforts.

Then she was at the edge of the cliffs. She could not see the water below because the sun had not yet risen behind her and the heavy mist still enveloped the coast. But she could hear the call of the gulls as they swooped through the mist and dove toward the water below. Was it her imagination, or was there a figure forming to her left? Iris stood transfixed as the figure took on human proportions and the sound of a human voice mixed with the cry of the gulls. She could not make out the words, but there was a mournful tone to the voice, as the figure turned and opened its arms toward Iris in supplication.

Could it be Sappho herself trying to tell her something? Iris shivered. Behind her the first shafts of light were piercing the sky above the crest of the mountains. The figure leaned away, raising one arm as if to shield her face from the sun. But it was not the sun that caused the fear, but another figure, larger, more solid than the first. It was the figure of a man that strode up to the lip of the cliff through the mist. The ghostly figure let out a scream and dispersed as the male figure walked through the space she occupied and advanced toward Iris.

Murder, thought Iris, the idea flashing through her mind with the speed of telepathy. Sappho was murdered by a man who walked the mountains with evil in his soul. But her knowledge did not cause the male figure to disperse like the first. Neither did the lightening sky seem to slow his purposeful stride. As the figure approached she could see that it was no apparition at all, but a mortal man: her brother-in-law, Dionysos Panagakis.

"Dionysos. What are you doing here?" She tried to sound authoritative, in control, while in actuality a growing dread filled her soul.

"I gotta talk to you, Iris." He was only a few yards away, his features taking on solid form.

"Stay where you are, Dion, or I'll call for help."

"And who's going to hear you? The other two are asleep and too far away to hear you."

"What do you want?"

"You. Ever since I laid eyes on you years ago I've wanted you. Sure, I married Phyllis. But it was you I always wanted. I want you even more than the gold, you understand? I can't even sleep anymore. I've got to have you."

"You're mad," cried Iris. "What would I want with you? Are you forgetting Phyllis? Or Dee? I love Dee, do you hear? What makes you think I'd waste my time with a pig like you?"

Dion lunged for her like an animal, pinning her arms to her sides before she had a chance to defend herself.

"You're mine, ya hear? It was all a mistake with Phyllis. I should have waited. Yeah, I didn't know. I should have waited for you."

Iris twisted in his grasp, trying to free herself from the madness in his eyes.

"I killed the last man who forced himself on me, Dion. And I wouldn't think twice of doing it again."

"Kill me" Dion snorted. "And how you gonna do that? With words? I'm going to have you, Iris, whether you want me or not."

Dion wrestled her to the ground, the sharp rocks biting into her back through the sweater as he tore at her jeans.

"No!" screamed Iris, clawing at his face with her free hand, ripping across his cheek and causing the blood to flow in long red lines. Dion drew back and dealt her a blow from his powerful fist, stunning her for a moment, giving him all the time he needed to rip the clothes from her body and enter her like a maddened bull.

Iris regained consciousness slowly, the image of Dion above her, his weight pressing upon her. With her free hand she groped along the ground and closed her fist around a jagged rock and waited, waited for the shiver to pass through his body and for the muscles to relax for a moment as he rolled to the side of her. With all her strength she turned and brought the rock down on his face, crushing the nose flat as he let out a bellow like a wounded animal.

Iris tried to jump to her feet, but Dion's arm reached out to grab her ankle despite his pain. The man is a demon, she thought in terror as she crashed to the ground beside him, her body lacerated by the sharp rocks.

"You'll never get away with this, Dion," she gasped, hoping to bring him to his senses.

But he was beyond reach, his breath coming fast as he scooped her up in his arms.

"You're a cunt like any other woman, aren't you? And to think I thought your thighs were paved with gold. You're just a cunt. And no cunt can stand in the way of Dionysos Panagakis."

And with one mighty heave he threw Iris over the side of the cliff, as the gulls screamed their alarm and the sun rose over the edge of the mountains of Lefkas.

III.
Keeper of the Keys

One

Phyllis Panagakis woke suddenly in the dark room. There was a whimper in the air and the drip of warm liquid on her arm. She fought herself to consciousness through the disturbing dream of her husband and found her son Jason kneeling on the bed next to her, crying, with blood running from his nose, down the face so like his father's and onto her arm.

"Jason, honey, what's the matter?"

She was fully awake now, taking the boy in her arms and dabbing at his nose with Kleenex. The boy could only sob in response, too terrified by the warm, sticky flow of blood from his nose. A switch was thrown in the hallway, casting a panel of light into the bedroom. A dark figure filled the door.

"The boy, what is wrong with the boy?" Sophia leaned against the door frame, her long grey hair loose around her stooped shoulders.

"A nosebleed, Sophia. He'll be fine," reassured Phyllis.

"I don't wanna die, Mommy." Fresh sobs broke out from the boy. "I don't wanna die."

"Oh, my angel Jason, of course not, honey. It's only a little nosebleed. Come on. We'll go to the bathroom and wash it off and you'll be good as new, OK?"

Phyllis cradled the boy into her arms and carried him to the bathroom. Sophia followed in her wake. How heavy he's getting, thought Phyllis. Her little boy. Next fall he would go to first grade and she wouldn't have him all day. She ran cool water on a washcloth and applied it to Jason's face as he stood on the closed toilet seat.

"You have a dream, boy?" asked Sophia, her dark eyes appraising the strong little body.

"Yes, Grandma." A shiver ran through his body and he sobbed once again.

"What happened in the dream, Jason?" pressed Sophia.

"Sophia, please." Phyllis held the boy close to her body. "It just upsets him more."

"No, it will help him. Tell me the dream, boy."

"Water, Grandma. There was water all over me. I looked up and there was water and I couldn't breathe. And Daddy was there, too."

"There, there, Jason. You don't have to talk," soothed Phyllis, stroking his back. How odd, she thought. I was dreaming of Dion, too. And Iris, of all people. There was water in her dream as well and a great sense of foreboding.

"You must keep him away from the water," warned Sophia, crossing herself.

"A little difficult on an island, wouldn't you say?" countered Phyllis, tired of the mysterious hocus-pocus from Sophia that frightened Jason. "Anyway, he's an excellent swimmer. I don't think one dream warrants yanking him away from the water."

"His grandfather knew the water, too. And the water did not spare my Andreas. He had dreams before he went out. Warnings. And he didn't listen."

"There, there, Jason." Phyllis ignored Sophia and continued stroking Jason's back until he relaxed in her arms.

"Where's Daddy?" he asked drowsily as sleep crept up on him once again.

"He'll be home soon, honey. Any day now. Then he'll take you out on his boat, OK?"

"OK," mumbled Jason, his love for the boat overriding his fear of the dream. "Can I stay with you, Mommy?"

"Sure, baby, I'm going to take you back to bed now, all right?"

Phyllis lifted Jason in her arms once again and laid him in the wide bed. He was asleep in moments. She treasured the nights he slept with her, his little body curved into hers in the dark. But as soon as Dion returned from Greece Jason would be returned to his cot in Sophia's room. Dion didn't like him sleeping with them. He thought the boy was too old for it and that Phyllis' attachment to him would threaten the manliness of his son.

"He sleeps," confirmed Sophia.

"Yes, he sleeps," agreed Phyllis, no longer angry at the older woman. "You tired?"

"No, I cannot sleep now."

"Want some iced coffee? I think there's some left over from dinner."

The two women prepared their drinks and carried the glasses out into the tiny back yard behind the stucco house, into the moist calm of the tropical night.

"You worry?" asked Sophia, sipping on the coffee laced with cream and sugar.

"Yes. It's been so long since we've heard from Dion. It was crazy for him to take off like that to Spain and Greece."

"Nothing we could do to stop him. The fever was in him. As long as there was some hope to do this thing, he would try. Maybe Kostakis will help him, maybe not."

"What got into him, Sophia? We had a good life. The tourists paid him well, and he could always join in the shrimp harvest if he needed more money. Or I could have gotten a part-time job once Jason was in school if the extra money was that important."

"More than money, Phyllis, more than money. He has to feel like a man. Like a Greek man. He doesn't want you to work. He must be a big man in the eyes of other men."

"Was Andreas like that, too?" Phyllis cocked her head thoughtfully.

"Not so much. He was just as stubborn. But it was not for the eyes of other men." Sophia touched the place between her sagging breasts. "It was the voice in here that he listened to. He was never at home in the company of other men. He like to be alone. To be quiet. He was a man of courage, though no one knew. Except me."

A slight breeze stirred the large leaves of the rubber tree.

"And Jason? How do you see him, Sophia?"

"He is both of them, so he will be sad. Like his father, a strong man. But the sensitivity is his grandfather's when he asks me why birds fly so high and die on the pier. Or who sings under the water to make the waves sound so beautiful."

"I know," whispered Phyllis. "Sometimes he's so much like Dion I can't tell them apart except for size. And then he's like a stranger. Nothing of me in him at all."

"No, nothing of you in him."

Phyllis swirled the ice cubes around her glass and felt terribly alone, an orphan once again in the world with no one with whom to feel connected. She tried to remember her dream, but could only recall that Iris was in it. But Iris as a grown woman, not the teenager she last saw. How did it happen? How did they lose each other? Easy, Phyllis told herself. They were so busy looking for love in the foster homes that they could not stand the risk of competing for affection with a sister. But it's mostly my fault, Phyllis chided herself. I was older. I should have taken more responsibility. But Iris had always been so pretty, so bright, so talented that Phyllis had feared that Iris would be chosen over her. And she had to face the fact of her own jealousy once Dion came on the scene. Then it was too late. She married and moved and Iris embarked on her own long wandering ways.

"I go in now," announced Sophia, easing herself out of the lawn chair, her aching muscles protesting the move.

"Good night," responded Phyllis absent-mindedly. "I'm going to stay out a while."

What a rare luxury, she reflected. To sit out in the middle of the night and just think, at a time when all the neighborhood children were asleep, when the traffic in front of the house had ceased and even the tourists had quieted down for the night. Only her and the night, with the scent of hibiscus and oleander in the air. This solitude was the last outpost of romanticism she had left in her. After years of marriage and motherhood she had ceased believing that the right man could make her life meaningful, because if Dionysos Panagakis was not the man of every girl's dream, who was? Phyllis smiled to herself, thinking of the girl she had been when he had sailed into her life, changing its course forever in a matter of days.

How could she have done anything else? She had been pathologically shy, locked into a boring job that only paid enough to keep her on the genteel side of poverty. And there he was, like a god, the hero of her dreams, treating her like a fairy princess and begging her to marry him. She blushed even now thinking of the way he made love to her, his hard body next to hers, gentle but powerful. She could feel how he held back, afraid that he would break her if he forgot himself. He terrified and thrilled her. But once Jason was born, something changed in Dionysos. He still made love to her, but not in the same way. He seemed to be elsewhere after the birth, as if his passion was intent upon her until his son was produced, and after that he turned away toward the water, the world and his private dreams. She became the mother of his son, and like many other mothers, became invisible as a woman to her husband.

But, she questioned herself, what else is there? You grow up, you marry, you have children. Even a few years of romance was more than most people got. She had a safe life, a predictable one with certain securities and small joys. Not adventurous, perhaps, but acceptable. Yes, acceptable. She was a plain woman of thirty-two with a dashingly handsome husband and son. It should be enough. And it was. Except for those dreams and the nagging doubts about the places in herself that she had buried along with her mother.

Two

Dionysos winced noticeably as he touched his swollen nose to test the progress of the healing. Still painful. And the pressurized air of the plane cabin seemed to irritate it even more, each breath a painful throb across his face. He breathed through his mouth to relieve the pain and was grateful that the small aircraft would land soon at Key West International Airport.

He carefully turned over in his mind the story he had prepared for Phyllis and couldn't help feeling a pride in his cunning. There was no way anyone could connect him with Iris' death. However maddened he had been in those moments before dawn on the White Cliffs of Lefkas, the sunrise seemed to return him to sanity. With the first light he felt the full impact of his action and broke into tears, the open wounds on his face stinging with the salt of his tears. He was horrified. What had he done? What had possessed him, pressed him to such extremes? Could one really blame Greece; the light, the ghosts?

He had rushed to the edge of the cliff but could not see the water clearly through the heavy morning mist. The only sound was the crash of water against the rocks and the screech of the circling gulls. No human voice or cry rose from the depths. Dion had looked around for a way down the side of the cliff when he heard a voice in back of him.

"Iris, where are you? Iris," the voice called. It must be Dee looking for Iris.

Dion panicked once again. He couldn't be found out. He had no reason to be here and the bloody mess of his face would tell the story all too clearly. He turned from the cliff and ran back the way he came, away from the little campsite that Dee, Iris and their guide occupied the night before. He moved quickly over the rocky surface of the mountain, knowing that they would soon come upon the scene of the struggle and realize that violence had been done. He ran until he thought his lungs would burst and stopped only once to bathe his bloody face in a mountain stream.

"Damn," he swore, realizing that his nose must be broken. He had to find a way to cover the injury, to find an excuse for his broken face.

By midafternoon he had made his way back to the channel between Lefkas and the mainland. He reclaimed his rented car and drove as fast as possible back the way he had come, except that he veered off before reaching Athens and crossed to Rafina. It was the only logical plan he could hit upon. He could claim that he wished to see his mother's home town before returning to America and had rented the car for the trip. He drove through the town so that he would know the familiar landmarks and then steered the car once again back along the highway that led into Rafina.

He took his time finding the right location. He needed a place that looked dangerous, where an accident could easily take place. His patience was rewarded. A curve in the road hid the stone wall of a vineyard that bordered close upon the road. Dion turned the car around so that he could build speed coming into the curve. His foot pressed down the accelerator and he held his breath as the car swung into the curve. With a quick jerk of his wrist, the nose of the car was pointed directly into the wall. Dion's other hand rested on the door handle. At the last possible second, he opened the door and flung himself clear as the car crashed into the wall.

Nodding his satisfaction, Dion dusted the grit from his hands and started his walk back to Rafina. His clothes were already bloodied to a suitable degree. And the car certainly would convince anyone that the driver was lucky to walk away with just a broken nose.

Dion smiled in spite of himself as he fastened his seat belt for landing. It had worked like a charm. Once back in Rafina, he called Kostakis to tell him of his misfortune. His cousin responded like a prince, dispatching a car to pick him up and take him to the best hospital in Athens. Kostakis' plump wife was at the hospital when he arrived, loaded down with flowers and sweets which she lavished on Dion with the care of a solicitous mother.

Kostakis also arranged a long distance call to Phyllis so that Dion could alert her to his plans for return. Dion had to be careful during the conversation because Kostakis was in the background.

"Hello, honey, it's Dion. How are ya? And Jason?" Dion nodded as if deeply engrossed in the reply. "Good, good. No, I'm all right. Had a little accident near Rafina seeing Ma's home town. No, I'm fine. Broke my nose on the steering wheel, but the doctor here says I'll be good as new. Doesn't even think I'll be scarred. Not that I care, but I know how you feel. No, really, I'm all right."

Dion shrugged mutely to Kostakis as if to say, women, what trifles they involve themselves with.

"I should make it before Iris, anyway. Iris. Your sister. Didn't you get my letter? You're kidding! No, really. It was the craziest thing. I met Iris here out in the islands with a friend of hers. Yeah, really. She said she'd stop by Key West on her way back to Hawaii. Can't wait to see you. Yeah, yeah. It's wonderful. She's quite a lady. Well, don't want to run up Alexis' bill. I'll be home in a couple of days. And make Iris stay a while, OK? Sure. I love you, too, baby. Bye."

Dion hung up the phone and smiled at Kostakis. "Great to hear her voice, you know? Thanks."

"It's nothing. I know how the women worry. At least you had good news for her as well as bad. It's good that the sisters will see each other again. In fact, next time you come to Greece, you bring your mother to visit with my mother. They should spend time together before it is too late. Or send your mother any time. I'll pay her way."

"You've been terrific, Alexis. Sorry for being so pissed off before."

"Forget it. That was business. And speaking of business, will that nose keep you from diving?"

"Not for long. The doc says I should wait a few weeks before going down. But I've got the other divers lined up and I still can skipper the *Rafina* all right."

"Good." Kostakis rested his well-manicured hand on Dion's shoulder. "We're counting on you."

"So am I," thought Dion as the plane started its descent.

Through the lightly scattered clouds Dion could see the dark string of islands surrounded by the swirling waters breaking over the coral reefs. And connecting them all for as far as the eye could see was the concrete ribbon known as Highway 1 that started at the uppermost tip of Maine and wound its way down the east coast and southern mountains of the United States to end, finally, at the last key in the long string of islands — Key West, Dion's home.

The island was inhabited by two contingents that enraged Dion: the hippies and the gays. While still in the Navy during the sixties, he would visit his mother and find hordes of long-haired, shiftless loafers wandering around the streets of Key West, openly begging from natives and tourists alike. They tried to camp on any available piece of land whether it was a public beach or somebody's lawn. They begged, smoked dope, screwed on the beaches and tried the patience of the friendly islanders to the breaking point. No overt action seemed effective in dissuading them from their chosen lifestyle. But the fashion changed once the war was over and economic considerations once more took hold of young minds.

The gays were another matter. Sleek young men paraded the beaches in the briefest codpieces, their finely muscled bodies toned and glistening with oil. They paraded for the sheer pleasure of it, to allow the rich middle-aged men the opportunity to appraise the merchandise. While many such gentlemen brought their expensive Disco Dollies with them from New York, faint and wan with generous doses of cocaine, others preferred to pick up their vacation treats on the island itself, the lure of the unknown being part of the holiday thrill.

There was one ritual at which all the island contingents seemed at peace, at a point of truce with each other. In late afternoon small clusters of people would make their way down to Mallory Square, opposite the harbor, and mill around waiting for the finale of the day's work, sport or sightseeing. Tourists reddened by too much afternoon sun, natives on their way home after work and a drink at a local bar, hippies who fell into the natural rhythm of ritual and Navy boys looking for a stray girl all crossed at the end of the day to watch the sunset, the sky turning from blue to peach and orange as the shrimp boats passed far out, readying the nets they would drop once the sun set to catch shrimp moving across the ocean floor in the night.

It was to this habitual gathering that Dion made his way

after his plane set down at the small airport in the late afternoon. He felt the difference in the air immediately, the humid sub-tropical climate and island breezes more sensual and real to him than the stark, mystical light of Greece. For once he did not mind the long-haired boys or the strutting fags cruising the beach for the night's entertainment. Instead he felt a sense of homecoming; the power that comes in knowing yourself a native and in command of the ground you walk upon. There was no mystery here, no forces ranging against him that he could not control. All the people he saw in front of him were safely human, with human passions and faults, comprehensible and predictable. Mists did not gather that gave off the call of past centuries and women did not give off auras that promised answers to questions only asked in dreams.

The red orb of the sun dipped below the tip of the horizon. The sky turned a vibrant yet moody purple. The crowd was pleased at the show and struck up an appreciative applause. Dion smiled, sticking the half-smoked cigarette in the side of his mouth to free his strong hands to join in the ovation as the last edge of the blood red sun disappeared behind the black line of the horizon.

"Your face!" Phyllis could not hide her shock when she rushed into the small living room that evening at the sound of the front door closing.

"I tried to warn you, honey." Dion touched his swollen nose self-consciously and ran his hand down the butterfly clamp on his cheek. "It looks worse than it is. Be good as new in a few weeks." He opened his arms to her and Phyllis allowed herself to be engulfed in his embrace. At least he was safe, alive, all limbs intact.

"I'm glad you're home, Dion. We've missed you."

"Spoken like a sailor's wife. Where's Jason?"

"With Sophia in the yard."

"Get him, okay? I've got a few things for him."

"All right." Phyllis left Dion in the living room and crossed through the kitchen to the back door. Sophia sat in a lawn chair in the early evening, rocking Jason in her arms and softly crooning an old Greek song. Back in Greece again, thought Phyllis as she stepped into the yard and approached the two figures that seemed like one large body in the night.

"Sophia. Wake Jason and come inside. Dion's home."

"Wake up, boy. Your father is home. Come, come, Jason."

She struggled to lift the groggy child from her lap. Phyllis helped lift him to his feet and led him back to the house, Sophia shuffling behind with great excitement.

"Jason!" Dion's face lit up with pride as the boy entered the room. He thought he could see a difference in size from a month before. His son. Yes, he would be a strong figure of a man.

"Dionysos," was all his mother could say as she cradled his wounded face in her gnarled hands. Tears were in her eyes, but Dion could not tell if they were tears of joy at seeing him or shock at his face.

"I'm fine, Ma. Just fine. Your sister says hello. She wants you to come visit, to see Rafina again."

"I am too old," said Sophia shaking her head. "I will not leave this island again."

"Don't be silly. Maybe we'll all go once we haul in the treasure, eh?"

"Treasure, Daddy? Where's the treasure?"

"We're going to dive for it, Jason. Then we'll be rich."

"Can I have all the toys I want, Daddy?"

"Sure, son. Anything you want on this whole damn island. Or the mainland, too."

"Thanks a lot, Dion," groaned Phyllis. "Just when we had him quieted down about a new bike. Thank God the televison broke so he can't get any more ideas for things he wants."

"Why don't you get the thing fixed?" asked Dion, loosening his tie and relaxing in his large black Naugahyde chair in the corner.

"No money," said Phyllis. "We just have enough for groceries."

"Get it fixed," ordered Dion. "We've got money from now on. Got a beer, honey?"

"Yes, there's a few left. I'll get one."

Phyllis went to get the beer while Dion unzipped his bag, pulling out blouses, bottles of wine, figs and colorful toys for Jason from his rich relatives in Greece. That's a switch, thought Dion as he distributed the gifts to his mother and son. Every peasant in Greece talks about their rich relatives in America and here I am begging favors from a wealthy Greek relative.

Dion sat in the circle of his family, the women and boy at his feet listening to his stories of the beauty of the Greek islands, the charm of Rafina, the grandeur of their cousins. Jason wanted to hear of the toys his cousins owned, Sophia about the

Easter Saturday Mass in the churchyard and Phyllis wanted to hear only of her sister, Iris.

"What's she like, Dion? Still beautiful?"

"She's good looking all right." Dion shifted uncomfortably in his chair as he started on his second beer. "You should see the guys turn around to get a look at her. But she just wanted to hear about you. Guess they should be turning up any day now, so you gals can gab your heads off."

"They? Who's with her?" Phyllis looked up at her husband as she sipped the strong-tasting wine from Greece. She liked the way it scratched her throat on the way down and seemed to warm her breasts from the inside out.

"Another woman. Someone she knew from when she lived in Hawaii. An older woman. A psychologist, I think. They're on their way back to Honolulu soon."

"She must have changed. Didn't have friends as a rule. Always was a loner, although people tried to get close to her all the time. People were always attracted to her. Did you feel that, Dion?"

"I dunno. She was sort of mysterious at times, talking about dreams and things she saw that weren't there. I just thought she was a little bit of a nut. Or maybe she's spoiled by that fancy education."

"No, it's real enough. She was that way long before she hit any fancy schools."

"When we going out on the boat, Daddy?" interrupted Jason, who was impatient with all the talk about somebody he didn't know.

"Tomorrow soon enough? I gotta give her a good once-over and take some measurements. Gonna need another boat, too, and equipment for the divers. We've got a lot to take care of, Jason."

"I'll help, Daddy," he volunteered, his small chest puffed out with pride, a miniature imitation of his father. The adults laughed. Sophia struggled to her feet and stretched out her hand to the boy.

"Come, Jason. It's time the young and old go to bed. You can see your father in the morning."

At first Jason protested but was coaxed into his room with the new toys and promises of nautical adventures the next day. Dion and Phyllis were left alone in the living room, listening to the chatter of the boy as he got ready for bed and the low crooning of his grandmother.

"Let's go out in the yard, Dion," urged Phyllis, the wine making her drowsy and loose-limbed.

"Sure." Dion grabbed another beer and followed his wife through the kitchen and into the yard. A few stars were visible in the night sky, but they did not shine with the crisp brilliance of the stars in the Greek sky. How long will I go on comparing the two, he wondered. This is my home. This is where I'll make my fortune. My family is here, not in Greece. He could even absolve himself of the rape and murder of Iris. It was on foreign soil, almost like a war zone. Yeah, that was it. More like battle conditions in a strange country. Soldiers were not considered murderers. And the women they took were all a part of it, too. No, he was fine. An unfortunate incident, nothing more. He was home.

"What are you thinking, Dion?" asked Phyllis in a soft voice. She was caught between two emotions; happiness at having her husband back again and a slight resentment that he was standing in the yard, making it smaller and less like her own private meditation space as it had seemed the other night. Silly, she chided herself, it's his yard, too. But should it be his, too? After all, the rest of the world was his. She did like to feel that one little corner of it was hers alone for her private wishes, dreams and memories.

"I was thinking how good it was to be home," he said with a conviction that surprised Phyllis.

"Really? I thought you got restless here, that you needed these trips."

"Not much any more. This ain't a bad place to be. I've seen a lot of the world, honey, and it's as good as any of it."

"Well," said Phyllis, sipping the wine. "Isn't that always the case? I'm the one who's dreamed about Greece since I was a little girl, and you're the one who gets to go and you could care less. Just business to you, isn't it?"

"If it means that much to you, Phyllis, maybe you should go with Ma. Get her to take up on Kostakis' offer and go along with her."

"'And who'd look after Jason?"

"You could take him, I guess. Though I don't much like the idea of him traveling around so much."

"Well," sighed Phyllis. "Guess we can't all get what we want, can we?"

"Did you hear something?" Dion turned toward the house.

"Hmm?" Phyllis was lost in thought about Dion. Did she

want him to make love to her tonight or not? What was it that she resented about him all of a sudden?

"The bell. I thought I heard the front doorbell," he said moving across the yard towards the house.

"I didn't hear anything," mumbled Phyllis, remaining in the yard. She drained the glass of wine and stared absently at the fronds of the rubber tree swaying gently in the soft breeze. Dion reappeared waving a yellow envelope in his hand.

"Telegram. For you."

"For me? I've never gotten a telegram in my life. Who'd be sending me a telegram?"

"Open it." Dion placed it firmly in her limp hand. "Only way you're going to find out is to open it. Maybe it's from Iris, telling you when she's going to get here."

"Think so?" Phyllis ripped open the envelope with her thumb and unfolded the message eagerly as Dion watched her face nervously. For a moment terror struck his heart. What if Iris wasn't dead? What if the telegram really was from her, exposing him to his wife? It was crazy. No one could survive that fall.

Phyllis let out a sudden shriek. The telegram dropped from her hand and floated innocently to the ground.

"She's dead!" wailed Phyllis, her hands helpless at her side.

"Who's dead, honey? What's wrong?" asked Dion, relief spreading through him. She's dead. She's dead. And I am safe. The message pounded through his body with the beat of his heart.

"Iris. She's dead." Phyllis collapsed in Dion's arms. "It's not fair, Dion. It's not fair. I just found her again. Now she's gone."

"What happened? I just saw her last week."

"An accident of some sort. On an island."

"Who sent the telegram?"

"Her friend, Dr. Hartman."

"An accident, huh?" Dion held his wife firmly. It was better than he had hoped. They believed it to be an accident and not murder after all. He was in the clear.

"I think so. She's coming here next week to bring me some things. Oh, Dion, why did it have to happen?" She was sobbing now, laying her head against his chest. "What's wrong with that place? You get in a terrible accident, Iris is killed. Evil. It must be evil," she mumbled, giving herself up to the comfort of her husband.

Three

Spring was in full force along the Keys. The stream of wealthy winter tourists gave way to the flood of solid middle-class working people who saved up all year for their two weeks of recreation in the closest they could get to paradise on a city clerk's salary. The "Beer and Bait" joints were booming. Children on spring vacation begged weary parents for one more ride in the glass bottom boat at the Coral Reef State Park off Key Largo.

On Key West the natives who made their living off the tourists spruced up for another season. The Old Town section was a prime target of the hordes. Craft shops, boutiques and galleries clustered next to each other in the ten-block area. Museums were also a popular attraction; they ranged from the cigar factory museum in Pirate's Alley on Front Street to Audubon House on Whitehead Street. There was conch stew and fresh oysters in one quarter and the famous Cuban black beans and rice in another. Any first-time visitor was bound to find satisfaction for any appetite somewhere on the small island that housed nearly 30,000 people.

But Dee Hartman had no intention of playing tourist on Key West the fine spring morning she landed at the airport. Her handsome features were drawn in a grim, purposeful line as she waited patiently at the baggage claim area for her suitcase. Her mind was on only one thing – to find out what sort of stuff Phyllis Panagakis was made of.

Dee claimed her soft green suitcase and hailed a cab to the Panagakis home. She looked vacantly out the window, barely taking notice of the impressive white Bahamian-style homes that lined the streets. In no time at all, the cab turned down a side street lined with unremarkable small stucco houses that were redeemed by the presence of lush, tropical green foliage and vibrant red flowering trees.

"Keep the change," said Dee as she handed the driver a five dollar bill and let herself out of the taxi before the rotund Cuban had a chance to open the door for her.

"Thanks," he shrugged, then pulled away as Dee walked up the short span of concrete to the door.

She rang the bell and the door was thrown open immediately by the woman Dee had seen smiling so kindly from the picture Dion carried in his wallet.

"Dr. Hartman?" she asked politely.

"Yes. But call me Dee, okay?"

"Sure, Dee. Come on in." Phyllis stepped aside to allow Dee to pass her into the relative coolness of the living room. "Make yourself comfortable."

"Thanks," responded Dee, sitting on the first available chair.

"Something to drink?"

"Love it."

"Iced tea? Or a gin and tonic, maybe?"

"Oh, gin and tonic, if you don't mind. I could use it."

"Sure. I'll just be a minute."

Phyllis disappeared into the kitchen, allowing Dee a chance to examine the room. A typical lower-middle-class home, decided Dee. Television in a prominent position facing into the room like the chairman of a committee facing his board. A large floral couch dominated one wall with its companion coffee table in blond wood; a few wicker chairs and that huge black Naugahyde chair that was oviously Dion's — the man's throne. But there were hopeful touches; the bookcase sported both Edith Hamilton's and Bulfinch's *Mythology*, some plays and a selection of novels that contained classics as well as more recent literary fare.

"Decided to join you," said Phyllis, returning with two large glasses of effervescent liquid with a wedge of lime floating near the rim.

"Thanks," said Dee, taking her drink and sipping it gratefully. "Well, I'm glad to meet you although the circumstances are hardly what I imagined two weeks ago."

"I know." Phyllis hung her head. "What a shock. I still can't get over it. To find her and lose her so fast. It's almost better if I had never known at all."

"Really?"

"You know what I mean," explained Phyllis. "After all these years I got used to not having her around, not thinking that we could get on again. Then, for a few days, I got so excited. Everything that was buried inside of me about Iris and our mother and the life we had together. Don't get me wrong. I love my family here. Dion and Jason and Sophia, too. But to think about Iris again and how happy we were before, well, before. . . ." Phyllis trailed off awkwardly and became painfully aware of how the cold glass was numbing the hand that held it so tightly.

"Before your mother's death?" suggested Dee.

Phyllis nodded and took a sip of her gin and tonic before responding, switching the glass to her other hand.

"Yes. So you know about that."

"From Iris. But how did it affect you?"

"My life stopped. I couldn't believe it. First my father died in the war, although I guess you're always a little more prepared for that. But we all pulled together after he died – mother and Iris and I. Mom went back to work as a secretary and I sort of helped to look after Iris more. I didn't mind, really. Not like some girls would. I always liked Iris, even though she was prettier and smarter than I was. But she didn't throw it in your face, you know? And I had the edge of being older. No matter how special a kid is, they're always grateful when an older one takes an interest in them."

"Speaking of kids, where's your son? And Dion, for that matter?"

"Oh, Dion had some business to take care of down by the harbor. And Sophia took Jason to the doctor's. They should be back soon."

"Something wrong with Jason?"

"I don't think so. It's just that he's getting nosebleeds lately and he's having trouble sleeping, having nightmares. Maybe it's just growing pains."

"Doesn't sound too serious," agreed Dee. "But you're smart to check into it."

"You have kids?"

"Yes, didn't Dion tell you? I have a son in high school."

"How nice. No, he didn't tell me much about you. All the excitement about Iris. And he's so wrapped up with this salvage deal." Phyllis sipped at her drink and felt the slight dull buzz as the alcohol seeped through her system. Should have eaten something, she reminded herself. "You must have been good friends."

"Indeed." Dee threw back her head and laughed. "I guess Dion really didn't tell you very much at all, did he?"

"No, he didn't." Phyllis looked at Dee quizzically, trying to figure out what she had said that was so funny. "But men are like that. They never give you the details you're interested in. Instead it's all about business deals and equipment. So what did he leave out?"

"That Iris and I were lovers," Dee said simply, though she watched Phyllis closely for a response.

"Lovers?!" The word was out before Phyllis could stop herself. Her eyes grew large like those of a child listening to a ghost story. Suddenly Phyllis looked ten years old.

"Yes," said Dee softly. "I loved your sister very much. We were going back to Hawaii together, to live together."

"How awful this must all be for you," said Phyllis, her natural kindness overriding her shock. "Did Dion know about you and Iris, you know, that way?"

"Oh, yes. He tried to take it in stride. But I saw that he didn't understand. Funny how he kept that from you."

"Not really. Sometimes he treats me like the Virgin Mary. He tries to keep me pure or something. The mother of his son and all." Phyllis drained the last of her drink and set down the glass with a clink on the table. "But I resent that he keeps anything about Iris from me."

"And he thought I wouldn't mention it, I suppose. As if I had something to hide, to be ashamed of, about loving her." Dee shook her head sadly and stared at her almost empty glass.

"Another drink?" offered Phyllis.

"Sure."

Dee was left alone again to collect her thoughts while the drinks were being made. Phyllis was a kind woman, Dee concluded, with a loyalty to Iris even though they hadn't seen each other in years. And there was that edge about Dion, how he treated her like a child and withheld information from her. She seemed to fill the wifely function for him and he seemed to give her little thought or consideration beyond that. Good. While no ardent feminist at the moment, Phyllis had the seeds of change in her. She was bright, loving, and emotionally unsatisfied. Dee was starting to put the pieces together.

"Here you go, Dee," said Phyllis handing the drink to Dee and sitting opposite her once again. "Tell me about Iris."

"Where to start?" Dee drew in her breath. "She was lovely, through and through. Unique. She had spiritual depth and insight that put other forms of learning to shame. A tough individualist and yet fragile. Too fragile for the evil she couldn't seem to leave alone. It's as if she were given all the gifts of the gods and then persecuted by divine jealousy." Dee lowered her eyes. "You'll have to excuse me. I always go off on some tangent when I think about Iris. She was simply the most extraordinary human being that I ever met. And I loved her. Passionately."

"Well, I believe you." Phyllis blushed. "I just don't know

women who feel that way about each other. Or I should say, who talk about it."

"You loved her, too. Don't let the sex issue distract you. Women love each other all the time. Some of us make love physically, some don't. But the point is that we love each other because we understand each other like no man has in our lives.

"I'm not backing away from the physical aspect. Iris was the most exquisite lover I've had. The lovemaking grew out of our shared attraction, our shared sympathies. It was a thrilling aspect of our love, but not the entire force of it." Dee stopped herself short, afraid she was pushing too hard, giving Phyllis too much to assimilate in one dose.

"Her accident must have been horrible for you. Were you there when it happened?"

"It was no accident."

"What? No accident? Then she isn't dead?"

"I didn't say that. I said there was no accident. Iris was murdered."

"No!" screeched Phyllis, her hands flying to her ears as if to shut out the sound of Dee's voice. "Who did it? Why?"

"That's what I intend to find out."

"How do you know it was murder?"

"We were camping on top of the White Cliffs of Lefkas, an island off mainland Greece in the Ionian Sea. It was part of the pilgrimage that Iris plotted for us. Anyway, we reached the campsite late in the afternoon after an exhausting climb. There was little we could do except sleep.

"When I woke up the next morning, just around dawn, Iris was gone. I didn't think twice about it. She liked to walk the hills before dawn. She said she saw things then, that an ancient power was at work at the moment of dawn. At any rate, I didn't worry. I got dressed and went out to look for her. I know she'd head over towards the cliff so I made my way in that direction, calling her name, because the mist was still so thick that I couldn't see very far in front of me.

"As I approached the edge of the cliff I heard the sound of someone running. It was a heavy tread, a man's tread. At first I thought it was Níkos, our guide, so I called out his name. But there wasn't an answer, just running feet. Then I was at the edge of the cliff and the light was starting to burn off the mist. I looked around and I was afraid. Still no Iris. And then I saw Iris' belt on the ground. And the blood. I screamed her name. But there was just silence.

"I ran back to the campsite and down the slope. Níkos was still asleep in his sleeping bag. I woke him up and made him follow me back to the edge of the cliff. By that time the sun had burned off the mist. And looking down the cliff we thought we saw something, a spot of color by the rocks. I knew it was Iris. And I fainted dead away." Dee stopped to catch her breath, to light a cigarette to calm her nerves. She looked over to Phyllis who was sobbing.

"Oh, no. No," she mumbled. "Did you catch the bastard?"

"No. Not yet. But we will."

"Do you really think so?" Phyllis looked hopeful.

"Oh, yes, I do think so."

"And the damn courts will probably let him off, right?"

"Who said anything about courts?" asked Dee archly. "I want to make *sure* there's justice. That has very little to do with the courts these days, wouldn't you agree? Direct vengeance is so much more satisfying. And just."

"Do you mean what I think you mean?"

"Precisely. I'm going to track down that killer and take care of him myself."

"Aren't you afraid of, well, of getting caught?"

"I like the way you think," smiled Dee. "You didn't try to convince me not to do it. You're just worried about getting caught."

"Of course."

"You're more like your sister than you appear."

"Thanks. Is there anything I can do to help?"

"Maybe. I don't know yet. But I'll keep you in mind."

"Then you have an idea who it is, or where he is?"

"Nothing I can talk about yet, Phyllis." Dee turned and sat opposite the younger woman once again. "We'll keep in touch. I have to go back to Honolulu. Toby, my son, and my patients can't wait much longer. But I'll be working on this the whole time, believe me. And before I forget, I have something for you." Dee reached inside the high neck of her blouse and lifted out a gold chain and a locket. She undid the clasp and held the locket out toward Phyllis.

"I think you should have this." Phyllis didn't recognize the locket at first, but as she took it from Dee's hand she let out an involuntary gasp.

"It's grandmother's locket! Where. . ." Phyllis looked up at Dee's face. "Of course. Iris must have given it to you, right?"

"Yes, she did. But I think you should have it."

"But she wanted you to have it."

"Because she wasn't in touch with you, I'm sure. It's a family heirloom. You keep it. Put me in your will if it'll make you feel any better about it."

Phyllis nodded and held on to the locket that was still warm from Dee's body.

"Thank you."

The women looked at each other with a deep understanding. A pact had been formed. Before they could speak the front door was flung open and Jason raced into the room followed by the slow-moving Sophia in her perpetual black dress.

"Mommy, can I have a Coke, please?" he asked climbing into his mother's lap and eyeing the stranger with interest.

"In a minute, Jason. I want you to meet a friend. Her name is Dee."

"Hi," he said with ease. "You just move in? Got any kids?"

"No, I'm just visiting, Jason. And yes, I do have a son. But he's in Hawaii."

Jason immediately lost interest in Dee.

"Sophia, this is Dee Hartman, a close friend of my sister Iris."

"Sorry to hear about the accident. I prayed for the girl. It's sad when the young go."

"Yes, it is, Sophia."

"Mommy, I'm thirsty," demanded Jason.

"He's very like his father, isn't he?" observed Dee quietly.

"Yes, very." Phyllis threw up her hands. "Okay, Jason. Why don't you go into the kitchen and have Grandma pour you something to drink?"

"Yes, come, boy. Let your mother talk with her friend."

Jason slipped from his mother's lap and ran into the kitchen.

"Wait a second, Sophia," said Phyllis as the boy disappeared. "What did the doctor say? Is he all right?"

"He says the boy is fine." Sophia swayed her head and upper body from side to side. "He can find nothing wrong. The boy dreams. He sees things. He may have a gift. It's too early to tell these things."

"At least he's all right, then. Good."

Sophia moved toward the kitchen as she heard the refrigerator open signaling Jason's intent to serve himself.

"We will see," cautioned the old woman as she hurried to

the kitchen to divert a sticky disaster on the kitchen floor.

"He has dreams, does he?" said Dee. "Maybe he gets it from his Aunt Iris, hmm?"

"Yes, there is something of everyone in that boy but me," said Phyllis in an irritated voice. "He's got Dion's body and will, his grandfather's poetic spirit, his aunt's visions and his grandmother's complete attention. Why does he need me at all?"

Dee looked at Phyllis with interest. A new idea was forming itself in her mind.

"Funny you should say that, Phyllis. Not many women would admit they resent their sons."

"Oh, I love Jason. But the older he gets the less he seems to need me." Phyllis shrugged and felt awkward about her outburst. "I'm sure you went through the same thing, didn't you?"

"Of a sort," agreed Dee, watching the other woman carefully for a moment. "Well, I have to go. I need to get to bed early tonight to help with this damn jet lag. I have to catch the early plane in the morning to connect with the flight in Miami."

"Oh, I wish you could stay longer," urged Phyllis.

"Thanks. But I can't. I'm late getting back to Honolulu as it is. But I'll call again before I leave and like I said, I'll keep in touch. It's not the last time we'll see each other, I promise you. Now, do you mind if I call a cab?"

"Of course not," Phyllis replied. "I'd take you but Dion isn't back yet with the car. I'm surprised."

"I'm not," said Dee calmly.

"What do you mean?"

"Oh, let's just say that Dion isn't comfortable around me."

"Because of you and Iris?"

"Yes, that mostly. I frankly would have been surprised if he'd been here. I'm just as glad. We had a chance to talk and get to know each other a little. I like you, Phyllis."

"And I like you, Dee." Phyllis blushed self-consciously.

Dee rose quietly to her feet. The visit was a success from her point of view. Phyllis Panagakis was no fool. Dion sold her short.

"And thank you for coming, Dee. And for sharing everything with me." Phyllis stood and reached out her arms to hug Dee in farewell and smiled. "You feel like family. And I'll take care of our locket."

"Fine," said Dee.

Phyllis released her grasp and took a step back. An hour ago she would have been horrified by the idea of women who were lovers. Yet after so short a visit with Dee, it seemed to make perfect sense to her on the emotional level, although the physical manifestations of that love still seemed rather obscure.

"I'll call the cab. The phone's in the kitchen."

Dee nodded and wandered over to the window to wait, staring out across the small, well-tended lawn to the houses across the street framed by the lush green foilage. She was unaware of the feverish, gold-flecked eyes that returned her stare anxiously from between the slits of half-opened white shutters of the house opposite the Panagakis residence.

The fresh scampi appetizer was placed in front of Dee Hartman, the aroma of fresh garlic filling her senses, as the crowds started to gather in front of the Pier House Inn dining room for the nightly sunset ritual. It was time to relax now that she had met Phyllis and had laid out the next steps in the plan. Her eyes grazed the tops of the shrimp fleet masts that were barely visible near the horizon against the sherbet-colored sky.

Phyllis was a potential ally, which made the whole scheme more elegant and more primitive at the same time. Dee smiled to herself, the lines deepening around the clear blue of her eyes. How calm I feel, she marveled. How patient, when I thought I would have been a ball of fire, aching for instant vengeance. On the contrary, the prolonged retribution — when the victim becomes anxious and then is lulled into a false sense of security as time passes — is better; there is time to plan and strike from the most unexpected and devastating quarter.

Dee patted the fat envelope that contained the pages she had dashed off that afternoon after leaving the Panagakis house. In the morning at Miami Airport she would have it weighed and sent express to Switzerland. As the sun set it cast the dining room in a rose glow, and flushed Dee's face with the color that, by turns, connotes modesty, love and revenge.

Four

As the summer wore on, Dion's anxiety over the death of Iris and possible retribution faded as the more immediate threat of Frank Taylor loomed before him. At first he had been mistrustful of Dee Hartman's visit and the motive behind her befriending of his wife, particularly when Phyllis innocently informed him that Dee believed Iris' death was due to murder and was not an accident after all. Not a week went by that a pale blue envelope with a Honolulu postmark did not make an appearance in their mailbox. What could they have to write about, wondered Dion. Memories of a dead woman should wear thin after a while. Maybe Dee was trying to seduce his own wife, he had thought at one point, but he discarded that idea too. What could happen with Dee in Hawaii and Phyllis safe at home in Key West?

So after a time Dion came to accept the long distance friendship and turned his attention to the more immediate problems before him. He had a year to find sunken treasure and he could not tolerate wasting even one day in worry about other things. With his background as a Navy diver, his familiarity with the waters up and down the Florida Keys and the documentation on the *Toledo* that he retrieved from the *Archivo General de Indias* in Seville, Dion was able to convince the Florida Board of Archives and History that they should grant him a year's franchise to explore an area near Crocker Reef opposite Windley Key along the Straits of Florida. He was convinced that the wreck had nestled in a curve of the reef further south than covered by previous explorations. With Kostakis' money Dion filed his $5,000 bond for the right to explore that area and prove his claim before the year ran out.

So far, luck had been with him. When he returned to Key West from Greece he was informed by his two divers, Carlos Lopez and Joe Phipps, that Frank Taylor had asked if they were available for another diving job. It seemed that he had his eye on the same area as Dion and was in the process of putting together backers for the venture. The divers informed Dion because he had promised a larger sum of money up front than Taylor and a larger cut of the profits if they were successful. They also remembered that Taylor had cut them out of the dive that hit the jackpot for him further down the Hawk Channel near the Matecumbe Keys.

Dion hurried to file his request and was granted the license. Just two days later Taylor showed up with his package deal; when he was turned down, Taylor became enraged and caused such a scene at the Board office that he had to be restrained by police. He called down curses on Dion and vowed to ruin him for poaching on "his" territory. Taylor had reached the point where the money to be made discovering the wreck was secondary to the search itself, the need to dive and to uncover wrecks regardless of the cost in money, family, health and sanity.

Dion Panagakis, on the other hand, still believed that he was in control of his faculties, that he chose the search rather than the other way around. His choice of the *Toledo* seemed eminently rational and he went about locating it in the most businesslike fashion. But he was held by gold fever as surely as the maddened Frank Taylor, and the fever spurred him on to even greater daring and larger successes.

The area that Dion researched was the richest underwater treasure chest in the world. During the three hundred years that Spain had maintained colonies in the New World, returning ships loaded with treasure passed through the narrow Straits of Florida and many fell victim to the high winds and hurricanes that whipped the area so fiercely. Many alternatives were sought to protect the treasure. Gold-laden galleons were guarded by an armada of armed war ships. Heavier cargo ships were pressed into service whose thicker hulls stood a better chance of surviving the rough Atlantic crossing in one piece.

Dion knew that these ships held the most fabulous wealth for two reasons. First, the vessels were loaded to capacity with the legitimate booty for the King of Spain. And second, passengers and crews were notorious smugglers, hiding gold, silver and other valuables to avoid the heavy "King's fifth" tax on all goods. Dion knew of the fake-bottom trunks that held bars of gold and the ploy of fashioning a ship's rudder in gold and painting it to escape detection by the King's tax collectors. The *Toledo* promised to hold such rich treasure. On the ship's manifest found in Seville, he learned that many wealthy passengers were aboard the ship when it went down.

A fleet had started out of Havana harbor toward Spain in July, 1714, seeming to navigate the fifty mile wide straits with ease. But a sudden hurricane darkened the sky and washed over the ships, dashing many of them against the sharp coral reefs of the Keys, splintering their hulls and filling their holds with sea water in a matter of minutes. Some of the ships went down in shallow water. A certain amount of salvage work was done by Spain that year using divers who had to rely on the span of one breath to accomplish their underwater retrieval of gold, silver and jewels for the King. Other wrecks sank nearer the lip of the reef and slipped into water too deep for even the best diver to reach. But in the twentieth century the development of scuba gear and rubber fin changed all that and opened the deeper floor of the ocean for treasure hunting once again.

By the time Dion Panagakis was afflicted with gold fever many wrecks from that 1714 fleet had already been salvaged by adventurers who had located them by hard work and research or just plain dumb luck. But no one had yet located the *Toledo*. Dion felt that it was his ship, his alone; that it had his name on it. He laughed when he heard of Taylor's rage. How could the man hurt him? This time Dion was going by the letter of the law. He did not resent the twenty-five percent the State of Florida would take as its share. It was worth the protection from other competition during his search.

The newly outfitted *Rafina* set sail from Key West in early May, Dion's heart bursting with excitement. He waved to his mother, wife and son on the pier. Jason cried loudly, inconsolably, at being left behind. Dion steered the boat down the Hawk Channel along the Intracoastal Waterway until they were opposite Bahia Honda Key, then steered the *Rafina* further out to sea, outside the edge of the coral reefs along the Straits of Florida. Lopez and Phipps lounged on the clear deck area smoking cigarettes and exchanging an occasional story between long, idle gazes out to sea. They were seasoned divers and knew that they would labor long and hard before any wreck was likely to be found. It was Dion who was fired by the hope of instant success, dreaming of sudden discovery.

From his office on Plantation Key, Frank Taylor was making plans to insure that Dionysos Panagakis would be kept away from the true site of the *Toledo* for months and hopefully an entire year. Unlike Dion, Taylor had made a number of exploratory dives in the Crocker Reef area prior to his attempt to get a permit. While Dion had been busy researching in Seville, Frank Taylor and two hand-picked divers made a series of dives from an inconspicuous pleasure boat. One of the divers had returned to the surface with an encrusted eight reales piece – strong evidence that a Spanish ship lay below. After further dives, they were able to recover a few shards of pottery and a huge anchor. Taylor was convinced. If this wasn't the *Toledo*, then it was its twin sister. It was fairly easy for him to raise the funds to continue the excavation, because of his success at other salvage efforts. But what he hadn't taken into account was Dion Panagakis.

Who the hell was this Panagakis, questioned Taylor, chewing on his fat stub of a cigar. A nobody. A fisherman. An amateur. And what dumb luck made him guess where the *Toledo* lay? Well, guessing the area and actually finding the site were two different things. Panagakis had exclusive rights for a year to find the location that Taylor already had pinpointed. Taylor just had to make sure that he wouldn't find it.

"'Scuse me, skipper. Ya busy?"

Taylor turned around swiftly to face the beefy man that hovered hesitantly at the door. He must be slipping. He rarely allowed people to sneak up on him like that. He was usually so careful about not turning his back to the door.

"I'm always busy, Murphy. More than I can say for you. Now what is it?"

"We done the job. That Greek's gonna go on some wild goose chase."

"Good, good. You do it in both spots like I told you?"

"Sure. Just like you said. We put the coins and some of that pottery by the wreck in the south part of the reef. We dumped the anchor and some more coins out further near the frigate."

"That should hold him a while," chuckled Taylor, scraping his hand across the iron-grey stubble on his chin. "I got this guy pretty well figured. He goes by the book. All that nice research and fancy equipment. And that pretty boat. He'll play it straight, criss-crossing that area in a grid. Whichever way he starts, he'll hit one of our little nests of *Toledo* treasure before he lands on the right one at the edge of his territory. He'll be months at either place, the sap."

"Yeah, can't wait to see him haul up some of that stuff and wet his pants with excitement."

"You'll see nothing, you idiot. I don't want anybody from this outfit anywhere near Crocker Reef, ya hear? We'll play nice, now, and keep our noses clean. You forget all about your expedition, ya hear? Just keep busy bringing up the rest of the stuff on the Matecumbes site. Ya read me?"

"Loud and clear, skipper. Loud and clear."

"Good. Now clear out. I got some work to do."

"Sure, skipper."

Murphy backed away from the threshold a few steps before turning and placing his battered blue cap on his head and stepping into the bright sun. Taylor yanked open the bottom drawer of his desk and drew out a flask of whiskey. He twirled off the cap in a single gesture and raised the bottle to the ceiling.

"To the luck of Panagakis. May he be bright enought to trip over an anchor the size of a house and choke on a few lousy gold coins."

He removed a cigar from the corner of his mouth and tilted back his head to receive the stream of whiskey down his throat.

On the fourth day of diving Dion slowed down. The first three days he had pushed like a madman, driving himself and the other divers nearly to the point of exhaustion. The *Rafina* was anchored a few hundred yards off the tip of Crocker Reef. Dion planned to comb the reef coral head by head, keeping careful record of the area they covered each day so as to not duplicate their search as they crossed the area. He wanted to operate the magnetometer himself and was impatient with the advice Lopez and Phipps tried to give him. But finally he was forced to listen to their more seasoned experience.

Dion was worried. He was tiring too quickly. He no longer had the stamina of a twenty-year-old, and the pressure below the water was causing his face to throb where his nose had been broken. But he pushed on in spite of the pain, guiding the magnetometer above the reef, anxiously awaiting the signal that would indicate the presence of metal below the surface, covered by centuries of silt and debris. Zipped in his wet suit for protection against the cold and surprise attacks from moray eels, Dion was oblivious to the beauty that swarmed around him: the schools of curious reef fish, the elaborate configurations of brain coral dappled by shafts of sunlight that filtered down to the shallow ocean floor. He was intent on one thing and one thing only: the uncovering of his *Toledo.*

On the second day he thought he had found something. The magnetometer indicated the presence of metal. Dion was alone, Phipps and Lopez out of sight around the bend in the coral reef. Dion's heart started to pound with excitement as he swam around the curve only to find a large torpedo shell crusted over with sea life. Just an old World War II practice torpedo, nothing more. Dion chided himself on his childish reaction. He must learn to control his impulses. He was just as glad that Lopez and Phipps were not close enough to have seen his exuberance.

Dion looked across the water, the sky a pale blue in the early morning light and decided to let up a bit. He needed the loyalty and good will of his divers if he hoped to bring the project to a successful conclusion. Since he was a little boy Dion had had trouble being a team player. But now that the stakes were so high, he had to force himself to learn new ways fast.

"Hey, Lopez," he called out. "Come here a minute, would ya?"

The younger man turned toward Dion and nodded. He was short like Dion, powerfully built across the chest, and his face and torso were tanned a deep, smooth brown from his life in the sun. As he came forward, Dion could see the gold crucifix catch the light and shine brightly around his neck.

"You want something?" Lopez's eyes were patient.

"Just wanted to ask you something. Would you mind manning the magnetometer today? I've had my fun the first couple of days, but I'd like to see how you handle it a while, okay?"

"Sure," nodded Lopez. "I've worked with lots of them. You've been doing okay, but the way you're going at it can tire a guy out pretty fast. I'll show you how to take it a little easy, eh?"

"Yeah. I could use a little lesson in that, too. What do you say we knock off early today and head into Plantation Key for a decent meal and some beer, okay?"

"Get no argument from me." Lopez returned the grin, his fine white teeth flashing in his dark face.

"Then it's a deal." Dion turned toward Phipps who was suiting up across the deck. "Hey, Phipps, could you do with a few beers and a decent steak tonight?"

"Who do I gotta kill?" retorted the slender, sandy-haired Phipps.

"I'll take that as a yes," shouted back Dion.

"Hey," said Lopez. "Doesn't Taylor hang out on Plantation?"

"Yeah," grinned Dion. "Guess he does at that."

Lopez gave a low whistle.

"You go look for trouble, don't you, man?"

"I think I can handle Frank Taylor all right. And what's he

gonna do? The law protects me like a fuckin' crown prince. Why, if we even see any of his boats around here we can call in the cops. And he knows it. And since he blew up at the Board office, I don't think he'd get too much sympathy."

"You should have been a bullfighter, man. You like walking in front of dangerous animals and seeing how close you can get before getting gored."

"Aw, don't worry," Dion slapped Lopez on the shoulder and turned to heft his scuba tank onto his back. "We're just going for a little steak and beer and any pretty little tourists who like romantic men of the sea, eh?"

"Okay," Lopez laughed and zipped up his wet suit. "The girls sound better than crazy Taylor any day."

The three divers plopped backwards into the water, a trail of bubbles tracing their path underwater. On deck one crewman kept an eye on the bubbles while the others took out clean shirts and lathered up their faces for a shave in anticipation of their night on the town.

Frank Taylor was knocking back his third Wild Turkey at Maggie's place by the Sunken Treasure Museum that night when Dion Panagakis and his crew walked in. Taylor had never laid eyes on Panagakis before, but he recognized Phipps and Lopez and it didn't take a genius to figure out that the guy with the puffed-out chest and air of authority must be the bastard that was trying to lay claim to his ship.

The group headed for the bar and didn't immediately see Taylor sitting in the corner. Their minds were on a drink and on checking out the place for any likely broads. Maggie's was the one place in town that offered decent food and drink and thus it ended up drawing a strange combination of locals and tourists.

It was Lopez who first spotted Taylor staring at them from the back of the room.

"Hey, Dion, see that guy over there? The mean lookin' bastard with yellow eyes?"

Dion looked over his shoulder casually in the direction that Lopez indicated.

"Yeah, I see him. But I can't tell ya if his eyes are yellow." Dion snorted.

"They're yellow, all right. Just like the streak down his back. Taylor's the kind of guy who gets his goons to do his dirty work for him."

"Oh, yeah? Sounds worse by the minute. Somebody oughta

teach him a lesson."

"I wouldn't try it," advised Lopez. "This is his territory."

"I don't see no signs, do you?"

"Hey, I thought we came in for a good time." Lopez was getting nervous. "Say, look over there. Phipps is warming up a couple of dames. Let's go over, eh? Check 'em out." In the other corner Phipps had corralled three college-aged girls who were playing up to the all-American looking Phipps. Dion glanced over quickly then returned his gaze to Taylor who was staring at him like a man possessed.

"You go ahead, Lopez. Save that blonde for me. I'll be over after I buy Mr. Hot Shot Taylor a friendly drink." Lopez shook his head.

"Can't leave him alone, can ya? Gotta needle the guy."

"He can take it." Dion turned to the bartender. "What's Taylor drinking tonight?"

"Wild Turkey. Same thing he drinks every night."

"Fine. Give me two doubles." Lopez moved away from the bar with his beer.

"See ya later, boss." Dion took the drinks and walked over to Taylor, his powerful body swaying from the shoulders, though the liquid in the glasses hardly stirred. He stopped in front of Taylor and looked down at him with a slight smirk on his face.

"Mind if I sit down?"

Taylor shot Dion a look of pure hate.

"Mister, you got some balls."

"Thanks," said Dion affably as he sat down opposite Taylor. "Have a drink." He pushed the glass of Wild Turkey across the table. Taylor eyed it for a minute then grabbed hold of the glass and, deciding that there was no point in wasting good whiskey, took a sizable slug without answering Dion.

"Well, Taylor, seems we got something in common now, don't it?"

"Mister, I don't even know who you are."

Dion smiled. "Come on, Taylor, cut the crap. You know who I am. I'm Dion Panagakis, skipper of the *Rafina*. Just thought I'd come over and pay my respects. You know, professional courtesy,"

"I don't mix with greaseballs." The smile on Dion's face flickered for a moment, but he kept control of his temper.

"Look, Taylor, I don't need nothing from you, get it? Okay, so you got lucky once. You got yourself a nice little treasure site down on the Matecumbes. Terrific. Just keep busy with that for the next year or so and stay out of my territory, understand? If I even see the wake of one of your fuckin' boats I'll have your ass in jail so fast you won't know what hit ya. The *Toledo*'s my ship, see? She's mine. And if the law don't scare ya, I've got a few tricks of my own. Get the picture?"

Dion's eyes were fixed on Taylor. Taylor's fist was clenching and unclenching around his glass as his head bobbed up and down. Damn, Murphy. Where was he now? He wanted this bastard decked so badly he could taste it. But he didn't dare take a swing without Murphy to back him up.

"Ha! You talk big with your crew lined up along the bar don't you, greaseball? Big man."

"Yeah, I'm a big man. I do my own fighting. Wanna step outside and see who's the greaseball? Man to man? Or is that too much for you? What's the matter, Taylor? Lost track of the boys? They having a party in the can or something?" Taylor took a look at Dion's physique and knew he would be a fool to take Dion on.

"Didn't know I got to you so bad, greaseball. Looks to me like you're scared."

Dion threw back his head and laughed. "Oh, that's a good one. Scared of a scrawny son of a bitch like you? You gotta be kidding. Shit. You're not even worth warning."

Dion stood up and drained his glass in one swift gesture, smashing the glass down hard on the table in front of Taylor. He walked over to Lopez and Phipps who were sitting at a table with the girls. All eyes were on Dion as he approached the group. Lopez slapped Dion on the shoulder as he sat down and signaled for another round of drinks.

"Brother, I ain't seen old Taylor so mad since he caught a diver pocketing a gold coin," said Lopez. "You just made yourself a lifelong enemy, my friend."

Dion shrugged. "Only way to be with bastards like that. Natural enemies. So forget it. Now, why don't you introduce me to these lovely ladies, eh?" Lopez waved his hand around the table.

"Let me see if I can remember. This is Candy, and Joan, and Carol, right?" The girls eyed Dion coyly, impressed with his bravado. Dion nodded to each one.

"Pleased to meet you. I'm Dion Panagakis, head of this, ah, little expedition. You're all my guests tonight, ladies, so let's have a good time."

"Well, thanks," said the dark-haired one named Joan. "But we're on our way up to Key Largo."

"Naw, stay here. Key Largo's just another tourist trap. Mix with the natives, see the real Keys." Dion leaned close to the blond named Candy that he had picked out for himself. "Tell your friend to loosen up. She needs a little more romance in her life, don't she, Candy?" Candy blushed, flattered at the attention from the dashing adventurer. At twenty, she thought older men were sexy.

"Maybe he's right, Joan. Who wants to see an old Coral Reef, anyway?" Joan was torn.

"Well, I don't know. What do you think, Carol? We got those reservations at the motel and everything."

"There's a terrific motel right here," said Dion before Carol had a chance to vote. "And tell you what. The rooms are on me. You'd be doing us a favor. After all that time at sea, we need the company of ladies, ain't that right, Phipps?"

"Yeah, yeah, he's right. It gets pretty lonely out there on the water day after day," agreed Joe, trying to keep a straight face. Thanks to Dion these chicks were practically in the sack. Joan threw up her hands in defeat.

"What the hell. If no one else cares, why should I? I guess I'm in no big hurry to get back to Miami."

"Atta girl, Joan." Dion flashed her a wide grin. "How about another glass of, what is that you got there? Wine? Fine. Wine again for the ladies." Dion leaned close to Candy, his mouth brushing her hair. "Did I tell you that I got a powerful sweet tooth, Candy?"

She giggled nervously, but stopped as she felt Dion's hand run up her thigh under the table. She was terrified and thrilled, but she didn't stop him. She thought of the diaphragm tucked away neatly in her purse and wordlessly gave herself permission to spend the night with this handsome stranger.

Across the room Taylor pushed back his chair from the table and stalked out of Maggie's without a backward glance at Panagakis. Let the fool have his little-boy victory. Taylor would have his revenge in the end.

Five

"Jason, I said go to your room, young man. Now! Do you hear me? Right now!"

Phyllis' face was flushed with rage. It took all her willpower not to strike the boy. She had told him three times that he had enough Coke and the minute she turned her back to put away some dishes he tried to help himself and brought down an entire shelf of the refrigerator onto the kitchen floor, glass and food flung in every direction.

"I didn't mean it, Mom, honest," argued Jason.

"I've told you a thousand times not to help yourself. What's the matter with you?"

"I wanted more," he retorted. "And Daddy said I could have anything I wanted from now on." The reference to Dion was the final straw. Phyllis' hand shot out and struck Jason across the face, the blow snapping his head back against the cabinet. He stood stunned for a second, then reached up to hold his head and ran out of the kitchen screaming.

"Grandma, Grandma!"

Phyllis stood planted in the middle of the mess on the kitchen floor, shaking with rage. She was not sorry for hitting the boy. He grew to be more like Dion every day; proud, defiant, assuming that women existed only to serve him.

"Phyllis, what you do to the boy?" Sophia stood in the doorway, a specter in black.

"I slapped him. He disobeyed me, Sophia. He made a mess and then threw it back in my face. He has to learn a lesson."

"But you should not hit the boy. Never. It was an accident."

"It wasn't for the accident, Sophia. It's for his attitude. He acts like I'm his servant." Sophia shook her head.

"We *are* the servants of our children, Phyllis."

Phyllis whirled toward Sophia. "I'm not, Sophia, not me. Maybe *you* like taking abuse. Maybe you get comfort from that damn icon of yours, but not me. If I thought I was put on this earth to serve Dion Panagakis and 'his seed' I'd kill myself."

Sophia backed away from the blast. She was shocked. Phyllis had always been such a good girl, but this summer she had grown short and spiteful. It was not good for Jason or her son to have a spiteful woman in their home.

"I know what it is with your husband away. Very hard. I know," offered Sophia. "Many times Andreas was away for the fish. Very hard." Phyllis gave a short laugh and stepped over the debris to the counter and poured herself a glass of wine.

"Oh, Sophia, you're on the wrong track. It's *better* when he's gone. When he's here all he does is fill Jason's head with nonsense about treasure and how rich he'll be. He's so damn self-important, the way he puffs out that big chest of his. And Jason thinks that's just great, that's the way to be a man. So he starts throwing his weight around just like his dear old Dad." Sophia laid a hand on Phyllis' arm.

"And this is wrong? That a boy tries to be like his father? What is wrong with that?"

"Plenty." Phyllis twisted away from Sophia's grasp. "They're both bullies. Selfish bullies. And you put up with it. Put up with it? Jesus, you encourage it."

"Men are different."

"Only if we allow them, Sophia. Only if we let them step all over us. Listen, Sophia, you spoiled Dion from the day he was born. And now you want to do the same with Jason. I'm not going to let you, you hear me? I won't have you interfering every time I try to discipline Jason, everytime I try to teach him a little respect. He's old enough to get the message, believe me. He's testing. He's testing me, he's testing you. And if I allow him to walk all over me now, he'll do the same to other women all his life. But I won't get anywhere if you keep crossing me. As long as he knows that all he has to do is run crying to you to get around me, I don't stand a chance."

Tears were filling the old woman's eyes. "Jason is all I live for. I love him, Phyllis. You tell me it is wrong to love my grandson? To turn him away when he cries?"

"No, no, Sophia, it's not wrong to love him, but what about yourself? Or me? Yeah, me. I wish you could be concerned about me sometimes, Sophia, and not just see me as the wife of your son."

Sophia was at a loss. Her daughter-in-law had changed into a different woman before her eyes. Ever since the death of her sister. It was wrong, it was morbid to mourn so long for one that had already been gone for so many years. The girl was unbalanced. She needed something to take her mind off this. Or maybe Dion wasn't being a husband to his wife? Sophia decided to take a different approach.

"Is it Dion, child? Is he not taking care of you?" Phyllis sat at the kitchen table and sipped her wine, looking absently into the yard.

"Oh, Sophia, I'm used to him ignoring me. Ever since Jason was born he's only been half there. He got his son. That's all he wanted from me. I know he doesn't want to make love to me anymore, either. And you know what? I don't care. I really don't care. No, Dion's just going along like he always has, I guess, only more so. It's me that's changing."

"Maybe you need to have more children," offered Sophia, naming the remedy she felt that she had been denied in her life.

"Oh, dear God, no. The last thing I need is another baby." Phyllis shook her head. "No, no, Sophia. Women drug themselves with child care, the endless, mindless drudgery of it all. Don't you see, I'm just waking up. I've been asleep most of my life. Dion married a sleepwalker. He *wanted* a sleepwalker. And that's what he got. But I'm waking up, Sophia. I'm thirty-two years old and I'm just starting to ask what I want to do with my life. *My* life, do you understand?" Sophia was worried by Phyllis' talk.

"But the boy—"

"The boy, the boy. What is it with you, Sophia? Always the boy. Or Dion. Don't you ever have a thought for yourself? Listen, why don't you do yourself a favor. Why don't you go to Greece and see your sister before she dies? You're forever talking about Rafina and your childhood and all that. You've got the perfect opportunity right now. Kostakis will send you the ticket." Sophia waved her hand.

"No, no, I am too old for such trips. And the boy needs me."

"The hell he does," retorted Phyllis. "He'll be in school full time soon. He doesn't need two women hovering over him all day. And you're not all that old, either. You'll be sorry if you don't see your sister, believe me. If I had only seen Iris before she died. Well, you know what I mean. Go, Sophia. What's stopping you?"

The old woman stood by the sink, wavering, undecided. "I will ask Dionysos what he thinks. When he comes home I will ask. If he thinks it would be a good thing for me then maybe I do it."

"Oh, Christ, Sophia. There you go again. Ask your son permission, like he owned your life. Your wishes count for nothing with Dion, and neither do mine. Maybe you're beyond reach, but I'm not.

Phyllis got up from the table and walked out the screen door into the yard, her yard, and fell to the ground in the sun. She smelled the strong odor of the ground still damp from the rain of the day before and felt the coolness on her back contrast with the hot sun that beat down along the top of her body. Hot and cold. Cold and hot. Where did the two meet in her body? Was there an even temperate zone that bisected her body through the middle, a balance point, a thin line on which she traveled her whole life, feeling neither hot nor cold, feeling nothing travel from one end of her body to the other?

She was just starting to step off that numb, nothing, unimpassioned line. And she finally had a friend who understood; Dee Hartman, her sister's lover. The women she knew in the neighborhood were totally wrapped up in their husbands and children, having nothing more exciting to talk abut than recipes for Key Lime Pie. But Dee was different. At first Phyllis was flattered that a bright professional woman like Dee would take the time to write her at all. She found herself looking forward to the letters like a school girl, hungry for news about places and ideas that charged her imagination. And after a while Phyllis realized that Dee really was interested in what she had to say, that she wasn't being patronized, but was being treated like a peer, an equal. Gradually, Phyllis relieved herself of her frustrations and her dreams through the letters to Dee. She told her of her passion for mythology and the fascination she had in the stories of people of different cultures. Instead of saying "That's nice," Dee sent Phyllis books on psychology, anthropology, mythology... and the catalog for the East-West Center in Honolulu.

Phyllis turned over on her stomach, pressing the sun-warmed top of her body into the cool earth and exposing her chilled back to the warming rays. A shiver passed through her body. Hot, cold, by turn, never allowing herself to become one medium, unfeeling temperature again.

The idea that she could go back to school, to do research in the area she loved, was a new concept for her. Where would she get the money? She doubted that Dion would endorse the notion at all, let alone cut into his precious treasure-hunting money to make it possible. Dee had suggested a scholarship and sent information on special programs for people returning to school after many years.

In any case, it would involve leaving Key West. She could start by going to the University of Miami. Or even Honolulu;

Dee could help her there. Phyllis started sending away for catalogs from around the country; she decided to apply to half a dozen and let fate take a hand. Whoever wanted her and could give her some money, well, that's where she would go. Next year. In the fall. In one year.

Phyllis sighed as a breeze swept through the yard. In a year Jason would be firmly in the routine of school. She couldn't decide which was better for the boy and for her; to take him with her wherever she went or to leave him in Key West with his father and Sophia. The three of them seemed like the true family anyway. She had just been the means by which they perpetuated themselves. Well, she had time to figure out that one. If Dion hit it rich on his treasure hunt he wouldn't care if she were there or not. And if he didn't make it, she didn't want to be there to suffer the inevitable abuse.

Phyllis squinted up toward the sun. It was near its zenith, almost noon. She pushed herself to her knees and brushed the loose earth from the heels of her hands. The mail must be here by now, she thought. The mail; her one link with the outside world, the world with all its possibilities. Perhaps there would be another catalog today, or a fat blue envelope from Honolulu with pages of inspiration and hope. Phyllis rose to her feet and hurried to the front of the house, her thoughts focused on the contents of the black metal box that hung beside the front door.

Summer was drawing to a close in Hawaii. The stream of summer tourists had let up as families headed back to the mainland to prepare their children for school. On the islands the teenagers cut back their hours of work at the Waikiki hotels, turning their minds back to football practice and homework, away from the long days on the beach courting vacationers, divorcees or service men on leave. They retreated back inland, into their own society of island teenagers, no longer an exotic attraction for high-paying guests but their own people once again.

In her office at the University, Dee Hartman paused from her work on a lecture about developmental psychology and leaned back in her chair, removing the glasses she was just starting to need for close work of any kind. She folded the tortoise shell frames shut with a snap and slipped the glasses into their leather case. Enough work for today, she informed herself. She was ahead of her self-imposed schedule and could afford to take the rest of the afternoon off. She was always ahead of schedule these days, as if she were trying to keep very busy to fill up the large expanse of time. Toby was hardly home anymore. At sixteen his time was devoted to his friends, football and his part-time job with a research team of marine biologists.

A year ago Dee would not have thought twice about Toby's absence. But then, a year ago she had had Iris.

Could it only be a year? Dee gazed out her window towards the mountains. Yes, just a year ago Iris and she had seemed so very happy and unconcerned with the rest of the world. Well, that had been a foolish mistake, because the world was fairly concerned about them. First, Harold. And then. . . .

Dee pivoted in her chair and jumped to her feet. And then there was Greece. Her blood began to boil the instant the memory hit her consciousness. And to think that bastard Dion Panagakis thought he could get away with it! The unmitigated hubris of the man. A swift justice was too good for him. For five months Dee had patiently laid her plans. For five months she courted Phyllis Panagakis from a distance, playing into her fantasies, firing her dreams and fueling her mounting frustrations with the megalomania of her husband.

Time, Dee reminded herself, was her ally. Vengeance guided through the intricacies of time can yield justice. And justice positioned opposite evil can root it out and destroy its seed into the future.

Dee walked around her desk and picked up two volumes on her way out the door to the secretary's desk.

"You leaving for the day?" asked Virginia, looking up from her typewriter whose electric hum obliterated the intermittent chirp of birds outside.

"Yes, Virginia, I am. Done and gone for the day." Dee placed the books on the edge of her desk. "Listen, if you have time before you go, could you send these to Mrs. Panagakis, please?"

"Sure. You want them to go book rate?"

"No, send them air mail. I want her to have them by the weekend."

Virginia reached over and placed the books on the blotter in front of her. "Oh, Japanese myths this time. And Polynesian. She must be some kind of special student, eh?"

"Let's just say that I think she would be an asset to the school. Interdisciplinary, you know."

Virginia smiled, her bright teeth echoing the white ginger

flower in her dark hair. "If she doesn't come, she can open a used book store in Florida and make a fortune."

"I don't know what kind of market there is for mythology on Key West," smiled Dee. "I think it's a little too hard-core American there to go in for it in a big way."

"I'll get them out, don't worry, okay?"

"Thanks, Virginia. See you tomorrow."

Dee walked out of the building and into the bright afternoon sun. Her old blue Volvo sat across the parking lot looking a trifle derelict. Time for a new car, mused Dee. She would give the old one to Toby and get another car for herself. She certainly could afford it and it was time Toby had a car of his own.

Poor Toby, she thought as she let herself into the car and started up the rumbling motor. He had come back from his annual two months in California with his father a wreck. No, just confused, she decided. His father showered him with all the things his sizable resources allowed: the use of a brand new car, a private wing in the expensive house in the hills. He had grilled the boy about football, proud of his son's accomplishment in that realm. But he wasn't as supportive about Toby's passion for sea life. Tom Hartman didn't think a marine biologist could make enough money to live in style, and Tom couldn't imagine that a son of his wouldn't be interested in power and money. He pressured Toby toward the law, but Toby held his ground. Of course Tom blamed his soft ways on Dee, and Toby found himself in the distasteful position of having to spend most of his time defending his mother to his father.

On impulse, Dee turned the car toward the valley rather than toward home. It was a sentimental gesture to satisfy a longing for celebration, no matter how melancholy. She wanted to visit Paradise Park again. Dee hadn't been back since she had been there with Iris the year before, at the height of everything good in their relationship. They had walked through the lush gardens, flowers in their hair, not needing to speak.

But such innocence wasn't enough, Dee knew now. They had been foolish in their happiness. They had thought that everyone would leave them alone because they weren't harming anyone. Only later did Dee realize that the love that she had with Iris threatened a great number of people. Dee thought that only prudes would be disturbed by their relationship, but it wasn't the sexual aspect that was threatening to others. After all, lesbian scenes were regular fare for male pornography. Men were so secure in their dominance that women together in a sexual way were only perceived as a diversion for their own tastes and not something sought after and satisfying for the women themselves.

So the sexuality was not what disturbed the order of the universe. No one really cared when Iris' mouth moved over her body with such lingering, soft wetness, her tongue flicking Dee on to ever greater excitement and pleasure. It was what grew out of that pleasure and satisfaction that was threatening: the notion of self-worth and autonomy that a woman's love could give to another woman.

Dee had experienced certain satisfactions in life with men, both sexual and emotional. She had felt appreciated, even secure in the arms of men. But never powerful, never like she was throbbing with the very stuff of the universe. To be "possessed" by a man was to be disinherited from the direct access to the world. To be possessed by a man was to become a satellite to his vision, and a woman could only lay claim to the territory that her man had carved out in battle with other men. No wonder they developed such theories of biological determinism; it justified their own behavior, their own aggression. It finally dawned on Dee that war existed because men enjoyed war, that war was necessary to notions of dominion and power over other creatures and that peace was defined as the resting space between wars and not as an ongoing state that reflected the harmony of forces, the best in what was attainable in human life.

"You're still here with me, aren't you, Iris?" Dee intoned softly as she sat on a moss-covered rock near a small waterfall. She rested in the beatific perfection of the park for an hour until the late afternoon sun dropped behind Diamond Head and threw the jungle in deep shadows. The chill of the air roused Dee from her reverie and made her remember the time and that Toby would be home from practice soon, hungry and anxious for his dinner. And after dinner Dee would write Phyllis Panagakis. It was time to prepare the way for her new "friend."

To her delight, Phyllis did find a blue envelope in the mail box when she rounded the house the day of Jason's outburst over the spilled Coke. Rather than enter the house and encounter the disapproval of Sophia, Phyllis returned to the back yard to read her letter in peace. She settled in the far corner of the yard away from the house and near the bougainvillea that edged the property, slitting the envelope with the long nail on her left hand and removing the pages from their envelope. A slight scent of jasmine rose from the paper to join the other fragrances of late morning.

Dear Phyllis,

With any luck at all you should be receiving two books today or tomorrow. Since you say you've read every book on the island that could possibly interest you, I thought I would send you a couple on mythologies that you have never mentioned: Japanese and Polynesian. If this sounds suspicious of me, you are right in questioning my motives. I want you to become interested in what Honolulu can offer you in the way of education and culture. It is a fascinating place and although it suffers from the ills of all fast-growth American cities, it still retains enough of the dignity of the old cultures to give it a sense of grace.

The Japanese and the Samoans, for example, are so different. One has such a strict, formal heritage that reaches back through centuries of ancestors, while the other, while quite old in its own right, has the feeling of an eternal present; much more playful and fleshloving than the Japanese. And yet the harmony achieved in the Japanese aesthetic almost seems worth the restraint. A Samoan can be lusty, but a Japanese understands eroticism.

Well, that seems a far cry from mythology, doesn't it? But I leave the other discoveries for you within the pages of the two books. What is interesting to me from a quick glance through them is that such wildly different cultures share some basic similarities. One would expect that they would both have creation myths. But that both have myths about the Great Flood is rather interesting. Do you think it is because both are basically island cultures? Or is the flood part of history? Or does it connote a universal image of the human mind, one of the archetypes that Jung describes? Your opinion is as valid as any other, Phyllis, since everyone seems to answer these questions from the vantage point of their own discipline, prejudice or spiritual base.

All this is to just goad you on, to get you thinking and acting on your very good idea about returning to school. As I've said before, you have a very good mind and to think that you are too old at thirty-two to set out and get what you want is pure rubbish. Look at me. I had a bachelor's degree, but I didn't go back and start on my doctorate until I was thirty-four. So it can be done quite nicely at your age. I'm living proof. And believe me, I had more trouble believing in my intellectual capacities than you do now. Yes, I lived a rather well-to-do upper-middle-class existence, but my brilliant attorney husband had me believing that I was dumber than dishwater. Hang in there, Phyllis.

Toby is doing rather well, since you asked. He seems to be returning to his old self now that school has started. It is an adjustment for him every time he comes back from California. But I'm proud to say that he not only looks like me, he seems to have more of my values than Tom's, so we get on most of the time. He's stuck on a lovely Chinese girl at the moment and he thinks I don't know that they're having sex. Thank goodness that he knows enough about contraception not to make me a grandmother. At forty-one I'm not quite ready for that role. Guess I still have the notion that one must be on the downswing of life to be a grandmother. And I feel nothing like a slowing down. On the contrary, my life has only gotten better these last years. There is no reason not to believe the same is in store for you.

I am concerned by what you tell me about your husband. To be quite frank, the man doesn't sound sane. When I was with him in Greece he seemed distracted and obsessive; not healthy signs. But as his search continues he seems to get more out of touch all the time. I feel I must warn you that I think that he is potentially dangerous and that violence is a real possibility with a man in his condition. Is there any way that he might be coaxed to see a therapist? From what you say I realize that he will probably not listen to you. But is there a mutual friend, or a co-worker of Dion's, that might be able to get through to him? I suggest that you consider this carefully, Phyllis, for the sake of both yourself and your son.

But to get on to other matters. I have a very large favor to ask of you. A very dear friend of mine is moving to Key West soon and she desperately needs a friend, though she resists the suggestion at every turn. She is from Miami, but is reluctant to go back there at the moment. You see, she suffered a horrible skiing accident in Switzerland and has been laid up for months in the hospital there with a series of operations and therapy. It has been a difficult time for her. She was a beautiful woman, full of life and vitality. Now, I am afraid that she no longer looks the same, nor can get around as she used to be able to do. There is a fear that she may be permanently disabled and she needs to adjust to this hard fact before she can return to her former life.

With your permission, Phyllis, I would like to give her your name and address although I am far from certain that she would even contact you. She writes me that she wishes to be alone for a time before returning to Miami. This is understandable, to be sure. But I am afraid that she will isolate herself too much. And knowing how kind you are, Phyllis, and how you may need a friend in the flesh, too, rather than just one through the mail, I thought it might be mutually beneficial that you two meet.

Please let me know next letter if this sounds all right with you. Oh, her name is *Cassandra*. I thought you might like the mythological flavor of that one. Cassandra Walton. I do think you would like each other. But I will not press the matter any further.

Meanwhile, I do hope things brighten up for you. I think of you often, with concern at times, I must admit. I sense that a great change will be coming to you. And I can only hope it is a change that will transform your life and urge you to a greater blossoming of your spirit.

But I must run. I have a patient to see tonight. And after that Toby and I will have our evening chat and I can be filled once again with the incredible world of the teenager. It's not the pimples and music and sense of rebellion that I mind so much. It's just their attitude that they are the first generation of the world to see things clearly, to feel emotions truly and that we adults are hopelessly in the dark about anything of significance in the universe.

Enough for now, dear Phyllis. I will write again very soon.

Love,
Dee

Phyllis looked up from the blue paper covered in Dee's handwriting and smiled. The words and more importantly, the spirit of the letter acted like a transfusion. Of course she would agree to see Dee's friend. For a moment she was curious about the connection between the two women. When she had visited in the spring, Dee had made no mention of a friend in Miami. Was she another of Dee's lovers? Or was she a school friend or professional associate? No matter. It would be interesting to find out what other kind of woman Dee would call a friend.

Phyllis was sure that she would be no ordinary woman at any rate, and Dee was right in perceiving that Phyllis hungered for the company of a kindred spirit on the island. Her slow process of awakening had its drawbacks; it made her lonelier than she had ever been before. While she was still a sleepwalker, a somnambulist, she had no perception of her own desolation. She had been numb to any life of the mind or spirit, unfeelingly absorbed in the daily care of Jason and the dull round of Sophia's life. But now, her mind and sense were stirring and she needed a friend, a confidant with whom to share herself.

Cassandra. Cassandra Walton. Phyllis folded the pages carefully and placed them back in the envelope, then stretched out on the ground facing the sun. Later, when Jason was down for his nap, she would pour herself a glass of cool white wine and give herself an hour to reply to Dee, granting permission to recommend her to Cassandra Walton, her new friend.

Three nights later as Phyllis lay sleeping alone in her wide bed in Key West, Dee Hartman sat at her desk in her home in Honolulu. Although it was only eleven o'clock, Toby had been asleep for an hour, exhausted from his day of football and sun. Dee sat at her desk, Phyllis' letter open beside her, a satisfied smile on her lips. After so much waiting it was time, at last, for action.

Dee drew a fresh piece of blue stationery from her desk drawer and unscrewed the cap of her gold-tipped fountain pen. First, she addressed the envelope with the air mail stamps affixed to the right corner, taking care to underscore "Air Mail" and "Switzerland." Then, with a flourish she scrawled the salutation and brief message:

My dear Iris,

Everything is in order. You may leave for Key West immediately. My heart is with you as always.

All my love,
Dee

Dee folded the jasmine-scented sheet and slid it into the envelope, confident in the knowledge that Iris would be joining her sister within the week.

IV.
Rapture of the Deep

One

Iris fingered the slim blue envelope before opening it as she sat on the terrace of the spa at Baden, 1,300 feet above sea level. Curious, thought Iris, how they measure their relationship to the sky by the level of the sea that at no point touched the landlocked country of Switzerland. She, who was so attuned to island existence, dependent on the very tides for a bearing on the world, had for five months laid in the mountains, healing.

The slight nature of Dee's letter could mean only one thing: it was time to leave the mountains and to rejoin her sister Phyllis on yet another island. It would be a delicate reunion. Iris would get to know her all over again before she would reveal her identity. It could be months yet. But she knew that Phyllis would not recognize her during the period of adjustment. No one would recognize her as the beautiful young woman whom Dion had thrown from the cliff. She was utterly changed. No longer would she have trouble with men following her in strange cities, begging for her favors. She now had the freedom of the old and ugly: to be able to move in crowds with impunity, with anonymity, in peace with her own thoughts and purpose. In this way Iris came to accept her deformity as a refuge. It was as if her body had been transformed into a cloister whose walls kept out the world.

This sense of peace and reconciliation was something new for Iris. It had not come to her immeditately after the fall. For weeks she could perceive nothing through the wall of pain that dominated her feeble existance. At first she had prayed for death as a release from the senseless, torturous agony. But death did not come to her easily. She felt the strong pull of life emanating from Dee and in the first crucial days it was that presence that made the difference. It was Dee who pulled her back from the tunnel of darkness that was death, an avenue into another life; pulled her back into the life she had known. But she had been changed, transformed into another entity.

Gradually her memory came back in flashes, in fragments. She would wake from the dreams of falling, reliving again those few seconds when she flew from the cliff, before she met the rocks and sea below her. Suspended, in free fall, she was Sappho reborn to an identical fate; she was Icarus falling with melted wings of wax; she was Lucifer, the most beautiful of angels falling from the grace of an intolerant god.

Miraculously, she did not loose consciousness as her body glanced off a shelf of rock and was deflected into the sea. She opened her mouth to scream, but was choked to silence with a wave of salty sea. The water carried her toward the cliff, throwing her against the jagged rocks, lacerating her flesh, crushing the bones of her shoulder and beating her face beyond recognition. Her hip had already been shattered by the rock shelf before she hit the water. Helpless in a body that would not obey her commands, Iris was tossed repeatedly against the face of the cliff. She tried to keep her head above water, gasping for air and beating the water frantically with her one good arm in an effort to keep afloat.

Somehow Níkos got to her before her strength gave out entirely. It was when his strong arm closed around her broken body that she finally fainted, giving herself up to his care, her conscious mind retreating from the battle with pain and the demands of the sea. The next time she regained consciousness she lay in the bottom of a boat, in Dee's arms.

"Dee, what?" She was too weak to speak through her swollen lips and broken jaw.

"Shh, shh, my love. We're almost at Patras. An ambulance is waiting there for us. And a doctor. We'll be in Athens before you know it."

Iris struggled against her body, needing to tell Dee about what happened.

"Shh, don't try to talk now. There will be time later."

"No, no, he'll be gone." Iris rolled her head from side to side. "Dion. It was Dion," she managed to mumble.

"Dion!" Dee stiffened as she held Iris in her arms. "Did you say Dion? Are you conscious, Iris? Do you know what you're saying?"

"Yes," she responded. "Dion. Rape. Threw me over." She was exhausted, could say no more.

"My God, my God," Dee held Iris gently in her arms. Dion Panagakis! How did he find them? She thought he was in Athens or on his way home by now. He must have followed them, doubled back. But why? To do this to Iris? He was a madman. She looked at Iris, a bloodied, tangled mess in her arms, and broke into tears. But she could not allow herself the luxury of plotting her revenge just yet. Iris' very life was in danger and all attention had to be focused on one end: to save Iris.

As soon as they reached Patras the doctor administered pain killers so Iris could rest unconscious as the ambulance raced toward Athens and the operating facilities they needed.

"Will she make it, doctor?" Dee asked.

"There is hope." The swarthy doctor shrugged slightly, his kind brown eyes resting lightly on Dee. "She's young and strong. If she wants to live, there is hope."

Dee held Iris' hand the entire trip, not daring to let go, to lose the connection. She concentrated with all her strength, trying to send that one message to Iris: Live, Iris. Live, my love.

Late that evening they arrived at the hospital in Athens, a team of doctors awaiting her arrival. Dee paced outside the operating room, unaware that Dion Panagakis had been admitted that very day for treatment of his broken nose and lay resting two floors above her surrounded by the generous care of the Kostakis family.

Hours went by but no one emerged to reassure or encourage Dee. There had been extensive damage to the organs and a great deal of internal bleeding. One lung had been punctured by a broken rib. Her chest had been caved in and Iris' hip had been totally shattered along with her right femur and arm.

And her head; her beautiful, magnificent head. Her nose, jaw and cheekbone had been crushed and she suffered a fractured skull as well. There seemed to be no part of her body or organs that had not been affected by the fall.

After six hours in the operating room the doctors filed out, weary from the long ordeal of holding Iris together. Dee grabbed the first one through the door.

"Doctor, tell me, will she live?"

"Yes, I think she'll make it." He tried to impart a confident smile to Dee. "We were able to stop the internal bleeding and remove the bone fragments that were lodged in dangerous areas. She's lost a great deal of blood and the trauma of all her wounds is enormous. But I think she'll live."

"Thank God." Dee's knees gave out and she leaned heavily against the wall for support. "She'll live."

The doctor hesitated a moment. "Are you a relative?"

"Yes, she's my niece. I'm the only one she's got."

"I see," said the doctor thoughtfully. "Come, sit down a moment. We must talk."

Dee followed the doctor's small, wiry frame through the swinging doors and into a lounge area.

"Coffee?" he asked, pouring himself a cup from a pot on a hot plate.

"Yes, I could use some more."

The doctor carried the two cups to a small table and took a long look at Dee's strained face before he began.

"As I said, I think she'll live, Mrs. Hartman. But she will be a very changed young woman."

"How changed?"

"It's too early to say with certainty, but she may never walk again. You must be prepared for that."

"But there is a chance she will?" Dee tried to hold back the tears that welled up in her eyes.

"A chance, yes. But it would take another operation and long therapy. And then there is her face."

"I know, I know." Dee was openly sobbing. "She's such a beautiful woman, but now her face."

"There, there, Mrs. Hartman. Plastic surgery can help her there. But she won't look the same again. A new nose must be constructed. And the entire right side of her face has to be rebuilt. That, too, is a long process. She can be made to look almost normal, I think, although perhaps not the same as she did before."

"I see," mumbled Dee.

"I am trying to say that she'll need a great deal of care over a long period of time. Let me be direct. This will not be inexpensive."

"How can you even mention money? Of course I'll see to it. Whatever it takes, I'll take care of it."

"Good. I didn't mean to insult you, madam, just to prepare you."

"Yes, yes. I understand."

"She'll need other kinds of help, too, as she recovers," he continued, taking a sip of strong coffee and then pushing the cup away from him. "First, the rape and then this disfiguring tragedy for one so young. Her spirit will need healing along with her body."

"Doctor, I'm a psychologist. I've already taken that into account."

"I see. Good. Let me continue. For the kind of care she will need, I recommend that she be moved when she is strong enough."

"To another hospital?"

"More than that. I recommend that she be taken to Zurich. There are surgeons there who can perform the operation on her hip and the nerves, as well as plastic surgeons that can reconstruct her face. But for her mind, she will need a doctor more like yourself. The Jung Institute is in Zurich, too. Oh, we can keep her alive here in Athens. But to fully heal her you might have to move her to Zurich."

"Funny, just last week Iris was teasing me about being a psychologist in Greece, how I would starve trying to ply my trade. That they have no use for psychologists in Greece, that all problems are religious problems here."

"I know what she means. But now I think she needs the doctors from her own culture to bring her back."

"Yes, whatever it'll take, doctor. Can you make the arrangements?"

"Yes, that can be done from here. With luck, she can be moved next week. I studied medicine in Zurich as a young man. Many of my former colleagues still practice there. She'll be in good hands, I assure you."

Dee stood up and started to pace around the table.

"If only I could stay with her."

"You will not be able to do so?" The doctor looked surprised.

"No, I have a son and a practice back in Honolulu."

"I see," said the doctor gravely. "Then no husband. . .?"

"Divorced," stated Dee cripsly. "And I don't expect any help from that quarter."

"Maybe I can help." The doctor pressed the tips of his fingers together as he turned over the problem in his mind. "I'll write to the wives of some of my friends and ask that they look in on her. They'll do this as a favor. They are kind people. She won't be left alone with just doctors and nurses."

"Thank you." Dee reached out her hand and squeezed the doctor's hand. "You're being extraordinarily kind, doctor. I can't thank you enough."

"Not at all." He shrugged slightly. "I feel ashamed."

"Ashamed?" asked Dee in surprise.

"Yes, ashamed for my sex at times."

"What a thing to say, doctor. Especially a Greek man, if you don't mind my saying so."

"Not at all. I understand. What that poor girl has gone through because of a crazed man. I see much in this hospital, Dr. Hartman. Disease is one thing. An affliction is comprehensible, unspecific, visited upon both men and women indiscriminately as part of the human condition. But violence, ah, that is another matter. The mutilated bodies carved up by knives or riddled by bullets or beaten by fists or pipes – these are not afflictions. This is something men do to each other and to women. Few people are rushed into an emergency room because a woman became violent and took her anger out upon them. Few, very few, my friend. It is men, my sex, that do this thing to their fellow human beings. That is why I am ashamed."

The doctor bowed his head in thought. Dee looked at his small, grey-streaked head and wondered briefly about his own store of tragedies. But she was restless and suddenly very tired.

"Excuse me, doctor, but may I see Iris?"

"Not yet, I'm afraid. She won't be conscious for hours. Why don't you get some rest? There's a pleasant hotel just a few streets from here; I think you'll be very comfortable there."

"Thank you again, doctor. I'll come back."

He rose to his feet and walked slowly to the door. "And tomorrow we can work out the details of the Zurich trip."

"Yes, fine."

Dee followed the doctor from the lounge into the dawn light that bathed the Athenian streets. Yes, she needed rest desperately, her limbs heavy with the strain and fatigue of the last day when she had not relaxed for a second, willing Iris back to life. Tomorrow she would make the arrangements to send Iris to Zurich. And tomorrow she would start her plan for vengeance.

After five days in the Athenian hospital, the doctors felt that Iris was strong enough to be moved. A special flight was arranged to fly non-stop to Zurich from Athens. The first class section of the plane was converted into a temporary hospital room where Iris could lay full-length with intravenous stands and oxygen tanks surrounding her bed like sentries. Both a doctor and a nurse were in attendance on the flight. Although Iris was heavily sedated, Dee winced each time they hit an air pocket and the plane dipped and hung weightless, suspended in air for a moment before regaining its course. Iris would moan, not so much from the pain, but from the memory of falling, reliving each time her long drop from the cliff of Lefkas.

An ambulance awaited them at the airport when they landed and Iris was whisked to the hospital that would become her home for the months ahead. The ride from the airport was relatively short, covering the few miles to the central city in less than fifteen minutes. Looking out the window of the ambulance through the heavy, dull rain Dee was struck by the contrast with the sun-fulled, chaotic disorder of Athens. Zurich seemed so grey and rigidly ordered in the cool drizzle of the afternoon. The houses they passed were kept in immaculate order and not one person they passed, regardless of their station in life, seemed in the least bit shabby. Zurich was a hard-working, bourgeois city, a child of the grim Reformation. And while it lacked the joy of other capitals, it did retain the Protestant virtues of cleanliness, hard work and honesty. At the moment, Dee was only concerned that the skills and determination of its doctors would cure Iris.

Once Iris was in her room, Dee was allowed to stay with her until she awoke. She unpacked some of Iris' things, laying out her copy of Sappho's poems so that she could see the volume when she regained consciousness. The room was light and airy and Dee tried to cheer it up even more by buying a fresh Alpine bouquet that she arranged in a graceful, hand-painted vase. She lit a cigarette and gazed out the window towards the mountains to pass the time when she heard Iris stirring behind her.

"Hey," said a weak voice. "Is there jasmine in that bouquet? Or are you around here somewhere, Dee?"

Dee's heart lept for joy at the sound of Iris' voice. She rushed to her bedside and reached out a hand to gently brush the short hair away from Iris' forehead.

"It's me, baby."

"Thought so. Say, ya got a cigarette?"

"Do you really think you should, Iris?" Dee looked doubtfully at Iris' face and the jaw that was wired shut.

"Sure. Let me try on the left side, okay?"

"If you insist." Dee lit a fresh cigarette and held it gently on Iris' left side to allow her to inhale.

"See, it works," said Iris proudly.

"Great," said Dee. "Now you can smoke. God knows how worried I was that you'd never smoke again." She was trying to tease, to lighten Iris' mood.

"Oh, I plan to get back to my vices as soon as posible. Soon as I get back on my feet, lady, look out."

Dee turned away quickly so that Iris couldn't see the

expression on her face. No one had told Iris yet that getting back on her feet was not something to take for granted.

"There's nothing I'd like better than you chasing me around the room, love." Dee turned back toward the bed, her face composed."Seriously, are you in much pain?"

"Yeah." Iris gave a crooked grin. "Everything I can feel, hurts. Bet I don't look so great, either."

"Oh, you'll heal up all right, Iris. Lucky you. You even get to pick the shape of your nose."

Iris was silent a moment."Don't try to soften things for me, Dee. Tell me straight out. I'm not going to look very good any more, am I?"

"I'll tell you everything I know." Dee swallowed hard and drew a chair close to the bed and sat down. "And that doesn't amount to much. About your face, well, it's going to take a few operations and you'll look different when they're all through with it."

"What else?"

"Your hip and leg were shattered. There's a lot of muscle and nerve damage. And, well, you're going to have to learn to walk again."

"Is there a chance I might not walk?" Iris' voice was quaking.

"Not with your spirit." Dee reached out and held Iris' good hand tightly in her own. "You'll make it. But it will take months of hard work. And determination."

"Dee, I can't let you take me on like this. It isn't fair."

"Stop it, Iris. I love you. And I don't stop loving you because you've had bad luck and need some help. What kind of love would that be, huh? Now, be serious."

Iris turned her head on the pillow and felt a fresh stab of pain through her skull. Everything seemed covered by bandages. She could only imagine what the remains of her body looked like.

"Ever since I met you there has been trouble for you, Dee. First, there was Harold and you became an accessory to murder."

"Hardly. You saved me from being raped and probably killed. That was pure self-defense in anyone's book."

"Okay. But how do you account for Dionysos? What is it about me that attracts these lunatics?" Iris gave a short laugh. "Well, guess I don't have to worry about attracting anyone very much anymore, do I?"

"Stop it, Iris."

"Guess you get what you ask for. When I was in Athens the first days men were following me everywhere. I prayed to be turned into a hag so I could be left alone. Guess I got my wish, didn't I?"

"Stop it, I said." Dee squeezed Iris' hand hard. "It's too early to tell anything at all. I just thank God that you're still alive. Nothing has changed between us, do you understand? Nothing."

Iris rolled her head back where she could see Dee more clearly. "My pretty Dee. You look so tired. You must have gone through hell this past – how long has it been? A week?"

"It's all right, baby."

"No, I'll tell you something. The best part of having a face called beautiful was that it seemed to give you so much pleasure. And now I can't give that to you anymore."

"Oh, Iris, that isn't the most important thing. Of course I appreciated the way you look. But that's not what makes me love you. That doesn't change, you hear? Want another cigarette?"

"What do you mean, another? I got two drags off that other one."

"Oh, you're getting better, all right. Here." Dee lit another cigarette and shared it with Iris.

"Dee, what about Dion?"

Dee stopped mid-puff and rose to her feet before she answered. "He's back in Key West, Iris. By the time I had my head clear, knowing that you were going to live, he was gone. There wasn't any point in pressing charges that couldn't touch him. All he has to do is keep out of Greece and he's a free man. And even if he were caught in Greece, I doubt we'd get very far in the prosecution. It's a case of your word against his. And he's the one with the powerful relative in Athens. And besides, he's a man. Need I say more?"

"Then he's going to get away with it?"

Dee's voice came back cold and hard.

"No, he won't. He's not going to get away with anything. If it's the last thing I do, Dionysos Panagakis will pay for what he's done to you."

"You thinking of killing him, Dee? What if you got caught? It wouldn't be worth it. And wouldn't they be suspicious of you, with the thing about Harold and all?"

"There are many ways to do a man in if you're clever. And

patient. No, I don't plan to pull any triggers myself. I have other weapons. A man like that makes a lot of enemies. I just have to find out where he's most vulnerable and then range the forces in such a way that he's his own undoing."

"But how?"

"I haven't worked out the details yet, my love. But I've taken some preliminary steps. On my way back to Honolulu I'll stop off at Key West like we planned, to meet your sister. I already sent her a telegram, notifying her of your death. I think it's better that Dion believes he was successful. I don't expect that he will hang around when I'm there. I just want a chance to see what kind of woman she is, how the family holds together, or doesn't hold together, as the case may be. The more we know about them, the better chances we'll have to get away with it."

"You really have been working this out, haven't you?"

"With every fiber of my being. The madness stops here. No more. No more violence inflicted on us or those we love." Dee caught herself as she looked down at Iris and saw the course of pain twist across her face. "Oh, honey, there's time for all this later. You need to be quiet now. The painkillers are wearing off, aren't they?"

"Yes," said Iris weakly, trying to smile in spite of the pain that was throbbing through her entire body.

"I'll call the nurse."

Dee left the room in search of a nurse and Iris tried to breathe evenly to relieve the pressure in her chest. She was alive; that much she knew. And she would stay alive. She still had the love of Dee, the hope of reunion with her sister and the promise of a well-calculated revenge.

Iris opened the blue envelope and quickly read the message from Dee. Yes, it was time to leave, to meet Phyllis and to enact the next stage of the plan. She adjusted the wool blanket that covered her legs as she sat in her wheelchair looking out across the mountains. The air was cool, but Iris forced herself to stay a little longer. She was trying to toughen herself up, to push herself a little further each day in her efforts to regain her strength. The long flight would be tiring, and the excitement of meeting her sister would put another strain on her still delicate system. Her one regret was that she would not see Dee yet. It would be too risky if they started appearing everywhere together. Dion was probably too preoccupied with his treasure hunt to notice, but if he got suspicious he could find out that there never was a death certificate filled out for Iris in Greece.

Mentally Iris began to pack and ready herself for leaving the spa. To her surprise she found that she would miss Zurich and Baden, and the people who had been so consistently kind during her long convalescence. She had to revise her prejudices against the little materialistic, landlocked country that she had been prepared to hate for the period of her recovery.

The devotion to duty in the Swiss was just as fervent as the devotion to the senses that she found in the Mediterranean. It was a more sober view of life, too be sure, but hardly less ennobling. It was a place where an exiled soul could find temporary relief from the violent swing of mood and politics in the larger world. Life seemed manageable in Zurich. People respected one another's privacy. Shopkeepers swept the sidewalks in front of their shops daily and a customer was always sure of receiving the correct change. There were few surprises in the street life of the city, but neither was there random violence or roving bands of thieves. A soul filled to overflowing could quietly bail out his spirit undisturbed in Zurich. It was a place where healing took place not in blinding flashes attended by miracles, but by patient, small steps of will aided by careful scientific procedures.

Iris underwent two operations on her hip and leg and three on her face during her first four months in Zurich. Every time she regained her strength from one operation, she was prepared for another. Skin was grafted from one part of her body to another. Metal was placed in her skull and a pin in her hip. Her entire face was remolded and her short hair started to grow back with a new dominance of grey.

Iris avoided mirrors for months. She had never considered herself vain before, taking for granted the gift of her beauty. She wasn't prepared for ugliness and the absence of grace in her form. The only thing that remained of her former beauty was her eyes, her otherworldly, remarkable green eyes that were all the more astonishing now that there was no other arresting quality to offset them.

By the end of the summer, the doctors decided to give her body a rest from operations and their attendant traumas. Iris was moved to nearby Baden where she could more directly benefit from the therapies connected to the baths. Her life during that period was given over to the healing powers of swirling waters and strong, gentle hands. She underwent a series of thermal, steam and carbonic acid baths for her paralysis. Sturdy young women administered underwater massage to her atrophied limbs. She drank mineral water and inhaled the mountain air. Gradually, the pain faded from her body, becoming an occasional visitor rather than a constant companion.

Then, shortly before Dee's letter arrived, Iris had started taking her first steps, first with a walker, then hopefully with a cane to take some of the weight on her weakened right side.

If she stayed at Baden, there was hope that she would reach the cane stage by Christmas. But Iris elected to leave the spa by the middle of September to take up residence in Key West. At first her doctor had been disturbed by her choice, but Iris convinced him that she needed to go back to the States soon to avoid depression. She had been under the care of a psychiatrist the entire time and he agreed that it might be time for her to go home. Arrangements were made with the hospital on Key West for Iris to continue her physical therapy there and Dee briefed a psychologist on the island about Iris should she need help in that area. Satisfied at last, Iris' doctor signed the release and Iris booked a flight.

The night before she left, Iris sat at her small writing table for the last time to write Dee her parting letter from Switzerland.

> My love,
>
> Everything is packed now, and all I have is one night of sleep between here and my arrival in Florida. I would like to say that I am fine and that you should not worry about me. But that would be misleading and a lie. I am not fine. My natural tendencies to withdraw from the world have been accentuated by my long months here. No one advised me to leave. I often dream of falling asleep forever in the seductive peace of the mountains, and most likely that is exactly what I would do but for one thing – you.
>
> Yes, you, Dee, who despite everything coax me back to the world of the living. It is because of you that I will leave my mountain and the steady, slow process of healing to venture forth once again into the tropical blazes of an island. It is because of you that I will also be rejoined with my sister whom I have put from my mind for too long, as I've put so much of life away from me.
>
> And because of you I am about to embark on a

full-bodied, bloodthirsty path of revenge. My visions and voices alone can not deal Dionysos Panagakis the blow he so richly deserves. I need to call into service all the cunning, iron will and ruthless determination that we women are so often accused of wielding and yet, in truth, so rarely use against those who do us the greatest harm.

How long will it be before we are truly together again? How many more trials must we suffer before we are granted the one simple thing which we always wanted and which has seemed so impossible to achieve; simple peace in our loving each other?

Thoughts of you never leave me. At least I have been there and can imagine you quite clearly at your desk, all business-like and professional with your rows of books behind you and your glasses perched on your nose. I can see you in your kitchen, making something wonderful for Toby who really doesn't care and could be just as happy with a hotdog, but he will grow to manhood and remember your care and love and maybe he will be one of the few men who *can* love, *can* understand. I can see you in Paradise Park with a fresh blossom in your hair. And the way you open to me in bed, the soft animal noises you make and the way you make me feel that no one since the beginning of time has been blessed with such a love. Will it happen, Dee? Can it happen again for us in that way with my broken body that can no longer arch over you with ease, or this cripple's gait that will not allow me to run across a room and into your arms?

In the morning I will leave Zurich, this home of exiles, and go to the island you have chosen for me. From the way you describe the island, I think I would like it best if I could rent a houseboat and live anchored in the harbor among the shrimp boats with a front row seat for the nightly theatrics of the sunset. I have been so much rocked in water these last months that it would seem quite natural to me.

I will become the Wild Woman of Key West, the hag, the visionary eccentric that bobs in the harbor. This is the last letter that I will send you as Iris. From now on I am Cassandra. I will arrive in a new place with a new name and a very ancient identity.

Everything I have learned during the months on Santorini among the witches, the months in the mountains with the doctors of the mind, I will bring with me. I will drag my reborn, broken body before the sleeping beauty of my sister. And we will all have our revenge.

In love and new glory,
your Iris

Two

The summer along the Keys was a hot one with little relief from the constant blaze of the sun. The unbridled enthusiasm that launched Dion Panagakis on his quest subsided as the days and weeks wore on with little tangible result for his efforts. The *Rafina* inched across the ocean, anchoring at intervals so that Dion, Lopez and Phipps could painstakingly comb the ocean floor for traces of the *Toledo*. Dion finally settled down to a regular routine of twenty days out at sea and seven off. Pushing any harder only wore the men and made them careless with fatigue. Three weeks away from women or their families was all they could tolerate with good humor.

Everyone but Dion, that was. Rarely did he spend his entire time off on Key West with Phyllis and his son. His usual pattern was to roll into Plantation Key with a few of the single crew men to pick up tourist women or one of the waitresses at Maggie's and spend a few days screwing and drinking while boasting of their adventures, about which only the tourists seemed impressed. The native girls knew better. They had brothers or fathers who drank, too, and talked of fabulous treasures just waiting to drop in their laps. But they would take in Dion and his crew anyway, finding the presence of a hard brown body and the fuzzing effect of too many beers a relief from the daily boredom of their lives. Those with larger dreams had left long ago for the mainland.

Dion was developing a strange fetish. He could only get aroused by blond women; young blond women who in some slight way were reminiscent of Iris. He did not perceive the pattern until Lopez kidded about it one afternoon while they were drinking in Maggie's. Two attractive young tourists walked in and sat at the far end of the bar. Dion looked up briefly but after one look continued his talk with Lopez who couldn't help but smirk.

"Hey, what's the matter with you Lopez? I say something funny?" asked Dion.

"No, man. It's what you just did. Those girls over there. You interested?"

"No, are you? Help yourself. You don't have to keep me company."

"No, no, that's not what I mean. Pretty nice looking girls, yes?"

"They're all right."

Lopez laughed out loud. "But the minute they walk in here I know you're not going to look twice."

"Oh yeah? Why?"

"Because they're both brunettes."

"So?"

"So, the only women you look at all summer are blond. You pass up better looking dark ones just to get in the pants of something with yellow hair. Boy, you something else."

"What's it to you? Everybody's got a right to their tastes, don't they? So I like blondes. Big deal."

"Hey, like I said. It's okay with me. This way I know my wife is safe from you, right? Don't bother me any. Just I read you like a book."

"Go on. Quit hanging around and go do your pitch. Maybe you can get both of them and have a little party."

"Not for me, man. I'm catching a ride down to Key West to spend some time with my family before we go out again. Why don't you come, too, eh? See your wife and kid. Be good for you."

"No, I want to hang around here. Might drop down in a day or two. Catch you then."

"Okay, boss."

Lopez threw a bill on the bar and strolled out past Dion, tipping his straw hat to the two girls on the end stools. Dion turned his attention back to his own drink and ran Lopez's comment through his mind. It was true. Dark women left him cold. He couldn't even make love to his wife anymore. At first he thought it was because he felt guilty about what he had done to her sister. Then he attributed it to Phyllis herself. She was different somehow. More bossy. She was giving him a hard time, questioning him all of a sudden. For the first time in their married life he suspected that she kept things from him, that she made plans separate from him. He grew mistrustful of Phyllis.

He would lie beside her pretending he was asleep and listen to her uneven breathing. She would often get up in the middle of the night to read in the living room or would go out alone into the back yard and just lay in the grass for hours. He watched her through the kitchen window once, just laying there in the moonlight as if in a trance. It gave him the creeps. It reminded him of the strange ways of Iris. And the oddest thing of all was that she never pressed him to make love to her. It was as if she no longer wanted him and was indifferent to his touch. Phyllis, who used to blush and tremble with the anticipation of passion if he just stroked her arm.

But it wasn't as if he were totally impotent. The mere sight of a young blond woman would get him hard. Like that silly coed Candy that he met the first time he had come into Maggie's a few months ago. He had played it cool and was sociable for a while, sitting around having drinks with the others. But he had a hard time keeping his hands off her thighs under the table. He wasn't as crazy as he had been in Greece, but he recognized a similar obsessive lust as he maneuvered toward her.

The second they got into the motel room he was on top of her, pulling off her blouse and skirt with the ruthless urgency of a teenager. He felt her grow stiff under him, afraid of his strength and insistence, but he didn't try to stop himself.

"It's okay, baby, just relax. Just relax."

"No, I really have to go to the bathroom," she said in a timid voice as he ripped off her panties in a single rough gesture. "I have to put something in, you know?"

"Forget it," snapped Dion, unzipping his fly and shoving into her before she had a chance to protest. He was dimly aware that he was hurting her, that she was dry and frightened, but he didn't stop. Once inside her, he wouldn't stop to save his life. Every muscle of his body was tensed with the force of his thrusts. He was grunting and straining like an animal, all his frustrations mounting to the moment of release when he finally collapsed, pinning her to the bed.

Dion hadn't thought twice about his reaction. He chalked it up to the fact that Candy was the first woman he had since the incident in Greece with Iris. Just a carry-over, he thought.

But it didn't stop there. While he was at sea he was fine. The gold fever took his entire attention. But once on land, he was on the prowl for women, trying to bed as many as he could. And always it was quick and brutal for him, giving the women little pleasure, as if he were punishing them for having a control over him.

Even the older men started to notice his predatory habits with women. At first they thought he was horny like the rest of them and was just letting off steam. But it was Lopez who noticed the single-mindedness of Dion's pursuit and made the first comment. Lopez was no angel and certainly wasn't above an occasional piece when he was away from home. But he basically was a family man and truly valued his wife and two children. Dion lacked that familial love. And a man who did not love his family was always a little dangerous in Lopez's opinion. He had seen Dion's wife and she had the look of a neglected woman, her face drawn and anxious. She seemed to lean away from the space that Dion inhabited, holding the boy against her like a shield. But Dion did not even seem to notice – or to care.

Lopez got more insight into the family life of the Panagakises than he had bargained for one autumn morning when he stopped by their home to take Dion down to the harbor. They had been in port a week for some minor repairs and were going to set out for the diving area again that day. He walked around the back way and found Phyllis sitting alone in the back yard, gazing into the distance above the tops of the trees, an open book in her lap. He was struck by the determination of her profile. She was not a pretty woman, but at the moment Lopez perceived a power in her that he had never noticed before. Rather than walking into the kitchen, he decided to approach Phyllis.

"Hey, Phyllis, how you doin'?"

The sound of his voice broke Phyllis' trance and she jumped to her feet immediately and advanced hesitantly toward Lopez; the shy, quiet woman once again.

"Oh, hello, Carlos. Is it that late already? I don't think Dion's ready yet."

"It's okay. I'm a little early."

"He's in the shower. Want some coffee?"

Lopez removed his straw hat and played with the brim in his hands. "No, I had breakfast with my family."

"How are they?"

"Oh, Anita's so big now. She started the junior high school. And Carlos is in the fourth grade. Everybody's fine. How about you?"

Phyllis sighed and cast her eyes down to her feet, seeming to study the grass that tickled her toes through the sides of her sandals.

"Jason's in school all day. I have more time to myself. I get along."

Lopez sensed the sadness in her voice but did not know what to do or say.

"You read much?" he asked, pointing to the book Phyllis held absent-mindedly in her hand.

"Oh, yes. Myths mostly. Things about different cultures. Anywhere but here." Her voice trailed off and she seemed to forget Lopez for a moment, but then turned her eyes toward him and looked frankly into his eyes. "Tell me something, Carlos. Don't you think there's something strange about Dion?"

Lopez took an involuntary step backward. He did not expect such a question from her and he was torn between being honest wth her because he liked her and being loyal to his boss.

"Strange? What you mean, Phyllis? You mean about the gold?"

"Not exactly. He's been gold crazy for a long time. But there's something else going on. He's jumpy, suspicious, short-tempered."

"Pressure, Phyllis. He needs to find the *Toledo* soon. Makes a man nervous. And all the diving. I'm used to it. But Dion isn't. He should be more careful. He forgets himself, pushes too hard. Always pushing. It's not good."

"No, it's something else, Carlos. A friend of mine, whose business it is to know such things, says he could be dangerous. Says he's at some sort of edge and that he could blow any minute. She said that he needs help. Professional help. But he won't listen to me. Think he'd listen to you?"

"Naw," Carlos shook his head and fingered the brim of his hat nervously. "I work for him. He's the boss. He'd never listen to me. But your friend's right. There's something not right with Dion."

"What have you seen, Carlos? Tell me."

"Oh, how he seems lost when he's not at sea. How he doesn't seem to want to come back here when we take a break."

"He sees other women, doesn't he?"

Lopez looked up briefly then turned his eyes away from Phyllis. "I can't answer that, Phyllis."

"You just did. Don't worry. It's no surprise. He may be odd now, but I didn't think he'd turned into a monk. And God knows he's stayed away from *me*. That's not what worries me."

"Then what does?"

"Oh, what to do with my life, I guess. Dion seems less important to me, too. I was just trying to confirm the feeling that it's the same for him. We really haven't talked about it. It just happened when he came back from Greece. And we both understood and neither of us tried to stop it or turn it around." Phyllis squeezed Lopez's hand. "Sorry. I'm sure you don't want to hear this, Carlos."

"No, that's okay. Hey, you know, I guess I could use a cup of coffee at that."

"Sure. Come on in the kitchen."

Lopez followed her into the kitchen, relieved that the conversation was over. Jesus, she must be some lonely woman to have to confide in him. He wasn't used to women talking about their lives to men. He took the cup from her hands and watched her clean up the kitchen in a slow, methodical way, putting dishes in the sink, wiping the counter with a worn pink sponge, her face expressionless and vacant once again, all the power drained from it, all the determination vanished.

"Ready, Lopez?" Dion strode into the kitchen.

"Sure, boss. All set. I got the tanks in the back of the pickup. Enough for two weeks."

"Good. Let's go." Dion turned uneasily toward Phyllis. "Well, good-bye. Tell Jason I'm sorry I couldn't stick around until he came home. Probably better this way. He puts up such a stink when I leave."

"Yeah, it's better," said Phyllis in a monotone. "See you in a couple of weeks."

"Bye." Dion was out the door. Lopez put down his half-full coffee mug and followed.

"Thanks for the coffee, Phyllis."

"Sure, Carlos. Any time."

He nodded briefly, then quickened his pace to catch up with Dion.

Once inside the pickup and around the corner Dion turned on Lopez. "What're you talking about with my wife, Lopez?"

"Hey, nothing, Dion. We just passing the time."

"I saw you in the yard. You weren't talking about the

weather. What's up, Lopez. Trying to make my wife?" Dion's eyes were slits focused on Lopez at the wheel, the gold flecks in them flat and hard.

"You crazy? Not me, man. Not me."

"Oh, yeah?" Dion still wasn't convinced.

"Hey, we were talking about you, okay? She's worried about you, man. Don't you talk to your wife? She'd tell you if you tried." Lopez shifted his eyes back and forth between the road and Dion leaning toward him at a dangerous angle.

"Me? What you got to talk about?"

"It's not my business. I know it's not my business. She just started talking to me. I didn't do nothing. What's the matter? Don't she have any girlfriends? I don't want to hear about her problems."

"What'd she say, Lopez?"

"She said you two not getting along. Thinks you both want out. That's it." Lopez breathed a little easier. Dion seemed to be cooling down towards him.

"Oh, she's had enough, eh? How about me? Jesus, what a spoiled cunt that one is. She's got one kid that my mother looks after half the time while she sits around the house with her nose in a goddamn book while I'm out bustin' my balls crawling around the ocean. Some hard life for her, right?" Dion leaned back in the seat, folding his arms across his chest as if holding himself in from an explosion. "The bitch. I'd kick her out right now except she'd take the kid. The fuckin' courts would probably give him to her, too. And she don't even care about him. But wait. Just wait. Once I hit it big with this *Toledo* I'll get rid of her all right. With all that dough I can buy the lousy court. What's she? She was a lousy receptionist when I found her. Ungrateful bitch."

Lopez swung the pickup into the harbor and nudged it close to the *Rafina* to load the tanks.

"I'll take care of these," volunteered Lopez as he swung out of the driver's seat and around the back of the truck. He was grateful to get out of the line of fire. For a few minutes there he had been afraid that Dion meant to take his head off. Phyllis was right. Dion was getting too touchy. If they didn't find that wreck soon they were all in for it from Dion. Lopez hefted two tanks on his shoulder and walked the few steps to the boat where Phipps stood waiting to receive them.

"Looks like you really stocked up," observed Phipps, taking the tanks from Lopez's shoulders.

"Yeah, we can stay out more than two weeks. So look out. I

think he means to do it. Hope we find her this time, too."

"He was on the warpath again?"

Lopez nodded curtly as Dion climbed out of the truck and made his way to the boat. "Yeah, watch it."

"Hey, Phipps. You load enough food for a couple of weeks?" demanded Dion, leaning toward the lanky youth.

"Sure, Dion. Just like you said."

"Good. Because this time we're staying out there till we find her. If we have to send to Plantation for more supplies, then we send to Plantation, ya hear? We're not coming back until we've nailed her." Dion jumped into the *Rafina* to the side of Phipps and made his way to the bridge. Phipps exchanged a long look with Lopez as he eased the tanks on the deck.

"Jesus. What's with him?"

"Family trouble," said Lopez, the gold cross on his chest catching the sun and obscuring his face from the other man.

"So why he's got to take it out on us, man? I don't need this kind of grief. If I want abuse I can go back to Taylor."

"Don't let him hear you say that, Joe. He'd throw you over the side for shark bait. And don't count on Taylor coming along to fish you out."

"I'm just a diver, man." Joe Phipps shrugged his lean shoulders. "I keep out of their little wars. They're both fucking loony if you ask me."

"Yeah, right, Joe. All the more reason to steer clear of him."

Lopez turned back to the pickup and grabbed another pair of tanks. He knew how to take care of himself. He would just avoid Dion as much as possible and keep to himself. Once in the water he was fine. He knew his business and underwater Dion couldn't nag at him. Poor bastard. He was getting as cracked as old Taylor. And just like Taylor he was going to lose his family and friends in his single-minded pursuit of treasure. And no matter how much treasure they hauled up they all ended up broken men with feverish eyes and hands like claws that clenched and unclenched with the impulse of their greed.

Lopez crossed himself quickly and thought of his wife, Maria, his little Anita and young Carlos. They would never be wealthy, but he had more than Dion. His wife loved and cared for him; his children, too. All his desires could be satisfied on the island of Key West. And unlike Dion, he truly loved his work; the slow patient examination of the ocean that only gradually gave up any secrets, but rewarded the faithful along the way with great beauty and wonder.

That's it, concluded Lopez as he silently passed the tanks

to Joe Phipps. Dion had no spirit, no faith in any God or any human being. He was a dead man obsessed with the treasure of dead men. He shivered slightly in the hot sun and turned quickly back to the truck before Phipps could detect his sudden discomfort and pallor beneath the smooth dark tan of his face.

"Here," ordered Dion, his forefinger tapping the map with impatience. "I want to go out deeper, over by the two hundred foot depth area."

"You just want to skip the area in between, then?" Lopez threw a sidelong glance at Phipps.

"Yeah. That's right. I'm tired of playing criss-cross and getting nowhere. I've got a hunch. It makes sense to me that the ship slipped off the edge of the reef a long time ago. Then it worked its way into deeper water. The current goes in that direction. Makes sense. Let's go."

Dion turned from the two men and went below deck to get his wet suit as the *Rafina* headed out to deeper water. For months they had combed the shallow area, never going below a hundred feet to explore the ocean floor. Now Dion wanted to double that depth and keep them out at sea till doomsday.

"He's fucking crazy," spat out Joe Phipps. "What's he trying to do, kill us? I don't know about you, man, but I'm taking my own sweet time this trip and taking as much rest as I need."

"Sure, sure," soothed Lopez, lighting a cigarette and squinting against the bright sun. "He's just talking. What's he going to do? Throw rocks at you down there? You go up when you need to go up. Pay no attention to him."

"Damn straight," agreed Joe, calming down now that he had the support of the older man.

The *Rafina* anchored far off the lip of Crocker Reef, bobbing lazily in the ocean far away from the path of excursion boats and houseboats rented by tourists to explore the keys. Over two hundred feet below the hull of the boat, Dion, Lopez and Phipps fanned out to explore the depths. It was darker here then they were used to and they had to work more slowly, using a lantern to probe the knots of coral on the sea floor while slowly passing the magnetometer over each coral head.

After a half hour Dion started feeling woozy and light-headed but he ignored his growing giddiness, attributing it to the greater depth and his unfamiliarity with the new pressure. He concentrated on the magnetometer although his mind began to wander and his body started feeling clumsy, as if he were slightly drunk. Instead of giving in to it, Dion concentrated all the more on the pattern of light that played across the coral from the lantern and the occasional shaft of sunlight that reached all the way to the bottom of the sea. He started seeing patterns in the formations, in the seaweed that fluttered out in the currents like hair from a mermaid, like Iris' hair. Dion was getting more woozy. He ran his gloved hand over his face mask. What was it that he saw? A woman's body? Iris? Could it be Iris laying there, her hair streamed out just beyond his grasp?

Dion veered off to follow the apparition around the corner of the reef. Lopez caught the quick gesture out of the corner of his eye and decided to follow. A few yards away Phipps was weaving oddly, throwing the beam of his lantern in a random pattern across the coral. Then it hit him. He was feeling lightheaded, too. But the others were worse. They were suffering from nitrogen narcosis, "rapture of the deep." The gas mix in their tanks wasn't right for this depth. What they were breathing was acting like an anesthetic. If they didn't pull out soon they could all be killed.

Lopez quickly swam over to Phipps and jerked him by the shoulder, causing him to drop his lantern and send it bouncing across the floor of the ocean like a child's ball. Lopez urgently jerked his thumb up in front of Phipps' mask and gave him a shove upward. At first Phipps resisted, but Lopez's wild gestures seemed to snap him from his hypnotic trance long enough to realize what was happening and to start his slow progress to the surface.

Once he saw Phipps was steadily making his way to the top, Lopez spun around in the water after Dion who had disappeared around the other side of the coral reef. He was getting clumsier himself and he knew he must find Dion quickly before he succumbed to the seductive intoxication. Rounding the curve of the mound, Lopez spotted Dion weaving along the ocean floor, swinging the magnetometer like a huge toy in large sweeps.

Dion was following the illusive figure of Iris that appeared and then disappeared in front of his eyes. She was mocking him, allowing him to come almost within reach and then dodging away once again. He had the notion that he could track her course with the magnetometer, that her gold hair would set off the metal detector. That she was the treasure. And where she stopped would be the site of the sunken *Toledo*. He felt a sudden pull on his shoulder and tried to brush it off. But it came again and Dion whirled to face the intruder, his free hand reaching for the knife in his belt. It was Lopez. And he was trying to pull him upwards, away from the image of Iris, away from his treasure.

Dion lashed out with his knife, narrowly missing Lopez's torso, and broke away to swim a few yards with the magnetometer stretched out in front of him. Then it went wild, the indicator registering the presence of metal. Lots of metal. Then Lopez was on his back again, trying to yank him away. Dion gestured toward the meter and Lopez stopped his struggle briefly.

Then they saw it. At first it had looked like an old timber or hunk of scrap metal from another ship. Crusted over and dimly visible in the dark, the two men made out the shape of an anchor, a huge anchor. The kind Spanish galleons used.

Dion was totally intoxicated now as he circled the anchor, reaching out his hand to touch it, caress it more tenderly than he ever touched a woman. It was Iris who led him to it, she was the key to it all, just like he always believed from the first day he set eyes on her. He had to throw her in the ocean back there in Greece so that she could wait here, underwater, to point the way to the treasure for him. It all made sense to him. And then he felt the sharp blow on his skull, and everything went black. The last image floating across his mind was the face of Iris, lit with an unearthly glow, a slight mocking smile on her face.

When he came back to consciousness he was laying on the deck, his head throbbing and his body heavy and lethargic. Lopez was kneeling above him, breathing heavily and Phipps was sitting a short distance away, blond head between his knees, his back rising and falling with the effort of his breathing.

"What?" Dion tried to sit up, but he fell back as the pain seared through his skull.

"Relax, man. Just relax. We almost died down there," gasped Lopez, easing himself back on his haunches and gulping in the air.

"What happened?" groaned Dion, throwing an arm across his face to shield it from the sun.

"Wrong tanks. We got the rapture. The rapture of the deep. You were crazy. Had to knock you out and breathe with you all the way up."

"But the anchor. There was an anchor, right?" gasped Dion.

He couldn't stand it if it all was just hallucination.

"Yeah, there's an anchor down there."

"Then let's get it," retorted Dion, struggling to a sitting position despite the pain. Phipps lifted his head for a minute and looked at Dion with a gaze of pure hate.

"Relax, you asshole. Lopez just saved your fucking life. Think you got time to thank him?"

"Yeah, thanks, Lopez." Dion blinked and tried to clear his head. "Guess I lost my head."

"That's okay. You couldn't help it. Jesus, I can't believe we were that dumb."

"Guess it was my fault. But I was right, wasn't I? With my hunch, I mean. Sometimes you just got to go by your gut." Dion decided not to tell about the figure of Iris that led him to the anchor. They would think he really was nuts. And he didn't want to explain who Iris was. Besides, the more he thought about it the less sure he felt that she was on his side. He found the anchor all right. But he almost got himself killed following her like some deranged madman. He turned to Lopez. "We got to get some rest. Then let's haul up that anchor. You remember the spot, don't you?"

"Yeah, I remember," nodded Lopez. "We should be okay on the tanks if we just go down fifteen minutes at a time. We do it this afternoon." His hand went to the crucifix around his neck.

"Right. Jesus, I can't wait till Taylor sees us sailing in with that thing," said Dion as his breath started coming a little easier.

"No guarantee it's from the *Toledo*," warned Lopez. "Lot of ships on the bottom around here. We got to wait to find more of the evidence, no?"

"It's the *Toledo*, all right. I feel it in my bones," declared Dion, resting against the side of the boat as it rocked gently on the waves. "It's the *Toledo*. And we'll all be fuckin' rich."

"I sure hope so," mumbled Phipps. "But gold doesn't buy anything for a dead man."

"Aw, cut your bellyachin', Phipps," snapped Dion. "We're sitting over the biggest treasure ship sunk along the Spanish Main and you're crying cause you're a little out of breath. Listen, pansy, you can get off this dive any time you like. I can have my pick of divers now. I don't need you. So just say the word."

"When the payoff's just around the corner? Are you kidding? What are you, another Taylor?"

Dion glared into the pale blue of Joe Phipps' eyes. "Just say the word, Phipps."

"Naw, I'll stay. I'll stay," he said, dropping his eyes to the deck and seething with his unreleased anger. "I want my cut. I've earned it."

"Yeah, well, just make sure you keep on earnin' it," retorted Dion. "Hey, Sammy," he called. "Bring me a cigarette, will ya?"

Lopez stood up and threw back his massive shoulders, working the stiffness out of his upper back and neck. He hoped Dion was right, that they had located the *Toledo*. It would be easier on all of them if they could work straight salvage instead of hunting for sites. And maybe Dion would cool off a little if he thought he actually had found his precious *Toledo*.

"I'm going to lay down inside a while," said Lopez, disappearing below and leaving the other two men to glare at each other across the hot, sea-washed deck.

It was Murphy who first spotted the *Rafina* pulling into Plantation Key. He had been lounging on the pier drinking beer and shooting the breeze with a few of the old timers, watching the tourists file in and out of the Museum of Sunken Treasure. Since the crew had been in just a few days ago, no one expected to see Dion for a couple of weeks. But as soon as Murphy could make out the ship he knew what was up and slapped old Nate Parker on the back, causing him to spill half his beer down the front of his faded blue shirt.

"What the fuck," sputtered Nate. "What's the matter wid you, Murphy?"

"Look, it's that Greek and his crew comin' in."

"You sure? They was just here last week."

"Yeah, I'm sure all right."

"Wonder if they got engine trouble or something. Or maybe that Panagakis got hot pants quick this time, huh?" chortled Nate.

"Naw, naw, bet it's something else. Bet they found something this time."

"Oh, yeah? Thought you said they was going to come up dry. Now you think they got something. Which is it, Murphy?"

"Look, you old coot. On the deck. See that? Looks like an anchor." Murphy was laughing out loud. "Whoa. Wait till old Taylor hears about this."

"Wait a minute. How come you so happy? Won't Taylor

piss blood if it's an anchor?" Nate was confused. Murphy just wasn't making sense. He never was a very bright guy, but he never seemed to get things exactly opposite before.

"No, not this time, Nate. Wait here. I'm going to get Taylor." Nate Parker was left puzzling.

"Guess Murphy's catching crazy from Taylor. The whole damn island is goin' plum crazy. It was better before the war, before all these guys got all them ideas about treasure."

"Right, Nate," piped up Sam McGee. "Better when it was just fightin' and mindin' your own business. But look there. Damn if Murphy wasn't right. It *is* an anchor. And that Greek looks like he jest give birth to it hisself."

The old men sat patiently on the dock as the *Rafina* cut through the water in the late afternoon light. And it was Dion, all right, standing in the prow of the ship, holding up the end of the anchor for everyone on shore to see. He looked like the figurehead on his own boat, like an explorer cruising into new territory, like God himself with a brand new idea about creation.

By the time Dion docked and swung through the door followed by old Nate and Sam, Taylor was waiting for him with two double whiskeys in his hand, and Murphy was leaning against the bar behind him.

"Here ya go, Panagakis. To your anchor."

Taylor pressed one glass into Dion's hand and raised his own glass in salute to the other man. The smile faded from Dion's face. He didn't trust Taylor's sudden good will.

"News travels fast, eh, Taylor? Why the congratulations?"

"Oh, let's just say that I'm a good sport, Panagakis. Like you said before, I got my little site that keeps me busy and in the chips. No reason you shouldn't have yours, too. Enough for everybody who's willing to work for it. The American way, right?"

Dion still didn't like the jolly good sportsmanship of Taylor, but he raised the glass to his lips and drank anyway, watching the other man closely over the rim of his glass. His yellow eyes gave no hint of what was going on behind them.

"I'm not home free yet, you know," said Dion testingly. "Got to make sure the anchor's from the *Toledo*."

"Yeah, right." Taylor nodded sagaciously. "Find anything else?"

"A coin. Gold. Right year." Dion couldn't resist the urge to boast in front of Taylor, of throwing his own good fortune into his face. "It's looking pretty good."

"A coin, huh?" Taylor raised an eyebrow. "Looks good. Suppose you already notified the state?"

"Sure did. Doing it all nice and legal," smiled Dion. "Just like you. A real straight shooter."

"That's smart," agreed Taylor, ignoring Dion's sarcasm and waving to the bartender for another drink. "But now you're going to have one of them state archeologists looking over your shoulder every day. Those guys can be a real pain in the ass. You'll get a kick out of it, Panagakis. You, with your eyes all sparkling for gold and then you see these guys just cream over a couple of pieces of broken pottery. It's okay, though. They count it up as part of their share and ship it back to Tallahassee so another bunch of guys just like 'em can get excited about it, too. And then they dust it all off real nice and put it back together and charge the tourists a buck to come look at it. Just another kind of peep show."

"Yeah, well, guess you're the expert on those kind of things, Taylor. I like the real thing, myself." Dion downed his drink and shoved the glass across the bar. "Thanks for the drink." Dion turned to the room and shouted out, "Everybody have a drink on me. No, a bottle on me. We got a Spanish galleon out there just loaded with gold and jewels and I want you all to celebrate with me. Everybody up to the bar."

Dion smiled widely as the gasp went through the room. The regulars rushed up to shake his hand and place their orders while the tourists hung back.

"You, too, mister. Have a drink," called Dion to a middle-aged man in the back who was eating chicken with his wife. The man looked embarrassed, but his wife was beaming at the handsome, romantic figure.

"Oh, Fred, he's talking to you. Let's have a drink. Thank the man, Fred," she urged.

"Ah, thanks, captain. And good luck," offered Fred at his wife's prompting.

"Atta boy," said Dion. "Hey, Brenda. Bring that guy and his wife a bottle of white wine to go with their chicken, okay? Though with Maggie's chicken they'd be better off with kerosene, what do you say?"

Old Nate Parker and Sam McGee got a good chuckle on that one. They were happy as clams sitting on the bar stool and lapping up the whiskey that Dion kept buying.

"Ya know," drawled Sam as the room grew hazy from too

much smoke and too much liquor. "That Greek fella ain't so bad, after all."

"Yeah," agreed Nate, tilting back his head and letting the warm whiskey tickle his throat and bob his Adam's apple pleasantly on the way down. "Old Taylor never bought nobody nothing when he stumbled on that wreck of his last season."

"Now he's turnin' around and buying the Greek a drink for finding the wreck he wants. Don't figure," mused Sam, who was always a trifle quicker at sniffing out something fishy than Nate. "Man like Taylor don't change over night."

"What's he gonna do?" said Nate, pleased at his free high. "Law's on the Greek's side. Maybe he just learned to accept it."

"Naw, naw. Don't figure. Look at Murphy. Looks like he jest swallowed the canary. Something's not right."

"Cut it out, Sam. You always was so damn suspicious of everybody. Comes from readin' all them mysteries. Ain't no mystery here. Enjoy yourself. Everybody else is. Hey, look at the fella. He's already movin' in on that girl in the corner. Boy, he sure can bird dog those gals, now, can't he?" Nate watched Dion move to the end of the bar and lean in towards the young bar girl who looked at him with frank adoration. Lopez was also watching.

"Hey, Dion," he said. "You want to call Key West, huh? Pass along the good news?"

"Not now, Lopez, I'm busy," said Dion, annoyed. "If you call, why don't you have Maria pass the word along. I got business tonight, okay? Ain't that right, doll?" Dion turned his back on Lopez to zero in on the girl. She giggled as he ran his hand over her arm.

Lopez sighed and took a swig of his beer. No way to get through to him now. He took his beer and pushed his way through the crowd cashing in on Dion's offer at the bar, then he strolled out onto the porch of Maggie's. He tilted back in one of the old wooden chairs that once was blue but now just carried old flecks of faded paint on its rough surface, worn brittle from alternating doses of sea air and sun.

It was the moment before sunset, when the last edge of the sun was just disappearing below the horizon. At home everyone would be applauding off the Square now, thought Lopez. Maria would be cleaning up the dinner dishes, maybe putting away the leftover black beans and rice for a lunch tomorrow. Anita would be doing homework and Carlos would be trying to talk his mother into letting him go out to play again before going to bed. If this was the *Toledo*, maybe they could get a new car next year. Or maybe they could have another baby. Maria would like that. She said she missed a baby. And it had been so many years since Carlos was in arms. If it was the *Toledo*, maybe they could have a new car *and* a baby. Carlos Lopez smiled and hummed a tune to himself. Why not?

Then he thought of Phyllis Panagakis and the sun dropped from sight, leaving a halo of orange in the sky where it had been. If it was the *Toledo*, what would she do? Would she take Jason and leave Key West to go back to the mainland and read books? No, Dion wouldn't let her do that. She would have to go alone. Could she do that? Lopez believed in the innate love that mothers had for their children. But he also believed that Dionysos Panagakis would not allow anything to stand in the way of what he thought was his. The sorrows of that woman were not over, thought Lopez, who in his heart believed that Dion was the stronger force.

But Carlos Lopez had no knowledge of the latent powers within Phyllis, nor of the forces that could be mustered by the strange newcomer inhabiting a houseboat in the harbor of Key West that very night, or the well-laid plans of a woman who unraveled people's minds thousands of miles away on an island in the Pacific. Lopez, the good man, rested easy that evening on Plantation Key, sipping his beer and dreaming gently about what riches could do for him and his family, unaware of the mounting force of three women who wove a web that would snare Dion Panagakis once and for all.

Three

Phyllis watched the pickup round the corner and heaved a sigh of relief. She always breathed more easily with Dion out of the house. And now she wouldn't have to deal with him for at least two weeks. Phyllis sat at the kitchen table and relished her time alone. Sophia was out shopping and Jason wasn't due home from school for an hour. She felt like talking with someone; someone who would understand her. But no one on Key West could fulfill that need; not yet, at any rate. So, instead,

Phyllis decided to take the time to answer Dee's letter and to let her mind spin out through the vehicle of writing. She got out her box of dime store stationery, poured a cup of warmed-over coffee and sat down at the formica top table in the kitchen facing out to the calm green of her yard.

Dear Dee,

Thank you for your wonderful gift! I love both books and really can't decide which is more magical, the Japanese or the Polynesian. You should see me. I grab a story like a quick fix between dressing Jason for school or making dinner. Short stories are the best thing for a housewife who only has snatches of time throughout the day. So the myths are perfect and I thank you from the bottom of my heart.

But I am more lonely than ever. It makes it worse having people around who have no sympathy or understanding. I feel less lonely when no one is here or when I am out in my yard. It is other people who make me feel strange. And my husband is the worst of the bunch.

You said something in you letter that has crossed my mind, too. I am afraid of Dion. I do not know what to expect from him. It is so much better when he is gone. I tried what you suggested. I spoke with a man who works with him, a diver named Carlos Lopez. You would like him. He is very gentle and loyal and loves his family very much. But he also works for Dion, so I don't think he really was the right one to talk to after all. He did agree, though, that Dion was acting strange, so it isn't just you and me who think so. But Carlos will not say or do more because he respects Dion as a boss and doesn't think he can say anything to him that will be taken seriously. I could tell that he was uncomfortable talking to me this morning so I don't think I will try that approach again. It isn't fair to put him in the middle. But I do need a friend so badly here.

Maybe I will have one, though, thanks to you. Your friend Cassandra Walton did call me yesterday. She sounds like she is not used to talking; her speech was so very slow and deliberate. I think that maybe she is shy, too. She has been on the island a few days and I think she is ready to have company. I will go visit her tomorrow morning when Jason is in school. As you know, she lives on a houseboat in the harbor. I think that must be difficult for her if she is not well, as you say. But I suppose I will find out more tomorrow.

You have been so kind and considerate towards me, Dee. I am grateful. Thanks to you I think now that there is a chance for a different life for me; that I can get away from here, start again, do what I want for the first time in my life. I think divorce is inevitable. I know now that Dion sees other women. That's fine. Maybe that can give me the grounds I need. What do you think? I am so ignorant about these things. And I do not want Jason in the middle of a tug of war between us. Would you think it inhuman if I just left him with his father and grandmother? Or would it be right to leave him with a man I think is unbalanced? I don't want Jason to grow up to be another Dion. But is it too late already? I don't know.

Do you believe in evil, Dee? Or is it all just sickness that needs understanding, care and treatment? And why is it always given over to women to heal the world? Sometimes I think that men will continue their brutality because they unconsciously count on women to make it all right again. What if we all said no? What if they were left to clean up after themselves for once?

Questions. One after the other. All I am these days is one mass of questions. Are there answers? It is so frightening to open up and admit that all these questions are inside of me and then at the same time not to know if there are answers. I turn to you as someone who has gone before me, who has gone through many of the things that I am just now beginning to feel. You seem so brave and accomplished. You tell me of all the pain you went through. It gives me hope. How lucky my sister was in having you, if only for a short time, before she died. How I wish I could have known her, too; to see her transformed and at peace for once in her life.

But am I any less aimless? She traveled the world, while I just went deeper inside myself, rooted to the same small town, the same small life for years.

I must go now, Sophia will be here any minute. And so will Jason. I don't want them asking questions about this letter, about you, about what I want. So goodbye, my friend. You sustain me.

Love,
Phyllis

Phyllis folded the pages of the letter with care and slipped them into the envelope as Sophia struggled through the door with a large sack of groceries.

"Oh, let me help you, Sophia," offered Phyllis as she deftly swept the stationery and letter into a drawer away from the older woman's eyes.

"Eh," grunted Sophia, allowing her daughter-in-law to take the package from her arms. "Too many people, now. Too crowded in the market. And all those boys who act like girls. It is a shame. This island is not the same anymore. It's good Andreas did not live to see all this."

"Now what's the matter, Sophia?" asked Phylis, sitting down to sip her cold coffee. She had heard it all before, but she thought she'd give the old woman a hearing.

"No family anymore. Everybody big shot. The store is owned by someone on the mainland. They charge prices only other people on the mainland can afford. What about us? We live here. We work hard. Nobody cares about the families. All the faces change so fast now. It is terrible." The old woman eased herself into a chair and nodded her head in agreement with herself.

"So go back to Greece, Sophia."

"Why you always trying to send me back to my village? Everybody is changed there, too, I think. And what would you do, you lazy girl? Would you look after the boy, eh? Cook meals every day? No. No. You would not. You are just like all those people in the store. Selfish. Ungrateful."

Phyllis looked at Sophia with hardened eyes. She no longer cared what Sophia thought of her. She no longer had any mechanism for guilt in the Panagakis clan.

"No, Sophia, I've just started to be selfish, as you call it. I am just starting to think of myself. It's you who is selfish. You and your son. You're the tyrant. I'll tell you something. From now on, I'm going to be more selfish. In fact, I'm going to leave the house as soon as I change and I won't be back till dinner time. That should thrill you. You'll have the entire afternoon to pamper Jason and poison his mind against me. You should be in your glory, Sophia. I'm doing you a favor. What would you have in your life if you couldn't find fault with me and report to your almighty son?"

Sophia recoiled from the vehemence of Phyllis' anger. The younger woman pushed herself from the metal edge of the formica table and stormed through the kitchen to her bedroom, neither expecting nor wanting a response from Sophia. There was nothing more to say. Her words had no currency in the Panagakis home. It finally hit her that she was the only one with any interest in change. Everyone else was content with things as they were. She had to get out. And waiting an entire year now seemed impossible. The letters from Dee alone could not carry her through.

She stood in front of the worn dresser in the bedroom shaking with her pent-up frustrations. The room was dark, the blinds drawn against the sun and heat of the day. I have to get out, she repeated to herself, unbuttoning the plain white blouse she wore. She opened her drawer, searching for another blouse, something that would come closer to reflecting the changes that were going on inside of her. But her wardrobe had not yet caught up with her awareness. Everything was plain, sensible; the clothes of a woman who tended a small child and never went out. Nothing in her drawers or closet hinted at a verve, a zest with her own body. Her clothes were convenient disguises, not signals to the world to take notice of her.

Then I'll get new ones, she told herself with a sudden satisfaction. I'll go down to the expensive tourist shops that Sophia abhors and outfit myself in something a New York woman on vacation would buy. I will buy a new outfit and I will go to this new friend and just get the goddamn ball rolling.

Phyllis slammed the drawer shut and started buttoning up her old white blouse. It didn't matter. As soon as she bought something else she would just throw it in the nearest trash can. Phyllis smiled at herself and caught her reflection in the dresser mirror. She wasn't that bad looking, was she? When she smiled like this there was some life in her face. She turned away from the dresser and was about to leave the room when a glint of gold caught her eye from the top of the dresser. Her grandmother's locket. She scooped it up in her hand as she left the bedroom. What was the point of keeping it locked up in the house all the time? She would start wearing it now, using it, like she was about to take her own life out of deep storage and start using it.

She heard voices in the kitchen as she emerged from the

bedroom into the hall. Jason must be home. And his grandmother was fussing over him. Fine. Phyllis turned on her heel and cut across the living room to the front door, slamming the door hard as she left and stepped into the bright sun.

A houseboat was perhaps not the best choice as a home for a woman who was just relearning how to walk. But for Iris it was the only choice. No matter that the rocking of the boat added another dimension of stress to her efforts to walk a straight line for ten feet at a time. The times she made it, the sense of accomplishment more than wiped out the disappointment of the failures. And she was getting stronger. The muscles in her legs learned to hold her steady with the swaying motion of the boat.

She kept the wheelchair for long journeys on the island, but on the boat she relied on the walker and the cane to stump around the deck like an old-time pirate on a wooden leg. She had been on board only a few days, but Iris felt secure and rested enough to call her sister and invite her to her new home. What a thrill it had been to hear her voice! Iris had been filled with a longing, a poignancy at hearing that voice from her childhood, that beloved voice that now was deeper, more weary and somewhat formal. And yet it had been enough like the voice she knew that it had transported her back to childhood. Iris wheeled herself out of the hotel where she made the call and returned directly to her houseboat, not bothering to do the shopping she had planned for the day. She just wanted to return to the boat, to be rocked by the motions of the waves and to sip a glass of wine as she drifted back in memory to the last time that she had heard that voice.

Iris had been up since dawn in anticipation of Phyllis' visit. She sipped her coffee on the deck, watching the rose light illuminate the sky above the island. A few fishermen were pulling out of the harbor for the day's catch, while the shrimpers had just recently returned, the men now sleeping below the decks, sleeping through the light of the day in wait for the night and the next catch. The pleasure boats were quiet, the tourists and the wealthy with time on their hands still asleep. They always missed the glorious part of the day, sleeping away the liquor of the night before, thinking the best to be had was dancing in smoke-filled rooms crowded with strangers, hoping to find a new face to wake beside them in the cruel noon light of the next day. Few of them ever met the freshness of the dawn alone, gave themselves the gift of the day, and thereby owned a part of constant creation that was available to all and recognized by so few.

But why waste worry on them, thought Iris. They are not evolved; there is no magic in them. Given everything, they had nothing. And here she was, who by all rights should be dead. She had risen again from the ashes of cruel flames, remolded and tempered to an even greater strength. She had lived to become an avenger, to be a lover. All less trivial occupations were burned out of her.

And soon the women she loved would come to her across the water. Today Phyllis, and soon it would be time for Dee to come. They must all be together for the final, culminating event when Dion would meet his fate and they would be reunited, the true family once again.

Until then there was this harbor and the small dailyness of lives on the shore. Iris pulled herself to her feet and practiced her rolling gait across the deck. Thump. The cane would strike the surface hard and then the slight hesitation as she swung her right hip up and around in a rolling motion and set her weak right foot to the side of the sturdier left. Then the moment of faith when the cane was in the air for a second, her body leaning dangerously to the left before it was caught once again – thump! – by the prop of the cane before the entire, laborious process was repeated and six inches gained.

The sun was at its zenith, the hot rays beating down on the deck of Iris' houseboat with a force that had been unimaginable in the cool mountain retreats of Switzerland. Iris was flushed and short of breath, but it was not due to the heat. In front of her sat her sister, Phyllis Panagakis, sipping a gin and tonic and looking at her with intense curiosity. She actually looked handsome in a tangerine sundress with thin straps that showed off her beautiful brown shoulders. Her hair could have stood a bit of styling; it was cut blunt and hung uninterestingly straight around her face. But the straw hat was attractive and framed her face in a flattering manner.

In spite of the heat, Iris was more covered than her sister. She wore light muslin trousers gathered at the waist and a loose Greek blouse with long sleeves. Her skin was white and uneven from the many operations and her retreat from the sun. She purposely chose the loose clothes to hide the twisted contours of her body. She, too, wore a wide-brimmed straw hat to shield herself from the sun and pair of dark sun glasses to further disguise her eyes. But at the moment, at least, Phyllis did not seem to connect her at all to her true identity.

"Have you ever lived on a houseboat before, Cassandra?" Phyllis asked pleasantly, wanting this quiet woman to feel at ease while at the same time Phyllis was hungry for the details of her life.

"No, I haven't. But I've always had such an affinity for the sea. I'm surprised I never thought of it before."

"I know what you mean." Phyllis looked past the other woman and glanced briefly at the shore. "I've lived on this island for years and it never occurred to me to actually live on the water. Maybe because of my family. I've only lived here with them. We needed a house with the baby coming. So we stayed with Sophia. It's absolutely wonderful here, though, isn't it?"

"Yes," agreed Iris. "It's the constant motion. Like being in the cradle again. And no traffic whizzing by your door. And when the mood strikes you can just lift anchor and drift out to sea. But of course you must be familiar with all that with your husband's boat."

"The *Rafina*?" Phyllis gave a short laugh. "Hardly. That's his private little toy. It was bad enough when he just used it for his fishing tours. But now that it's the flagship in his treasure fleet there's no place for me on that boat at all. Not that I'd want to. It doesn't have the same feel as this boat. This feels like a home. His is all for sport or adventure. The manly pursuits, you know." The last sentence was spoken with a sneer.

"Don't you get along?" asked Iris innocently.

"No. I don't even feel married anymore. Just as well. He's such a stranger."

"Divorce?"

"Soon. Just the details, now. How I'm going to do it."

"I see."

"Look, I've been doing all the talking and I'm really very boring. I want to hear about your life, Cassandra. Dee didn't tell me very much, but I bet you've seen a lot more of the world than I have. Tell me about it."

"In some ways, I've seen more, I guess. What do you want to know about? Greece? The islands? The mountains of Switzerland? Hawaii? Manhattan? Does it matter?"

"Oh, yes, it matters," said Phyllis with conviction. "I have to believe that there's more out there than this life. There must be. Dee gives me a hint of it. And you're a friend of hers. Tell me, oh, just tell me about your favorite place in the world."

"All right," said Iris, pouring herself another gin and tonic and twisting the slice of lime into the glass. "But it isn't just geography that makes the difference in a place. It's the spirits that inhabit a location. Places where you can have access to stronger powers. They must be here, as well. You just have to know how to look for them, how to read your own dreams, how to listen to the wind." Iris smiled to see the rapt expression on her sister's face. After all these years the tables were turned. As a little girl she would sit spellbound listening to Phyllis tell her stories of the ancient Greeks. And now here she was listening like a hungry child to the stories of her own travels and encounters with the strange forces of the earth.

"My favorite place on earth is Oia on the island of Santorini in the southern Aegean. It was there, in solitude during the course of a winter that I learned to speak to the dead and to learn the secrets of death and recurring life; how matter turns into spirit and is illuminated by a certain slant of light at the right time, in the right place with the proper attention being paid. I can't tell you any more.

"But other things I can tell you. About the winding stairs that lead from the sheer edge of the cliff down to the boiling water below. The harbor that was formed by a volcanic eruption that swallowed up an entire civilization. You can still hear the moaning of the people caught off guard in that terrible moment.

"Or do you want to hear of the streets lined with fruit and olive trees or the courtyards shaded by pomegranate trees? How about the ruins of a medieval Venetian fortress on a promontory along the cliff? Do you want to hear of the island women's talent for embroidery that encrusts curtains and tablecloths? Or their weaving, the constant weaving of women that produces bedspreads and rugs, making everyday things full of the texture of care? Ancient patterns are passed down from generation to generation of women. I have seen a workhouse where old women, bent over and fragile in their black shawls instruct young girls on large looms to carry on the unbroken tradition that has been going on for thousands of years.

"A line unbroken of women. Yes, a line of women who pass along magic and knowledge of healing and curing as well as of vengeance and death. They know power. The real kind of power. Not the kind that is written into history books that are revised after each battle between arrogant men. No, the power of life and death and immortality. The only real kind of power. The power beyond history, notions of time and culture, all that illusion. And it was on Santorini that I learned about this. Maybe for you, it will be Key West."

Iris turned her gaze fully upon her sister who sat spellbound across from her, the drink forgotten in her hand, the liquid almost pouring out of the glass. Dee had been right. Phyllis was ripe for all this. She was making an impression.

"My God," muttered Phyllis when she regained her voice. "Who are you?"

Iris threw back her head to watch the gulls circling above the harbor on the lookout for fish. Beside them off the port side an old man in a rowboat plunged his hand into the water and yanked up a sponge, slapping it a sharp blow with the paddle he held in his other hand.

"Phyllis," she said simply. "Can I freshen up your drink?"

"I think I'm dizzy enough without it."

"Are you sure?"

"Oh, all right," said Phyllis passing her glass across to Iris for a refill. "It really doesn't matter when or in what shape I go home anyway."

"Tell me about your island, Phyllis. What makes it different from other islands?"

"Oh, I think you'll get the picture in a day or two. It does have a romantic past with the piracy and all. It's a mixture of Cuban and Creole and American military. And loaded with tourists and drug smugglers. A lot of homosexual men and some artists. That's about it. Not very magical to my way of thinking. Not like this Santorini that you talk about."

"Are you sure?" asked Iris archly. "Maybe you're not looking in the right way. Tell me. Are there any places that particularly attract or repulse you on the island? Any place which you definitely notice, no matter how many times you've been by it before?"

"Let me see." Phyllis took the fresh drink from Iris' hand and furrowed her brow in thought for a moment. "Well, there's one touristy place that I like. It's the old Geiger place on Whitehead Street. They call it Audubon House now. You know, where Audubon stayed when he sketched the birds of Florida. It's just such a great old house, filled with 18th and 19th century antiques. I've gone back a lot. It's so peaceful there."

"No," said Iris with authority. "That's not it. I'm not talking about museums that reconstruct somebody's idea of history. What place makes you feel something? Something like terror but also like you're on the brink of a great discovery? Think."

Phyllis looked puzzled for a moment. She was straining with the effort. She wanted to please Cassandra. It was how she felt with Dee, sort of coaxed to stretch into a higher level of herself. Then it hit her. Of course. Her shoulders relaxed and she looked up at Iris and smiled.

"I got it. Hemingway's House."

"The writer's place? What's so special about it?" asked Iris, surprised.

"It's like what you're talking about. A place that scares me, but also holds an answer. Listen, it isn't all that special in itself. It's an old Spanish-style colonial house, stuffed with Spanish furniture and things. In back of the house is the studio that he used when he was writing there during the thirties. And a swimming pool. I think that dates from his time as well."

"What else?" probed Iris.

"It's eerie somehow. All those trophies hanging around. The stuff from Africa, relics from the Spanish Civil War. A real he-man type of place. It reminds me of Dion, my husband. It feels like he thinks, you know?"

"And this frightens you?"

"Yes, yes it does. There's so much violence in that kind of masculinity. And a great deal of selfishness. I just feel it when I'm near that house. And then to see all the people line up to take a tour. People who idolize the man. And I think not so much for what he wrote but for the image he projected; that hateful, macho male image. And I think it's coming back into fashion. That's what scares me."

"I see," said Iris, slowly sipping her drink and trying to put her sister's fears into perspective. "All right. Now we have the fear. Something is there that scares you, that you have to fight in your own life. Now, what is there in that place that offers hope, that has something of you in it?"

"The cats," Phyllis answered promptly.

"Cats?"

"Yes, dozens of cats. They're supposed to be descendants of Hemingway's cats. They seem to be everywhere, all over the property. On the grounds. Sitting on chairs. They're real haughty with the tourists. It's like they really run the place and just allow humans in during certain hours."

"And this appeals to you?'

"Sure does. I suppose Dee would say that I identify with the cats. A female image. How they seem protective of their terrain."

"Not to mention their magical and occult significance," added Iris, a strange plan forming in her mind. "Cats are favorites as familiars."

"Oh, you mean witchcraft, don't you? But on Key West?"

"Why not Key West?" demanded Iris, taking off her sunglasses for a moment and focusing the blaze of her wondrous eyes on her sister. "Remember what I told you. It's not so much the geography of a place as it is finding the exact way to tap into the spirits of the region. There are spirits here just as surely as they are in Greece. Don't romanticize places halfway around the world. Everything is always available to you everywhere. Learn that, Phyllis. Learn to identify and to use your power. From what you say, there's something for you on the grounds of this Hemingway House. You must take me there sometime with you. Perhaps I can help you find what it is that calls you. And how you should answer."

"Of course. If you really think so." Phyllis gave a short laugh. "My, my. I came here for a friendly visit and here I am about to dabble in witchcraft."

"Don't laugh. And don't tell me you just came for a friendly visit to do a favor for Dee. You needed to come. You needed desperately to see who I was and what I might offer you."

Phyllis' face fell from laughter into a serious mask. How could this woman know her so well? What signs did she read? Could she really be in touch with occult powers?

"How do you know about me? I haven't told you that much."

"You don't need to tell me. Do you think words are the only way people learn from each other, learn about each other? It's clear that you are a woman who needs to find a way out of her present life into a much larger life. You need help. You need guidance. You need the confidence that you can have a better life and that you deserve to go out and get it. It doesn't take witchcraft to see that. But maybe I can help you find your own mystery, although only you alone can solve it."

"Yes, yes, that's it. But what about you? You had such a tragedy yourself. I really thought I could help you in some way, too. And here you are offering to help make my life right."

"You'll help me, believe me. By solving your problem you will also solve mine. It'll all become clear to you later. I think we've talked enough about it for now."

"I see," she mumbled, trying to find another topic of conversation.

"But there are other ways you can help me, if you really want to."

"Yes, of course. What can I do for you?"

"Come and visit me," said Iris.

"Is that all? I'd love to come. Sure I wouldn't bother you?"

"No, nothing of the sort. It's time I started learning to be social again. And I like you."

"Well, thanks. I'd love to come. I could even make it every day, if you like. Jason's in school now." Phyllis laughed her short laugh once again. "Maybe it's a good thing after all that Sophia won't go to Greece for a visit. Now I can leave the house any time I want without having to worry about Jason. Maybe I am luckier than I've been leading myself to believe."

"And I am lucky, too, that you feel that way. Bring your books. Maybe you can read me your favorite stories and we can get silly drinking gin and tonics in the afternoon."

Phyllis reached out and touched Iris' knee. "It's so good to have a friend again."

"I think we both have been lonely too long, Philly," said Iris quietly, looking with longing into her sister's eyes and wishing the masquerade could be ended.

"What did you call me?" said Phyllis, straightening in her deck chair.

"Phyllis," said Iris.

"No, no I thought you called me Philly."

"Did I? I don't know. Does it matter?"

"My sister used to call me Philly. When we were children." Phyllis' eyes brimmed with tears. "My sister Iris. She's dead. And now you're calling me by the same name."

"How extraordinary," commented Iris, cursing herself for the slip. "Maybe in some way I'm meant as a replacement for her."

"Maybe." agreed Phyllis. "If only I could have talked to her, made contact. But what's the use? You're right. Ever since I met your friend Dee I've started thinking in a different way. And she claims that everything changed for her since she met my sister Iris. So the circle comes round. And maybe I can help you as you help me. I get dizzy with all this turning round and round."

Iris smiled at her sister. "You look pretty in your apricot dress."

"Oh, thanks." Phyllis blushed beneath her tan. "It's new. Just today, on my way here, I bought it. Nothing I owned seemed to suit me anymore."

"And that locket. I can't take my eyes from it. It's quite attractive. Is it an antique?"

"Yes, my grandmother's." Phyllis' hand went to her throat. "I just came into it myself. I've decided to wear it. A lot."

"Good," approved Iris. "You should. You should do more that makes you feel happy."

"Thanks. I think I will," said Phyllis brightly. A thought crossed her mind and she was serious once again. "Tell me, Cassandra, would you ever want to go back to Santorini where you found your magic, as you call it?"

"No, I don't need to go back any more." She touched her hand to the place between her breasts. "I have it all here; now wherever I go Santorini is inside of me. The volcano is in my soul, the voices of ancient Greeks come to me in my dreams, Atlantis lives on in my mind and in my heart the love I have always known pulses on through my entire system. When you make that connection you'll feel the same way, Phyllis."

"Really? What makes you so sure, Cassandra?"

"Because we are of the same family, Phyllis. We recognize each other. You'll know this, I promise you."

Phyllis sighed and settled back into her chair. "And the crazy thing is, I believe you."

"Good. You should."

The two women were silent for a moment as they looked out across the water.

"It's getting late," muttered Phyllis absent-mindedly as she turned over Iris' words in her mind.

"Not really. Why don't you stay for the sunset?" suggested Iris.

"Oh I don't know if I should..."

"You said it didn't matter what time you got home or in what shape. Have you ever seen the sun set from the water here?"

"No, I haven't. All the years I've lived here and I've never watched the sunset from the harbor. Always from land. Landlocked. All these years, looking out across the water. Never riding on top of it."

"Then it's settled. You stay. No one can reach you or call

you. We'll just sit here and be quiet for a while and get to know each other. Really know each other, okay?"

Phyllis looked at the bright eyes in the twisted face of the other woman and nodded her head in agreement. "Yes. That would be nice. More than anything else in the world right now, that's exactly what I would like to do."

The two women entered into the silence as the houseboat rocked gently with the constant motion of waves. The pale blue sky turned dark and then tinged with an apricot not very different from the hue of Phyllis' dress, then turned once again, this time to indigo, before Phyllis tore herself away from the shared peace she found on the houseboat of Cassandra Walton and returned to the small stucco house on shore that she had grown to regard as her prison.

From the moment she entered the door she knew something was wrong. Sophia rushed toward her, not with a rebuke, but with great excitement, her old cheeks tinged with color. And Jason. He was still up and was converging on her as well.

"Phyllis! Where you been? News, such news, child."

"Why, what is it?" responded Phyllis taking an involuntary step backward. "Why is Jason still up?"

"Treasure, Mommy. Daddy found the treasure." Jason was bouncing around the living room like a helium balloon on a short string.

"What?"

"Yes, Phyllis. It is true. We got a call. Just a little time ago."

"From Dion?"

"No," said Sophia. "From Mrs. Lopez. Her Carlos had called her. They found the anchor of the ship and a coin. It must be the site of the ship Dion wants."

"I see," said Phyllis, who wasn't sure initially how to respond. A sense of foreboding welled up inside of her as well as the hope for freedom.

"Aren't you happy?" Sophia was suspicious of Phyllis' subdued reaction. It just served to make her more convinced that her daughter-in-law did not want the best for her son.

"Oh, it's just so sudden, Sophia. None of us expected him to find it right off like that. I mean, he just left. Are they sure it's the *Toledo*?"

"It is the ship. It is the ship." Sophia waved her gnarled hand with impatience. "Mrs. Lopez is happy, celebrating. Why not you, child? What is wrong with you?"

"Why should I be happy? Maybe Mrs. Lopez has a reason to be happy, but not me. Dion didn't call, did he? No, not Dion. His family isn't important enough to call. He sends someone else to do it if he even took the time to think of that. And for Carlos the money will bring his family things they all want together. Not for Dion. He'll spend it for what he wants. And we're supposed to be grateful. And praise him. Tell him what a goddamn hero he is. Well, not me, Sophia. Not me anymore. All I want from that man is out. Fine if I get some of the money, too. But I'm not counting on it. God knows he loves that gold more than he does any of us. So let the gold keep him comfortable, cook his meals, raise his son. It's his choice. And I'm going to stop trying to save him from his own choices."

"You become a bad girl, Phyllis," scolded Sophia as Phyllis stormed from the room. "Where you go tonight, eh? You find someone else, maybe?"

"No," Phyllis whirled toward Sophia in the doorway. "But if I had it wouldn't be any of your business. No, I just found a friend. Think of it, Sophia. There's someone who cares more for me after knowing me one day than any of you do after all the years I've lived with you. Think of it, Sophia."

Jason stood between the two women, looking from one to the other, calculating who had the power. Phyllis saw his dilemma and once again saw the scheming side of Dionysos appear in his son.

"What's the matter, Jason?"

"Don't you want the treasure, Mommy?"

"Is that what's bothering you, Jason? Let me ask you something. What would you rather have, a long trip with Mommy and a new place to live, or to stay here with Daddy and Grandma with the treasure?"

"Phyllis . . ." objected Sophia.

"No, Sophia, let him answer. He's more cunning than we give him credit for. He is his father's son, as you're so fond of saying. Come on now, Jason, what would you like better?"

The boy glanced quickly again between the two women and planted his feet firmly on the ground.

"Daddy and Grandma and the treasure. But if you had the treasure, Mommy, maybe I could go with you."

"See," said Phyllis to Sophia. "Are you satisfied, Sophia? You've done a good job. His affection can be bought, too. Just like his father. You've raised the same son twice. Congratulations." Phyllis leaned down toward the boy. "It's all right,

Jason. I'm not mad at you. I love you. You can't help it. But always remember, I love you. No matter what happens, I love you. When you're old enough maybe you'll understand, if there is any of me in you at all. Or maybe you won't understand. I have no control over that. You always have a home with me, no matter where I am, do you understand?" Phyllis straightened up and looked at Sophia for one long moment.

"I'm leaving, Sophia. I'm not gong to live here anymore. Oh, it might be a few days yet, so that I can make arrangements. And even after I'm gone I'll come for Jason now and then. I won't be denied that. I may be gone before Dion decides to come home, maybe not. I have no control over his comings and goings. And soon, he'll no longer have any control over mine. That's it, Sophia. I'm going to bed, now. I am very tired. I have nothing more to say."

Phyllis turned her back on the room and entered the small dark cave of her bedroom. She turned on the small dresser lamp and was surprised for a moment at her own reflection in the dresser mirror. The new dress was flattering. She looked so out of place in the frumpy bedroom hung with cheap reproductions and a Greek cross.

I'm better than all this, Phyllis told herself with a new conviction. I know better. I don't have to settle for this anymore. Mother taught me finer ways to live and to think. It's time I woke up. And thanks to Dee Hartman and Cassandra Walton, I am waking up. She unzipped the back of the dress and stepped out of it carefully, hanging it in her closet in a corner away from the offensive drabness of her other garments.

I'll leave them all here, she told herself, start new with clothes, too. Everything new. She turned back to the dresser and caught her reflection once again. Except this locket. This is the one old thing that means something. A symbol, the only thing that was passed down the line of women in her family. She touched the locket lightly and looked at her body in the mirror. It's a good body, she concluded, liking her form for the first time in over a decade. Nothing wrong with it at all. Here was Cassandra Walton, a cripple, who thought more of herself than Phyllis did. It made her ashamed. She would trade places with Cassandra any day to have her wisdom, her power in the world.

Phyllis undressed quickly and was about to slide into her bed when she hesitated. She could hear Sophia and Jason in the other room. And suddenly the bed she shared with Dion seemed repulsive. She quickly stripped the blanket from the bed and grabbed a pillow. She would sleep in the yard, the one place on the property that she felt was hers. It was the first step out of the house. Under the stars, in the clear night she would sleep and start learning to listen to her dreams.

Back on board the houseboat Iris had just finished the laborious task of changing her clothes and putting on her nightgown. What used to be an unconscious act now was a study in patience. She had to support herself with one arm while the other would claw at her trousers to get them off. And she usually forgot one item on the other side of the small cabin and would have to heave herself up and stump across the short distance with a half dozen of her swaying, cane-propped steps. But she was happy, despite the pain that would shoot through her system in sporadic bursts, unannounced and unrelievable save by time.

She sat at the small breakfast table and spread a few sheets of stationery in front of her, trying to gather her impressions to convey them to Dee. Outside, the shrimp boats were coming to life, the men calling to each other as they readied their nets for the evening's catch. Iris clicked on the small lamp over the table and in the pool of soft light she started her letter:

> Dear Dee,
>
> Today, I saw my sister Phyllis for the first time in nine years. It was wonderful and sad at the same time. Sad, because of all the time that we did not have together. I have not known any of the things that have happened to her from the time she was a girl. And now she is a woman. One forgets. I still had the image of her in my mind as a girl just out of her teens. And before me was a woman whose kind face was edged in sorrow and resignation. But the spark is still there; you were right. And I think she will be able to join us. She stayed the entire afternoon, right up to and through a glorious sunset that we watched together in silence.
>
> I owe this to you, Dee. Through you I have become reunited with my sister. Looking back, I cannot believe how we let Dion come between us. But it doesn't matter any more. I will not allow it to happen again. I only feel badly about the deception. I watch

her and I want to reach out and enfold her, sob on her breast and speak of all the pain we've both been through. But that, too, will come. In one afternoon we have become friends. I think we will see each other every day from now on. Already we have plans to visit places on the island. And I want to lift anchor and sail her out to sea and along the line of Keys.

And how about you, my love? I miss you terribly and want this time to pass quickly although I am savoring my new independence. Who would have thought that the day would come when I would rejoice about being able to take myself to the bathroom?

But seriously, I think that in another month it will be time for you to come here. I sense a gathering of forces happening very quickly now. Phyllis is right on the edge already. Dion is an unknown, of course, but it appears that he has the reputation of a hot head and has shown recent bizarre behavior that will work to our advantage. So I would say mid to late October should be right. I hope this will not be a strain on Toby or your patients, to lose you for weeks at a time twice in one year. But if all goes well we will all be back on your island again soon.

I have so much to say, but I grow tired. Tomorrow I will mail this and probably start another letter right away. It is the way I am, always needing and wanting this constant line to your attention, to your heart.

All my love,
Iris/Cassandra

A shrimper passed silently beside Iris' houseboat as she folded the letter into the envelope. A sudden splash startled her for a moment until she realized that it was just the nets being lowered into the water. She could imagine the tightly packed webs unfolding in the water as the net hit the floor of the bay. In a few moments, all would be still again and the unsuspecting catch of pink gold would ensnare itself within the mesh of the still, patient net.

Four

The morning after Dion and his crew sailed into Plantation Key with the Spanish anchor on their prow, they were preparing to sail back to the site of their find. The strain and excitement of their find was showing on them, however. Phipps' head throbbed with the after-effects of too much booze, and Dion suffered from a lack of sleep following a night of sexual athletics with the blond waitress. But his maniacal energy drove him on as he forced the men back to the job of salvaging the wreck. In fact, only Carlos Lopez seemed at the top of his form that morning, having retired early the night before after calling his wife in Key West. He had tried to caution her that the evidence was not yet conclusive that the wreck they found was the *Toledo*. But the excitement of treasure was in his voice and it was just the sort of news that she was waiting to hear.

The divers labored in long shifts the entire next week, carefully sifting through every bit of silt and debris surrounding the area from which they dug the anchor. Dion switched to an electrolung instead of regular scuba tanks so that he could stay under longer by recycling his breathing gas supply. An air lift was lowered to the sight to suck great quantities of the loose bottom silt up to the surface where it could be sorted on deck. And overseeing the entire process was the state archeologist, Deryl Simpson, who examined each shred with care in search of evidence to confirm the wreck's identity.

Simpson was just the sort of man that irritated Dion. He was small, precise and exacting, never saying or doing anything that was not carefully thought out beforehand. Dion hated the fine sandy hair that was carefully combed over the balding top of his head, the pale eyes and the moist, pursed lips that puckered slightly before he spoke.

After a long four-hour dive one afternoon, Dion heaved his aching body against the side of the ship and lit a cigarette to relax when Simpson came and sat next to him on the deck.

"Something on your mind?" asked Dion, knowing he'd have to wait ten minutes if he let the other man warm up to a subject.

"Why, yes," affirmed Simpson, working his mouth in a spasmodic rhythm. Dion frightened him and he had waited until the last possible moment before confronting him with his doubts.

"Well?" prodded Dion, taking a long drag on the cigarette.

"Frankly, I'm beginning to have my doubts."

"Doubts? About what?"

"About the *Toledo*. I'm not entirely convinced that she's down there."

"What do you mean, not down there?" Dion straightened up and leaned threateningly toward the other man. "Listen, you worm. Two weeks ago you said the pieces we brought up were definitely from the *Toledo*. How about the pieces of pottery that got you so excited, huh? And the other coins. Now you tell me you made a mistake?"

"No, calm down now," said Simpson waving a hand weakly in Dion's direction. "I still think they came from the *Toledo*. But nothing I've seen since confirms that there's a wreck down there. You're not finding any large cannon, or beams, or pieces of the hull. It's strange that you locate these little bits and pieces but nothing larger, of a more substantial nature."

"How about that anchor? That big enough for you?"

"It's another piece, do you know what I mean? Nothing substantial from the body of the ship itself has come to the surface."

"Tell me straight, Simpson. Quit beating around the bush. If you had to lay bets on what's going on, what'd you say?"

"The way I see it, it could be one of two things. I could be convinced that the ship was broken into pieces either during a long, arduous sinking or it was scattered underneath the water once it settled. You know, half of it falling off as the shelf of the reef gave way and washed part of it further down the straits. Either of those things would account for the fact that the anchor lays in a different place than the body of the ship."

"Is that what you think happened?"

Simpson hesitated. "No, no, I don't think so. If the anchor broke off from the rest of the wreck, why would there be pottery at the sight? And gold? It seems to me that cargo wouldn't enter the water until the hull gave way. And that'd be much later than the severing of the anchor. That leaves only one other possibility."

"Yeah, what's that?"

"That you've been duped, Mr. Panagakis. That someone has planted these items to make you believe that the *Toledo* is here when it is actually at a very different location."

Dion jumped to his feet, grabbed Simpson by the collar and

drew him up to his face. "Liar! You goddamn liar! It's there, I tell you. I know. I know. I was led to the site. It's gotta be down there, do you hear?"

"Fine, fine, if you want to continue, by all means, continue." Simpson's eyes were wide with fright. "I may be wrong."

Dion started to calm down after his outburst and loosened the grip he had on Simpson.

"Yeah, yeah, but what if you're right?"

"You see," offered Simpson, "everything you found was very near the surface. In the last week you've brought up nothing new. When you can think about it dispassionately, doesn't that seem a little odd to you?"

"Taylor." Dion spun around and looked back toward shore. "It's gotta be Taylor. The son of a bitch. That's why he took it so well. That son of a bitch planted the damn anchor and he's just sitting back and laughing up his ass at me. I'll find him and make him talk, the bastard. And so help me God, if he did that I'll kill him. Do you hear me? I'll kill the bastard."

Dion turned away from Simpson and started ripping the wet suit from his body as he made his way to the cabin.

"Phipps! Lopez! You keep working the site, do ya hear? I'm taking the launch and checking out something in Plantation. I'll be back tonight or I'll send word. Just keep working. Understand?"

Lopez and Phipps looked at each other in surprise as Dion disappeared into the cabin. Simpson leaned heavily against the side of the *Rafina*, trying to catch his breath. Below the deck Dion pulled on his clothes in a rage, Taylor's mean yellow eyes clouding his vision along with the image of Iris' mocking smile, the apparition that led him to the site that almost killed him and now appeared to be a fool's trap of another nature.

That afternoon Dion burst into Maggie's like a renegade from the Old West. Sam McGee and his crony Nate Parker sat alone at the bar. A tourist couple sat in the back, eating Maggie's chicken."

"Where's that fucking Taylor?" demanded Dion as his eyes swept the room.

Sam and Nate looked at each other a moment before answering the fuming Dion.

"Ain't seen him in a coupla days," offered Nate. "Maybe he's hangin' out at his office."

"No, I just came from there. There's just that idiot Murphy

sitting around. Claims he doesn't know where Taylor is."

"Guess he don't." Nate shrugged. "Taylor don't tell nobody 'bout his comin's and goin's. Have you tried his salvage site?"

"Not yet," said Dion, signaling the bartender for a shot. "But that's where I'm heading next. Sonofabitch. I'll track him to Cairo if that's what it takes."

"He done something to you, son?" asked Sam, shifting his pipe to the other side of his mouth.

"Not sure yet but I'm goddamn gonna find out. There's some suspicion that he seeded that wreck to throw me off my *Toledo*. If he did, he's a dead man, do you hear? A dead man." Dion threw back the shot in one motion and signalled for another. Sam let out a low whistle.

"Whoa! Seeded wrecks, eh? Well, I gotta say it wouldn't surprise me none. Fact is it makes more sense than him bein' so buddy like to you a few weeks back. And that Murphy grinnin' like a fool when you drug in that there anchor. I think you got something there, boy. You see, Nate, my suspicion's right after all. I don't want you on me 'bout those mysteries again, ya hear?"

"You mean you thought that right away? For Chrissake, why didn't you let on to me? I've lost weeks fuckin' around that wreck."

"Well, you ain't the type that can be approached, if ya know what I mean. Besides ain't no proof that Taylor done it. Guess you gotta dig him up before you go jumpin' to any conclusions."

Dion downed his second drink and threw that glass roughly across the bar. "Yeah, well, that's just what I'm going to find out, old man."

"Why don't you try Miami?" offered Nate. "Seems he was talking about needin' to go to Miami on some business a while back. Or maybe it was Tallahassee. Don't remember."

"Big help," said Dion as he headed for the door. "But if he's not at the salvage site I'll tear both them damn towns down looking for him, the bastard. He'll rot in hell before he touches one timber on the *Toledo*."

Then he was gone, leaving the two tourists with their mouths open, their chicken cooling on their plates.

Meanwhile, Phyllis Panagakis was enjoying the most Eden-like time in her life since childhood. At her new friend Cassandra's urging, Phyllis practically moved onto the houseboat, only returning to her home every other day to take Jason on outings. And rather than feeling like an intruder, Phyllis felt truly useful. She was happy when she could drive Cassandra to the hospital for her physical therapy, then help her practice walking back on board the boat. And sometimes Phyllis would stock up on groceries and they would pilot the boat out of the Key West harbor and along the Intracoastal Waterway, stopping as the mood struck them to investigate whatever struck their fancy.

The second week together they laid anchor just off Big Pine Key within the waters of the National Key Deer Refuge, and spotted three of the small, rare large-eyed creatures stare out at them for a few curious moments before bounding away to safety in the dense foliage of the park. Phyllis and Iris were thrilled by the sighting and stayed up half the night talking of animals and magic and the poverty of a life that did not include other creatures.

But as if by instinct, they never ventured further north than the Matecumbe Keys. Neither was prepared to run into Dion Panagakis. Phyllis had yet to confront her husband with her decision to leave him, although she did know that Sophia filled his ear with a tale of woe when he finally called one night and Phyllis was gone. She was never sure when Dion would make an appearance, and each time she approached the house to pick up Jason, she would hold her breath in anticipation. The meeting was inevitable, a necessity before she could fully launch herself on her new life. But she dreaded the acting out of that very scene that would bring her freedom.

It was in late October, on a Friday afternoon, that Phyllis finally confronted Dionysos. She was coming to pick up the boy for a weekend cruise on the houseboat to Fort Jefferson in the Dry Tortugas in the Gulf of Mexico. But as she walked up the front walk, she knew that he must be home. An air of tension hung about the place and the living room blinds were still drawn tight. Phyllis' heart beat quicker and she fought the urge to turn and run back down the path, back to Cassandra and the comfort of the home on the water. She took a deep breath and pushed into the front door, trying to make her voice sound normal.

"Jason, honey. Where are you?"

There was silence for a moment and then Dion appeared in the doorway leading from the bedroom onto the hall.

"Where the hell you been?" he demanded as he took a few

threatening steps in her direction.

"I might ask you the same question. But I really don't care. Where's Jason? We're going on a trip."

"The hell you are. I sent him to the movies with Ma. I want to talk to you alone."

Phyllis fought the urge to retreat a few steps from Dion. She did not want him to smell her fear of him.

"But he was looking forward to the trip, Dion. Why do you have to disappoint Jason just to get at me?"

"That's a good one. As if you cared a damn about him. You've deserted him and now you're crying. Don't make me laugh."

"I want a divorce, Dion." said Phyllis, deciding to get it over with as quickly as possible.

"A divorce, eh? And I suppose you want a nice little piece of the treasure action to go with it?"

"No, I don't care about your damn treasure. I just want a few thousand dollars to get myself started again, back in school somewhere. You can keep all the rest."

"Really? And how about Jason?" sneered Dion, his hand resting lightly on the knife he always wore in his belt.

"I'd like to take him with me, Dion. But if it won't work out I'll go without him. Or we can share custody."

"What grounds you going to use about this divorce, huh?"

"Let's make it polite, Dion. You give me a little money and we'll just let it dissolve. Or I can start slinging mud and bring up the other women you see."

"You bitch. Who's been talking to you?"

"Does it matter? You can't deny it. You make no secret of it. And I can quite truthfully testify to your refusal of marital rights to me. It won't be a pleasant trial, I can guarantee."

"So help me, Phyllis, you won't get Jason. He's my son. Get out, but I get Jason."

A new idea began to form in Phyllis' mind, a way of revenge. All along she had been ambivalent about taking Jason or leaving him with Dion. But seeing Dion now she knew she must take the boy away from Dion's influence.

"I don't think so, Dion. I think any court would give me my boy. He's still so young. And with your record of financial irresponsibility, absence and ways with other women, I think it's pretty safe to say that I'll win. You'll get him a few weeks in the summer. Not enough time to fill him with your poisons."

Dion's hand shot out and struck Phyllis a blow across the

mouth. A small trickle of blood seeped from the corner and spattered on her fresh new dress.

"Bitch. Goddamn bitch. We'll see who gets Jason. Who's this woman you been staying with, eh? I hear she's a friend of that Dee Hartman. Another dyke, maybe? Oh, brother, let the courts hear about that. They won't want you anywhere near the kid. Is that what you've been up to, Phyllis? Just like that damn sister of yours. Nothing but a bunch of dykes. We'll see who gets Jason. We'll see."

"Thanks, Dion." Phyllis dabbed at her mouth with her hand as she looked at Dion with pure hate. "You just strengthened my case. Want to hit me again so there can be no mistake?"

All Dion's frustrations welled up inside of him. He drew back his powerful arm and let fly at his wife's face with a crushing blow to the jaw that sent her sprawling across the room.

"You asked for it, Phyllis. You goddamn asked for it. Now get out. Get out of my house and never set a damn foot in here again. Nothing, do you hear? You get nothing. No Jason. No money. No house. Just get out. And let any damn court try to tell me different. I settle my own scores. Soon as I find Taylor, he'll get what's coming to him. And then I'll come back and settle it with you, understand?"

Phyllis staggered to her feet, dazed from the blow.

"You better watch your step, Dion."

Dion threw back his head and laughed. "Oh, that's good. You threatening me? Don't make me laugh. Just get out of my sight."

Phyllis walked haltingly to the door, leaning against the wall for support until she could regain her equilibrium from the blow. "You'd be surprised, Dion. You'd be surprised."

And without a backward glance, Phyllis was through the door and down the path leaving Dion alone in the living room of what was once their home.

Phyllis' anger and thirst for revenge had not subsided by the time she reached the harbor and climbed into the small boat that would carry her across the water to the houseboat anchored further out. But the pain in her face had started to distract her and she worried that perhaps Dion had broken something after all. She had to get to Cassandra. Cassandra would know what to do next, how to handle Dion and Jason and her escape into her new life. But as she approached the boat she noticed two figures on the deck instead of one. It was another woman. And for the first time Phyllis felt a stab of jealousy. She had grown to feel that Cassandra was her own private friend, who required nothing from anyone but her. And particularly now, fresh from her encounter with Dion, she wanted Cassandra to herself.

But as she approached the side of the boat, the other woman turned and bestowed upon her the kindest of smiles. It was Dee. Phyllis' face lit with a smile and was surprised as Dee's face melted into an expression of worry.

"Phyllis! My God, what happened to your face?" demanded Dee.

At her exclamation, Iris struggled to her feet and tried to peer over the edge of the boat to get a better look at her sister.

"What is it?"

"A message from Dion," replied Phyllis ruefully. "I'm not sure if it's broken or not."

"Come up and let's have a look." Dee reached over the side to grasp Phyllis' hand, then turned her face to the light and examined it closely.

"The bastard," she muttered. "Can't stop himself from brutalizing women, can he?"

Phyllis winced from Dee's probing as Iris looked on anxiously.

"Think it's broken, Dee?" asked Phyllis.

"No, don't think so. But you're going to have one hell of a bruise and black eye." A thought crossed her mind. "Listen. Did you report this to the police?"

"No, I didn't think to." Phyllis stared at her blankly.

"Well, that's the first thing you've got to do." Dee looked over at Iris with a knowing half-smile. "Stay a minute and have some juice. But then I want you to climb right back in that boat and go the nearest police station and fill out a report. You need to get official papers filled out on the guy. For your own protection."

"Of course,"agreed Phyllis. "I wasn't thinking."

"Who does at such times? But we have to learn to snap out of it if we hope to stop being victims."

"I'll go in a minute," said Phyllis. "I just need to rest a bit. But anything I can do to nail Dion, I'm all for."

"And we'll help you," assured Iris.

"What a surprise to see you, Dee," said Phyllis as she eased into a chair. "I didn't know you were coming."

"Surprised me, too," said Iris innocently.

"Yes, well, I saw a little clear spot in my schedule and I decided on the spur of the moment to come and see how you both are doing. It seemed all was well until you pulled up a few minutes ago, Phyllis."

"I'll be all right, Dee. Don't worry. But what do I do next? About divorcing Dion?"

"Okay, let's look at the facts," said Dee. "He's shown that he hits you. Anything else?"

"Oh, yes, there's more. Besides seeing other women, I guess he's been strange these past months. Even his men are uncomfortable around him. And now he's trying to hunt down this Frank Taylor and is threatening to kill him."

"What's this?" said Dee, her interest piqued by this recent piece of news.

"Oh, I heard about it the other day from Mrs. Lopez, the wife of one of Dion's crewmen, when I picked up Jason at school. Seems Taylor might have seeded a wreck to throw Dion off the track of the *Toledo*. So he's trying to find Taylor and make him tell if it's true or not. If it is, then it looks like Dion means to do him in."

"Lovely bunch of fellows, aren't they?" mumbled Dee. "So Dion hasn't found Taylor yet?"

"No. But Mrs. Lopez says that Taylor found out that Dion was after him and is laying low right here in Key West. And Mrs. Lopez doesn't know that Dion's here now, too. Neither did I until today," she said, passing her hand across her sore jaw that was starting to swell painfully.

"Well," said Iris with pleasure. "So both of them are on the island and neither one knows the other is here. What a nice meeting that one would be, huh?"

"Perfect," agreed Dee.

"What are you two talking about?" asked Phyllis.

"We'll tell you when you get back," assured Dee. "Now I think you better get going while your bruises still look convincingly fresh."

"Oh, all right." Phyllis rose to her feet and maneuvered back into the small boat with Dee's help. "I have a feeling there's something you're not telling me, Dee."

"When you get back, Phyllis. We'll talk then. All of us," assured Dee.

"I'm counting on it," said Phyllis. "You and Cassandra are

the only ones I trust in the world."

Dee and Iris watched as Phyllis' boat skimmed across the water to the dock.

"It's all happening, isn't it Dee?" asked Iris softly as she held Dee's hand tightly.

"Yes, even better than we thought."

"At last I can stop this deception with Phyllis. It's been difficult."

"Think she'll join us against her husband? She ready?"

"I can almost guarantee it. Especially after what he did to her today. And I have the place."

"Really?"

"Yes. At the Hemingway House. That's where the forces seem to gather for Phyllis. I've been there. It's perfect. We should arrange it for late afternoon, after the last tour. The employees are busy in the front mansion. For a little while there's no one in the back studio building or near the swimming pool. That's the place. That's the place Phyllis would be capable of doing things she's never done before."

"And this Taylor?"

"He's our man, all right. And our bait."

"Think we can find him?"

"I think so. I hope so. If we ask around enough in the right way in the sailor's bars I'm sure we can turn him up."

Dee smiled at Iris and held her hand to her breast. "Have I told you that I love you and that I've missed you so very terribly these months?"

"Only about six times in the hour that you've been here."

"Then I haven't told you enough, Iris." Dee looked across the water to the speck that was Phyllis. "She won't be back for at least two hours, wouldn't you say?"

"No, I guess not." Iris grew uneasy and withdrew her hand from Dee's grasp.

"Don't be afraid, Iris." Dee looked deeply into Iris' liquid green eyes. "I want to hold you, make love to you. What's so frightening about that?"

"Dee, you know why." Iris avoided the other woman's eyes.

"You're not in pain, are you?"

"Not much any more. I just, well, I don't want you to be shocked. And I don't want your pity."

"Pity? Never. I need to hold you. When are you going to believe that it wasn't just your beauty that made me fall in love with you?"

"I'm trying, Dee, I'm trying. It's not that I don't believe you. I guess I'm not fully adjusted to myself any longer. I can't make my body move the way I want it to."

"Then let me touch you, my love. Let me just hold and caress you."

Dee stood and drew Iris to her feet, then walked with her to the cabin. Silently she eased Iris back onto the bed and drew the flowered curtains over the windows. Iris' eyes never left Dee as she slowly undressed and then lay next to Iris, pressing against her while slowly drawing the clothes away from Iris' body. Dee was careful not to move too quickly and avoided looking at Iris' body and making her self-conscious. Instead, she slowly took Iris into her own flesh until Iris relaxed into the embrace, whimpering softly with her own sadness, love and thanksgiving.

"It's time you know everything, Phyllis," said Dee.

"Yes," agreed Iris. "Come over here by me."

Phyllis moved her chair near Iris on the deck of the boat. It was late afternoon. In the harbor the shrimp boats were preparing to sail.

"You being here isn't a coincidence, is it Dee?" asked Phyllis.

"No, no coincidence," Dee responded.

"Didn't think so." Phyllis looked from Dee to Iris. "Once my head started to clear I got to thinking. You know, Dee, I kept waiting for you to write something about tracking down Iris' killer. And you never did. And something in me wouldn't let me ask. It's like I knew by instinct how much I could take at a time."

Iris reached out and took one of Phyllis's hands. "Go on," she urged softly.

"That's why you're here, isn't it? You know who he is. And how to get to him, right?"

"Yes," said Dee. "And so do you."

The awareness that had started to manifest while Phyllis sat in the police station burst to the surface.

"Dion!" she screamed. "It's Dion, isn't it?" Phyllis tore her hand from Iris' grasp and jabbed both fists into her temples in a fruitless attempt to keep the knowledge from spilling out.

"Yes," confirmed Iris. She took hold of Phyllis' wrists and pulled them away from her head. "What else do you know? Look at me, Philly. Look in my eyes."

Phyllis looked up into the translucent green eyes. She saw a tiny reflection of herself, small, like a child. Like the Philly of twenty years ago.

"Iris," groaned Phyllis. "Oh my God. Iris." Phyllis slipped from the chair and buried her face in her sister's lap, sobbing.

"There, there, Philly," soothed Iris, stroking her sister's hair with her gnarled hand. "It's all right now. We're together. It'll be all right."

Suddenly Phyllis stiffened and whirled around. There was a madness in her eyes, a wildness Iris had not seen since her stay on Santorini.

"I'll kill him. I'll kill him for what he did to you."

"Easy, Phyllis," said Dee. "Remember what we talked about months ago. There will be justice. I guarantee you. You'll have your chance to confont him. As will Iris. But let's leave the killing to someone else."

"Who?" demanded Phyllis.

"Frank Taylor," said Iris. "You gave us the vital link this morning. Putting those two together can only lead to death."

"But what if Dion kills Taylor. Then what?"

"We'll be there to help assure it's the other way around," said Dee. "And if there is a slip up, then Dion would be put away for murder. Either way, he'll get what's coming to him."

"No," said Phyllis slowly. Her manner became very cool and determined. The riot in her head began to focus. "He must die. Prison wouldn't be enough. He must die. But first he will know what true justice means."

Dee looked at Iris anxiously to see if she caught the sudden change in Phyllis' mood. But Iris' attention was riveted on her sister.

"I know this is a lot to take in one day," ventured Dee. "Perhaps you should take a sedative. I have some in the cabin."

"No, I don't need it," said Phyllis slowly, holding Iris' hand tightly. "I'm very calm now. I know what must be done."

But could she do it? Jason. The little Dion. True justice would eliminate the line of Panagakis. Like Medea, who paid back the treachery of her husband with the bodies of their sons. She had to insure that neither Dion nor his son would ever victimize another woman. Never again would a sister in blood or spirit be terrorized by a Panagakis. Never again. But could she do it?

"Phyllis, are you all right? Phyllis, look at me." Iris tugged at her sister's arm.

"I'm fine," said Phyllis slowly. "Dee, Iris, I'm fine. Now, what do we do next?"

"Lay out plans very carefully," said Iris. "And bind ourselves to each other in a pact of love." Iris reached out and grabbed a hand of each of the women and pressed her lips to them with passion.

The fading sunlight caught the silver threads that ran through Iris' hair, turning them a glowing peach, creating a halo around her head visible from shore. The stance of the three women suggested a religious painting of the Renaissance, edged in peach and gold in the subdued light; or a page from an illuminated manuscript if, indeed, a Christian document could accommodate such disparate qualities of spirit, beauty and ancient pagan terror upon the water.

Five

Iris woke before dawn while the two other women slept. It took great effort to move her awkward body so as not to disturb the others and to prepare a pot of coffee to take with her onto the deck while waiting for the first light. She had to be ready and alert for any last minute power she could glean from the spirits of the dawn. For today was the day. Today Dionysos Panagakis would meet the fate he had created for himself.

It was no ordinary morning. It was October 31st. Halloween. In the United States it was just another party day when people dressed in costume and went to parties in costume. Children could rake in candy and vent frustrations with unfriendly neighbors by soaping windows, stringing toilet paper in trees and sticking toothpicks in doorbells to keep them ringing for hours like the bells of doom.

But for Iris the day held a more potent meaning. She was well aware of the more ancient ritual of the day, the Witch's Sabbath, when old wise women were at the height of their powers and the irreverent did well to be wary. At midnight the souls of the dead would walk again and men's hearts grew cold.

Iris sat at the rail facing east, sipping her coffee with these thoughts running through her mind. The first pale light behind the buildings on shore brought out their shape against the horizon. Small shafts of light edged the inky water of the bay, giving the ripples of water a sheen like obsidian, that crystalized form of volcanic lava, and made her think once again of Santorini and the bay formed by volcanic eruption.

She breathed the morning air deeply and gradually felt all the powers she knew in Greece infuse her system and send a tingle through her body that for a few moments was free of all pain. Once again she felt sound of body with the strength of the Furies. She inhaled deeply, entering into the pleasure of that strength and then caught her breath in a sharp gasp. Blood. The unmistakable smell of blood filled her nostrils while a haze clouded her vision, turning the water a rosy hue.

Tears sprang to her eyes and Iris was plunged into sorrow. And still the blood-letting was not over. There was still violence to be done. She bowed her head and rested her chin against her chest. Then the sun edged up over the jagged backdrop of trees, houses and television antennas and spilled generously across the water, illuminating a path from the shore to the houseboat. The heavy weight lifted from Iris' chest and she raised her head once again and stared across to the source of the light. And while the unrestrained joy did not return, the sorrow lifted and she was left with the foreknowledge of what would take place that day and she accepted it all without judgment, without elation or sadness, without desire for anything but for what the prevailing forces perceived as justice and how she was to play her part as an agent of those spirits.

On the island, in the Panagakis home, Sophia was rising with the first light of dawn as she had done every morning of her sixty-five years. But this particular morning she did not rise refreshed and ready for the tasks of the day. It had been a disturbing night. She had been plagued by dreams and a sense of foreboding that was only intensified by Jason's restlessness throughout the night. More than once she woke to his whimpering in the room and she had to take him in her arms and stroke his forehead before he could fall asleep again. Finally she took him into the bed with her and held him close until the morning.

It was not good for the boy, all these problems in the family, thought Sophia. His mother gone, driven out by his father. While Sophia did not care for Phyllis' behavior during the past summer it made her cringe when Dion told her that she was banished from the house and was not to see Jason under any circumstances. Her loyalty, as always, was with her son. But something inside her felt the violation done to a mother by such a decree, and for the first time an element of doubt entered into her perception of Dion.

He is not himself, Sophia told herself as she pulled on her shapeless black dress and shuffled into the kitchen. He was drinking too much. And his gold had made him a little crazy. He would listen to no one and his temper was terrible. All he could talk about was this Taylor and what he would do to him if he was found. He was still asleep in his own room. Or passed out, to be more accurate. Sophia stirred the orange juice in the glass pitcher with a large wooden spoon and crossed herself quickly to ward off the sense of dread she felt descend upon her from an unnamed source.

"Where's my hat?" demanded Jason, still half asleep and dragging his white admiral's coat behind him.

"In your closet, boy. But look what you do. Here, give me your coat. You get it all dirty. Why you have it out today?"

"Halloween, Grandma. Don't you remember? I'm going to dress up like an admiral."

"Oh, yes, yes, I forgot. This Halloween. You drink your juice and Grandma will get out your coat and white pants." Sophia sighed. "Dress up in your good white suit. You will be ruined by the time you come back from school. Then Grandma must make it clean all over again, yes?"

Jason grasped the glass of juice with both hands and drained it in one long series of gulps. "More," he commanded, holding out the glass at an angle for a refill.

"Good boy," smiled Sophia. "Drink juice. It is good for you." She poured a second glass and left him in the kitchen, his sturdy little legs planted firmly apart as he tilted back his head for the juice while she returned to the bedroom to search out his starched white suit.

Back on board the houseboat Dee opened her eyes with a quick flutter and for a moment did not know where she was. She had been dreaming of making love with Iris in the lush setting of Paradise Park. It had seemed so real to her that upon waking she had trouble deciding whether it was a dream, a memory or a vision of what was to come. But when she was able to focus her eyes in the shaded light of the cabin she saw that Iris was not in her bed and that Phyllis lay sleeping fitfully across from her in another bunk.

As quietly as she could, Dee swung her legs over the side of the narrow bed and drew on a light robe over her lace-trimmed nightgown. She knew she would find Iris on deck and wanted a few minutes with her before Phyllis awoke.

When she opened the door onto the deck she saw Iris staring out across the water toward shore. Dee moved up behind her and slid her hands across Iris' shoulders and hugged her back against her body. Iris' right hand moved up Dee's arm and caressed her.

"Good morning, love," whispered Dee softly, bending her head down to speak directly into Iris' ear.

Iris turned her head to look directly at Dee. For a moment Dee was taken aback. Iris' remarkable eyes were glowing with light that could not be entirely attributable to the new dawn. In them she saw sorrow and infinite patience, weariness and yet hope. Finally, Iris could focus on Dee alone and the little lines around her eyes deepened with her slight smile.

"Good morning, love, yourself. Sleep well?"

Dee brushed the hair back from Iris' forehead. "Not really. As soothing as your boat is, I can't rest easy until this is all over."

"Yes, I know. And it will be over. Today. Then we can sleep. Coffee?"

Dee took the cup from Iris' hand and brought it to her lips. "Are you frightened, Iris?"

"Of course. I'd be a fool not to be. But we've been careful; it's now up to the fates. And I think they look kindly upon you and me. At last. I think we've earned it."

"Yes, I think so, too. And I hope you're right."

Iris turned her back to the water. "Is Phyllis up yet?"

"No, not yet. But she's restless. She'll be joining us soon, I'm sure."

"Poor Phyllis," murmered Iris. "Poor, tragic Phyllis."

"We'll be there for her, Iris. She won't fall through the net again. We'll catch her."

"I know, I know," agreed Iris. "But there are some things over which we are powerless."

"We've done the best we could," said Dee. "Now, do you want any breakfast?"

Iris shook her head. "No, I'm not hungry yet. Let's wait for Phyllis. Just sit here with me, Dee. Let's just be quiet together for a little while."

"All right," said Dee softly. She sat down on the deck next

to Iris' chair and laid her head in her lap. Iris' hand gently stroked Dee's head, tracing the contours of her skull as they both followed the course of a swooping sea gull with half-closed eyes.

On Whitehead Street young Tom Mason pushed open the door to Hemingway House and started the morning rounds to make sure everything was in order for the tours that would start at ten. He walked slowly through the rooms, taking in the familiar trophies and generously proportioned furniture, making mental note of which rooms required dusting that day and which could wait. They were short-handed with Nancy out sick the past few days and little hope that she would feel well enough to come back today.

Satisfied that the main house could pass inspection, Tom walked into the back yard and around the swimming pool to check the condition of the studio. A little dusty, he concluded. And the famous writing desk could use a polish. People noticed that desk. They liked to think of Hemingway standing over it and composing great books. Tom took pride in keeping the desk shining. It was important. People dreamed into that desk, buffeting it with visions of romantic glory in just wars and virile men who made the earth move for compliant, adoring women. It was a tradition worth honoring as far as Tom was concerned. And most of the tourists who passed through the studio agreed with him.

Coming back around the pool Tom noticed a scattering of leaves and paper floating on the water. He hesitated a moment, but decided it was something he couldn't let go. He spun on his heel and went around to the back of the studio, jumping over a slow-stalking cat to get the long pole with the net on the end. Walking up and back around the circumference of the pool, he skimmed the offensive debris off the water and shook out the net over the lawn. It had only taken him ten minutes, but he was far enough behind his usual schedule that he had to hurry to make up the time and get himself presentable before the first group of tourists would arrive. He hurried around the back of the studio one last time to return the pole and then rushed back to the main house at a half trot.

After a few moments the ripples caused by Tom's net calmed down, leaving the surface of the water smooth as glass, disturbed only occasionally by the slight breeze that broke through the protective screen of trees and swooped down the pool that lay clear and untroubled down to the fine lines of the cracked bottom.

Back in the Panagakis home Dion was struggling through a net of nightmares to consciousness in the heavily draped bedroom. He had been dreaming of Iris again, something he hadn't done for weeks. He had thought that he was finally rid of her, but her image would not leave him alone. In his dream she wore the same mocking smile that she displayed underwater while leading him to the site of the anchor. And mixed in with that image was the memory of the two old men he met in Rhodes; the old man who predicted visions of gold and his skeptical friend who blamed it all on too much ouzo.

Dion turned over on the disheveled bed and to his surprise found that the sheets were soaked through with sweat as they had been in Greece when his obsession with Iris kept him in a constant fever. His head ached from all the drinks of the night before during his pursuit of Taylor through the bars of Key West. He had not located Taylor yet but he was fairly sure the man was on the island. He felt it in his bones. He knew he was closing in on him. But the image of the old man in the dream kept popping up in his mind as he tried to shake himself awake.

What was it that he said? Dion wracked his brain. Anchor. He did say something about an anchor. And Dion certainly did find that. But he said something else about a blond woman who kept him from the gold. Was it Iris? Had her image led him off the track by leading him to the anchor? There was something else. Something about the one who found the anchor was different from the one who hauled the gold up on deck. Now if it was Taylor who originally found the anchor and then planted it, that was fine because it would mean that Dion could be the one to haul up the gold. But if he, Dion, was the discoverer of the anchor, then what? Would Taylor get the treasure? Or somebody else?

Dion shook his head and lumbered to his feet. Stupid. What was he doing wasting time on junk like that? Time was wasting. Time was money. He could trust Lopez to keep the dive going but he had to find Taylor in order to know whether the site was dry or not. That fucking Taylor.

Dion walked into the kitchen and found Sophia washing dishes. She turned at his entrance and gestured to the kitchen table.

"Sit down, Dionysos. I have coffee for you. I get you some

breakfast. Now you just sit."

"Okay, Ma. But just coffee. I don't want nothing to eat right now, okay?"

"Oh, but Dionysos, you need your food. You are not eating right."

"I said just coffee, Ma. That's all I want."

Dion sat heavily at the table and shuffled aimlessly through a pile of mail and magazines that were spread out on the surface.

"He just come, the mailman," explained Sophia as she poured a mug of coffee for her son. "I not get a chance to sort it out yet."

Dion didn't answer as he thumbed through the utility bills and advertisements for sales at the drug store. One envelope with no return address had his name on it but carried no stamp or postmark. Curious, Dion turned the envelope over in his hand and ripped it open. Inside was one sheet of white paper with the words, "If you want Frank Taylor go to Hemingway House back by the pool at 5:30 this afternoon."

Dion jumped to his feet and ran to the front of the house.

"What is it, Dionysos?" called Sophia.

Satisfied that no one was in sight, Dion returned to the kitchen and sat down. "You see anyone deliver this letter, Ma?"

Sophia shook her head. "No. Just the mailman, Dionysos. I don't see anyone else this morning. Something wrong?"

Dion tapped the table impatiently. "No, it's fine. I finally got the information I need. I just wanted to know who delivered it, that's all."

"Is this trouble, Dion?" asked Sophia with a tremor in her voice. She didn't like the violent swings in her son's moods.

"Naw, naw, everything's fine, Ma. I just have some business to take care of about this dive, that's all. Don't wait dinner for me, ya hear? I might be late tonight. Or I might end up going back to the *Rafina*. So don't worry. I might not be back for a while, okay?"

Sophia hung her head and didn't answer. It was no use. She knew that Dion was keeping something from her, something that was not good. But she kept her silence, feeling the old shroud of sorrow descend once again over the house of Panagakis.

Phyllis lay awake in the cabin, her brain a mass of conflicting passions. During the past two days she tried to squelch any lingering shreds of maternal sympathy. But time and again images of the infant Jason would flash through her mind, alternating with the loathsome form of Dion.

Outwardly, she had kept control, laying their course carefully with Iris and Dee. She kept her own plan to herself, knowing they would not go along with it and not wanting to implicate them. If she did this, it was her burden alone. She had given life to Jason and she alone could take it away. She was prepared to face the consequences – to go to jail, to give up her own life. It didn't matter.

Phyllis rolled out of bed and started to dress. She would get Jason out of school. Until she saw him, touched him, she wouldn't know if she could go through with it or not. And today was the day she must know.

On the other side of town, in the Cuban section, Frank Taylor was just starting to stir. His pattern the last few days was to sleep most of the daylight hours and then go out at night to meet other men who dealt in illegal trades. Besides the treasure business, Taylor had his hand in the lucrative drug traffic that flowed through Key West. In fact, the treasure fleet served as an excellent cover for his other enterprise that yielded a return on a more consistent basis than the floor of the ocean.

He rubbed his bloodshot yellow eyes and reached for the half-pint bottle of whiskey on the scarred night stand. Just enough to get him started. Today he was going to make an exception to his pattern. He had to go out in the late afternoon and meet a connection. A mainlander from Miami with some big bucks. A woman. Someone who could cover her tracks, a doctor of some sort. She was an odd one. Didn't want to meet at her hotel, which was smart. And she didn't want to come to the Cuban section because she might attract attention there as well. And the harbor was too public and crawling with cops. So she hits on the Hemingway House where they could meet and make it look like they were both tourists.

Taylor chuckled as he lifted himself from the grey sheets of the bed and ran his hand across the stubble on his chin. He'd have to get cleaned up a bit first. He'd never pass for a tourist the way he looked now. He needed a shave. And some fresh clothes, polyester if possible. It would be like a costume party for him. It was Halloween, after all, wasn't it?

All he had to do was duck out and get those clothes and then cut over to Whitehead Street. Panagakis would never look for him in the tourist section. And for all he knew the guy might have finally given up and gone back to his precious ship to keep diving. He was hardheaded enough to keep pumping a dry well hoping to hit a gusher.

Tom Mason was tired. For some odd reason they had had more visitors than usual demanding tours through the House that day. And of course being short-handed didn't help at all. He was obliged to take every other group himself and since he really couldn't trust Maria to keep her eyes peeled, he lived in constant fear that someone was ripping off mementos in rooms he couldn't see. A lot of kids... some of them in costume for Halloween. He spotted two big game hunters whose attraction to Hemingway was understandable. But also ballerinas and cats and little girls dressed as "ladies." He felt he was losing control of the situation and he didn't like it. Almost five o'clock now. Just one more tour and then he could lock up the place, keep it safe for one more day; safe from the greedy hands, the unthinking demands of the public.

Iris and Dee had just arrived and joined the last group that Tom Mason was forming in the hall of the big house. Maria had one more after him and that was the one they had targeted Phyllis to take. Dee and Iris followed Tom Mason as if totally enthralled with his every word. But they also purposedly held back, slowing down the group and making much of Iris' handicap. She pretended that walking was a greater effort than it really was and Dee hovered over her at every step as Iris thumped along with her cane and demanded frequent rests. At first Tom Mason tried to be his official cordial self, but his patience had been stretched to the breaking point and he wanted no more delays. Finally, on the second floor of the main house Iris feigned a near collapse and sat down hard on a chair near the balcony.

"Are you all right?" demanded Dee, bending over Iris with a smile.

Tom Mason hurried over the seated Iris. "Are you ill? Do you need a doctor?"

"No, I don't need a doctor. But if you don't mind, I would like to sit here for about fifteen minutes to regain my strength. I know I shouldn't have pushed myself, but it's our last day on the island and I would have been distraught if I had missed this tour. I hope you're not angry with me."

Tom Mason stood up to his full height and nodded curtly.

"Not at all. You rest there and I'll come back to check on you before we close up. Just stay calm, Madame. Take all the time you need."

"Thank you," said Dee demurely. "You are so kind."

"It's nothing, nothing at all," he assured her and turned quickly to catch up with the group that was straggling downstairs unguarded.

"Here," said Iris. "Help me out onto the catwalk. Then you better go greet Taylor."

Dee opened the windows onto the balcony and helped Iris onto the long ramp that connected the second floor of the main house to the upper level of the studio.

"Are you sure you're all right here?" asked Dee, concerned.

"I'm a lot safer up here than on the ground once Dion gets here. You better go. Phyllis should be in the studio now with the last tour."

"Take care, love," said Dee. She turned quickly and doubled back through the bedroom, leaving Iris leaning on her cane suspended above the pool and patch of yard between the two buildings.

By the time Dee reached the studio, the tour group was emerging. And at the tail of the group was Phyllis – with Jason in tow.

"What's he doing here?" demanded Dee as she drew Phyllis aside.

"I had to bring him. You'll see. You'll see." There was wildness in Phyllis' eyes.

"Let go, Mommy." Jason was squirming in Phyllis' grip.

"Phyllis, how could you?" moaned Dee. "This could spoil the entire plan."

"He must know about his father," said Phyllis evasively with tears in her eyes as she stroked Jason's head. "Hush, baby. Hush."

"Not here, Phyllis. Whatever possessed you?" Dee looked up to Iris for help.

"There's no time to quarrel," called down Iris. "Keep him in the studio."

By now the tour had returned to the main house and the women were alone except for the ever-present felines that stalked around the pool with restless strides.

"All right," said Dee, revising the plan fast. "I'll take Taylor to the second floor of the studio. There's plenty to keep Jason occupied on the first. Understand, Jason?" She crouched down and looked straight at the boy. "I want you to stay on the first floor until you're called, understand? You can play with anything you like. But stay there until we call you."

"Why?" demanded Jason.

"I can't tell you now. But please do as I say."

Jason looked up at his mother, who still held him in a vise grip. "Okay. But I want ice cream when I come out."

"Okay, Jason. We'll have ice cream," assured Dee as she pried him from Phyllis' arms and pushed him toward the door. Phyllis watched him as if in a daze.

"Isn't he just like Dion? The little admiral..."

"Phyllis, snap out of it," ordered Dee. "What's the matter with you?"

Just then Frank Taylor walked out the back door of the main house, almost unrecognizable in his new yellow shirt and bright blue trousers. He spotted Dee immediately and strolled over to her in a cautious manner, sizing up the other woman beside her.

"It's all right, Mr. Taylor," said Dee as he approached. "We're alone."

"Yeah? You didn't say nothing about another woman."

"We'll conduct our business inside, Mr. Taylor. My friend here will stay outside and make sure we're not disturbed."

"A lookout, eh?" Taylor shifted his weight and eyed Phyllis. "Guess it ain't such a bad idea. Let's get going, Doc."

"One moment, Mr. Taylor." Dee's eyes went to the knife Taylor wore on his belt. "Would you mind removing that weapon? I'd feel safer if you did."

Taylor's hand went to his belt protectively. "I always wear it," he protested. "I ain't goin' to use it on you."

"Please. As a gesture of good will."

Taylor's eyes narrowed as he examined the women. Satisfied, he drew the blade from the leather case on his belt and handed it to Dee.

"Okay, Doc. If it makes you think better."

"Thank you," said Dee as she handed the knife to Phyllis. "Hold this while we're inside."

Phyllis nodded and clutched the blade to her breast.

"Shall we go, Mr. Taylor?"

"Yeah, Doc, let's go."

Dee and Taylor disappeared into the studio, leaving Phyllis alone in the yard near the pool and Iris hovering above.

"Philly, are you all right?" Iris leaned out as far as she dared from the catwalk. Phyllis turned her face upward, tears streaming down her cheeks.

"It's so hard, Iris. So hard."

"It'll be over soon. Then we all can go to Hawaii."

"It must be done. Must be. For all of us."

"Dear Philly," Iris stopped abruptly. Dionysos Panagakis had just walked out the back door of the house. He scanned the yard until he spotted his wife on the other side of the pool.

"Phyllis!" he called. "What the hell are you doing here?"

"Settling with you once and for all." The sight of him aroused her passion for revenge anew.

"I got business here," he responded.

"So do we," said Iris from her perch. Dion's head snapped up, seeing the twisted form on the catwalk for the first time.

"Who are you?" he demanded.

"Can't you guess, Dion?" she said smoothly. "Come closer. Look into my eyes."

Dion took a few uneasy steps forward and felt a growing unease. Those eyes! They were so familiar. And yet the face, that pieced-together, contorted face held nothing familiar at all.

"Think back, Dionysos. Think back to a misted morning on the White Cliffs of Lefkas. Look into my eyes. And remember."

Dion looked up into her eyes once again and stepped back in horror.

"No!" he croaked. "It can't be you. You're dead."

"No, she isn't," hissed Phyllis from the other side of the pool. "But you will be soon."

"It's taken long months of continual pain, but I lived. I lived to see this moment, Dionysos Panagakis." Iris spat out his name with disgust.

"You can't prove it. You can't prove a thing. And we're in the United States, not Greece. You can't touch me, Iris. You've been a curse ever since I laid eyes on you in Lesbos. Yes, I wanted you. And, by God, I had you. But now you're nothing to me, do you hear? Nothing! Nothing but a sorry cripple. But you can't touch me, do you understand?" Dion's eyes were wild, the gold flecks in them giving off a wicked gleam.

At that moment Jason shot out of the studio.

"Daddy," he called. "Did you come to take me trick-or-treating?"

"Come here, Jason," commanded Phyllis, pulling the boy back against her. Dion was too absorbed to acknowledge the presence of his son.

"How about Frank Taylor?" taunted Iris. "Don't you have a score to settle with him? He did seed your wreck, you know. He's the only one who really knows where the *Toledo* lays. And he can outwait you. He knows. And your time is running out, Dionysos. Your time is running out."

"Liar!" he screamed. "The *Toledo* is mine and I'll kill Taylor if he won't tell me where she is."

"Go ahead and try," said Iris evenly. "He's right here."

"Where? Where's Taylor?" Dion sank to a crouch and drew the knife from his belt in preparation.

Phyllis looked up at her husband, the man she had lain next to for ten years, the father of their son. His face was twisted in an ugly sneer of hate, a murderous gleam in his eye as he readied himself to do battle with the man who took what he wanted.

"Mommy, let me go," demanded Jason, squirming against her in his efforts to release himself from her iron grasp. "Let me go. I want to go with Daddy. Let me go!"

Slowly Phyllis looked down at the petulant face of her son, contorted in frustration, trying to get away from her. The little admiral. The little Dionysos. It was inevitable. He was his father's son. Her duty was clear.

"Dionysos," she called to him, tightening her grip on both Jason and the knife. "You won't die alone. I can't allow it, do you understand? You won't hurt me anymore. You won't hurt my sister, or any woman again. And neither will your son."

"Phyllis, what are you doing?" said Iris in a panic. She struggled to her feet, but knew there was no way to get to her sister in time.

"How like your father you are," Phyllis said clearly with great deliberation, looking down at her son. "Are you watching, Dion?" she called in a shrill voice. And with one fluid gesture she ran the blade across Jason's throat.

It happened so quickly that Dion had no time to stop the act. A jet of blood shot out from the open wound as the boy let out one strangled gasp and slumped forward. With perfect calm, Phyllis threw the knife away from her and swung the boy into the pool, where he floated, face down as plumes of red spread out from his body, haloing the small white body in blood.

"No!" screamed Dion, throwing himself into the pool on top of his son. "No! No! Not my son!"

"Yes, your son," hissed Phyllis. "Your precious son and seed into the future. It's done. You're done. Your time has run out, Dion. You are finished."

"Phyllis, get away from him," yelled Iris helplessly from the catwalk. "He'll go for you next."

"It doesn't matter, Iris." Phyllis stared up at her sister vacantly. "I'm ready to die. I killed my son." And in a second the cold avenger dissolved in tears and stood, immobile on the lawn with the cats circling around her.

The commotion finally reached the inside of the studio and Taylor leapt from the door as if to make his escape. But he stopped short at the sight of Dion flaying the water with the body of his son and screaming curses at the woman who stood transfixed by the side of the pool.

"Panagakis!" he exclaimed and looked back wildly at Dee who emerged behind him. "What's going on? What's he doing here?"

"I wouldn't know," said Dee, trying to maintain calm through her horror. "But if I were you, I'd pick up your knife and be ready to defend yourself. Dion seems to have gone mad."

Without another word Taylor scooped up his knife from where had Phyllis had thrown it and tried to edge his way around the pool. But Dion caught sight of him out of the corner of his eye and let out a bellow like an enraged bull.

"Taylor! You son of a bitch. It's you. You're in on this. My son's dead. And now you're taking my treasure. I'll kill you, Taylor."

Dion dropped the limp form of his son, lunged for the side of the pool and heaved himself up onto the concrete. Taylor jumped back from the side of the pool and looked around frantically for an escape route.

"Hold on, Panagakis. Hold on. Don't go jumpin' to any conclusions. I don't know nothing about your kid. Now you just calm down."

"Tell me," screamed Dion. "Did you seed that wreck, Taylor? Did you?"

Taylor circled back and away from Dion, his knife out in front of him. "Now I think we should have a talk, Panagakis. It's not too late. There's enough for all of us, don't you see? Christ! And the *Toledo* ain't the only ship in the sea."

"But she's mine!" shouted Dion, drawing his knife. "She's my ship."

"Okay. Okay. We could be partners. I can tell you where she is. Partners, okay?"

Dion lunged at Taylor, swinging his knife in an arch. "Then you did do it! You seeded her. Tried to make a fool of me. And now you want to be partners, eh? Partners! When you tried to rob me of my ship?!"

"Yeah, I did it," sneered Taylor, avoiding the sweep easily. Dion was a wildman, his fighting broad and unfocused. "Yeah, I did it, you big stupid greaseball. You're easy to fool."

"I'll kill you!" screamed Dion, lunging once more for Taylor and passing him wide, leaving his side exposed. In a flash Taylor drove his knife into Dion's side below the heart, then pulled up the blade with a twisting motion as if he were gutting a fish. Dion let out a bellow and lashed out with one last effort, catching Taylor's upper arm with his knife, but causing no real damage.

"You asked for it," croaked Taylor as he withdrew the blade and allowed Dion's body to slump in front of him. "You asked for it, you bastard." Taylor brought up his knee under Dion's chin and snapped him back, throwing the body back full length on the grass, Dion's torso opened up through a two-foot slash, his life spilling from him onto the ground.

Tom Mason stepped through the back door of the main house to check out the source of all the noise and was frozen in his tracks.

"My God, my God," he sputtered. The crippled woman was leaning over the catwalk. At the head of the pool stood two women with their arms around each other while in the pool drifted a small body clad in a bloodstained admiral's uniform, the water tinged pink. And at the other end of the pool lay a dead man with his guts spilling out and another man standing over him, a gory knife in his hand. Mason didn't know whether to run for protection or take command.

"Call the police," ordered the blond woman as she disentangled herself from the other woman. "Call the police, do you hear?"

"What happened?" stuttered Tom Mason.

"A madman," said the blond woman. "He was mad. He killed his own son and then turned on this other man."

"That's right," piped in Taylor, wiping the blade clean against his pants leg without thought. "He came for me. Ask around. This guy's been telling everyone up and down the Keys that he meant to kill me. Should have been locked up. The lady's right. He's crazy."

"No," wailed Phyllis. "I killed my son."

"Quiet!" Dee grabbed Phyllis' hand.

Tom Mason felt weak in the knees and his stomach grew queasy. He was afraid he was going to vomit.

"Yeah, police. I'll go call the police." Mason rushed back into the house and into the bathroom to heave before he could steady himself enough to place the call.

Once he was gone, Taylor turned to the women.

"I don't know what kind of game you're playing, but you better back me up."

"Don't worry, Mr. Taylor," said Dee smoothly. "We'll vouch for your action as pure self-defense, won't we?"

"But what about me? I killed my son. I must pay," chanted Phyllis.

"I'm getting out of here," said Taylor, uneasy. "I don't know who's nuts." He started for the main house.

"Oh, Mr. Taylor," said Iris. "Don't be so confident. I know what you're thinking. But you won't live to bring up the treasure of the *Toledo*, either."

Taylor, Dee and Phyllis looked up at Iris in amazement.

"Are you threatening me, lady?" asked Taylor.

"No, Mr. Taylor. This is not a threat. Merely a prophecy. The *Toledo* is not yours any more than it was Dionysos Panagakis'. You will simply be killed within the year, much too soon to salvage the wreck. That's all."

Taylor looked at the unblinking stare from Iris' green eyes. "I don't believe in all that crap," he sneered.

"Neither did Dion Panagakis," said Iris wearily as she rested on her cane. "And I foresaw his death to the hour."

Taylor gave a slight shudder and took a step toward the house. "Bitch," he spat out.

"No, Mr. Taylor. More like witch. But it doesn't matter what you think. Your doom is already written."

Taylor slammed into the house, leaving three women alone in the yard with the two bodies.

"Now what?" said Phylis softly. "Now what?"

"We all go home," said Dee. "All three of us."

"Home?"

"To Hawaii," said Dee. "We all have a home there."

"But I've killed my son," said Phyllis. "And I must pay for it."

"But there's no proof," insisted Dee. "We can say Dion did it."

"But I know I killed him. I want to stand trial."

"Insane. Temporary insanity. No jury would convict you," said Dee.

"It's up to them, then," said Phyllis. "I must submit myself to justice. But no matter what they decide, I will mourn my son the rest of my life."

"Let her be, Dee," said Iris quietly. "It is her destiny. But one day she will join us again. My beloved sister. My Philly."

"I think I hear the police," said Dee. A distant wail grew. "Do you want to go in?"

"No," said Phyllis. "I'd rather stay out here. They'll come for us quick enough. But I feel stronger in the yard."

"She's right," agreed Iris."And I'm so tired." Iris eased back into the chair on the catwalk and faced the back door of the main house.

A few moments later when police burst through the door they saw what appeared to be an old gnarled woman sitting high above them, her cane extended in front of her like a scepter. Below, two women flanked the pool, while a dozen cats prowled around them. They all seemed to be looking onto the scene of a bizarre entertainment prepared for their benefit: a gutted man and a boy floating in the pool on a late tropical afternoon; the end of a lineage, and the beginning of a story that Hemingway forever was afraid would be written.

Also available from Alyson

Don't miss our free book offer at the end of this section.

☐ ONE TEENAGER IN TEN: Writings by gay and lesbian youth, edited by Ann Heron, $4.95. One teenager in ten is gay; here, twenty-six young people tell their stories of coming to terms with being different, of the decision to [illegible] — and whether to tell friends and parents, and what the consequences were.

☐ THE LAW OF RETURN, by Alice Bloch, $[illegible]. The widely-praised novel of a woman who returns to Israel, reclaims her Jewish heritage while also claiming her voice as a woman and as a lesbian. "Clear, warm, laughing and moving" writes Paula Chester. "I want to read everything Alice Bloch writes," adds [illegible].

☐ BETWEEN FRIENDS, by Gillian E. Hanscombe, $6.95. Frances and Meg were friends in school years ago; now Frances is a married housewife, while Meg is a lesbian involved in progressive politics. Through letters written between these women and their friends, the author weaves an engrossing story, while exploring many vital lesbian and feminist concerns.

☐ ROCKING THE CRADLE: Lesbian mothers: A challenge in family living, by Gillian E. Hanscombe and Jackie Forster, $5.95. A look at both the social and personal aspects of lesbian motherhood; the complications of artificial insemination by donor; and how children feel about growing up with lesbian mothers.

☐ DECENT PASSIONS, by Michael Denneny, $[illegible]. What does it mean to be in love? Do the joys outweigh the pains? Those are some of the questions explored here as Denneny talks with a gay male couple, a lesbian couple, and a straight couple about all the little things that make up a relationship.

To get these books:

Ask at your favorite bookstore for the books listed here. You may also order by mail. Just fill out the coupon below, or use your own paper if you prefer not to cut up this book.

GET A FREE BOOK! When you order any three books listed here at the regular price, you may request a *free* copy of *Talk Back!*

BOOKSTORES: Standard trade terms apply. Details and catalog available on request.

Send orders to: **Alyson Publications, Inc.**
PO Box 2783, Dept. B-32
Boston, MA 02208

– – – – – – – – – – – – – – – –

Enclosed is $_______ for the following books. (Add $1.00 postage when ordering just one book; if you order two or more, we'll pay the postage.)

☐ Between Friends ($6.95)
☐ Coming To Power ($7.95)
☐ Decent Passions ($6.95)
☐ Iris ($6.95)
☐ The Law of Return ($7.95)
☐ One Teenager in Ten ($3.95)
☐ Reflections of a Rock Lobster ($4.95)
☐ Rocking the Cradle ($5.95)
☐ Talk Back! ($3.95)
☐ Young, Gay and Proud ($2.95)
☐ Send a free copy of *Talk Back!* as offered above. I have ordered at least three other books.

name: ______________________________

address: ______________________________

city: ______________ state: ________ zip: ________

ALYSON PUBLICATIONS
PO Box 2783, Dept. B-32, Boston, Mass. 02208

This offer expires December 31, 1984. After that date, please write for current catalog.